HEARTS OF SAWYERS BEND #4

IVY LAYNE

GINGER QUILL PRESS. LLC

Also by Ivy Layne

THE HEARTS OF SAWYERS BEND

Stolen Heart

Sweet Heart

Scheming Heart

Rebel Heart

Wicked Heart

THE UNTANGLED SERIES

Unraveled

Undone

Uncovered

THE WINTERS SAGA

The Billionaire's Secret Heart (Novella)

The Billionaire's Secret Love (Novella)

The Billionaire's Pet

The Billionaire's Promise

The Rebel Billionaire

The Billionaire's Secret Kiss (Novella)

The Billionaire's Angel

Engaging the Billionaire

Compromising the Billionaire

The Counterfeit Billionaire

THE BILLIONAIRE CLUB

The Wedding Rescue

The Courtship Maneuver

The Temptation Trap

Chapter One

NASH

The day my brother got married was the worst day of my life.

It didn't start out that way.

When it started, I thought it was going to be another typical day with my family. Long stretches of boredom punctuated by bursts of irritation. My family was frequently both boring and irritating. Despite our differences, I loved my parents, so for them, I tolerated the boredom and irritation.

My brother Tyler was a different thing altogether. Tyler I avoided completely. I tried to stick with that tactic when it came to his wedding. I had no interest in watching him marry some society airhead in a spectacle that would easily run seven figures. I wasn't going to suffer through a tedious weekend I'd never get back when they'd be divorced in a year.

I had my strategy all planned. I'd have a last-minute emergency meeting. In Tokyo. Maybe I'd miss my flight back. My mother put an end to that. I'd learned over the years that firm boundaries are the key to loving Claudia

Kingsley. Very firm. As in, sky-high and rock solid. Once Claudia knew she couldn't yank my chain, we'd settled into a comfortable affection that worked for both of us.

Then Tyler proposed to Parker Sawyer and my mother decided my boundaries could go to hell. She wanted her whole family at the wedding of the century and wouldn't accept anything less. I managed to get out of the engagement party and rehearsal dinner but agreed through gritted teeth to attend the ceremony and reception.

Skipping the engagement party was the biggest mistake of my life.

After, my mother's words rang in my ear. *You have to meet her, Nash. I really think Parker will be the making of your brother. She's perfection. You're going to love her.*

For once, my mother was right, 100%. And 100% wrong. Parker Sawyer wouldn't be the making of Tyler. He was a lost cause. He was greedy, jealous, entitled, and excelled at the kind of manipulation that kept everyone around him dancing to his tune. No woman could be the making of Tyler. He'd destroy anyone foolish enough to tie herself to him. That's what Tyler always did with his toys.

My mother was wrong about Parker and Tyler, but she was right about one thing. I was going to love Parker Sawyer.

For the rest of my life, I'll never forgive myself for waiting until the wedding to meet the bride. The first time I set eyes on her, she was heading down the aisle on her father's arm, her slight, fragile form elegantly sheathed in a white satin column of a dress, its spare design highlighting her small stature, her pale hair in a refined knot that accentuated her stunning features.

Everything about her was understated beauty, except for her eyes. A golden hazel, they glowed with serenity. And deeper, beneath the shell of perfection, there was a spark, a hint of life that was nothing as serene and orderly as her exterior suggested.

I'll never know how I alone saw it—Parker's secret chaos, the wild spark she hid so well. See it I did, and as she walked down that aisle I experienced the first moment of genuine regret in my life, a sense of something precious slipping through my fingers, gone before I could make it my own. My heart ached, an unfamiliar sick pulse in my chest, loss spreading through my limbs, saturating my soul.

So much regret in that one moment. I make it a policy not to have regrets. I make decisions, and I move forward. If I fuck up, I try not to do it again. Simple and efficient. I don't waste energy dwelling on things I can't change. Until Parker.

There's nothing I regret more than turning down my mother's invitation to Tyler's engagement party. I have no doubt that if I'd been at that engagement party, I would have left with Parker.

Unfortunately, at the time I wasn't speaking to our father and all my mother's pleadings fell on deaf ears. I was done helping them enable Tyler. If I'd known my father wouldn't live more than a few months after the wedding, if I'd known who Parker would be to me, I would have come to the engagement party. I would have taken one look at Parker and changed all of our lives, instead of putting us through what came later.

Thunderstruck, I watched Parker proceed up the aisle, something elemental inside me demanding I leap from my seat to steal her for my own. I couldn't compute, couldn't reconcile the ultra-civilized wedding unfolding before me with the raw, primal need to seize Parker, to make her mine.

3

Vows were spoken. Tyler pressed his mouth to Parker's. My stomach turned.

The bride and groom left the church in a spray of soft pink flower petals.

I headed straight for the bar.

Two whiskeys and I wasn't any closer to getting my head on straight. Something inside me had shifted, a puzzle piece moving and another sliding into place. I'd seen Parker for only a moment and I knew. She was meant to be mine. And she was my brother's wife. Not just any brother, she was Tyler's wife. Fucking Tyler. Even Parker's formidable shell wasn't enough to protect her from the insidious poison that was Tyler.

She'd chosen him. I tried to remind myself of that through whiskies number three and four. *She had chosen him.* She probably thought she loved him. It wasn't my place to tell her who she should love.

That feeble protest didn't get very far. I'd grown up with Tyler, after all. I knew exactly how charming he could be when it served his purposes. Parker, my Parker, likely had no idea what she'd done in marrying my brother.

I held it together when my mother tracked me down and dragged me to the receiving line to congratulate the happy couple. Tyler wasn't the only Kingsley who could pull off charming. I'd almost convinced myself I'd imagined everything I felt as I watched Parker walking down the aisle.

Love at first sight is a child's fairy tale. I knew nothing about this woman, and she was married to Tyler. Not a choice that spoke highly of her character. I'd been momentarily deluded, had been having a weird moment and had fixated on this woman, my brother's bride. I'd made more of her than she was.

4

Parker Sawyer—no Parker *Kingsley*—was just a woman. She was my sister-in-law. She was married to my dickhead of a brother. She was no one special.

Then my mother pushed me at the bride and groom. Parker leveled her practiced, cool smile on my face as she slid her hand into mine. The moment we touched, the second her eyes met mine, we both went still, and that spark, the wild flicker of chaos in her depths, flared to life. Reflexively, her fingers tightened on mine, her breath caught in her throat. Wonder suffused her face, her body tilted forward, closing the distance between us—

I don't know what would have happened if my mother hadn't cut in, her voice shrill, manic in her excitement. "Nash, this is Parker! I can't believe you haven't met—"

Her voice faded. Everything faded as the light in Parker's eyes dimmed, filmed over. Her hand slid from mine, her cool shell pulled tight around her. I caught the flash of awareness in her eyes as they flicked over Tyler, my mother, my father, before landing on me.

The tiniest burst of anguish, sharp and desperate, and then it was all gone. The light in her eyes, the soft touch of her skin on mine. I made some excuse and headed straight for whiskey number five, my heart pounding in hollow thuds of loss.

I'm not proud of what happened next.

Not proud, but in that whole clusterfuck of a wedding, what happened next is the one thing I don't regret. I'm self-aware enough to know I *should* regret it. It was an asshole move. I never said I wasn't an asshole.

I'm more like my brother than I want to admit. When I see something I want, I'm ruthless. I was going to walk away from Parker Kingsley. I had to. I'd seen that flare of awareness in her eyes. And I'd seen it dim as she made her choice.

But she hadn't made a choice. Not really. Not until she knew what she was giving up.

Like I said, I'm not proud of what happened next. At least I can honestly say I didn't plan it.

It was a happy coincidence that I, six whiskies deep, strode down the darkened hallway, determined to get the hell out and away from this fiasco when who did I see but the bride herself coming toward me. Parker's shoulders were slumped, her eyes fixed on the carpet.

If she'd been looking where she was going she would have had time.

Time to escape.

Time to see what was coming and run.

Whatever had caught her attention, she had none left for her surroundings, which made it so incredibly easy to slide my arm around her shoulders and yank her into a dark supply closet.

I didn't say a word. I didn't have any words to say. This sliver of time was all we'd ever have, and I wasn't going to waste a minute of it on words. The dark settled around us, the sounds of the party cut off as I pulled Parker close, bending my head to her small frame.

The back of my fingers brushed her cheeks, warm and smooth. Her lips were fuller, softer than I'd expected, parting as I brushed her mouth with mine. Parker didn't shrink away. She didn't protest. She tilted her head back, wound her arms around my neck, and kissed me.

That kiss was fire, burning me from the inside out. Her eager mouth demanded mine, Parker as desperate as I was to make the most of every second we had. The only seconds we'd ever have. Parker's kiss was like nothing I'd ever imagined—the low groan in her throat, the desperate way she nipped at me, her teeth sinking into my lower lip, her tongue sliding against mine.

I barely had a thought for how her passion would translate to sex. This kiss was so much more than a prelude to something that could never be. For the first time, a kiss wasn't about an end goal. Wasn't about the first step to fucking.

This kiss was all we had and it was everything.

Everything I'd never imagined I wanted.

Everything I knew I'd never have. Not now. Not ever. And not because of me. I would have done anything to have Parker. Burned every bridge, laid waste to the party outside our dark closet. I have no limits when it comes to Parker, even then, after one kiss.

No, we'd never have more than this one kiss, because of Parker. Because of what happened next.

Someone in the hall must have tripped, bumped into the door, rattling it in its frame. Parker startled, tearing her mouth from mine, twisting her body away as I fumbled for the light switch, slapping it on and casting us both in harsh fluorescent light.

Flags of red stood out on Parker's high cheekbones. Her breath hard and fast, eyes wide and panicked. Her serene, perfect shell was gone, shredded by our kiss.

"I thought— I thought—" Her voice caught on a choke and she finished weakly, "I thought you were Tyler."

Disappointment stained the beauty of that kiss, the promise of everything I felt between us. "No, you didn't." I wasn't going to let her lie to me. I couldn't do anything about the lies she told herself.

Parker drew in a harsh breath and let it out, shoulders slumping in defeat. "No." She shook her head. "No, I didn't. I knew it was you. I wanted—" She caught herself, cutting off whatever she'd been about to say. "I can't. I just married your brother. And I'm not that kind of woman."

"You could be," I pushed. "You could take my hand and walk out of here with me." Something flickered in her eyes, and I pushed harder. "Take a chance, Parker. Take a chance with me and I promise you won't regret it."

I was insane. Definitely. I was insane. The look Parker gave me said she agreed. Still, she squeezed her eyes shut and drew in another breath, her fingers tangled together in a grip that left her knuckles bone white.

My heart stopped beating, my breath frozen in my lungs as I waited, balanced on a precipice, every cell in my body straining for the words I needed. Words that would give me hope. Give us a chance, a future—give us anything. I would have taken anything.

An eternity later, Parker opened her eyes. Wiping beneath her lashes to clear away the hint of tears, she whispered, "I can't. I'm sorry, Nash. I can't."

That was it. Her final answer. Parker wrenched open the door and disappeared back into her wedding reception. That was the last I saw of Parker Sawyer for a very long time.

Parker Sawyer was a bomb.

I don't mean a bombshell, though she could fit that bill when she wanted to. No, Parker was a bomb, as in *an incendiary device*. She fell into my life out of nowhere and exploded, changing everything. My mind, my heart, my life. The goals I thought I had and the dreams I thought I wanted. Nothing was the same after Parker.

And now I'm here, again, Parker Sawyer falling like a bomb into my life once more. This time into my bed. In the moonlight, her skin is incandescent, her hair almost silver, her mysterious gold and green eyes closed in sleep. She reminds me of a fairy, of some mythical creature who lives in moonlight, who'll turn to dust at the first touch of dawn.

But Parker isn't a mythical creature. She's a woman. And now that I've touched her, made love to her, she's mine. I know what I suspected all those years ago. This woman was made for me.

The night I fell in love with her, I let her get away. This time, there's no escape. Parker can run—she'll bolt the first chance she gets—but it won't work.

I have a plan, and this time, when all is said and done, Parker will finally belong to me.

Chapter Two

NASH

Parker Sawyer blew up my life the day she married Tyler.

She blew it up again the day she finally left him.

Between those two events, five years went by. Five long years in which I saw Parker only a handful of times. Each one was a punch to my gut. The first came at my father's funeral, only months after her marriage.

My father died unexpectedly, as vigorous and sharply intelligent at seventy as he had been in my youth. It turned out his heart was less vigorous than we'd thought. On a night like any other, he'd been sitting beside my mother reading a book before bed. She got up to get him a cup of tea, and when she came back, the steaming mug in her hands, he was gone.

We'd been at odds the last few years before he died. He wanted me to join the company he'd built, always dreaming he'd hand it over to his son. I wasn't interested. To his disgust, I'd fallen in love with code before I was old enough to drive. When I earned a spot at MIT, he'd cut me off, fully believing I'd balk at figuring out how to pay for college and come crawling back, my hand outstretched for a tuition check to the college of his choice.

You'd think he'd have known me better than that. My heart in my throat but determined to make it work, I'd taken on terrifyingly huge student loans and dove into my studies. I once heard someone say *when you have a choice, always bet on yourself.* That's what I did, starting my first company out of my dorm room, then leveraging that into another opportunity, and another. Dorm room startups were all over the place, but only a handful got anywhere. Mine did. My heart might have belonged to code, but my head for business came straight from my father.

Somewhere between the day I'd driven north to Cambridge and the end of my sophomore year, my father and I had mended fences. He called to congratulate me after reading an article about my latest venture. He didn't offer to pay my horrendous student loans, but he did give me something even better. He told me he was proud of me.

After I graduated and moved West to Silicon Valley he threw another tantrum, claiming I'd promised to work for him after college instead of fooling around with these startups. We both knew I hadn't promised any such thing, but that hadn't stopped my father from shouting down the house to get his way. I walked out and another few years went by.

We were like that, hot and cold. I was his favorite son and the son he refused to discuss, depending on his mood and how annoyed he was at Tyler. Eventually, I reached a point where I was able to love him without expecting his approval. In the months after Tyler's marriage, he'd been pressing me to work for him again, maybe finally realizing that Tyler would never fill that role.

I thought we had time to work it out, and I'd ignored him. It never occurred to me that the clock would stop. That one day I'd get a call from my mother, hear the tears in her voice, and learn he was dead. I was in shock. I couldn't get it through my head that he was gone. That we'd never have time to mend what had broken between us.

I came home at my mother's call and took charge. She was lost, and Tyler was sucking up all the attention he could, riding the drama like this was a soap opera and not our lives. I couldn't tell how much he truly cared we'd lost our father. My guess was, not that much.

At the funeral, he flirted with the caterer in plain sight, ignoring his wife completely. Parker appeared not to notice. Parker stayed by my mother's side, holding her hand, often whispering in her ear, quiet and calm, her eyes shadowed, clearly grieving where her husband was not.

I let her take care of my mother and I took over everything else, handling the funeral arrangements, helping my mother with paperwork, and all the financial details that had been my father's domain. Parker never interfered, focused on making sure my mother was eating, helping her choose her clothes for the funeral, doing anything else my mother needed to function in those first awful days.

Watching them together, I realized that my mother hadn't just gotten a daughter-in-law when Parker married Tyler. In Parker, she'd gained a true daughter, one who loved her far more than her youngest son ever could.

Parker and I barely spoke. She tended to my mother and I handled everything else, but every time my eyes met Parker's golden-hazel gaze, hers filled with concern, warming me to the core of my grieving heart. In the months since her wedding, I'd almost convinced myself–again–that she was nothing special. And–again–the second I saw her, I knew that was bullshit. She wasn't just special, she was everything. Everything except *mine*.

Not that I could do anything about it. Even if I'd been inclined to seduce my brother's wife under my mother's roof, I sure as hell wasn't going to do it when my father had just died. Even I wasn't that much of an asshole.

I wish I could say the same for Tyler, who disappeared down a hallway with the caterer halfway through the reception after the service. I glanced around to find Parker at my mother's side, unaware her husband was fucking someone else only feet away. I wouldn't be the one to tell her. Maybe if I hadn't wanted her for myself.

As it was, I couldn't be the one to break them apart. Parker had chosen Tyler, and while my brother might not take his marriage vows seriously, I did. I'd fucked a lot of women in my time, but never the married ones. I wasn't going to start with my sister-in-law.

Tyler reappeared less than fifteen minutes later, his hair a mess, shoulders loose and his mouth twisted in a smirk that said he knew something no one else knew. Parker was too absorbed in my mother to notice and my mother was in no shape to pick up on anything.

Did Parker ever drop the serene shell encasing her? Did she let out that spark inside her with her husband? Did he know how to fan it into flames?

Did Tyler see what I saw in Parker? If she'd been married to any other man I would have sworn he did. How could he miss her secret wildness? The mischief, the adventure. The hunger for more. But Parker was married to Tyler, not any other man, and while I knew he valued her enough to have married her, I'd bet every penny I had that he'd never bothered to look beneath her surface, never seen her depths.

Parker was a woman waiting to become, and when she became whatever she was destined to be, she would be magnificent. I don't know how I knew that. I just did.

I waited until my mother was occupied with a distant relative to approach her. I wasn't going to seduce her, but I wasn't going to ignore her either.

Standing at Parker's side, I asked in a low voice, "You okay?"

She stiffened and looked up at me, her eyes hesitant, our connection snapping into place, as strong as ever. Instead of answering, she shook her head. "You?" she asked.

"Not even close." I wasn't going to lie to Parker. I didn't need to.

"I'm so sorry about your father," she whispered.

"Yeah, me too. Thanks for taking such good care of my mother."

Parker nodded, pressing her lips together before she said, "My mother died when I was nine. I like being around Claudia. I'm glad I can help her right now." Parker drew in a breath, letting it out in a short, gusty sigh. "She really loved your dad. He was a good man."

My throat closed. I couldn't have forced out a word if you'd put a gun to my head. Shoving my hands in my pockets, I nodded again.

Everything felt so wrong. I know a reception after the funeral is pretty standard, but it felt like a fucking cocktail party. A weird one where my aunt and my father's attorney were eating baked brie together while they chatted about tennis.

The only thing that felt real was my short conversation with Parker. So real I couldn't stop myself from asking, "Are you okay? Not about this. In general. Are you okay?"

Parker went stiff again, freezing utterly for a few long

seconds before her head bobbed in a forced nod. "Of course," she said, "I'm fine. Everything's wonderful, except for you know—"

Neither of us believed a word she said. I wasn't going to lie to Parker, but I had no doubt she'd lie to me. She had to lie to me. It was the only way she could keep lying to herself.

I let it go. There was too much going on to push Parker about her marriage. It was not the fucking time.

Looking back at those days of weirdness—of grief and shock and everything being wrong, only one thing strikes me as truly strange. My absolute assurance that while it wasn't time to push Parker, that time would come.

I had no reason to think that was true.

But I didn't think it. I knew it. Knew it to the marrow of my bones.

My job wasn't to push. Not yet. That would come later. For now, all I had to do was wait. Whatever came next, it had to come from Parker.

If I seduced her away from Tyler, she'd never be mine. Not really. Not the way I wanted her.

Once I had my mom on her feet, I left. I went back to my company, back to my life, and I forced myself to put Parker from my mind. I tried not to listen when my mother filled me in on little bits and pieces from her and Tyler's life. Tyler was playing polo again. Tyler had bought a boat. Tyler and Parker were sailing in the Greek Islands.

No mention of Tyler having any kind of employment. I didn't ask my mother who was paying the bills. I knew the answer. My father, no fool, had left his assets to my mother, but the bulk of them were in trust, and I was one of the trustees. Tyler was not.

My father died before we got back on good terms, but

even when we disagreed, he knew he could trust me not to piss away the family fortune on sports cars and elaborate parties as Tyler was undoubtedly trying to do. My mother insisted she could handle him, promising that Parker was keeping Tyler in line.

Annoyed beyond reason, I'd snapped, "He's her husband, not a toddler. She shouldn't have to 'keep him in line'. He should keep himself in line."

My mother had only sighed. "You know how he is, darling. I thought marriage would settle him down, but—" Another sigh.

"So he's still fucking half the eastern seaboard every chance he gets?"

"Nash! Language!"

That was her attempt to evade my question. Since it wasn't a real question, I let it go. Parker was not my business. Aside from partnering her in a board game the Christmas before she moved back to her hometown, we hadn't spoken more than a few words in years. If this was the life Parker wanted, who was I to argue?

If I could have excised her from my heart, I would have done it in a second. I couldn't understand why I belonged so completely to a woman I barely knew. Countless lovers had told me I was afraid to commit. That I was married to numbers, to code and dollar signs. Maybe they were right.

I'd thrown myself into work after I graduated, and as I'd become more successful I'd gained a level of celebrity. Or notoriety. Either way, it all came with a wide selection of beautiful women eager to be seen on my arm, to take their turn in my bed. I took full advantage. I wasn't saving myself for Parker. It wasn't like she was waiting for me, considering she was married to my brother.

Every time my mother asked me to come home, I threw

up business as my excuse. Always business as I hopped from one company to another, building them up just to sell and jump to something else, every time narrowing my focus, honing my experience until I was in reach of my end goal.

I was finally there. My current startup was positioned to change the future of AI technology. I was in Boston to meet potential investors for the next stage. I wasn't sure I liked the Boston team, but I was trying to keep an open mind.

I was heading out the door to meet a few of them for a drink, when my phone rang. My mother. I almost didn't answer. When I heard her first words, I was damn grateful I had.

Chapter Three

NASH

"**N**ash, I'm worried about Parker."

"What's wrong with Parker?" Alarm spiked through my chest.

Sounding flustered, my mother went on. "Nothing. Yet. I think. It's just—" Her words spilled out in a rush. "I need you to go to New York. To the Hamptons."

"Why? What's going on?"

"It's... Well..." She drew in a breath. "I want to tell myself I'm making something out of nothing, but you know how your brother can get."

"What did Tyler do?" I asked, already mentally rearranging my schedule to make time for a trip to the Hamptons.

"I don't— Nothing yet, but— He's my son—he's Parker's husband—I'm sure he'd never—."

"Mom? What happened?" I was holding on to my temper by a thin thread.

"Nothing yet," she said for the second time. "And I want to think nothing will, but he's been different since he came back from North Carolina without Parker. Angry, and drinking too much. Entertaining women in the house. In my house! While his wife is away! I told him I wouldn't stand for it, and he laughed at me. I'm ashamed to admit it's why I came to Paris."

"Mom, you should have told me," I admonished gently. I'd been waiting for her to give me a reason to kick him out. It was her house, true, but I didn't like the way he took advantage of her.

"I thought I could handle him, but I don't know how to talk to him when he gets angry. He raises his voice, and I just didn't want to be there. I didn't have to worry about leaving Parker with him, so I went. But now—"

I hated the idea of my mother being afraid in her own home. She wouldn't use those words, but I heard it in her voice.

She was afraid of Tyler. Afraid of her own son.

I'd spent so many years brushing him aside, blowing off my unease over his behavior, but now I couldn't deny it. Hearing the fear in my mother's voice, I couldn't brush it aside anymore.

"Why are you worried about Parker? I thought you said she stayed in North Carolina?"

"I just got off the phone with her and she said she was on her way to the house in the Hamptons to talk to Tyler. I know you're in California, but—"

"I'm in Boston," I interrupted. "I came east for a meeting. I didn't bother to tell you because I knew you were in Paris."

"Then you're close." My mother exhaled a long breath of relief. "Can you get there? He hasn't been alone at the house, and I don't want her to walk into something— I don't want her hurt, and I don't—" My mother's voice was uncertain and rough with pain. Quietly, she admitted, "I don't want her to fight with him without someone there to keep him... To make sure he doesn't... "

A chill raced down my spine. Tyler was spoiled and demanding, selfish and thoughtless, but he wouldn't hurt anyone. He'd never hurt Parker. Would he?

I was already on my way out the door. "Mom, I'll call you back later. I'm on my way."

I hung up and called the investors I was supposed to meet, then made another call and got lucky. The helicopter pilot who'd dropped me off earlier was at the airport and didn't mind taking on a last-minute charter. We were in the air half an hour later and landed on Long Island not two hours after my mother's call. I could only hope I'd get there in time.

The car I'd ordered was waiting for me at the helipad. I'd tried calling the house, but if Tyler was there, he wasn't answering. As the phone rang over and over, I reassured myself. This was probably all for nothing. My mother was overreacting. Tyler was a self-centered asshole narcissist with the temper of a cranky three-year-old, but he wouldn't hurt anyone.

I couldn't shake the sound of my mother's worry. She wasn't a woman who got worked up over little things. She was the last person to think badly of Tyler and she adored Parker. How could things have changed so much that she was afraid for them to be in the same room together?

Mental discipline is not something I struggle with–not usually–but I couldn't shut off the stream of doubts running through my head.

By the time I reached the house and saw the modest rental car by the front door, my heart was in my throat, my gut tight with nerves.

The front door was unlocked. I let myself in, relief

washing through me at the silence in the house. One light was on in the entryway, casting a golden glow over the papered walls and dark wood floors. See, everything is fine. Nothing to worry about.

The house was at peace in the quiet evening, just as it should be. The scent of cut flowers and salt drifted in the air, the familiar scent of home–

A shout carried from above. A woman's voice. Parker. Another woman, and Tyler. Then Parker again. A deep thump, like something falling over. I flew down the hall, racing up the stairs, the doors flashing by until I reached Tyler's room.

Tyler stood in the doorway, stark naked, an equally naked woman beside him, her arm flung around his neck.

Parker was in the middle of the hall, one hand pressed to her cheek, shoulders slumped, tears streaming from her eyes.

What. The. Fuck?

I reached her side and pulled her hand from her face. Her cheek was already swelling, the skin red and tight. What the fuck? I was going to fucking kill him. With gentle hands, I turned Parker to face the end of the hall and the stairs to the first level.

"Meet me in the kitchen," I said in a low voice. "Walk away and let me handle this."

Parker gave a stiff nod and strode down the hall, her straight back the last thing I saw before I turned to my brother.

"She's stepping out of line," Tyler drawled, "giving me shit about who I can fuck. She left *me*. I told her we were going home, and she said she was staying, so I came home. I don't know why she thought I'd sleep alone."

He flicked the dark waves of his hair off his forehead

and leaned into the naked woman behind him, reaching around to grope her hip. "Get rid of Parker, would you?" he said to me. "I've got business to take care of up here, and I'm not putting up with this marital spat bullshit. She wants to be a wife? She can come home and be a wife. She's going to stay down there in the boonies? Then this is how it's going to be."

White-hot rage erupted in my skull, blinding me. I didn't decide to do it. I just did. Lunging forward, my fist caught him in the jaw. Tyler flew back, taking the naked woman with him. They sprawled in a tangle of limbs, Tyler's shout of outrage muffled as they scrambled to get back to their feet.

"You had that coming," I said. "I'll go take care of Parker. Mom can deal with you when she gets back."

I left him there without another word. One more minute staring at his smug face, and I might have killed him. I couldn't erase the sight of Parker's red cheek, the tears streaking her cheeks.

I'd known he was cheating, but I'd never imagined he'd lay a hand on her. If I'd known, I would have done everything differently. Everything.

I found Parker in the kitchen, a neat pack of ice pressed to the side of her face. Crossing the room, I pulled it away gently, wrestling for control of my fury. The idea that anyone had hurt her made me want to kill.

And yeah, I get the irony—violence begets more violence and how was me hitting Tyler any better than Tyler hitting Parker? I don't give a fuck about that. It just was. If I hadn't needed to take care of Parker, I don't know what I would have done to my brother.

"Has he done this before?" I asked, dreading what she might say. Her silence was answer enough. "How often?"

"Not– He–" Her head dropped as she studied the granite countertop. "Only a few times, I swear. I told myself it wouldn't happen again, and then it did and–"

"Did you know about the cheating?"

Her head shook. "I should have. I should have known, but I–"

I shoved a cut crystal glass in her hand. She stared down at the amber liquid inside.

"Whiskey. You could use a drink."

Parker shook her head. "I can't. I have to drive–"

"I'm driving. Wherever you're going, I'm driving."

Her eyes flicked to mine, the golden hazel heavy with longing and regret. She shook her head again. "Nash, I can't. This is–" She drew in a short breath. "I can't."

I nudged the hand holding the glass closer to her mouth. "Give me a little credit, Parker. We have time for the rest later. For now, I'm going to get you home to your family, if that's where you want to be."

She nodded immediately. I was relieved to know she had somewhere safe to go. I couldn't bear the thought of her being on her own, and she was right–It wasn't time for us. Not yet.

Parker tossed back the whiskey. "He's still upstairs?"

"I'm assuming. I hit him," I confessed.

A tiny smile curved the corner of Parker's mouth. "Good. Let him see what it feels like."

"I'm happy to do it again," I offered, my heart squeezing at the vindictive edge to her voice. This wasn't the way I would have wanted her shell to crack, her sharp words revealing the spark of the Parker she hid inside. Proper Parker would have scolded me for using my fists, but the real Parker, the Parker I loved, was glad he knew what a fist to the face felt like.

I had to shut down that train of thought, or I'd get stuck on the knowledge that Tyler had dared to hit her, and I'd go back and kill him, my better impulses be damned.

Parker set the empty glass of whiskey on the counter with a decisive click, interrupting my thoughts.

"I love your mother, and I'm going to hate breaking her heart, but this is over. I'm going to file for divorce as soon as I find a lawyer."

I kept my face impassive—a feat of will considering the pure joy exploding through my heart—and reached for my wallet. Pulling out a card, I handed it to Parker. "Angelica Walton. She's based in Manhattan. She's the best, a fucking shark, and she's waiting for your call."

Parker took the card, turning it over in her hands. "How long have you been holding on to this?"

"Two and a half years," I said, braced for her to be furious at my presumption.

"That's a long time to hold on to a business card," she said musingly, before tucking it into her pocket.

"I know you." Considering the amount of time we'd spend together, I shouldn't know her at all. But I did. Parker didn't argue with that claim. Nor did she argue when I finished, "I know you and I know Tyler. I knew it would come to this, eventually."

Looking at her red cheek and bruised eyes, I amended, "I never thought he'd hit you, Parker. I never would have left you with him if I thought he'd hurt you."

"I know," Parker whispered. "I never thought he'd hit me either until he did. And I never thought he'd do it again until he did that, too."

"This is what we're going to do," I said. "You're going to get your things and we're going to get in your rental car. You're going to call Angelica while I give you a ride into the city and make sure you can get home before you run out the clock on that will of your father's."

Parker's eyes flashed to mine. Was she surprised I knew about her father's will and the reason she'd moved to North Carolina? She shouldn't have been. Even if I hadn't had a personal interest in her, Parker was family, as close to my mother as a daughter. For that alone, I would have kept an eye on her.

I finished, "Once you figure the rest of this out, you and I are going to have a talk. Later. Not tonight."

Parker did exactly as I suggested, picking up her purse and keys from the table by the door and leading me out to the car. She didn't resist when I plucked the keys from her hand and slid into the driver's seat. The only time she argued was when I told her to call Angelica.

"I've never met the woman, Nash. I'm not calling her at this hour on a Friday night!"

Parker had a point. She had no way of knowing that Angelica was a friend, one of the few who knew about my feelings for my sister-in-law. I hadn't been lying when I said Angelica was waiting for Parker's call. Angie would be thrilled to handle Parker's divorce.

I placed the call and Angie promised to meet Parker first thing the next morning. Satisfied, I escorted Parker to the hotel I'd arranged and checked myself into a room on another floor. There was only so much temptation I could handle. If Parker was filing for divorce, I wasn't going to muddy the waters by inviting myself into her bed. Not now. Not yet.

The next morning, I took Parker straight to Angelica's office where she and Angie shared breakfast and planned her exit from Tyler. Satisfied Parker's marriage was finally moving in the right direction—straight off a cliff—I put Parker on a plane to North Carolina, sure her family would keep her safe from Tyler.

For the first time in almost six years, I knew what it was to hope.

Parker had taken her first step to freedom. Her first step toward me.

Chapter Four

PARKER

What I was about to do felt wrong, on so many levels, but I didn't see another choice. Before I could talk myself out of it, I picked up the phone.

Nash answered in two rings. "Parker, is everything all right?"

"Yes," I said automatically. "No," I amended, more honestly. "I'm all right," I reassured him. I couldn't forget the stark pain in his eyes when he'd looked at my face after Tyler hit me that last time.

I knew Nash felt responsible, though that was absurd. Tyler was responsible, and so was I, for staying with him as long as I had.

I still couldn't explain why. Why had I stayed? Angie kept telling me I needed to see a therapist, but I wasn't ready for that. I was ready to be divorced and my husband was being a royal pain in the rear end about it, as he was about most things.

"Parker?" Nash prompted.

"Sorry, I was just gathering my thoughts. Thank you, by the way, for referring me to Angie. She's amazing."

"I know," Nash agreed. "I was college roommates with her wife's brother, so I've known her for years. I knew you'd like her, and she's the best divorce attorney I know." His tone shifted. "What can I do for you, Parker?" A simple question, but in those words, I felt the weight of everything that was Nash. The fact was, nothing was simple with Nash, and it never had been.

What can I do for you, Parker?

I already knew Nash would do his best to give me anything I asked for.

How did I know that? And why would he?

I couldn't give an explanation. I just knew. The same way I knew that if Nash had ever asked me for anything, I would have bent over backward to make sure he had it. But he never would. And he never did.

Nash gave. He didn't take. Another difference between him and his brother.

"I need to go to your mother's penthouse to get the rest of my things," I said in a rush, embarrassed that I hadn't been able to accomplish this simple thing. "I have everything from the house in the Hamptons, but there were a few things I left in New York. I, uh, I wouldn't bother if it was just clothes, but some of it is personal. Things I don't want to lose."

A necklace my mother gave me when I turned nine, not long before she died. A little clay kitten my sister Sterling made in school. There was also some jewelry I didn't want to abandon. I might need it. I had bills to pay, after all. Angie was wonderful, but she wasn't cheap.

"Do you want me to go over there? Pack up for you?"

"No, that won't work. I need to go myself." I didn't want

to explain why over the phone. If I did, Nash might think I was crazy. "I tried last week, after Claudia mentioned Tyler was in Florida, but not long after I got there, he showed up and tried to stop me from leaving."

"What happened?" Nash asked, his voice sharp. "Why didn't you tell me you were in New York?"

I dodged the second question and answered the first. "The housekeeper was there. She offered to call security for me, and Tyler finally backed off. But I don't want to put her in that situation again. Angie's process server finally caught up with Tyler in Newport at a friend's house a few days ago. As far as I know, he's still there, but I'm uneasy about going to the penthouse by myself. Is there anyone you can recommend for security? I'd ask Griffen but—"

I stopped, too ashamed to tell Nash about the wave of humiliation that hit me every time I thought about asking my brother Griffen for help. He would. I had no doubts about that. But then, not only would Griffen know how much of an ass Tyler was, everyone he called for help would know, too.

I felt stupid enough for putting up with Tyler for so long. I couldn't stand the idea of my brother and his friends knowing I was an idiot. Nash had seen us at our worst, and what he hadn't seen for himself, he was smart enough to figure out. I didn't have anything to hide from Nash.

"I understand," he said, his voice soft.

"I just don't want him to know how weak I was," I confessed, my words almost inaudible, spilling out before I could stop them. My cheeks heated, and I was desperately glad Nash couldn't see my face.

"Parker, you've never been weak. Put that thought right out of your head."

As if it was that easy. I wish. Still, I couldn't stop myself from talking. "I keep telling myself to forget about anything I left behind and just move on. I don't want to see him again. I don't want to drag this out. I just want it to be over. I don't want to be his wife anymore, Nash."

Those words came from somewhere deep inside, raw and true. The words of my heart. Not the cool politeness I showed everyone, but my real truth. I didn't want to be Tyler's wife anymore. I wanted–

No, I couldn't go there. I couldn't put into words what I really wanted. Not yet. Maybe never.

"I don't want you to be his wife anymore either," Nash said, "and not just for my own reasons. He's already proven you're not safe with him."

Nash's words were heavy with the weight of everything between him and Tyler. As far as I knew, the last time Nash saw his brother, he'd hit him. Tyler had threatened to press charges, but according to Claudia, nothing had come of it.

My mother-in-law and I spoke often. I'd been terrified she'd hate me for divorcing Tyler. She adored her youngest son, babied him and indulged his every whim. Tyler was hers. I was only Tyler's wife.

In the years of my marriage, Claudia and I had formed a friendship that had turned out to be stronger than the weight of my dissolving marriage. When I told Claudia I was divorcing Tyler, she'd only sighed, said she was afraid it would come to this, and asked if I had a good lawyer.

I probably could have gone to her for help, but it didn't feel right to put Claudia in that position. She was disappointed in Tyler and heartbroken that our marriage had fallen apart. I wouldn't ask her to betray her son. Nash, on the other hand, didn't give a damn what Tyler thought.

When I first met with Angie, I'd felt like I was on a runaway train, everything speeding in one direction.

Divorce. Such a big word. Even when I'd felt the first cracks in my marriage, I hadn't contemplated divorce. I wasn't like my father. I wasn't going to run through husbands like they were tissues.

Angie had filed for me and started the ball rolling. Tyler found a way to slam on the brakes. It had taken weeks for Angie's best process server to track him down. Tyler had hopped around the country staying with one friend, then hitching a ride in another's private plane and staying with them for a few days. Rinse and repeat. He'd been smart enough to use cash instead of Claudia's credit cards. It might have taken weeks to find him, but Angie's guy had, and the divorce papers had been officially served.

Not that Tyler had acknowledged that fact. He continued to refuse to engage his own attorney. He refused to take my calls. He refused to have anything to do with the process of getting divorced. I couldn't force him to move any faster, but I could pack up the last of my things so I never had to set foot in his home again.

"When can you get here?" Nash asked.

"I can be on a flight this afternoon," I said. "Do you have someone I can hire?"

"You don't need to hire security. I'll escort you to the penthouse."

"You're in New York again?" Claudia hadn't said, and I knew Nash lived in Northern California and spent most of his time there.

"I am. I've had business here over the last few months. When I talked to my mother yesterday, she mentioned that Tyler was in Newport, and planned to stay through the weekend. I think you'll be clear, but I'll come with you anyway, just in case."

"Does late this afternoon work for you?" I asked, relieved I was finally going to be able to retrieve the last of my things.

"Consider it done. I'll see you in a few hours."

"I owe you one, Nash."

"You don't owe me anything, but I'm going to collect anyway," he promised, in a voice of liquid velvet.

A shiver ran down my spine at those words. I wanted to pretend it was a shiver of worry. Maybe fear. It absolutely should not be a shiver of anticipation. Or worse, one of need.

No. Just no. Nash was my brother-in-law. He already had tension with Tyler, their rivalry of long-standing well before I came on the scene. Any relationship I had with Nash would only make everything worse.

And how would I explain it to Claudia? My feelings didn't control me. I wasn't Tyler, demanding to have every-thing I wanted, just because I wanted it. Nash was not for me, and he never could be. I'd shut that door the day I married Tyler.

Once this was over, I'd never see Nash again. All of a sudden I realized that while I'd see him when I was in New York, that might be the last time. We'd have no reason to cross paths again once I was done with Tyler.

That thought shouldn't have left a weight on my heart. And the weight shouldn't have lifted an hour later when I got a text from Nash asking for my flight number and arrival time.

I tried to put Nash from my mind as I set my own plans in motion, packing a light carry-on and calling my family's lawyer to let him know I'd be absent from Heartstone Manor for at least twenty-four hours. Every night spent away from Heartstone Manor had to be logged with Harvey and verified with our housekeeper, to ensure we stayed within the bounds of our father's will.

My father had been dead for four months, but he'd designed his will to control his children from the grave. We'd never been close. Pretty much everyone who met Prentice Sawyer agreed he was a bastard. I'm not going to blame my father for my decision to marry Tyler, but I couldn't deny that my desperate need to get away from Prentice had played a big part.

Compared to Prentice Sawyer, Tyler Kingsley had seemed like a prince.

My father came from a long line of wealthy and powerful men. My ancestor, Alexander Braxton Sawyer, had fought in the Revolutionary War and came out of it owning a huge chunk of Western North Carolina. Every head of the family since then had devoted himself to expanding the Sawyer empire, with moves into logging and mining, real estate, and, more recently, transforming Sawyer Enterprises into a diverse organization that had interests in corporations across the globe.

Prentice had been raised to think he was the master of the universe. Nothing that happened in the course of his life led him to think any different. Except maybe his murder. I wondered if he was looking up at us from hell, fuming that someone had finally gotten the better of him.

Not a charitable thought, but that was one thing I didn't feel guilty about. My father had spent most of his life acquiring and hoarding wealth while running through wife after wife, siring as many children as he could.

He'd also devoted a decent amount of his energy towards setting those children against one another. His idea of parenting was to isolate us, taking from one and giving to another, rewarding and punishing us for reasons only he knew.

By the time I married Tyler, most of us had moved out of the family estate, Heartstone Manor. We barely spoke, as distant as strangers. Until Prentice died, I hadn't seen Finn or Griffen in years. Now, according to the terms of his will, we were all forced to live at Heartstone for the next five years, under Griffen's authority.

As a final *screw you* to all of us, Prentice had left everything to Griffen, the eldest son he'd exiled years before. He'd set aside money in trusts for the rest of us, on the condition that we live at Heartstone Manor for the next five years. If Griffen kicked us out, or we were gone for longer than fourteen days per quarter, we lost our inheritances and were banned from family property.

Griffen got the house and the company, but no cash, though in his video will Prentice had encouraged him to help himself to the trusts left to the rest of us.

Generally, I tried not to guess what my father was thinking, but if I had to, I assumed he'd envisioned saddling Griffen with the rest of us, forcing us to watch as Griffen drained away our inheritances.

The joke was on Prentice. He'd assumed Griffen was as selfish and greedy as he himself had been. Instead, he was still the big brother I'd adored as a child. Loyal. Loving. Funny and affectionate. Instead of stealing from his siblings, he'd dedicated himself to making Heartstone Manor a home. To making us a family.

Being home with my brothers and sisters had changed everything for me. I'd watched Griffen fall in love with his childhood best friend and it hadn't taken me long to realize that I'd rather be alone with my family than anywhere with Tyler. Tyler, for his part, loved the idea of me inheriting a chunk of the Sawyer fortune but hated living in the small town of Sawyers Bend.

Well, I was done with Tyler. He could jet around the world, sponging off his friends for the rest of eternity. All I wanted was to start a new life in Sawyers Bend. I just had to tie up the loose ends of my old life first.

One last trip to New York and I'd be finished with Tyler Kingsley forever.

Chapter Five

NASH

Parker stepped to the curb at the airport, looking as coolly perfect as she always did. Not at all like a woman who'd jumped on a flight at the last minute and spent two hours trapped in a hot plane on the tarmac due to weather delays. She stood on icepick navy heels, her pale blond hair up in a neat twist, a sleek dark linen sheath skimming her slender body. She scanned the vehicles jockeying for space at the curb.

I popped open the driver's door of the car I used when I was in the city, standing and letting out a sharp whistle. The smile of welcome on Parker's face was all I needed to make this little venture worthwhile.

I met her as she stepped to the street, drawing in a breath of her perfume as I pressed my lips to her cheek in a perfectly appropriate kiss.

"Thank you, Nash," she said, as she passed her bag to me and opened the passenger door. I knew she was thanking me for more than storing her luggage in the trunk.

"Anytime, Parker. You know that."

"I do," she said when I got back in the driver's seat. "And

it means a lot. I know this is... Complicated."

Complicated didn't cover it, but I was betting that time would *un*complicate things. We just needed a little more. For now, I was content to be beside Parker, greedy for her company, happy just hearing the sound of her voice.

"When was the last time you talked to mom?" I asked.

"A few days ago. She sounds like she's having a wonderful time in Paris."

"She is. Do you remember her mentioning Martine? A friend she went to school with?"

Parker thought for a moment. "I think so. Didn't she marry a man who lives in a chateau with an actual moat around it?"

"You have a good memory. I forgot about the moat. She did, and she invited Claudia to stay for a few weeks. So, Claudia didn't tell you about the poodles?"

"No!" Parker turned to me, a bright smile on her face, her eyes dancing. "Tell me! What poodles?"

I spent most of the ride entertaining her with a story I'd heard the night before from my mother, involving Martine's very spoiled poodles, and a party that ended with most of the guests in the pool. Fully clothed. At least it hadn't been the moat.

Parker was giggling by the time I was done. I'd pay a million dollars to hear Parker laugh like that at least once a day. No, more. It had been a lifetime since I'd really heard her laugh. Being the one who gave her that? I couldn't put a price on it.

"Was Claudia angry?" she asked, her eyes bright with amusement.

"Not once she'd found her bracelet at the bottom of the pool. Then she thought the whole thing was a 'hoot', as she put it."

Parker let out a sigh. "I miss her. I'm so glad she's having fun, and it's better she's not here, but I miss her."

I knew Parker had lost her own mother before she'd turned ten, and my own mother had always longed for a daughter. The two of them had been close for years. This was exactly the kind of time a woman probably wanted her mother close by, and Parker must have felt like she had to pull away from Claudia. I glanced over at her pensive expression as she watched the city fly by.

"She misses you too, Parker."

Another sigh. "She's disappointed about the divorce."

"Not the way you think she is."

Parker turned her serious eyes to me. "What do you mean?"

"She's disappointed in Tyler, not in you. She thinks you're doing the right thing."

"Is that you guessing? Or did she say that?" Parker pressed.

"She said it," I told her with complete honesty. "She's feeling guilty that she encouraged you to stay for so long."

Parker reared back, her eyes going wide. "Does she know about–" Her hand fluttered up to wave at the side of her face.

My jaw clenched at the memory of her swollen cheek. I shook my head. "No. Not unless you or Tyler told her." Something occurred to me. "You told Angie, though. Right?"

"Yes, of course. She took pictures. She, um, said she might ask you for testimony." Parker thought for a second. "That's not what she called it. An affidavit? I don't know. I was a little overwhelmed when we went over all of this. I'd been thinking about divorce for a long time, but thinking about it and doing it are not the same thing."

I knew what she meant. Turning into the parking garage

of my mother's building, I waited for the gate to scan the tag on my car. Parker fell silent as we parked and rode the elevator to my mother's floor.

Years before, when the building went co-op, my father purchased a spacious apartment. A few years later, he'd purchased another, right above the first, and finally the penthouse, directly above the other two.

One massive renovation project later, he'd been the proud owner of one of the largest penthouses in the city of New York. Now that he was gone, my mother didn't need all this space, but I doubted she'd ever sell it. When I'd asked, she told me, "I raised my family here, and while to others it might be a prime piece of New York real estate, to me its our home."

Parker and Tyler had lived here for much of their marriage, but Parker didn't spare the rooms more than a glance as she headed down the long hall to the suite she'd shared with Tyler. Realizing I was following, she turned, a faint flush on her cheeks.

"You don't have to come all the way. I mean, you can wait in the sitting room, or ask Carla to bring you tea. I'm just packing some things."

I studied her flushed cheeks, curious. If I didn't know Parker, I'd have thought she was planning to pack away some goodies she could sell for cash. It wouldn't be the first time a suitcase left this house heavier than it should be thanks to someone's light fingers. People could be very weird, including, maybe especially, the very wealthy. But Parker would rather starve than make off with some of my mother's endless supply of expensive knick knacks.

I had to know what she was up to. Fortunately, I had an excellent reason to follow her to her suite. "I'm here to watch your back. I can't do that over tea in the drawing room. The front door isn't the only way into this place."

"I know but–" She shook her head, exasperated with herself, I think. Or me. It didn't matter. Either way, she wasn't going anywhere without me. Thanks to our teenage escapades, Tyler and I knew every way to sneak out of this place. And how to sneak back in.

With a sigh of resignation, she turned back down the hall, pulling her sleek metal carry on behind her on silent wheels. I hated that she flinched when she pushed open the doors of the suite she'd shared with Tyler. The sitting room was immaculate, with no sign anyone had ever occupied the space, the chair pushed in to the delicate writing desk just so, the fireplace laid with logs no one ever burned, especially not in July.

Parker kept moving, passing through the sitting room without giving it another glance. She came to a stop in the bedroom, picking up her suitcase and laying it open on the bed. A few trips to the closet and she had most of the case filled with a variety of odds and ends. A few scarf boxes, some shoes, carefully stored in protective bags.

When she was finished with the clothes, she stood in the middle of the room, hands on her hips, and made a slow turn, her eyes scanning the room from floor to ceiling. Turning to me, she said, "Don't judge," her cheeks flushed pink.

Before I could ask what she meant, she dropped to her knees beside the bed and shoved at the mattress, pushing it back until she revealed the box spring. Curious, I leaned over her to see her carefully detach a piece of the box spring cover to reveal a hollowed-out section containing a wooden box.

Opening the box, Parker let out a sigh of relief. Inside, I

spotted several small velvet boxes–ring boxes, I assumed–and a few larger boxes that likely contained bracelets and necklaces. And, curiously, a clumsy, brightly colored ceramic cat. If not for the comically oversized whiskers, I'm not sure I would have known what animal it was supposed to be. Parker stroked a finger over the little cat's head.

"Did you make that?" I asked.

Parker's head shot up, and I wondered if, for a moment, she'd forgotten I was there. "No, my little sister Sterling made it. We had a kitten once." Reaching for a scarf she'd taken from the closet, she wrapped up the ceramic cat as if it were the most valuable item in the box. I had a feeling that, for Parker, it was.

"The rest is jewelry," she continued. "Things Tyler bought me, mostly." A guilty look at me before her eyes skipped away. Standing, she crossed her arms over her chest, almost hugging herself. "I asked your mother if she'd take them back, but she refused. She was adamant. So I'm taking them." Parker's chin lifted, as if she was braced for me to argue.

"You should," I agreed.

Parker's arms dropped to her sides. "Even though your mother paid for all of this and not Tyler? Or me?"

I slid my hands in my pockets. "Once, years ago, I asked my mother what the deal was with men giving women jewelry. I was barely a teenager and couldn't imagine getting something so useless as a gift. Why not a car, or video games? You know, the important stuff."

Parker let out a surprised laugh. "I can see diamonds being low on the list of acceptable gifts for a teenage boy."

I smiled at the memory. "My mother said that my father gave her jewelry because she liked it and he loved her. But that, historically, there were a lot of reasons men gave women jewelry. To showcase wealth and status. As an investment. And often, women preferred jewelry for the security it provided. A woman might not have her own bank account or property, but if she had her jewelry, she had assets to work with. If she needed them."

I inclined my head at Parker's small hoard of black velvet boxes. "I don't know how accurate my mother's grasp of history is, but she knew what she was doing when she told you to keep anything Tyler gave you."

Parker just stared at me, her eyes filling with tears. "You think so?"

I couldn't do it. I couldn't stand there and watch her cry. Crossing the room, I pulled her into my arms, stroking a comforting hand down her back. "I know so," I assured her. Her back hitched against my hand. "You know my mother loves you, don't you? She thinks of you like a daughter, Parker. That isn't going to change."

Parker pulled away, abruptly turning and striding past me to the bathroom. She emerged a few seconds later with a tissue, wiping away her tears. "I wish I was sure about that. Tyler is her son. I wouldn't blame her."

"I would–" I began.

"Don't," Parker interrupted. "This is hard for her, too."

"I know. But it's hardest on you."

Parker's shoulders jerked in a hard shrug. "I married him."

"So you deserve it? That's bullshit. Don't blame yourself, Parker."

She wasn't listening to me. Kicking off her heels, she dragged a chair over to a built-in bookcase filled with a handful of books and shelves of decorative objets d'art. Climbing on top of the chair, she reached for a high shelf, teetering on her toes, her hand groping blindly behind a wide vase before she let out a little triumphant cry and stepped down, another small velvet box in her hand.

Her cheeks pink, she crossed the room to tuck the box into her cache of jewelry. Then she moved the chair to another spot on the bookcase and retrieved yet another small velvet box. After that, she revealed a hidden panel in her dresser. Another in Tyler's. I helped her shove the mattress off the box spring on the other side and she removed two more boxes. When she was finished, the wooden box she'd revealed first was packed full.

Arranging the contents so nothing would be damaged, Parker closed the suitcase and engaged the lock. Sliding her feet back in her heels, she turned to me, and explained, "Tyler was stealing. From me, from Claudia. Selling them for cash to gamble or just flash around. So I started hiding things. And sometimes he would break things. Things that meant something to me."

"That's why you hid Sterling's kitten?"

Parker nodded. "Looking back, I keep asking myself why I didn't get out sooner. But it all happened so slowly. Once I realized it was bad, it had been going on for so long, and I just didn't know how to fix it."

"You're fixing it now," I said.

A slow nod. "I am. Better late than never, I guess." She moved back to the bed, straightening the mattress, then the coverlet, trying to remove the evidence of her scavenger hunt. I helped, going to the other side of the bed to tug at the sheets we'd rumpled when we'd moved the mattress on that side.

Not the most innocent scene for Tyler to walk in on, I'll admit. Parker's suitcase in the corner, both of us making the bed. I wasn't surprised he immediately launched into an attack. I was surprised by Parker's cool response.

Chapter Six

NASH

"I knew it," Tyler shouted, jabbing a finger at Parker in accusation. "I knew you two were fucking! Wait until I tell mother about this. She won't be on your side when she finds out you're fucking Nash, you little whore." Tyler's eyes shone with fury, his face twisted in rage, all directed at Parker.

I didn't like that at all, but I wasn't going to miss an opportunity. While Tyler glared at Parker, I slipped my phone from my pocket, set it to record, and propped it up on the end table beside me.

Parker faced Tyler, arms crossed over her chest once more, her shoulders straight. She may have been wrestling with divorce, but she was definitely done taking Tyler's shit. "Tell Claudia whatever you want, Tyler. There's nothing going on with Nash. I asked him to accompany me while I picked up the last of my clothes, in case you showed up to pitch a fit. And here you are. Pitching a fit. Quelle surprise." Dropping her arms, she propped one on her hip and raised her chin. "Who's tipping you off?"

Tyler sent her a smug grin. "Wouldn't you like to know?"

Parker sighed. "Yes, I would, because Claudia should know if her staff is feeding you information. Or is it someone in the building?"

"I'll find out who it is," I cut in. And I would. Parker was right. If someone on my mother's staff was feeding Tyler information behind her back, my mother had a right to know. "For now, let's get you to the airport. You have a flight to catch."

Tyler pinned those furious, dangerous eyes on me. "You son of a bitch. You fucking kiss-ass, interfering son of a bitch. Do you think you can take my wife away from me? Not a fucking chance. She's not going anywhere."

I was expecting a tantrum. I wasn't expecting this. Tyler wasn't just pitching a fit. He was furious. In a rage. A chill hit my gut at the thought of him alone with Parker while he was like this.

I'm here, I reminded myself. No one is going to touch Parker, least of all Tyler.

I'm used to rolling with the punches. I'd had a plan for Tyler's inevitable tantrum, and it still applied. Calmly, I said, "I've discussed this with Mom, and if you agree to a simple divorce, if you make this easy on Parker, I'll sign one of the family trusts over to you."

Tyler stared at me, uncomprehending. "You're bribing me with my own inheritance just so you can fuck my wife? Not happening. Stick your dick in her if you want, but you're not going to pay me off to get me out of the way. Parker belongs to me. I'll never let her go—"

"She isn't a thing you own, you asshole—"

"Nash—" Parker cut me off, the concerned surprise in her expression snapping my mouth shut. I never let Tyler get under my skin. Grinding my teeth together, I forced my temper under control.

48

"You can drag out this divorce," I said tightly, "but no decent attorney will take on Angie Watson for free and you don't have any cash of your own. If you plan on stonewalling Parker, I suggest you find a way to pay because in situations like this, only the lawyers win."

"No one is winning here, but me," Tyler said, oblivious as always to the practicalities of life.

Making one last effort to simplify the situation, I explained, "Mom is not going to foot the bill for you to make Parker miserable. Not a chance."

"It doesn't matter," Tyler said, trying to stare Parker down. "Parker's going to drop the whole divorce idea. We can live apart while this will of her father's plays out, and then she can come home."

"Are you serious?" Parker asked with a huff of exasperation. "You just got the divorce papers after weeks of dodging service. What about that makes you think I want to work things out?"

"Call off your bitch. There isn't going to be a divorce." Tyler's fingers curled into a fist at his side.

A low growl rumbled in my throat. Tyler shot me a wary but resentful glare before loosening his fingers. His attention back on Parker, he whined, "I can't believe you had me served at Phillip's house. All of my friends were there. I came back to the city to get away from all the pitying looks. You didn't have to be such a cunt about it."

"You didn't leave me another choice, Tyler." She let out a short sigh. "I'm asking you, please, let's just make this simple."

"Simple?" Tyler sneered. "You want this to be simple? I'll give you simple–Your dad dies, you come into millions, and now you're trying to scrape me off. Good fucking luck.

You're my wife. Mine. For better or worse, remember? Well, this is worse. And you're not going anywhere."

Parker flinched at the malice in his voice. I expected her to back away, but she raised her chin and glared back at him. "Yes, I am. I'm done with you. I'm done with our marriage. You can drag this out, rack up tens of thousands of dollars in legal fees, and when it's all over, I'll still be free of you. Don't put us through that. I know you don't care about me, but think of your mother. Just sign the papers and let's both move on."

"Not a fucking chance. You want a fight? You think you can beat me? Well, game on. I'll make you pay for trying to walk out on me." Tyler's face twisted in a sneer, his mouth opening to spew more venom.

I cut him off. "Move aside and let Parker leave, or I'll make you move." Tyler only stared at me in disbelief. "I'll give you ten seconds to move." No response. I started to count. "Ten. Nine. Eight–"

Tyler stayed where he was, arms crossed over his chest, his chin pushed out in a belligerent stance that gave me a vivid flash of him as a child, angry that I'd eaten the last biscuit at tea. He'd always been a whiny brat. Not much had changed.

When I got to *five*, he jumped me. Turning on one foot, I pivoted, letting his momentum carry him past me. Closing a hand on his wrist, I used that momentum against him, swinging him around and twisting his arm until it was behind his back and he couldn't move without a gasp of pain.

To Parker I barked, "Go, meet me in the lobby. I'll be there in a minute." Parker hesitated, then grabbed the handle of her suitcase and left the room, her heels hitting the hardwood in brisk clicks until the sound faded away.

I wrenched Tyler's arm up a little higher. "You're a real piece of shit, you know that? Bad enough that you were cheating on her, but you hit her and you expect her to come back? Just let her go, man. You don't love her, anyway."

"And you do?" Tyler grunted against the pain. "Forget it. She's mine and she's not getting a divorce. And I'm telling my lawyer I found you in bed together."

I rolled my eyes. Shoving him onto the mattress, I stepped back. "This is a waste of time. If you come for me again, I'm going to knock you the fuck out. Do you understand?"

Tyler just glared at me. I nodded. "You understand." I picked up my phone and strode for the door. Tyler didn't follow.

Parker waited in the vestibule outside the front door, watching for the elevator, her toe tapping on the marble floor. Her warm hazel eyes lit with relief as I closed and locked the front door behind me. If Tyler came after us, the lock would slow him down long enough to give me a warning.

"I recorded all of that," I said. "Angie might be able to use it."

Parker nodded, her eyes focused on the elevator, her toe tapping faster. The light went off, and the doors opened. Parker rushed in, jabbing at the 'Close Door' button the second I was inside, her eyes fixed on the still locked front door of the penthouse.

"It's okay, Parker. He's not coming."

It was as if she couldn't hear me. She didn't relax until the elevator began its descent, letting out a long gusty sigh, her shoulders slumping forward in exhausted relief. I wanted to pull her into my arms again, wanted to promise her everything would be alright.

Now wasn't the time. Despite her relaxed posture, I knew Parker's guard was up, her perfect, polished shell back in place. Nothing was getting through. Not even me. Maybe especially not me. I could live with that. For now. We had time.

The elevator door slid open on the lobby floor. I gestured for her to exit ahead of me. "Let's get you to the airport."

I could only take so much temptation. The sooner she was out of New York and back in Sawyers Bend, the better.

Chapter Seven

PARKER

Dawn peeked through the grey sky, the rays of light from the rising sun filtering through the clouds, the overcast sky the only hint of the storms that had canceled my flight the night before. I leaned on the window, the glass cool against my cheek, and resisted the urge to look over my shoulder.

There was no one there. Well, there was an entire gate packed with people waiting for their flight, but no one who meant anything to me. I was just one more anonymous traveler, wishing they were anywhere else. I gave in to the urge and shot a quick glance over my shoulder at the crowd.

No Tyler.

Of course, he wasn't there. How would he know where to find me? And why would he bother to look? Despite his angry words the day before, Tyler didn't really want me. Certainly not enough to chase me to the airport and try to stop me from leaving.

I couldn't help the cool wash of relief as I scanned the crowd and saw only strangers.

I knew about Tyler's temper before we got married,

knew he could throw a fit and sulk when he didn't get his way. I'd hoped he'd grow out of it, hoped he'd learn to communicate like an adult. I'd hoped we'd finish growing up together.

None of that had happened.

Tyler had no interest in growing up.

Tyler's temper had never frightened me. Not even the three times he'd hit me. I'd been furious and deeply ashamed, but I hadn't been scared. Not until he'd stared me down the day before and sworn he'd never let me leave him.

Why did he suddenly care so much? Was it the money? Was he hanging on for his cut of my inheritance? If that was it, I wasn't sure his bet would pay off. I didn't think Griffen would drain our trusts, but I couldn't quite believe there was anything in there to be drained.

Logic told me that Griffen would have given us a heads-up if Prentice's will was a scam. My heart said that leaving money to his children did not fit anything I knew about my father. Promising us money if we did what he wanted and then yanking the rug out from under us once he had what he wanted? That was vintage Prentice Sawyer.

I flinched inwardly, remembering the venom dripping from Tyler's voice as he'd given Nash permission to have sex with me. *Stick your dick in her if you want, but you're not going to pay me off so I'll get out of the way.* Maybe this wasn't about me at all. Maybe this was about Nash.

A knot of disgust hardened in my stomach. I'd picked a winner of a husband. He didn't care who I slept with as long as I was still his wife. Like I was his toy to lend out. *You're my wife. For better or worse remember? Well, this is worse. And you're not going anywhere. You want a fight? Game on.*

Yeah, I'd picked a winner. Getting married had been the

easy part. Tyler had made it clear that as impossible as our marriage had become, leaving was going to be as difficult as he could make it. I scanned the crowd one more time, and I had to ask myself who I was really looking for.

Was it Tyler? Or was I hoping–

No.

Definitely no.

Not going there. I shoved that thought far, far into the back of my brain, just as I had every day since my wedding.

Nash was not going to show up at the airport, professing his love for me like the hero at the end of a rom-com. Why would he? We weren't anything to each other.

A lightning quick stab of agony sliced through my chest, stealing my breath. I forced air into my lungs. It hurt, but it was true. Nash and I weren't anything to each other. Especially not now.

Nash wasn't here. I'd left him asleep, laying on his stomach, one knee hitched to the side, the sheet pooled around his waist to reveal his muscled back, his broad shoulders, the wave of dark hair falling over his stubbled cheek. I squeezed my eyes shut, banishing the image from my mind.

It was a mistake. It could never happen again.

Nash had saved me. More than once. I wouldn't repay him by screwing up his life any more than I already had. I was leaving Tyler to save myself, but dissolving our marriage would drive wedges into his family. Wedges between Tyler and Claudia. Deeper wedges between Tyler and Nash. And it was all my fault. I wouldn't make it worse by pursuing my soon-to-be ex-husband's brother.

Assuming Nash wanted to be pursued. He'd gotten what he wanted. It was pretty arrogant of me to think he'd want more. I didn't have anything to offer a man like Nash, except complications and trouble.

A disembodied voice announced my flight, and the mass of people around me stood in rough unison. The air filled with the rustling of bags and murmuring voices. I stepped through the door onto the plane, my heart and head flying in different directions, grateful to be leaving New York, leaving Tyler, and anguished that my brief time with Nash was over.

We'd never have a reason to see each other again. Not now. And that was as it should be. Of course, it was. I just had to keep reminding myself. I was on to a new phase in my life. A new beginning. There was no room for the past or dreams about things that couldn't happen. I should be happy. Right?

Should be, but wasn't. Instead, I was exhausted and depressed, and deep down the only place I wanted to be was back in that bed, curled into Nash, body wrung out and my heart finally at peace.

No, Parker, I lectured. *You have to move on. There's nothing for you here.* I checked that I had my things, and rolled my carry-on to the end of the line, telling myself that all I wanted was to get on that plane and go home.

Most of that morning passed in a daze of flights–New York to Atlanta, Atlanta to Asheville, followed by the drive from Asheville to Sawyers Bend. Fueled by caffeine and drained from a sleepless night, I didn't notice much. I just wanted to get home, take a long, hot shower and cry myself to sleep.

Unfortunately, I didn't reach Heartstone Manor until mid-afternoon. Griffen was waiting when I walked in the door from the garage.

"Parker!" When I met his green eyes, they were bright with relief. I wasn't used to having anyone other than Claudia looking out for me. But here was Griffen, the big brother I'd missed all those years, and he'd been waiting for me to come home. He'd worried. He was glad to see me. The emotion in his eyes settled around me like a hug before he made it to the end of the hall and enclosed me in his arms. Griffen always gave good hugs.

I squeezed back as he asked, "You okay?"

"Okay, just tired." I didn't want to talk about New York. Griffen wasn't letting me off the hook that easily.

"Come back to my office. We'll get some food in you, and you can tell me how it went."

My stomach sank, and my cheeks flushed. I definitely wasn't telling Griffen everything about my trip. I didn't miss Griffen signaling over my shoulder to Savannah, our all-knowing, all-powerful housekeeper.

"Have you eaten yet?" she asked, head cocked to the side, strawberry-blond curls escaping her tight bun to riot around her face, her sharp eyes taking in my pale cheeks, the circles under my eyes. My empty stomach prodded me to shake my head, *No*. "I'll send something up," she said with a nod before disappearing down to the kitchens.

"I'm going to run upstairs and change, wash my face," I told Griffen, abruptly desperate to get out of this suit. "I'll be in your office in ten minutes."

Griffen gave me another squeeze and kissed my cheek. "Fair enough, I'll just carry your bag up."

I was too exhausted to argue. Griffen hefted my carry-on and jogged up the back stairs to the family wing without another word, setting the bag down on its wheels at the end of the hall. "See you in ten."

"I won't be long," I promised, my stomach growling now that I'd thought of food. In my room, I pulled my suitcase to the closet and caught sight of myself in the mirror.

My blond hair in a tight twist, the navy suit–I hated

everything I saw. Fingers trembling, I pulled at the buttons of my jacket, at my silk blouse, yanked at the tab on the back of my skirt, shoving it off. Shoving it all off and leaving it on the floor until I stood in front of the mirror in a plain white bra and cotton underwear and just stared at myself.

Blond hair tumbled around my shoulders, flat and creased from the too-tight twist. My skin was pale with fatigue, shadowed under my eyes, tight with strain. I didn't like this Parker. I didn't want to be this Parker anymore.

I didn't know what Parker I wanted to be.

Liar, a little voice in my head whispered. *You know what Parker—who's Parker—you want to be.*

That wasn't happening.

All I had was me, standing in my underwear, not knowing what to do next.

I had no clue.

Not about the next stage of my life. That was a problem for later. For now, I was going to have lunch with my brother, and then maybe a nap. Maybe in the garden where I could let the heat of the summer sun chase off the chill that had settled inside me after the encounter with Tyler.

I was home, and I was safe. Tyler couldn't hurt me here. I'd left my marriage with little more than my clothes, the jewelry, and a few belongings, but I had a roof over my head and a home with my family for as long as I needed it. That was far more than a lot of women in my situation had. I could figure out the rest later.

I leaned down to pick up my discarded suit out of habit. My fingers grazed the navy silk and pulled back. No. Just no. I'd deal with that later, too.

I turned to my closet and pulled out a bright red gauzy sundress I rarely wore. Too casual. Too whimsical. Tyler had hated it. He'd liked me elegant, his pearl set in platinum. I liked pearls and platinum, but sometimes I wanted to be a poppy or a Zinnia, vibrant and alive instead of cool and luminous.

The truth was, I wanted to be whatever I felt like. I wanted to live in the moment, instead of carefully crafting an image to protect myself. I hadn't realized what a trap my life had been. First with my father, trying so hard to be perfect enough to escape his attention, desperate to get away and too blind to see I was trading my father for Tyler and another kind of prison.

But Tyler had finally been served the divorce papers, and I'd collected the last of my things. Two small steps closer to real freedom.

It was finally sinking in—I didn't have to protect myself. I didn't have to be perfect for anyone. For the first time in my life, I could just be me. Whoever the hell that was.

I drew the light fabric over my head, pulled a brush through my hair, shoved my feet into a pair of cute white ballet flats, and left the closet, the navy suit crumpled on the floor behind me. The rest of my life was a lot to take in. For the moment, all I wanted was some food and the unfamiliar comfort of my big brother looking out for me.

Chapter Eight

PARKER

Griffen was waiting when I got to his office, a tray of sandwiches and a pot of tea on the coffee table in front of the fireplace. I sat opposite him on the sofa, taking in the view of the gardens through the French doors on the far side of the room, the grass emerald green under the July sun.

"I'm starving," I admitted, rubbing a hand over my stomach. "Too much coffee this morning–

"–and airport food is terrible," Griffen finished for me.

Despite my empty stomach, I reached for the pot of tea first and poured a cup for each of us. I doctored mine with milk and sugar before lifting it to my mouth, inhaling the familiar scent of bergamot and black tea with a hint of lavender and vanilla. My favorite blend.

Savannah was a genius. She knew everything about everyone living in Heartstone Manor and used her inside knowledge to take care of us. Savannah was making us into a family again as much as Griffen was. It was in her blood. Her mother, Miss Martha, had been the housekeeper of Heartstone Manor for most of my life. After my mother died when I was nine, Miss Martha was the closest any of us had to a mom.

"How was New York? Did you get what you needed?" Griffen asked, concern heavy in his eyes.

I sipped carefully at the hot tea, shrugging one shoulder slightly so I didn't spill. I loved Griffen, had loved him since I was a child, and he'd been my affectionate, fun-loving older brother. As a girl, I'd thought Griffen could solve any problem, right up until our father and brother had conspired to exile him from not just the Sawyer family, but from Sawyers Bend itself.

And Griffen had left. He'd walked down the long drive to the road, only a backpack slung over his shoulder. None of us had seen him again until a few months ago. At twelve, I hadn't understood how he could abandon us. Now that I'd run in my own way, marrying Tyler to create a new life away from Heartstone and my father, I thought I understood why Griffen had taken off and not looked back.

In my heart, I wasn't ready to let go of all those years apart. I wasn't ready to trust him completely. The little girl in me wanted to answer his question with the truth, to tell him everything, let him hug me and promise nothing would ever hurt me again.

I hadn't been a little girl for a long time, and no matter how much I wanted Griffen's comfort, I couldn't bring myself to tell him everything. It was enough that I knew how badly I'd screwed up my life. I didn't want to lay it all out for Griffen.

"I left a few things in my room, things I didn't want to leave behind."

"And you have all of it?" he asked carefully.

"I do. Everything is good now," I said with a faint smile. And just for a second I had a horrible vision of Tyler, and what he would have done if he'd caught me alone, packing up valuables he would have wanted for himself. Valuables he'd have felt entitled to, the way he felt entitled to me. If Nash hadn't been there...

I remembered too late that Griffen was highly observant. Years in the military and working in private security had only honed that skill. He didn't miss the way my smile dissolved. "What happened?"

I answered even as I was shaking my head in a negative. "Tyler came home. I think someone in the building tipped him off. He was—" I searched for the right word, something that would convey my concern, but was still low-key. Griffen had enough going on. He didn't need to worry about Tyler. I cleared my throat. "He was upset."

Griffen wasn't buying it. "What did he say?"

I should have known that wouldn't be enough for Griffen. "That he wasn't going to let me go."

"Did he threaten you?" Griffen asked, as if his question was nothing more than casual curiosity. I knew better. Griffen might have been away for years, but he was home now and he was determined to keep his family close.

Someone out there had murdered our father. Our brother Ford was in prison for the crime, but no one believed he'd done it. After Prentice died and Ford was in jail, someone had come after both Griffen and our brother Royal and had killed Ford's ex-wife, Vanessa.

Logic said it all had to be connected. We all thought Vanessa's killer was the same person who'd assassinated my father, but we didn't have any proof. We didn't know why. We didn't know anything, really, except that our father and Vanessa were dead, and any of us might be next.

Griffen wasn't taking any chances. Whoever had killed our father and Vanessa wasn't done with the Sawyer family, and Griffen had no intention of letting another Sawyer get hurt. He was on high alert for anything that could be a threat.

Tyler absolutely fit that category.

Every instinct I had told me to hide everything; The failure of my marriage. What an asshole my husband was. That he'd hit me and promised to make me pay for trying to leave him. My instincts told me to hide it all and pretend everything was perfect.

That's what I'd been doing my entire life. Pretending to be perfect.

I couldn't do it anymore. Not just because I was wasting my life hiding behind that shell of perfection. I was shriveling inside, dying a little more every time I gave a polite smile and pretended that what I wanted didn't matter.

This wasn't about me. It was about the family. Griffen couldn't keep us safe if we hid threats from him and my soon-to-be ex-husband was a threat, as much as I didn't want to admit it.

Setting my teacup on the tray, I folded my fingers together and rested them on my knees. "He didn't make a specific threat, but he was clearly angry about the divorce."

"What did he say? Exactly," Griffen asked slowly.

"I don't remember word for word. Nash, my brother-in-law, came with me. I was worried Tyler might be there. Nash recorded everything Tyler said. He's going to send the recording to Angie."

Griffen raised an eyebrow at my dithering. I'd gotten out of the habit of being upfront. Life with Tyler was easier if I was indirect. He didn't respond well to confrontation. But I wasn't living with Tyler anymore, and Griffen wasn't going to yell at me if I was blunt.

Bracing myself, I laid it out, "He said he'd make me pay

for trying to leave him, and that he wasn't going to let me go. That if I wanted a divorce, I'd have to fight him for it."

His voice so neutral, it sent a chill down my spine, Griffen asked, "Did he touch you?"

"No," I breathed in a rush of air and sound. "No."

Griffen didn't say anything. His green eyes weighty on mine, he read every nuance of my expression. After a long moment, he nodded. "And before? How many times?"

I'd never told Griffen that Tyler had hit me. I'd never told anyone except Angelica. I could barely absorb it myself. Nash knew, only because he'd been there the last time when I'd caught Tyler in bed with that woman and told him I was leaving him. By the time I'd made it home, my cheek had sported a nice purpling bruise.

I'd tried to hide it with makeup, but it had been Griffen's job to see through such things. I should have known he'd figured it out. "Only three times," I said.

"And the last was in June?" Griffen clarified.

I gave a short nod. "Twice while we were together. And then the last time when I went to tell him I wanted a divorce."

"He won't touch you again," Griffen promised.

I picked up my teacup with a steady hand and took a long sip, letting the hot liquid warm me, and waited for relief to come. Griffen and his security staff would protect me from Tyler. I knew they would. And yet, something in me couldn't relax.

I'd never seen that expression in Tyler's eyes before. Hate and the clear intent to hurt me. He wasn't going to let me go. He wasn't going to give up. I knew it to the marrow of my bones. Despite the heat of the tea, a shiver ran down my spine. Once, I would have said Tyler was too lazy and self-absorbed to cause me any real harm. After that scene at the penthouse, I wasn't sure.

"I called your lawyer," Griffen said, changing the subject.

My eyebrows shot up my forehead and my spine went straight. "You called Angelica? She's not your lawyer."

Griffen's mouth quirked on one side. "I know, but I'm your big brother and a nosy bastard. She wouldn't tell me anything, just so you know."

"Don't badger Angelica," I said. "You'll waste her time and run up my bill."

"Eat something, Parker," Griffen ordered, nodding at the plate between us.

Obedient, I picked up a sandwich and took a bite. Cheddar and roasted chicken with some sort of peppery greens and a spicy mustard that made my taste buds tingle. My mouth watered and for a few minutes, all I could think about was filling my empty stomach.

I almost didn't hear Griffen over the sound of my chewing when he said, "Your bill is what I called her about. I told her to send everything to me."

I chewed furiously, swallowing hard. Griffen was already shaking his head when I opened my mouth. "Griffen, no. This isn't your–"

"It *is* my responsibility. One hundred percent. I'm paying every single one of those bills. This is me telling you what's going to happen, not me asking your permission."

"Bossy," I grumbled under my breath.

"Damn straight."

I sipped my tea, trying to hide the warmth in my chest at his determination to take care of me. I couldn't remember the last time anyone had. Aside from Nash. And Claudia.

But this wasn't the same. Griffen was my big brother. He was family.

"Griffen," I tried to protest, my words catching in my throat.

"Parker," he countered. "Do you have any money?"

Chapter Nine

PARKER

I froze, the sandwich lifted halfway to my mouth, unexpected tears pricking my eyes as the fierce heat of a flush hit my cheeks. Money. I was ashamed to answer Griffen. Despite my expensive clothes and jewelry, Tyler and I never had much cash. Claudia seemed to pay for everything, money appearing just when we needed it and disappearing to cover our bills. Tyler refused to consider getting a job, finding a career, or doing anything other than flitting around entertaining himself.

When I'd suggested that I find some kind of employment, he'd been livid. That conversation was the first time he'd hit me. I might have gone behind his back or pushed harder if not for that. He'd lost it, his eyes hot with rage, screaming so loud that flecks of spittle flew from his mouth as he'd ranted. I was useless and stupid, and if I got a job I'd be even more of an embarrassment than I already was.

I'd protested, insisting we had to do something, that we couldn't go on running up bills we couldn't pay, living as if we had millions when, in reality, we had nothing. I'd made the mistake of reminding him that Claudia was covering everything. That had ignited a whole new level of fury and he'd whirled around, leading with his fist and catching me hard on the cheek.

I'll never forget the way the room had tilted, the carpet slick under my feet as I tumbled into an awkward heap. He'd kicked, catching me in the back and then the ribs, knocking me off balance. I'd scrambled on my knees, seeking shelter behind the couch before I'd slipped out of my heels, gotten to my feet, and sprinted for the stairs. I'd locked myself in our room, terrified Tyler would come after me.

He hadn't. I'd lay curled on the floor, hiding in the closet, waiting, but he never came. I don't know where he went, but I didn't see him for three days. When he came home, it was as if nothing had happened. I wasn't brave enough to bring it up. My face was still swollen, my ribs spiking in pain every time I moved, my back so sore I'd been sleeping on my stomach. Every time I thought about confronting him, the pain reminded me to keep my mouth shut.

"Parker," Griffen prompted. I avoided his eyes, afraid I'd see pity. I wanted to refuse, to say that I could handle this myself, but I knew I couldn't. I'd sold some jewelry to pay Angelica's retainer and first invoice, but the second was still tucked in my purse, more overdue by the day.

I'd spent more than one night laying in bed, a tight knot in my stomach, staring at the ceiling as I tried to figure out where I was going to get the money to pay it and all the invoices to come. The tight knot loosened, just a little, at the realization that Griffen had already solved that problem for me. I'd planned to find a jeweler and see what I could do with the pieces still packed in my carry-on. If Griffen insisted on paying Angie, I still had a little safety net.

"If Tyler is prepared to be a pain in the ass," Griffen said, "there are limits to what we can do to push your divorce through." Griffen raised an eyebrow in question.

"He is absolutely prepared to be a pain in the ass," I confirmed.

"Then one thing we have on our side is money. I'm covering Angelica's bills. I looked her up and her reputation is impeccable. Tyler is going to have trouble finding anyone willing to take her on, given his lack of funds."

A true smile spread across my lips. I picked up another half sandwich, my stomach still rumbling. "That's what Nash said."

"Sounds like a smart guy."

"Smart doesn't quite cover it. Not when it comes to Nash," I said and took a hefty bite of the sandwich.

"Your brother-in-law doesn't have a lot in common with your husband, does he?" Griffen poured us both second cups of tea.

I laughed, slapping a hand over my mouth so I didn't spit crumbs at Griffen. "They're polar opposites," I said after I swallowed. "They've never gotten along, as far as I know."

Griffen picked up his teacup and leaned back in his chair, propping an ankle on his knee. "I'm glad he was able to help you out."

"Me too," I agreed.

He hesitated, and I knew I wasn't going to like what he said next. I was right. "I want you to ask Angelica to send me the video footage from yesterday. Security needs to see it."

"Griffen–" I started to protest, horror soaking me in ice at the thought of our security team watching Tyler threaten me–his ugly words, my weakness–everything I wanted to keep a secret.

"Parker, we need to know what we're dealing with."

"Just you," I whispered. "Please? I don't want anyone else to see it. I don't want them to think I'm—" My voice faded away. I couldn't bring myself to say the words. Weak. Stupid. Pathetic. A victim.

This was my home. Here, I just wanted to be Parker, not Tyler's wife.

Griffen gave a sharp nod. "Just me. I promise."

"Okay." I set the rest of my sandwich on the plate, my appetite gone.

Griffen changed the subject to his wife, Hope. She was asleep, in her second trimester of pregnancy and still unable to resist a nap in the afternoon. Hope and Griffen had been childhood friends, then bitter enemies, when she'd ended up being the catalyst for his exile. In a million years, I never thought they'd end up married, much less deeply in love and eagerly anticipating the birth of their first child.

Watching Griffen with her, his tenderness and casual affection, the way we always seemed to stumble in on them kissing or cuddling, had been a big part of my decision to leave Tyler. I wanted that. Not with Griffen, obviously, but with someone. Someday. I had to divorce Tyler first.

As if she'd heard us talking about her, Hope appeared in the doorway just as I finished my tea. Giving her a hug on my way out, I wandered to the terrace behind the house, wanting to stretch out somewhere comfortable. Not in my room. I didn't feel like being inside.

I lay down on one of the lounge chairs looking out over the green lawn. The formal gardens of Heartstone Manor were barren, the squares of the parterre design defined but empty. For some reason no one understood, my father had ignored the state of the house in the years before he died. He'd fired the groundskeeper, along with most of the Manor staff, and let the estate fall apart around him.

Hawk Bristol, our current groundskeeper, was also head of security. After someone tried to run Griffen off the road, he'd decided security was a higher priority than the gardens. No one argued.

It was still beautiful, even without the flowers and decoratively trimmed shrubs. July in the mountains was just about perfect—the trees every shade of green, the skies electric-blue, the breeze chasing off the heat before it could build to unbearable levels.

I tried to relax. I was home. I was safe. I didn't have to worry about paying Angelica. I'd dodged Griffen's question about money, and he'd let me off easy with his questions about Tyler. He'd wanted to push. I was glad he hadn't. I needed a break.

I needed to remind myself that everything was okay. For now. The sparkle of the pool caught my eyes, and I drifted, letting the sun soak into my skin and warm my cold, stiff bones. The thick cushion of the lounge cradling me, I dropped my head back and watched the deep green leaves of the forest swaying in the breeze.

I'd lived all these years with Tyler and never quite understood how much I missed Heartstone Manor. Growing up here hadn't been easy. My father had been distant, demanding, and cruel. My mother had been everything he wasn't, but she'd died when I was nine. After that, we were mostly on our own. Miss Martha tried to keep an eye on us, but she couldn't parent ten children and run the estate.

I'd been lonely, grieving, deeply afraid of my father, and desperate for a different life. So desperate I hadn't realized that my home wasn't the problem. I loved my home. It was

Prentice who made everyone miserable. Now that he was gone, I could remember everything I loved about this place. Some of my siblings resented the will's dictate that we all live here for five years, but not me. For the first time in my life, I was happy to be exactly where I was.

A child shouted, another following behind. Then the rumble of a voice, older but not adult. I cracked my eyes open, shifting my gaze back to the pool to see my brother Tennessee and his girlfriend Scarlett, her long red hair flames in the bright sun. They were joined by Scarlett's two boys, August and Thatcher, and Savannah's young son, Nicky.

Seconds later, a shout and a splash drifted across the gardens. My eyes slid shut, my lips curling into a satisfied smile. Tenn had fallen in love with Scarlet in the blink of an eye. We were all still reeling from their lightning-fast courtship, but no one could deny they fit each other to perfection. I'd never seen him so happy.

It had been a special kind of fun to watch my too-serious brother fall head over heels for his ready-made new family. Fun and wonderful, but also another reminder of everything I was missing by staying with Tyler.

I drifted off, dozing in the sun, lulled by splashing from the pool and more shouts as Tenn tossed the younger boys in the water over and over. Hours later, I woke to the soft touch of Savannah's hand on my shoulder.

"Sorry to wake you, Parker, but dinner's in fifteen minutes and I thought you might be hungry." I blinked up at Savanna's kind smile. "I'm so glad you're home and every-thing went all right in New York."

Shifting to sit up, I set my bare feet on the cool slate terrace. Savannah reached out a hand, and I took it, letting her help me to my feet. I wobbled a little and laughed. "I can't believe I fell asleep. I feel like I was away for a year instead of two days."

"I know what you mean," Savannah said. Flinging her arm around my shoulders, she gave me a quick squeeze and a gentle shove in the direction of the terrace doors. I changed for dinner as I usually did, but not into a cocktail dress. Instead, I traded my red gauzy sundress for a white poet's blouse and a pair of ocean-blue capris.

My stomach fluttered as I walked into the dining room, expecting a third-degree. All I got were words of welcome. No one asked about Tyler or what I'd been doing in New York. Everyone left me alone, even my usually nosy aunt Ophelia and always bitchy cousin Bryce. I found myself back in my room early, my eyes heavy and my body desperate for more sleep.

I washed my face, pulled on a camisole and loose cotton bottoms, and crawled into bed, wishing I was already asleep and not sure what to do about the hollow space under my heart. A hollow space exactly the shape of Nash Kingsley.

Damn it. I wasn't supposed to miss him.

It didn't even make sense. Why would I miss him?

As if he was reading my mind, my phone chimed with a text message.

You get home okay?

I tried not to overthink it. I really did. I typed and erased my answer three times before I settled on–

I did. Had lunch with my brother and fell asleep on the terrace.

I'm jealous you had a nap without me. Neither of us got any sleep last night.

My body heated at the memory of what we'd done

instead. For a second, I could taste him, salty and sweet under my lips, could feel him moving against me.

I almost dropped my phone.

I was being ridiculous. It wasn't like the phone could somehow transmit my lustful thoughts to Nash. Wouldn't that be humiliating? Shaking away the idea, I answered–

Thank you for everything.

His reply took a minute. When it came I puzzled over his words for days.

Anything you need, Parker. Always. See you soon.

Chapter Ten

PARKER

My rooms were in a state of organized chaos. I was trying to focus on the *organized* aspect instead of the chaos. I'd woken this morning with that familiar knot of anxiety in my stomach. Yes, Griffen had taken on the burden of paying Angelica, but he'd made a good point.

I didn't have any money, nor did I have access to any. Not of my own, at least. I'm sure Griffen would have given me anything I asked for, but I was twenty-seven years old. I couldn't live with the humiliation of asking him for an allowance like I was a child instead of a full-grown adult.

I was familiar with the queasy burn of humiliation after all these years married to Tyler. I could do without that from now on, thank you very much. I'd get a job. I'd have to, sooner rather than later. But not today. I still had to figure some things out, like what I was interested in, and if I was qualified for anything. I'd finished college, possibly a point in my favor, but I'd been a dual English and French major with a concentration in French poetry and literature. Not the most useful skill set in the job market.

Before I tackled the issue of employment, I'd go after low-hanging fruit—the contents of my closet. Tyler had loved to shop. Especially since everything we bought went on Claudia's limitless credit card. I can't deny that I loved shopping too. It was possibly the only thing Tyler and I had in common. I'd only felt a twinge of guilt at spending Claudia's money. She'd always been so generous, so enthusiastic about my choices. Some of the best times I had with her were our shopping trips.

Claudia wouldn't mind what I was about to do. She'd be glad I was making lemonade out of lemons. I hoped. I couldn't bring myself to mention my plan during our brief conversation the day before. She'd been on her way out and had called to let me know that she'd secured Tyler an attorney, but with strict instructions that she wasn't paying for anything beyond an uncontested divorce on my terms.

Dryly, and a little sad, she'd admitted that she didn't have much hope that Tyler would agree. I'd cried a little when we got off the phone, grateful Claudia still loved me. She'd been the best part of my marriage to Tyler, by far, and it eased my worries a bit to know she wasn't angry with me.

Turning to face the chaos, I took in the piles of clothes on my bed. The dressing room was empty, the contents covering every surface in my suite. Like most of the family suites in Heartstone Manor, mine was divided into two spacious rooms, a sitting room and an adjoining bedroom with a generous dressing room and bath.

I loved my rooms. When we'd moved into Heartstone after my father's death, Tyler had insisted on redecorating. It was one of the only times I'd flat-out refused him. My mother and I had decorated my suite eighteen years ago, just before she'd died. She'd known she didn't have long, and she'd wanted me to have the 'grown-up' room I'd been asking for, had wanted to create it with me, before she was gone.

With Miss Martha's help, we'd poured over home design magazines together, carefully crafting a design esthetic that was probably too adult for the nine-year-old I'd been but was perfect for me now. Done in a midnight navy, with snow-white trim and crown moldings, and brushed gold accents, my rooms were both elegant and inviting. A deep green velvet sofa and chairs faced the fireplace in the sitting room, now with a flat-screen hanging above instead of the oil painting of sunflowers that had been there when I was a girl.

My childhood desk was still in the corner, with an ancient chair pushed in front. I'd have to find a new chair if I ended up using the desk, but the desk itself was another thing that had been too much for a little girl, but fit me now. Wide and deep, with curved legs and no drawers, it appeared light and airy but gave me plenty of space to work. At the moment it was heaped with suits. So many suits.

The pile of suits was arguably ridiculous. I hadn't had a proper job since I'd interned for my father after my freshman year in college. But these weren't business suits, they were the kind of suits I'd wear to lunch at the club, or to a board meeting for one of the charities I'd been involved in. I'd have to go through that pile carefully. Maybe I should keep them until I figured out a job, in case I needed them for work.

Purses covered the sofa and chairs. Again, so many purses. Why had I thought I needed so many? The answer was that I hadn't, but living with Claudia and Tyler, it was hard not to accumulate things. I felt a little guilty that Claudia had paid for all of this. If I was going to sell them and make a profit, I should give her back the money. I wasn't going to. For one thing, she wouldn't accept it. And, more realistically, I needed it.

That morning, I'd driven into town to open an account at the local credit union. Until then, I hadn't had an account that Tyler didn't also have access to. If I was going to build a nest egg, I didn't want him stealing it out from under me.

A knock sounded on my open bedroom door. I turned to see my younger sister Sterling leaning against the frame. "Did your closet explode?" she asked, strolling into the room.

"Kind of." I hesitated, not ready to explain. But this was Sterling, my baby sister who'd always loved me, even when I married Tyler and left her here alone with our father. Sterling, who had drunk her way to the bottom of a bottle before our father died, and had, so far, pulled herself back out through sheer grit. Sterling, whose first real relationship had ended a week ago when she discovered her new love had used her to get revenge for his father.

No matter how strong my instincts were to shut her out and pretend everything was fine, I couldn't do it. If I couldn't trust Sterling, who could I trust? I sank onto the edge of the green sofa, nudging a few purses out of the way. Sterling followed suit, sitting on one of the matching chairs beside my end of the sofa.

"I'm going through everything to see what I want to keep."

"And what are you going to do with the rest?" Sterling asked, scanning the room, taking in the piles of dresses, rows of shoes, and so much more.

"I, uh— Well, Tyler wasn't working and neither was I, and we don't, I mean, I don't—"

"You're broke," Sterling finished, putting me out of my misery.

A weak smile lifted my lips. "Basically. I need to get a

job, but that's going to take some time to figure out. For now, I thought I could sell some of this stuff so I have a little cash."

Sterling's smile could have eclipsed the sun. Bouncing a little on the edge of her seat, she rubbed her hands together. "Parker, this is going to be a lot more than 'a little cash'. A lot more." She gave the pile of purses beside me a more careful assessment. "Have you sold anything before? Consignment or an online auction or anything?"

I shook my head. "Never. Have you?"

"Oh, yeah," she said with relish.

I raised my eyebrows. "Really? When? Why?"

Sterling let out a laugh, rolling her blue eyes to the ceiling. "After Dad died, Griffen cut me off. He told me to get a job if I wanted money because he'd give me room and board, but not another dime. I got the job at the Inn, but it wasn't a lot of money and I realized I didn't even like half of my clothes, so I figured out how to sell what I didn't want. You just lucked out. I know exactly what to do with this stuff to get you top dollar."

I sank back into the sofa in relief before a stab of guilt hit me. "I've been taking money from Griffen. Not a lot, but I didn't want to use Claudia's credit cards and—"

Sterling was already shaking her head. "No, Parker, it's not the same. I was pissed at Griffen at the time, but he was right. I needed to get my shit together. Griffen didn't cut me off because he cared about the money, he did it to shock me out of the mess I'd made of my life."

"I don't want to take his money," I said, Sterling's stark explanation making me feel less like a screw-up. We'd both messed up our lives, but if Sterling could come so far in only a few months, maybe there was hope for me, too.

"I know what you mean. And hey, maybe you'll find a

job you like. I loved the Inn for a while, though I like working for Quinn. It's quiet. I like the quiet right now."

She stood and paced around the room, examining the shoes and purses with what I now realized was a practiced eye. After a minute, she straightened and turned to me. "First, we have to figure out what you want to keep. Once we have that worked out, we can start selling the rest of this."

"You'll help me? You don't mind?" I asked, the daunting task suddenly something to look forward to.

Sterling slid onto the sofa beside me, knocking a pile of purses to the floor. Her arms wrapped around me, pulling me close, surrounding me with her gardenia and lily scent, the same one my mother had worn, wreathing me in love.

"Of course, I don't mind. I was going to throw a party to celebrate you leaving the dick-head, but selling all this stuff is way better. It'll be a sister project."

I leaned my head into hers, my throat tight with emotion. A sister project was exactly what I needed. "Thanks, Sterling," I whispered into her hair.

"Anytime, babe," she whispered back, sitting up. With an avaricious gleam in her eye, she asked, "Did he give you any decent jewelry? Because I have a guy for that."

"That's what I went to New York for. I wasn't going to leave my jewelry for Tyler, but I don't know what to do with it. I sold a few pieces the last time I was there, so I could pay my lawyer, but I know I didn't get what they were worth."

"I've got you covered. Is there anything you want to keep?"

"I'm holding on to my ring to give back to Claudia—it was hers—as well as a few family pieces she should have, but the rest I don't care for. Tyler's taste was gaudier than mine."

Sterling rolled her eyes as she stood. "Not a surprise. So, is your closet empty?"

"Completely. Except for underwear and bras, that kind of thing. Where do we start?"

Sterling made a beeline for the mountain of dresses stacked on my bed. She flipped through the first few, checking the labels, before turning back to me. "Are all of them this quality? In terms of wear and designers?"

"Pretty much. The most worn dresses are the ones I wouldn't want to sell, anyway."

"Excellent." Propping her hands on her hips, Sterling raised her chin in my direction. "Strip off so you can try some of this stuff on." Not waiting for me to respond, she crossed the room and closed my door, flipping the lock. That was enough for me. I pulled my dress over my head, standing there in panties and a bra, and surveyed the pile along with Sterling.

She picked up the dress at the top of the pile, holding it up in front of herself. "This one?"

I didn't have to think. The cream silk cocktail dress was sedate, even for me. I shook my head. Sterling picked up the next and tossed it at me. Tags dangled from the neckline of the formal gown. Fashioned of wispy lengths of green and blue chiffon, with delicate silver threads woven throughout, it was a dress for a fairy princess. Cocking my head to the side, I took another look at the deep, rich colors, the bold decolletage.

No, not for a princess, this was the dress of a fairy queen. I'd bought it in Paris, years before, and had never worn it. Tyler had hated it, always demanding that I dress in a severely elegant style that provided the ideal background for his more colorful fashion sense. He wanted me to be admired, but not so much that I drew attention from him.

"Try this one on," Sterling ordered, reminding me of Griffen in her bossiness. "Why haven't you worn it? It's perfect for you." She scanned me from head to toe once I'd pulled the dress over my head. "I wish I was as tall as you. And as slender. I couldn't pull that off in a million years."

I laughed. "Maybe, but I'll never fill out a bra like you do."

"True," Sterling said, nodding sagely. I wasn't much taller than Sterling, but my small frame made it seem like I was. Wearing heels all the time didn't hurt either. In contrast, Sterling was barely 5' 2" and all curves, with a bombshell figure I'd envied ever since she hit puberty.

I handed back the fairy queen dress and Sterling set it in a new pile I thought of as my keepers. She picked up the next dress and immediately chucked it into the 'sell' pile, not asking my opinion. I didn't argue. Grey and boring, I'd happily never wear it again.

I wouldn't have guessed Sterling could be so efficient. In less than an hour, we'd sorted the mountain of dresses on my bed into three piles; Sell, Keep, and Maybe. Sterling sent me to my closet to hang up the 'Keep' pile, and ruthlessly dealt with the 'Maybe' pile, bringing me only two of the Maybe dresses before she helped me finish hanging the keepers and dragged me over to the stack of suits on my desk.

I fought her on the suits. I knew I couldn't keep them all, but I was worried about getting rid of too much and then needing to buy clothes for a job I didn't have yet. Sterling shook her head in disagreement. "I'll pick out everything you could wear to work at the Inn. That's a good benchmark since I doubt you'll work anywhere more formal than that. I'll save one or two suitable for a more social event, and the rest have to go. Trust me, in such good condition and with these designers, they're worth more for re-sale than they are in your closet."

I chewed on my lower lip, about to argue, when a knock sounded on the door. Glad I'd pulled on a robe during our last trip to the closet, I called out, "Who is it?"

Chapter Eleven

PARKER

"Savannah," came the response.

At my smile, Sterling unlocked the door and ushered Savannah inside before closing and locking it behind her. Savannah came to an abrupt halt just inside the door, her eyes wide. "What happened in here?" she asked, a little breathless.

"Fundraising," Sterling answered, succinctly.

Savannah nodded, sagely. "Good idea. Want some help? Or food? Tea? I realized you both missed lunch and wanted to see if you needed anything." With a confidence that spoke of long familiarity, she added, "Plus, I was curious."

I'd known Savannah my entire life. We were the same age, and until a few years ago her mother, Miss Martha, had been the head housekeeper at Heartstone Manor. In my father's household, there were clear lines between help and family and I had been no rebel. I'd known better than to get too attached to Savannah.

Forging a real friendship wouldn't have been good for either of us or for Miss Martha. While we hadn't been best friends, we had been friendly. I couldn't think of anyone I would rather have running our lives now. Far more than staff, Savannah was family. With my father gone, I could finally treat her that way without worrying she'd pay a price for my affection.

"We'd love something to eat," Sterling threw out, "Have you had a break? Wanna hang out and help me make Parker try stuff on? She has a killer wardrobe, even if most of it isn't her style."

"I'm not sure I know what my style is," I added with a shrug.

"Not this stuff," Sterling said, raising an eyebrow at Savanna in invitation.

Savannah gave us a slow smile back. "Actually, I missed lunch and I have some time before I have to get organized for dinner. I'll be back. Hot tea or iced?"

"Hot," Sterling called after her. "With those little butter cookies? The ones with the sugar on top?"

"On the way," Savannah called back, the door shutting behind her.

When Savannah returned, pushing a cart stacked with silver-lidded plates and a steaming pot of tea, I was wearing a black suit Tyler had picked out for an event I'd long forgotten. She took one look at me and raised an eyebrow, "Who died?"

Sterling flashed her a smile. "Right?" Twirling her finger in the air, she ordered, "Take it off and put it in the 'Sell' pile. You're not an undertaker or an accountant. How something this expensive can be this blah is beyond me."

Stripping off the suit and carefully hanging it back up, I agreed. "I haven't met any undertakers, but none of the accountants I know would be caught dead in something this dull."

"Do you know a lot of accountants?" Savannah asked, handing me a plate with a mini quiche and a delicate fork.

"Not really," I admitted, "only the Kingsleys' accountants, who came to the house a few times a year. Porter Kingsley didn't go to people, people came to him."

"Was he an asshole like Dad?" Sterling asked.

I choked back a startled laugh. I wasn't used to everyone talking so openly about what a bastard our father had been. Shaking my head after I managed to swallow, I said, "No, he was nothing like Prentice. He could be a hard ass. He butted heads with Nash all the time because Nash didn't want to join the family business. And he mostly ignored Tyler, because he didn't have the patience to put up with him. But he was kind to me, and he was so sweet with Claudia. He really loved her. I don't think she'll ever get over losing him the way we did."

My phone chimed with a text. Without realizing I was doing it, I looked at the screen, expecting to see Nash's name. Because we'd just mentioned him. Not because I was hoping he'd text me. Of course not. Why would he? He wouldn't.

As if to punish me for my idiotic fantasies about my brother-in-law, my husband's name showed on the screen. I tapped the message, dreading what I would find.

you can't imagine what i'm going to do to you when you come crawling back to me. tell your bitch to back off. i'm getting a new lawyer and we're going to destroy you. by the time we're done, you'll be begging me

Begging him for what? Mercy? For him to take me back?

He didn't say. I sure as hell wasn't going to ask. My skin prickled with goosebumps.

you can't imagine what I'm going to do to you

Did he know how those words would worm into my brain, sending icy tendrils of fear around my heart? How they'd come back to haunt me at odd moments, to remind me I still wasn't free of him? He must. He was trying to scare me into giving in.

It wasn't going to work. If I went back now, I'd never leave. I drew in a slow breath, trying to chase off my sudden unease.

"What is it?" Sterling asked, her worried tone drawing my eyes from my phone.

Shaking my head, I took a screenshot of the message and sent it to Angie. "Just Tyler being an ass. I don't understand this. He doesn't have anything to gain by staying married to me."

"Except your father's money," Savannah said, quietly.

"But inheritances aren't marital property, according to Angelica. And I won't get anything for another five years. And that's assuming there's any money in those trusts at all."

Sterling lifted her chin in agreement. "It would be just like Dad to promise us all a big inheritance if we did what he wanted and then stiff us in the end."

"And it isn't like Tyler to plan long term," I said. "He lives in the moment. A payoff in five years might as well be a lifetime." I shook my head. "I don't think this is about the money."

"Then what do you think it's about?" Savannah asked.

I was beginning to think I knew, though I couldn't bring myself to put it into words, much less say his name.

Nash.

I didn't believe that Tyler had suddenly realized he was deeply in love with me. I'd come to doubt that Tyler was capable of love at all.

Refusing to let me go so he could win an imagined victory over his brother? That made a lot more sense.

I put my phone down and finished my lunch, determined not to let Tyler ruin this time with Sterling and Savannah as he'd ruined so many things already. For hours, I managed to forget about him completely.

Forgetting Nash wasn't as easy. He crept in to my thoughts as I sipped tea and laughed with Sterling and Savannah, as I changed for dinner and got roped into an unexpected game of soccer with Scarlett's boys and my sister Quinn.

Maybe it was because Nash was on my mind. Or maybe it was because he was never far off it, despite my efforts to put him in the past.

I woke in the dark of night, long after the moon had set, when only the stars lit the sky. Closing my eyes, I wished more than anything to slide back into my dream.

Dream or memory? Or something in between...

My head was filled with Nash. My body hummed as if I could still feel his hands on me, his mouth gliding over my skin, the full, deep pleasure of him moving inside me. One night hadn't been enough. How had I possibly thought it could be?

I hadn't meant for it to happen. I'd scheduled my flight home for early evening, but the weather had thwarted my plans. Sitting beside Nash in his car, I'd frowned at the message on my phone. My flight was canceled due to inclement weather. I'd noticed the rain, but hadn't registered the way the wind had kicked up since we'd been inside.

"Problem?" Nash had asked, eyeing my phone.

"My flight was canceled," I explained. "I'll have to call and get on another—"

"I'll take you to my place. You can sort out your ticket there."

His offer had sounded so innocent, it hadn't occurred to me to say no. And even now, after everything, I still believed Nash hadn't had any ulterior motives. We hadn't planned it. It just happened.

The storm shut down all the flights out of the city. The best I could do was a seat on a plane leaving early the next morning. Nash offered me his spare bedroom, far more convenient than a hotel would have been. We'd cooked dinner, steak and asparagus, working together in the kitchen as easily as if we'd been doing it for years. A bottle of wine with dinner, some conversation, and when I'd bumped into Nash in the kitchen, plate in hand, my breasts brushing his chest, I hadn't pulled away.

We stared at each other for an endless moment, the sense of possibility, of anticipation building with every breath. I could have dodged, could have stepped back with an awkward laugh, and let the moment die.

I didn't. I'd set the plate on the counter with a rough clatter and lifted my mouth to his.

I'd only had a kiss like that once before. On my wedding day. Rough and hungry, seductive finesse and raw need. That first time, I'd been a virgin. Young and stupid, I hadn't realized what Nash had to offer. I'd had no clue.

Tyler and I had kissed and touched—enough that I thought I knew what I was getting into. But our joining had more in common with an arranged marriage than a romance. Tyler wanted me to wait for our wedding.

I hadn't understood why a man like Tyler would want a virgin bride until it was too late.

Nothing like an innocent bride who didn't know her own body, or what she should expect. Over the years, I'd had very little sex that I'd enjoyed and a whole lot that I tolerated, at best. Sex with Nash was not remotely in the same category.

A little wine, the warm buzz of companionship, and I jumped at the chance to touch Nash. Literally. I'm not sure he expected my enthusiasm, but he took full advantage. Just remembering the way I'd pulled at his clothes–getting him mostly naked before we made it out of the kitchen–had my cheeks burning and my nipples peaking.

Laughing, he'd scooped me up and carried me to his bed, laying me out on the crisp, white sheets and worshipping every inch of me until I was screaming his name, begging for release. He gave it to me. Again and again. I hoped it was as good for him as it was for me. I didn't have enough experience to guess. The whole thing had my head spinning until I didn't know which way was up. We'd had sex three times. How, I don't know. I didn't think men could do it that often. It couldn't be normal.

Why would it be? Nothing about Nash was normal. And none of that mattered.

I scrubbed my palms over my face, trying to banish the lingering heat from my dream. I'd taken advantage of Nash and I couldn't bring myself to regret it. Especially since I finally knew what sex was supposed to be like. I thought all those romance novels were lying. Until Nash, the only orgasms I'd ever had came from my own fingers.

Was it any wonder I was dreaming of him? That was probably the best sex I'd ever have, for the rest of my life. My heart sank at that idea. Would I be waking from sleep, dreaming of Nash, decades from now?

How depressing. Surely there was a man out there who was as good as Nash. I'd settle for half as good. A quarter.

My gut answered with a firm, no. There wasn't anyone as good as Nash.

I rolled over, folding my pillow and shoving it under my head. Fine, then my next partner would be sub-par. I'd learn to live with that because Nash was my past. I was moving on from all of them, except Claudia. My future was here, in Sawyers Bend, with my family. I'd have to settle for my memories–every orgasmic minute of them–because I'd never get the real thing again.

Letting out a pathetic sigh, I tried to fall back to sleep, minus the sex dream this time. The last thing I needed was to be hung up on a man I couldn't have. Or any man, for that matter. I'd gone from my father's house to Tyler's. It was time to stand on my own two feet, just Parker, no man involved.

Squeezing my pillow, I let out another sigh. In the light of day, my newfound independence felt powerful. In my bed, in the dark, it mostly felt lonely.

Chapter Twelve

PARKER

T he small, borrowed printer on my desk hummed, spitting out a page and chugging along to the next. It was slow, and I didn't have color ink, but it worked and it was free, so I wasn't complaining. Sterling, currently on pause selling her own things, had given me the rest of her shipping supplies, along with the printer Griffen had let her use when she was actively selling her stuff.

I was extremely pleased to note that I'd had seven successful sales so far and was about to use the last of my borrowed supplies. A few days before, Sterling and I had taken a field trip to Asheville to sell some of the smaller pieces of jewelry Tyler had bought me. It hadn't amounted to much money–Sterling refused to let me bring more, insisting that I'd get a better price when we could go to her guy in Atlanta–but it was enough to put a little cash in my pocket. Enough that I wouldn't have to borrow money to replenish my shipping supplies.

I did a little dance before I carefully folded a linen suit around a piece of tissue paper and wrapped it in another, sealing the package with a gold sticker I'd gotten from Sterling. Attractive presentation, she'd instructed, went a long way in warding off buyer complaints. I didn't know if my buyer would care, but I liked how pretty the suit was in its tissue wrapping. It would be fun to open if nothing else.

Folding the packing slip and setting it on top, I slid everything into a padded envelope and sealed it, smoothing the mailing label on the front. Selling my things wasn't going to change my life, but it was forward movement. At least I was taking action on something instead of sitting around waiting for Angie to call and tell me Tyler had agreed to sign the divorce papers.

So far he was agreeing to absolutely nothing. He'd fired the lawyer Claudia had found, declaring that he wouldn't be bullied into abandoning his marriage. That was exactly how he put it. Because in his mind, I was the bully, and he was the poor, innocent victim being forced from his wife's side.

Yeah, right. No one who knew either of us would believe it, but that was the story he was telling himself and anyone else who would listen. I reminded myself that it didn't matter. I had a life to live and Tyler's lies weren't going to stop me.

And speaking of having a life to live, before I took the packages to town to mail, I had one last thing to do. Stacking my packages on the front passenger seat of my car, I closed the door and went back in to the house. I made my way to Griffen's office and knocked lightly.

Both he and Hope called for me to come in at the same time. When she saw it was me, Hope stood. "I have to check in with Savannah on some things. I'll get out of your way."

"You don't have to leave–" I started to say, but she squeezed my arm and smiled as she passed me.

"I know. I lost track of time. I didn't realize until you knocked that I'd told Savannah I'd come down to see her half an hour ago. I won't be long. Unless you need me?"

Hope waited, and I knew if I wanted her to stay, she would. I almost asked her, a little nervous to start this conversation with Griffen. But I'm a grown woman and I don't need to use my sister-in-law as a buffer, no matter how tempting the idea.

"No, we're good. Thanks." With another smile and an affectionate squeeze to my arm, she was gone. I faced Griffen with a flutter of nerves in my stomach.

"Everything okay?" He asked, gesturing to the empty chair in front of his desk. "Do you want tea? Lunch?"

"No, I'm good. I just have a few questions." I sat in the chair opposite Griffen, hearing the high pitch of my voice. Ugh. I hated being nervous, especially when I shouldn't be. This was Griffen. He'd been nothing but kind since he came home. I had no reason to be nervous. Still, I was. Shifting in the chair, I smoothed my skirt over my knees and tried to figure out where to start. I'd practiced this, dammit.

Before I could say anything, Griffen did. "How are things going with Tyler?"

"Angie didn't tell you?" I asked, tartly.

Griffen grinned back at me, unrepentant, and shook his head. "She made it very clear that I could pay your bills, but she wouldn't give me any info without your express permission. Easier to ask you."

I shook my head. "Nothing to report. Claudia got him an attorney on the condition that he doesn't oppose the divorce. He fired that attorney and sent me a lovely text message I screen-shotted and sent to Angie. He has a little time to file the next thing—I can't remember what it's called.

Notice of Appearance, I think? And if he doesn't, we can ask for a court date to get a judge to rule."

"So you're in a holding pattern?" He clarified, his brows pulled together.

"Basically. There's nothing I can do to force him to move any faster." I let out a gust of air I'd been holding. "I'm trying not to be frustrated about it. Angie is doing everything she can."

Griffen nodded. "How can I help you today?" he asked, his words going a long way to ease my nerves. He hadn't said, *What do you want*, but *How can I help you?* Griffen's help was exactly what I needed.

"I need a job," I said, bluntly. "Sterling is helping me sell some of my things, but that's only a stopgap. I need a career." I glanced to the ceiling, inwardly cringing at that word. *Career*. "Maybe that's too ambitious," I confessed. "I need to work and earn money. I'm tired of depending on other people."

Griffen folded his hands in front of him, his expression grim for a long moment before it cleared and he smiled. "I don't like you selling your things," he began, holding up a hand to stop me when I would have protested. "But that's your business, and it's good problem solving, so I'm not going to get on your case about it."

"Thanks," I said, dryly.

"What kind of job do you think you want?" he asked, head tilted to the side, all his attention focused on me. I thought of the child Hope carried, and what a wonderful parent my oldest brother would make.

I shrugged one shoulder, grimacing helplessly. "I have no idea. I don't really know how to do anything. That's the problem. I can plan a party, and shop, and pack really well for a long trip. That's about it." I wished desperately for some skill I could offer, but I had nothing. My degrees were useless, and I had no life skills.

"Are you interested in working at the Inn? The position Sterling left is still open."

"She might want it back," I protested. Sterling had quit the Inn when she'd broken up with Forrest, who was currently the Inn's CFO. I'd expected Tenn and Royal to fire him when he'd admitted he'd come to Sawyers Bend for revenge, but Sterling had asked them not to and they'd reluctantly agreed. Apparently, he was a pretty good CFO, even if he'd been a terrible boyfriend.

"She might," Griffen agreed, "And while I understand why she wants the peace and quiet of working for Quinn, I know Royal and Tenn are hoping she'll come back."

"It might be a while, so maybe I could fill in until she's ready," I offered doubtfully. In truth, I didn't really know what went into event planning, but the sound of it didn't fill my heart with excitement. Not that it mattered. I needed a job, and I wasn't in a position to be picky.

Griffen considered that for a moment. "What do you think about helping Hope and me? Trying out a little project management?"

That sounded interesting. "What kind of project management? I've never done anything like that before."

"With this kind of project, neither have we. I talked to Harvey," he said, referring to the family attorney and the person in charge of administering our father's will and the trusts he left behind. "We need to move forward on updating both the housekeeper's cottage and the gatehouse. I know Hawk says he's fine with the mice and the outdated plumbing, but I'm not. And Savannah and Nicky need more than their rooms off the kitchens. They're a family. They need space."

"What would you want me to do?" I asked, intrigued. I liked houses and design, though I didn't know how to do much renovating myself.

"To begin with, take a good look at both spaces and put together a report on what you need. Security is still an issue. Hawk doesn't want contractors all over the property distracting his team, but he's vetted Billy Bob, and they have experience with this kind of thing."

Billy Bob were brothers who worked around town as jacks of all trades. Savannah had called them in to help her get the house ready for all of us to move back, and they'd been around ever since. Heartstone Manor was one of the country's finest examples of Gilded Age design, but after our father had stopped maintaining it, entire sections had fallen into disrepair. Nothing was dangerous or structurally unsound, but outside of the family wing, half of the light switches didn't work, and the plumbing could be questionable at best.

"Are they done in the guest wing?" As far as I knew, Savannah had them up there trying to get us at least one functioning guest room. She'd somehow managed to set up one of the guest suites for Scarlett and her boys, but the others were dark and unfurnished, with barely a workable bathroom between them.

"Not by a long shot," Griffen said grimly. "But the room at the end of the hall is in decent condition if we need it. I'm more concerned with the cottage and gatehouse at this point. I'd rather get livable quarters for Savannah, Nicky, and Hawk than prepare for a house party we aren't planning to host any time soon."

"So basically, you want me to assess both spaces, tell you what I think they need, ask Billy Bob what they think, and get the renovations started?"

"Exactly." Griffen leaned back in his chair, a satisfied smile on his face. "Does that sound like something you'd be interested in?"

I let myself consider it for a moment and discovered that, yes; it sounded exactly like something I'd be interested in. I was great at organizing things, and I had a good eye for design. "How would it work?"

Griffen leaned forward and pulled a blank notepad in front of him. "I'd want you to keep track of your hours, along with a general note on what you've been doing during those hours, as well as any expenses. I'll put you on the Heartstone payroll as day staff at the rate Savannah is currently paying new hires. It's not a fortune, but we pay a decent wage, and you get health insurance."

I nodded. I had to start somewhere and a decent wage with health insurance sounded way better than no wage. I hadn't even thought about health insurance. Claudia had set up a policy when Tyler and I got married, and it was past time I made other arrangements.

"I'll do a preliminary assessment on the cottage and the gatehouse, and then call in Billy Bob to see what they think," I said, already planning my first steps. "Then we'll have to have a meeting about the budget."

"Sounds good. When you take a look, keep in mind that we don't need to go over the top, but I want the quality of the renovations to be in keeping with the main house. No cheap materials or that kind of thing. I haven't gone through them since we moved in, but I recall the basic structures are sound. Hopefully, most of what you have to deal with will be superficial."

"I'm on it," I promised, my heart swelling at the realization that I had a job, and it was one I thought I'd be good at. It wasn't long-term, but that was okay. I wasn't sure I was ready to find a career quite yet. This would get me started, and it would put some cash in my bank account. I leaned forward to rise, and remembered the other thing I'd wanted to talk to Griffen about.

"One more thing," I said, mentally crossing my fingers for luck. "I have a request."

Griffen's green eyes brightened with surprise. "Really? Lay it on me."

"I want to get a kitten. For Sterling. But also for us to share."

I saw immediately that Griffen didn't need any further explanation. He remembered. I hadn't been sure if he would. It had been so many years ago.

Not long after my mother died, Sterling had found a kitten. I have no clue how a kitten had found its way onto Heartstone Manor's grounds, but this one had. Tiny, its grey fur patchy and its eyes barely open, the kitten had stumbled into Sterling's arms one afternoon and it had been love at first sight for both of them.

We'd tried to conceal the kitten from the adults, but Miss Martha had eventually discovered what Sterling was hiding in her bedroom. Once she knew, she was in on the game, but it hadn't been long before our father had discovered what we were up to. Once he did, in vintage Prentice fashion, he'd taken the kitten from Sterling and given it to me.

The only thing Prentice Sawyer liked less than disobedient children was children who were bonded to each other, against him. Taking the kitten she loved from Sterling and giving it to me might have worked to divide us, but as much as I'd loved that kitten, I'd loved my sisters more. Especially Sterling.

I'd taken the kitten and kept it in my room, but every

night I snuck out and brought it to Sterling for love and cuddles. Then, one day, the kitten was gone. We never found out what had happened to it. Sterling, barely eight years old, had been inconsolable.

"Dad was a monster," I said, remembering holding her slight body as she'd sobbed.

"He really was," Griffen agreed. "First she lost her mother, then Darcy, and he couldn't even let her keep one tiny kitten." He let out a sigh that I guessed was part melancholy at the memory and part despair at the thought of being overrun with pets once the kids got wind there was a kitten in the house. Griffen shrugged in resignation. "Good thing I like animals."

"I thought I'd take Sterling to the shelter if that's okay. We could share the kitten to start, keep it in one of our rooms most of the time. This house is way too big to let a kitten wander freely. At least until it gets used to the place."

"Exactly what I was going to suggest." He opened his drawer, rifled around, and pulled out a credit card, sliding it across the desk toward me. "It's the house card. Put any kitten-related expenses on this. And stop at that office supply store next to the pet store and grab anything you need to keep organized for the renovations. I think Sterling gets off at two today. If you leave now, you can swing by Quinn's place and pick her up."

I stood, more excited than I'd been in a very long time. My traitorous mind flashed to Nash, that sheet pooled at his waist, his long muscled form. Okay, the most excited I'd been in relation to things that did not have to do with Nash.

Stop thinking about Nash, I ordered my rebellious brain.

Considering that I'd never see him again, a kitten and

some office supplies were probably as much excitement as I was going to get for a long time. I wasn't going to complain.

Nash aside, a kitten and some office supplies sounded pretty damn good. I headed to town to get Sterling, a smile already curving my lips at the prospect of surprising her with a kitten.

Chapter Thirteen

PARKER

From across the room, my phone chimed with a text. I glanced over my shoulder, then down at my hands, submerged in a bucket of dirty water that reeked of something that was supposed to be lemons, according to the picture on the bottle. Somewhere under the acrid stench of chemicals there might have been a hint of lemon. The stuff smelled awful, but it was amazing at cutting through years of grime and dust. I'd get to the phone in a few minutes. As soon as I was finished scrubbing this section of tile.

Yes, I, Parker Sawyer, was scrubbing tile. I'd never admit to a single soul that I hadn't done this before. Or that I'd spent some time on the internet figuring out how one went about cleaning. Tile, wood, brass, and stainless steel. The cottage had it all.

Lucky for me, for Griffen, and for our budget, both the cottage and the gatehouse were in better than decent shape. The electrical needed work, and we needed new fixtures in the bathrooms, updated appliances and counters in the kitchens, but otherwise, what they really needed was elbow grease. Enter me and my currently submerged hands.

I pulled my scrub brush from the bucket and went back to work. The cottage had a cramped bathroom off the kitchen, beside an equally tiny bedroom, and a more spacious full bath on the second level, attached to the main bedroom. Every room in the cottage was designed in the same style; Dark oak-paneled wainscotting along the lower half of the walls and creamy white walls above, with dark beams cutting across the ceilings.

Only the bathrooms were different, both done in floor-to-ceiling vintage white subway tile. Though the tile hadn't been vintage when it was installed. When the tiles were clean they'd be gorgeous. At the moment, not so much.

I'd finished one wall, the smallest, and the sight of the gleaming, bright tiles sent bubbles of happiness through my heart. I told myself I was being silly. I'd started with the narrowest wall. It was just tile. The warmth inside me said it wasn't silly at all.

It was the first thing I'd done in a long time that felt good. Like I was making the world around me better. Maybe earning my own place in it. I hadn't known that mattered to me. Apparently, it did.

I wasn't sure I wanted to scrub tiles for the rest of my life, but for now, it felt great. Flexing my hand around the brush, I took in my red knuckles and shrugged. I felt great, except for my hands. I needed to get some gloves. I had to remember to ask Savannah.

I liked imagining her and Nicky moving in, once we had the place livable. They could make a home here. When Savannah had taken the job managing Heartstone Manor, she and Nicky moved into her mother's former rooms off the kitchen. Griffen had taken one look and deemed them too dark and cramped for a mother and young child, no matter that Miss Martha and Savannah had lived in them when Savannah was growing up. At the time, the cottage had housed the head groundskeeper, and the gatehouse had stood empty.

Griffen hadn't bothered trying to unravel our father's reasoning on that one. A mother and child needed more room than the crusty old groundskeeper, but that probably hadn't occurred to Prentice. It didn't matter now. As soon as Billy Bob and I had this place in shape, Savannah and I could go through the attics looking for furniture to fill it. Whatever we couldn't find, we'd buy.

Savannah could take the main bedroom upstairs, with its tall windows and elegant dark beams. The bed and bath on the first floor were small, but Nicky could make them his own, and while the room wasn't spacious, it was more than big enough for a young boy. And when he outgrew it? We'd figure that out later. For now, Savannah and Nicky needed a home.

I wanted to give something back to Savannah, to repay her for everything she was giving to us. Heartstone Manor felt like a home for the first time I could remember. Even when my mother had been alive, Prentice cast a dark shadow over the house. His temper, his impatience. His constant manipulations.

That thought usually twisted my face in a scowl, but not anymore. Instead, I thought of Sterling and the sweet, tiny, fuzzy black kitten she'd fallen in love with at the shelter. I'd peeked over her shoulder to study the little ball of fluff in her arms and had fallen hard myself. How could I not? Sterling had filled out the paperwork, written a check to the shelter—refusing to let me put it on Griffen's card as he'd suggested—and we'd headed to the pet superstore to get supplies.

For some reason I didn't really understand, they wouldn't let us take the kitten with us, but it worked out for the best. By the time our new pet was ready to go, we had our rooms set up in two versions of kitty heaven. Two litter boxes, cat treats, food, toys, and all the goodies we thought a kitten had to have.

If this worked out, I might have to get another kitten. We were sharing parenting responsibilities, but the kitten and Sterling were clearly in love. Shadow liked me well enough, but she loved Sterling. And as I'd expected, the kids in the house—Scarlett's two boys, August and Thatcher, and Savannah's Nicky—were all dropping not too subtle hints about a puppy. Or another cat. Even a snake.

No one jumped on the idea of a snake, but Griffen was considering a dog. Maybe. He said once we all got used to the kitten, we could talk about adding another pet. That promise was holding the kids for now. I shook my head, still convinced we'd end up with a menagerie. I didn't think Griffen would mind.

Tapping the scrub brush dry on the side of the bucket, I set it on the tile floor and stood, my palms going immediately to my lower back. I needed a massage. Too bad I couldn't afford one. Washing my hands in the sink, I reassured myself that while I couldn't afford a spa day, I did have a nice big tub in my bathroom. A hot bath before bed would be almost as nice as a massage.

Picking up my phone absently, I thought about lunch. Did I want to waste time walking back to the Manor and cleaning up to eat in the dining room, only to get filthy again when I braved the first-floor bath to see if I could get the stains out of the sink?

My stomach growled, putting in a definite vote for lunch, waste of time be damned. Or I could sneak in the back door without cleaning up and see if I could grab a snack. I was warming up to that idea when I saw Griffen's text.

Drop by my office when you have a minute.

I texted back, *Have you eaten? I was about to head over for lunch.*

Want to eat in my office?

I wanted to eat lunch with Griffen, but still didn't want to waste an hour cleaning up. It wouldn't kill me to ask—he could always say no.

Could we eat on the terrace? I'm too filthy for the house and still have more cleaning to do.

I'll meet you there with food in 20m.

Loving Griffen was a surprise after so many years apart, but he made it easy. Until I came home, I hadn't realized how starved for love I was. Without Tyler between me and my siblings, I was soaking in their affection, letting them make me whole in a way I'd never been.

I wasn't alone anymore. It was still sinking in, but every time my family did something to remind me they cared, it was like I had another piece of me back where it belonged, though I'd never known how much of me I was missing.

Once, a summons to the office would have had me shaking in fear. Now I smiled to myself, looking forward to lunch with my brother, not a bit of worry to spoil my happy anticipation.

I spent another ten minutes making notes on the

cottage. I'd met with Billy Bob right after breakfast and they'd left my brain spinning with ideas—what we could save, what I needed to replace, how to schedule the work. Fortunately, they hadn't blinked an eye at my taking over the project, and, unlike me, they actually knew what they were doing.

Washing my hands once more, I reminded myself to get a bottle of hand lotion and some work gloves as I strode down the gravel path winding through the sprawling green lawn on my way to the main house. I'd always loved this walk. The cottage was tucked against the woods, far enough away that the Manor didn't loom over it, and close enough to make walking back and forth convenient. From this side, the guest wing of the Manor jutted out at an angle, the windows sparkling in the sun, the granite streaked in places from the ivy Hawk had removed before it could pull the whole place down.

Passing between the pool and the gardens, I spotted Griffen on the terrace, Hope beside him, one of Savannah's food carts piled with covered dishes. They both gave me curious smiles as I approached, Hope's head tilting to the side.

"You weren't exaggerating," she said. "Did you transfer the dust from the cottage to your clothes?" Her words could have been cutting, but that wasn't Hope, and her warm, welcoming smile turned them into an affectionate tease.

Lifting my hands before me, I countered, "Maybe, but at least I washed my hands. Twice. Though after scrubbing the tile, my hands are probably the cleanest part of me."

"I bet you're hungry." Griffen slid a covered plate my way after I sat at the table in the empty chair.

"You'd be right," I agreed, my mouth watering as I pulled the cover off and set my eyes on a tall club sandwich on toasted bread. Hope put a glass in front of me, filled with freshly made lemonade. "I love you guys," I said around a bite of sandwich.

Hope sipped at her ginger ale and smiled. "Savannah and the cook did all the work." After finishing a much smaller bite of her own sandwich, she mused, "I like this cook. I hope Finn doesn't run her off."

"Agreed," Griffen said with a slight scowl.

Our brother Finn was a professional chef, though he refused to cook for the family. Unfortunately, he also had a temper and extremely high expectations of the family cook. Griffen had told him more than once that if he ran off another cook, either he could take over the job, or he could get out. Since then, Finn had kept his mouth shut.

My lunch disappeared in lightning speed. Slouching back into my chair, I sipped deeply of my lemonade and closed my eyes. I couldn't remember the last time I'd been that hungry. I'd only grabbed a coffee for breakfast, eager to get to work, and I'd been at it all morning.

"Things going well at the cottage?" Griffen asked.

While he and Hope finished their food at a more mannerly pace, I filled them in on my progress and everything Billy Bob had suggested. When I was done, Griffen gave me a wide smile.

"We knew you'd be perfect for this. If you need help with the cleaning—"

I shook my head. "The house staff has enough to do. Maybe when we're done, and it needs a final polish before Savannah and Nicky move in."

Before our father's murder and the attempts on Griffen and Royal, we could have just hired temporary help for a few days. Now every staff member had to go through extensive background checks. It wasn't worth the effort when I had two hands and could do the grunt work myself. "I've got it," I reassured them.

Griffen nodded, sharing a long look with Hope that I didn't understand. Sometimes it seemed like those two could have whole conversations just with their eyes. "I asked you to come by my office partly to check in, but mostly to share some information and ask for your input."

I straightened, wiping my palms on my shorts. "What's wrong?" My eyes popped from Griffen to Hope, but they gave away nothing.

"Nothing's wrong," Griffen reassured, before changing the subject. "Any progress with Tyler? Have you talked to any of the Kingsleys?"

I shook my head. "Nothing new with Tyler. He's still running out the deadline on the motion he's supposed to file. I talk to Claudia every few days, but that's it."

I didn't mention Nash. Why would I? It wasn't like we'd spoken. Or texted. I was trying not to feel resentful about that. *See you soon.* Why would he have said that? Unless he was just being polite.

Shut up Parker, I ordered myself. *Stop obsessing and move on.*

I was trying. I really was. But Nash Kingsley is not a man you just forget. I should know. I'd tried hard enough.

Chapter Fourteen

PARKER

"Why do you ask?" I tried to keep my voice neutral, as if it didn't matter and there was nothing to worry about. I don't know who I was trying to convince, Hope and Griffen or myself.

Griffen cleared his throat. "We got an interesting message from your brother-in-law."

"From Nash?" We all pretended we hadn't heard my voice crack. I swallowed and forged ahead. "Why would Nash contact you?" A horrible thought occurred to me. "He wasn't... checking in on me, was he? He's been very kind but–"

The thought of Nash checking up on me with my brother sent a scalding wave of humiliation across my face.

Griffen shook his head. "No, nothing like that. In fact, he didn't mention you at all."

Somehow, that was worse. Ugh. Why did I even care? Taking a slow sip of my lemonade, as if I couldn't possibly be concerned about Nash, I asked, "What did he want?"

"Do you know anything about his business?" Hope raised an eyebrow.

I shook my head. "Not really. Only that he works in tech, has started and sold off some startups, and he makes a big splash whenever he has a new company." There, that sounded appropriately detached, didn't it? Like I cared, but only a little.

I wasn't going to think about that pic I'd seen of him on an online gossip site attending a gala in New York last weekend, a tall, glamorous woman on his arm. The press loved Nash Kingsley–his ambitious startups, his bad-boy persona. Last year they'd gotten a shot of him on his motorcycle, his dark hair mussed, his black leather jacket well worn. I'd saved that one, hiding it on my phone among pics of a vacation Tyler had hated so he'd never find it.

"He's made some interesting advances in tech," Griffen said, "but his latest venture has the potential to be ground-breaking. For the last year, he's been working with his own team, under strict secrecy, while looking for investors to bring it to the next level."

"I didn't think Nash had to work that hard to find investors." As far as I knew, the money people would kill each other for the chance to own a slice of one of his companies.

"Usually, he doesn't," Hope explained, "but with this project, he's looking for a long-term commitment, and investors he wants to work with personally."

"He's not going to sell this one?" I asked, more curious than I wanted to admit.

"I'm guessing not," Griffen filled in. "We've had feelers out for a long-term tech investment. Something new and interesting, and not something that's going to the highest bidder as soon as it has proof of concept."

"Did you find Nash, or did he come to you?"

"A little of both," Hope said, pulling the cover off

another plate to reveal a selection of cookies. Helping herself to a gingersnap, she pushed the plate my way. I wasn't going to turn down a chocolate chip cookie.

"The thing is," Griffen continued, "part of our interest is in bringing new industry to Sawyers Bend. This is a desirable place to live, but we're lacking in jobs, aside from the tourist industry. Prentice closed the quarry and mill, but there are other options. Something like Nash's new venture is exactly what we're looking for. It'll start small, especially as he's still in the development phase, but it has the potential to provide the kind of jobs we'd like to attract."

"And we have office space already available for him," Hope added. "As long as you're okay with it."

My eyebrows shot up. "As long as I'm okay with it?"

"Of course," she said, with one of her gentle smiles. "I know he's been kind to you, and you're still close to his mother, but you're also trying to start a new life away from the Kingsleys. This is a good fit for us, but family is more important than business. If Nash being here is a problem, we'll say no."

I stared at them, reeling.

Nash in Sawyers Bend?

Family is more important than business?

I didn't know how to make sense of either of those things. "What I think doesn't matter."

"It absolutely matters, Parker," Griffen said. "I'm not Dad. The company is important, but there's more than one way to make a profit. If you don't want us to invest with Nash, we won't. Simple as that. There are other opportunities. Your happiness is more important. By far."

His green eyes were steady on mine, heavy with love. While my head wanted to doubt, my heart couldn't. His face said it all, and I knew without question that if I said I didn't want Nash around, Griffen would turn him down and that would be the end of it.

Was that what I wanted?

Did I even have to ask?

This is a bad idea, the cautious side of me warned. *Nash is the past, remember?*

Was this what he'd meant by *See you soon?*

My head spinning, my gut took the lead. "If you think it's a good investment and you're excited about it, don't let me stand in your way," I said, my ears ringing with shock.

What was I doing?

I didn't care, I was doing it anyway.

"Nash hates Tyler, so he's not going to help his brother, and I don't want to punish him for something that isn't his fault."

"He'd be here, at least to start," Hope said, cautiously, with a quick glance at Griffen. "Either staying at the Manor or in the Inn. He's ready to move his team and get going as soon as he makes an agreement with his investors. Would you be okay with that?"

To my own ears, my voice sounded tinny and thin, like it was traveling down a wire from very far away. "The Manor is probably easier than the Inn, now that we have a real guest room. Less driving back and forth for you two."

Sure, I was thinking about convenience. Absolutely. This was all about the deal and business and not at all about the heady prospect of having Nash under my own roof. Because that would be insane.

He's your brother-in-law! my sensible side screamed.

Not for much longer, my gut reminded me.

And this isn't about me, right? There was no reason I had to avoid Nash, was there? Of course, there wasn't.

"You're sure?" Hope asked, a speculative gleam in her eyes.

I blinked, taking a bite of my cookie for cover while I reeled in my scrambled thoughts. "I'm sure. Really. My problems are with Tyler, not his family. If Nash's company is a good fit for Sawyer Enterprises and you're a good match for Nash, there's no reason for me to stand in the way."

Hope's lips curved in a satisfied smile. "I'm so glad. I think this will work out well for everyone."

I glanced over to see Griffen's eyes narrowed on me, no hint of his wife's satisfied smile on his own face. "And if there's a problem, you'll let us know? You promise?"

"I promise." For the first time in my life, I believed I could. With my father, no way. But Griffen was entirely different. He'd back me up if having Nash around was a problem.

Assuming I was willing to tell him exactly what kind of problem Nash could be.

Did I think Nash was going to be a problem?

I took another bite of cookie, savoring a sweet chocolate chip as it dissolved on my tongue. No, Nash wasn't the problem. I was the problem, pining and obsessing, checking for texts, and scanning gossip sites when I should be putting Nash out of my mind.

I'd meant it when I said I wouldn't be the one who stood in their way. Nash wouldn't be a problem, and neither would I. I could keep my hands, and my mind, to myself.

Of course, I could.

Absolutely.

How hard could it be?

It wouldn't be long before I found out.

Chapter Fifteen

NASH

Sitting across the negotiating table from Parker's brothers wasn't exactly like being in front of a firing squad, but it was close. The housekeeper, a tall woman with strawberry curls and sharp, suspicious eyes, had led me through the main hall of Heartstone Manor and back to Griffen's expansive, wood-paneled office.

Heartstone Manor wasn't what I'd expected. I knew about the house and its history, knew that it was one of the only Gilded Age mansions still in private hands, and the only one of its size that had never been opened to the public. From what I could find out about Prentice Sawyer's will, it never would be.

It was as grand as I'd expected, with soaring ceilings, ornate woodwork, and sparkling chandeliers. But most of the artwork was missing and the silk wallpaper was faded. Some of the rooms we passed on the way to Griffen's office were bare of furniture. Weird. Parker had alluded to her father behaving oddly in the last few years of his life. Was this part of it? Impossible to know at this point.

I'd entered Griffen's office to find him coming around

from behind his desk, hand extended. A friendly overture, but his eyes were as sharp and suspicious as the housekeeper's had been. While it might make this negotiation harder, I was glad. Someone should be sharp and suspicious on Parker's behalf.

I wasn't worried for myself. I was going to get what I wanted from the Sawyers. There was no room for failure. The stakes were far too high.

For the first time, my goals had nothing to do with business. That Sawyer Enterprises was looking for an investment in emerging tech just as I had an eye out for investors was pure coincidence. If they turned out to be the right fit for my new company, all the better. But I wasn't here for the company.

My new venture was the culmination of all my years of work, the endgame for all of my professional aspirations. I'd never have another idea like this, and never one so perfectly timed to the market. And still, all of that came in second place to Parker.

I was going to get my foot in the door at Heartstone Manor. I had to. If my new tech was the way in, so be it. That didn't mean I wasn't going to negotiate the hell out of this. If I had to choose, I'd choose Parker. I didn't see any reason I couldn't have both.

Griffen gestured to an armchair in front of his desk. I took it, nodding as he sat, joined by a woman on his left. A man I guessed was one of his brothers was on his right. The other Sawyer stood and extended his hand.

"Royal Sawyer. Nice to meet you."

I shook, nodded again, and transferred my gaze to the woman. Hope Sawyer, if my guess was correct. She stood, and taking in the curve of her stomach, I knew I was right. Her hand was deceptively strong in mine. After introducing herself, she met her husband's eyes for a quick flash before she spoke.

"It's good to have you here, Nash. We're looking forward to discussing your tech, and how we can benefit each other, but it would be foolish to ignore our personal connection."

Her words surprised me. Not just that she'd taken the lead in the meeting, but that she'd pushed business to the side at the start. I'd heard the Sawyers were ruthless in business. Prentice Sawyer had a brutal reputation, and in the brief time he'd been at the helm, Griffen had become known as a fierce negotiator.

Eyeing Hope, I could guess where some of that came from. Some of the people I talked to said she was merely his assistant, but a few had noted that Hope was just as savvy as her husband. Royal was new to Sawyer Enterprises, and still an unknown, but I couldn't imagine Griffen and Hope would have let him into the family business if he hadn't had something to bring to the table.

In response to Hope, I said, "It can be complicated when business and family intersect."

She inclined her head in agreement. "Sometimes it's good, more often it brings trouble. Your company seems to be exactly the investment we're looking for, but Parker's happiness is our highest priority."

"And have you talked to Parker about this?" I asked.

Hope had me off balance. I hadn't expected them to come out of the gate telling me business was a secondary concern. Had they asked Parker about me? Had she told them she didn't want me here? A long moment of queasy uncertainty kept my mouth shut. I waited for Hope's response.

She shared another look with Griffen before he said, "We did talk to Parker."

That was all. I couldn't remember the last time I'd struggled for composure. I wasn't going to ask what Parker had said. Griffen's eyes met mine, his gaze curious, calculating. The best I could manage was calm and collected. In all my arrogance, it hadn't occurred to me that Parker might not want to see me.

For a split second, a vision of Parker as I'd last seen her filled my mind. Moonlight hair spread across my pillow, her golden and green eyes closed in sleep, a satisfied smile still curving her lips. I hadn't needed proof that we belonged together, but now I had it.

That night had been magic. Not just her body moving with mine, the bright and brilliant pleasure of her touching me, her cries as she came apart in my arms. No, all of it was magic. Cooking together, laughing over dinner, that unexpected kiss. I wanted more. I couldn't believe Parker didn't feel the same way.

What did she say? It was possibly the most important question of my life, but I wasn't going to ask. Griffen made me wait. Finally, after tossing a glance at the ceiling, silently asking someone up there for patience, Hope took pity on me.

"She said her problems are with your brother, not you, and she'd never want to stand in the way of us working together."

Talk about being damned by faint praise.

It wasn't the enthusiastic welcome I'd hoped for, but at least she hadn't asked her brother to send me away. I could almost see her, that polished, perfect shell firmly in place as she gave her permission for my presence. I was looking forward to pulling her into a dark corner and messing her up a little. I loved her polish, but I loved her even more with her lips swollen from kisses and a pink flush in her cheeks, that wicked sparkle in her eye.

My memory of a freshly kissed Parker fueling me, I went on the offensive. They'd started with the personal. I was going to finish it. "I don't know how much Parker has told you about my relationship with my brother, but we've never been close. He's a special breed of asshole. If I'd met Parker before the wedding, I would have found a way to talk her out of it."

Hope drew in a breath of air and leaned forward. "Did you know he'd–" She cut off with a glance at Royal. I understood in an instant.

Griffen and Hope knew Tyler had hit Parker, but Parker hadn't told Royal. I gave a sharp shake of my head. "Absolutely not. He had a million faults I knew about, but I never thought he'd go that far."

Royal's attention moved between Hope and me, but he kept his mouth shut. If Parker hadn't confided in him, I wasn't going to share her private history. To Hope, I said, "If I'd known how this was going to end, I would have stopped the wedding." I looked away, glancing through the tall french doors to the barren gardens beyond, gathering my thoughts. "My mother and I both feel responsible for everything she's been through."

"It's not your fault," Hope said, her voice low, gentle. Griffen made a rough sound in his throat.

"Disagree," I countered. "Right now, it feels very much like our fault. We knew he could be an asshole. We knew he was probably cheating. We knew he was irresponsible and immature. We knew enough."

Hope shook her head. "Parker is a grown woman. She can decide for herself, and she did. You went above and beyond to help her move the divorce forward. You can let yourself off the hook."

Another rough noise from Griffen. I met his hard, green eyes with a nod of agreement. "It wasn't enough, but I plan to make it up to her."

Those green eyes transformed to jade ice. Griffen leaned forward. "If we come to an agreement, and at any time after that, Parker tells me your presence here is undesirable, you leave. No questions asked. Understood?"

Chapter Sixteen

NASH

"Understood," I said immediately. "I have no interest in making Parker uncomfortable in her own home."

"Fine." Griffen gave a decisive nod. Sitting back, he picked up a folder from his desk and flipped it open. Hope slid an identical folder my way.

I picked it up as she said, "Do you want coffee or tea before we get started?"

"I wouldn't mind coffee," I said, opening the folder. Hope tapped at her phone for a minute, then set it down and opened her own folder. Royal did the same.

"As you can see," Griffen began, "We're not interested in an investment as much as a joint venture. We have appropriate office space, and when we get there, an adjacent location that can be retrofitted for manufacturing and assembly if we decide not to send that overseas."

It only took me a few seconds to take in the value of what he was offering. My team was small at the moment, but it was going to grow. By a lot. Eventually, there would be a hardware component, and while some of it would likely be manufactured overseas, one of my sticking points with investors was the insistence that, at a minimum, the final assembly would happen in the US.

Sawyer Enterprises had an office/industrial park in a prime location and they were willing to dedicate the most modern building to what could be our joint venture.

The location was ideal in some ways, and less than perfect in others. On the downside, Sawyers Bend was an hour from the airport, though the office park was on the highway, exactly in between. And while the area did have its own airport, there were few direct flights, potentially adding hours to any travel.

On the upside, the proliferation of video conferencing meant we were all traveling far less. And this area of the country was a magnet for people who liked the outdoors. As a tourist destination, it had plenty to offer employees in their free time. The cost of living wasn't cheap, but it was a fraction of what most of my team was paying in Northern California. Most importantly, I'd discussed Sawyers Bend with my people and all but two had agreed to make the move. The two that had declined would stay on working remotely.

Rifling through the proposal in the folder, I said, "I wasn't looking for a corporate headquarters. I had my eyes on a cash infusion to get us to the next level. I'm not sure I want a partnership."

Royal pulled a sheet of graphs from his folder and pushed it my way. "If you take a look at these projections, I think you'll find–"

And we were off. What followed wasn't the toughest negotiation of my life, but it was the most fun. I could see what Griffen, Hope, and Royal were after. It wasn't just about money, it was about bringing something to Sawyers

Bend. Jobs. Industry. The future. I respected that. And I wanted what they were offering. I just didn't want to give up too much to get it.

It ended, as all the best negotiations do, with each of us giving up something and gaining most of what we needed. And little did they know, I won on the most important point of all. Once we'd hammered out a basic agreement, I'd leaned back in my chair and propped my ankle on my knee as if I didn't have a care in the world now that business was out of the way. "Looks like I'll be in Sawyers Bend for the foreseeable future. Any suggestions on a place to stay?"

"You'll stay here," Griffen said.

It wasn't a question. Perfect. He wanted me here so he could keep an eye on me. Excellent. He could keep an eye on me all he wanted as long as I could be close to Parker. Living under the same roof was ideal, even if that roof was larger than some hotels.

"Works for me," I agreed easily. "I need to fly back to California, make some arrangements. I can be back by the end of next week. Does that work for you?"

"Absolutely," Hope said, beaming as she held out her hand. "We'll have a preliminary agreement drawn up in the meantime."

Griffen's smile wasn't quite as sunny as we shook on our new partnership, but he exuded a satisfied air. As he rose to walk me out, he said, "Stop at the gatehouse before you leave. Hawk, our head of security, will brief you on the rules."

"Rules?" I had an idea what he was getting at. I wasn't far off.

"Griffen's father was killed in the Manor, and we've had a few attempts on Griffen and Royal," Hope explained. "Security is tight."

"No visitors that haven't been screened," Royal filled in. "Hawk's team opens any packages–things like that. It's not that hard to get used to."

"Is the security going to be a problem?" Griffen asked.

"No, it seems sensible." It might have been a problem if I hadn't already known what I was getting in to. Parker had told me the precautions they were taking. I was happy to put up with them if they'd keep her safe. I'd been relieved to know Tyler couldn't take her by surprise. Without that, I wouldn't put it past him to ambush her.

I came around the corner into the entrance hall of the Manor to find Parker standing there, her mouth hanging open, eyes fixed on me.

"Nash?" she asked in confused wonder, her polished shell nowhere in sight. A hand raised to her hair in reflex and I saw her. Really saw her. This was a Parker I'd never imagined, and it took everything I had not to toss her over my shoulder and take off with her.

Her pale hair was pulled back in a messy bun, strands falling out to stick to her sweaty face. A pair of dusty, smeared overalls dwarfed her slight frame, the tight grey tank top beneath displaying toned shoulders and lean, strong arms. She was a mess from head to toe and the most beautiful thing I'd ever seen.

Her golden-green eyes narrowed on her sister-in-law. "You didn't tell me he was coming today," she hissed, color staining her cheeks.

Hope grinned at her and shrugged a shoulder. "Griffen asked me not to."

Parker transferred her ire to her brother, who gave a shrug identical to his wife's and grinned. "I wanted to meet him on my own. You're too nice."

I imagined I could hear her teeth grinding together. For

a second, I wondered if she was going to stomp her foot or throw something at him. From one breath to the next, she pulled herself together and aimed a blinding smile my way. Without looking at her family, she ordered, "You can go. I'll walk Nash out."

I didn't hear what they had to say about that. I only had room for Parker. She crossed the wide hall and stopped in front of me, shifting her weight, suddenly uneasy now that we appeared to be alone. I wouldn't have been surprised to find Parker's family lurking around the corner, eaves-dropping.

Her hand went to her hair again. She pulled it back, waving at her overalls. "Sorry I'm–"

"You don't have to apologize." I tucked a strand of hair behind one ear, my fingertip tingling at the brief contact. "You look gorgeous."

"You need your eyes checked," she said, tartly. "I'm managing the renovation of the old groundskeeper's cottage for Savannah and Nicky–our housekeeper and her son–and for the moment, the bulk of the work consists of cleaning decades of grime."

"And you're doing the cleaning?" I asked, as Parker opened the front door and led me outside. She shut the door firmly behind us, smirking through its solid weight at the eavesdroppers she'd just cut off.

"I am. Easier than trying to get temporary help cleared through security. And easier on the budget."

"Budget?" I wanted to hear every detail of her life.

Her eyes gleamed. "I have plans for Savannah's kitchen, but the counters I want are pricey. I moved most of the cleaning budget to the kitchen. It's going to be fabulous."

"I didn't know you knew how to handle a renovation," I said.

Parker gave a sheepish shrug, her eyes still bright. "I didn't. I don't. I'm learning as I go. Billy Bob are doing most of the work." At my confused look, she explained, "Savannah's cousins. They're joined at the hip, and everyone has been calling them Billy Bob practically since birth. They've been talking me through what I don't know."

She looked away, then back as I took her hand, tangling her fingers with mine. A flush hit her cheeks. "I had to look up how to clean tile on the internet. Kind of embarrassing."

"Not embarrassing," I said, squeezing her fingers in mine. "Resourceful."

"It's not running a company or inventing new technology." Her eyes were on the courtyard, avoiding mine.

Did she feel insecure? Like she wasn't good enough because she didn't have an impressive job? "Are you having fun?"

Her eyes swung to mine, uncertainty chased out by surprise. "I am. Is that enough?"

I couldn't resist dropping her hand and sliding my arms around her, pulling her close. I didn't care who was watching. "I don't know, sweetheart. Is it enough?"

Her body melted into my side, a smile curving her lips. "You know, I think it is enough. For now."

Holding back the intense need to take her away somewhere private, somewhere I could finally get her alone, I settled for dropping a kiss on her forehead. "Are you really okay with me staying in the Manor?"

Parker swallowed, then nodded.

"Good," I whispered against her temple. Straightening, I stepped away, every cell in my body protesting the lack of contact. Soon. It was almost time. Not yet. "I'll be back in ten days. Don't forget, you owe me dinner."

"I can't cook!" she protested, laughing, one hand

outstretched. I grabbed it, hauling her in to press my lips to hers in a kiss far more chaste than what I really wanted. Her family was behind that thick door, but I'd heard what Griffen said about security. There were eyes everywhere.

I wasn't ready, but I stepped away. It was time to go. For now.

"We'll figure it out. See you soon, Parker."

Chapter Seventeen

PARKER

Knock, Knock. I knew that quick rap on the door. A smile was already spreading across my face as I looked up to see Savannah, Sterling behind her. Savannah held up a bottle of wine. "We've come to rescue you from your drudgery. Nicky's in bed and I picked this up on sale yesterday."

Without waiting for me to respond, she pushed the door open and came in. Sterling followed, two glasses in one hand, a bottle of seltzer tucked under her arm, and Shadow perched on her shoulder.

"Shadow thinks he's a parrot," I said, wanting to reach for our kitty, but conscious of the clothes I was wrapping for shipment. No cat hair allowed. I finished packing the dress and sealing the envelope, stacking it neatly by the door before I gave in to temptation, and plucked the kitten from Sterling's shoulder before I sank into one of my soft velvet armchairs.

"She likes riding up there." Sterling rubbed at her shoulder. "But her claws are a bitch."

"Tiny, but fierce," Savannah commented, "kind of like you two."

"I'm not fierce," I protested, nuzzling Shadow's soft head, soaking in the rumble of her purr, outsized and deep compared to her delicate little body.

"You're fierce on the inside." Savannah took a spot on the sofa and popped the cork on the wine, pouring it in two glasses and handing me one.

Sterling flopped down beside her and opened her seltzer. "How's the great clean-up going? Griffen said you've been working your ass off."

Savannah's mouth twisted in an awkward smile. "I feel weird about you cleaning the cottage."

"Why?" Sterling challenged.

"First, because it's going to be the nicest place Nicky and I have lived, and it feels like too much. But I love it, so I want it for us. And second, because I work for you. You shouldn't be cleaning my house."

"Whatever," Sterling scoffed, but I waved away her comment, understanding where Savannah was coming from.

"Get over it," I said, sipping my wine and trying to keep Shadow on my lap instead of climbing my shirt with her needle-sharp claws. "Why shouldn't you have someplace nice to live? You work hard. This place feels more like a home than it ever has. Part of that is our father being gone, and Griffen and Hope, but a huge part is you. You make magic happen every day."

"Trust me," Sterling cut in. "We want you to be happy. We want you so happy you never leave us."

"I'm not going anywhere," Savannah said. "But–"

I held up a hand to stop her. "And second, I asked Griffen for a job. He offered me something at the Inn–"

"My old job?" Sterling interrupted.

I couldn't tell if she was annoyed, her expression revealing only curiosity. "Yes," I admitted, "But I wasn't sure if you'd want to come back–Tenn and Royal want you back, you know–" At that, Sterling shrugged but didn't comment.

"I turned it down. I didn't want to work at the Inn. I wanted this project, and I knew it would come with grunt work and getting dirty. I'm not looking to scrub toilets and floors forever, but this is different. Did I show you the marble I found for the counters?"

"No! Show me!" Savannah's excitement dimmed as soon as the words were out. "Isn't marble more expensive than granite?"

"Usually," I said, grabbing my tablet and scrolling for the picture I'd taken at the vendor's warehouse the day before. "But your kitchen isn't huge and the L-shape counter and farmhouse sink let us use smaller pieces. This was ordered for a client who changed their mind at the last minute and their measurements were an exact fit for yours. It was a win-win. We get marble at less than the cost of granite and Victor doesn't have to sit on marble countertops he can't move."

Savannah took the tablet and scrolled through the pics, taking in the white marble cut with bands of light gray. "This is going to look gorgeous with the sage green cabinets and those dark floors."

"I know," I agreed with glee. "And I got the stains out of the sink in Nicky's bathroom, so we don't need to replace that. I'm going to use that money and the savings on the counters to upgrade the tub in your bathroom."

Savannah handed back the tablet, shaking her head. "It's too much, Parker."

"Shut up." Sterling nudged Savannah's knee with her

own. "It's not. Griffen set a budget and Parker's staying inside it. No one wants you living in a shit hole. Especially after you've been stuck in the basement."

"The basement isn't that bad," Savannah protested.

"It's not that great either," I said. "When you're in the cottage, I'm going to talk Griffen into letting me re-decorate those rooms for the staff lounge he said you wanted. And we have to find time to go through the attics and see if there's anything you can use in the cottage. That way I can figure out how much of the budget I need for furniture."

"There are some really great pieces up there that would be perfect for Savannah's cottage," I heard from the doorway.

We looked to see Hope at the door, my sister Quinn beside her. Hope was already wrapped in a fluffy robe, her eyes tired, her hand resting on her abdomen over the swell of her pregnancy. Quinn had changed since dinner, out of the clothes she'd worn guiding a canoe trip on the river and into faded yoga pants and a loose t-shirt. She glowed with health, her dark hair shiny and her vivid blue eyes bright against her tanned face and pink cheeks.

"We brought an extra bottle of wine," she said, holding it up. "Can we crash the party?"

"Of course," I said, glancing behind them. "Where are Avery, Scarlett, and Daisy?" If we were having an impromptu girls' night, I didn't want to leave out our other sister or Daisy and Scarlett, Royal and Tenn's girlfriends, who'd both become part of the family.

Hope dropped onto the armchair opposite mine and propped her feet on the ottoman. "Daisy and Royal are on a date, Tenn and Scarlett are at the putt-putt with the boys—I think they were getting ice cream after—and Avery is still at the brewery." Craning her neck, she spotted the cabinet in the corner hiding my mini-fridge, electric kettle, and snacks. "Do you have another of those seltzers in there? Or water?"

"I should." I got up and crossed the room to the cabinet. Savannah, in her brilliance, had outfitted all of our rooms with drink and snack stations so we didn't have to go all the way down to the kitchens if we wanted a quick treat or a cup of tea. I'd spent some of my first meager paycheck on a single-serve coffee maker. I wasn't much for breakfast, and I liked to do paperwork from my online clothes sales in the morning, but I needed my coffee.

I opened the mini-fridge and checked the contents. "Pear or clementine?"

"Does it make a difference?" Quinn asked, pouring a glass of wine from the already open bottle. "They all taste the same."

"Pear," Hope said, reaching out to take the can. "They all taste the same, but the pear smells the best." She took a sip of the seltzer before she went back to the previous subject. "I was in the attics this morning and there's a queen-size bed you should look at for the cottage. It has matching bedside tables, and there's a wardrobe that could go with it. I don't know what the closet situation is."

"It's not bad actually," I said. "There was a small sewing room off the bedroom. Since no one sews anymore, Billy Bob is converting it into a walk-in closet."

"Really?" Savannah's eyes were wide. "That'll be fantastic. I figured I'd have to find a clothes rack or something."

Dealing with closets in a house this old was a problem. Both closets and bathrooms had changed so much in the last hundred years. What was luxurious in 1900 was far too small now. The family suites had been remodeled years ago, but Prentice hadn't bothered with the staff's rooms.

"How long until Savannah and Nicky can move in?" Hope asked.

"Not for another month, at least." I sent Savannah an apologetic glance. "Some of the electrical needs to be updated, and a few of the pipes are shot. Billy Bob are working on it."

Savannah shook her head. "I don't care. A month would be great. Just let me know when you want to go check out the attics for furniture and I'll be there."

"Tomorrow after breakfast?" Hope asked, explaining to me, "I want to come with you and show you some of the things I found. We have a meeting at eleven with your brother-in-law, but I'm free before."

"After breakfast works for me," Savannah said.

"Me too," I added.

Quinn looked up from her lap, where she was playing with Shadow. "Hold up and rewind for a sec. Why do you have a meeting with Parker's brother-in-law?"

I shrugged a shoulder, not sure what to say. I was all over the place on the subject of Nash Kingsley. I kept my mouth shut, deciding to let Hope field this one.

With a glance at me, she said, "We're going into business together. He'll be back in Sawyers Bend next week. Moving into the Manor, actually."

Quinn sat up, displacing Shadow, who loudly complained and picked her way across Quinn's legs to Sterling, her favorite human. Quinn looked from me to Hope. "What? Moving into the Manor? Are you okay with this? Is he a dickhead like Tyler?" Hearing what she'd said, she winced at me. "Sorry."

"Don't apologize, Tyler is a dickhead." I couldn't help but smile.

Why did it feel so good to say that to my sister? Because

I could finally stop pretending? Pretending to be perfect, pretending my marriage was wonderful when it was anything but. It felt so good to say it out loud, I said it again. "Tyler is a dickhead." I savored the sound of that for a millisecond before I finished, "Nash is different. He's the one who connected me with my divorce lawyer."

Quinn studied my face for a moment. "Yeah, but did he do that for you or to stick it to his brother?"

At that, everyone's eyes landed on me. I fought the urge to squirm or jump to Nash's defense too quickly. It was a good question. How much of that scene had been for me and how much for Nash? I didn't know, I wasn't living in Nash's head, but I could make a realistic guess.

I topped off my glass of wine and took a deep sip before I answered. "I think it was a little of both, but mostly for me." Considering, weighing how much of the truth to tell, I took a risk and let it out. Kind of. "The part that was for me was also for him. I think." I took another big sip of wine. "I don't know. Maybe I'm wrong."

"You're not wrong," Hope cut in. Her eyes on me were assessing. "Are you sure you want him in the house?"

I knew what she was asking. I lifted a shoulder in a faint shrug. "I do," I admitted, my throat tight at what I was saying. "But I feel like I shouldn't."

"I have no idea what you're talking about," Quinn complained, looking from Hope to me.

Sterling's eyes narrowed on my face and she jolted forward. "Holy shit, you have a thing for your brother-in-law!"

I covered my face with one hand and wailed, "Don't say it like that! It sounds terrible. He's my brother-in-law! I'm not even divorced yet. I might never be if Tyler gets his way."

"Forget about that. Tell me about Nash! What's he like?" Sterling demanded of Hope. "Is he hot? Is he an asshole? If he's an asshole I'm beating him up."

A giggle slipped out of me at the idea of pint-sized Sterling trying to take on Nash. "He's not an asshole. He's a really good man," I protested.

Sterling waved me away. "I'll get to you. I want to hear what Hope thinks."

"I only know him from our meeting and a few calls and emails since then."

"Yeah but you're good at reading people," Quinn added, "so what did you think? You must have liked him or you wouldn't have offered him a room in the Manor."

"Is he hot?" Sterling asked again.

"Don't you remember from Parker's wedding?" Quinn asked.

Sterling rolled her eyes. "Prentice grounded me for something–I don't even remember what–and he wouldn't let me go."

To stop the questions, I handed Sterling my phone, open to that pic of Nash on his bike in the leather jacket. Sterling let out a low whistle. "Please tell me you've slept with that man. He's seriously hot. Like so, so hot."

She handed my phone to Quinn, who let out a low whistle. "I remembered him being good-looking, but damn."

They both glanced up and spotted the flush on my cheeks. I could feel the heat, my guilt out there for everyone to see. Sterling hooted in glee. "Oh my God, you did sleep with him! When? How was it?"

Chapter Eighteen

PARKER

I clamped my lips together and refused to answer. Hope gave me a pitying look before glaring at Sterling and Quinn. "Stop badgering her."

Quinn leaned into Sterling and said in sotto voce, "Wait 'till she finishes that glass of wine and ask her again."

I didn't have it in me to glare at Sterling. I wanted to talk–I did–but this was a lot. I wasn't sure how I felt about Nash. I definitely wasn't ready to share.

"I like him," Hope said, pulling their attention from me for a blessed second. "He's a tough negotiator, but he made it clear that Parker was his priority. I think–" She bit her lip and stopped.

Quinn nudged her foot. "What? Tell us!"

"This is my gut talking, but I have a feeling he wanted the deal with us, but he would have given more to make this happen. I think he wants to be near Parker."

"No," I said, that idea turning my stomach upside down and inside out. "He said he was still looking for investors, that he was more selective than usual with this one. You were the right fit, that's all. It's a coincidence."

Hope shook her head. "I agree that it's a good fit. We're all satisfied with the way it worked out. But nothing about this is a coincidence."

"You can't know that," I said desperately, not sure what it all meant.

"No, I can't. But they didn't ask what I know. They asked what I think," Hope pointed out.

"Wait," Savannah cut in, looking at me. "How do you know so much about Nash's investors?"

"I, uh, I–When I was in New York, we had dinner after my flight got canceled, and we, uh, talked."

"Talked?" Sterling smirked. "Is that what the kids are calling it these days?"

If I'd had something to throw at her, I would have beaned it straight at her head. Instead, I took another long sip of wine, draining the glass. Before I could stop her, Quinn refilled it.

"Is that when you slept with him?" Sterling pushed.

I nodded, unable to get myself to answer the question out loud, and drank more wine.

"Was it good?" Savannah asked, one strawberry blond eyebrow raised. "Please tell me that man is good in bed."

"Did you see him when he was here?" Sterling asked.

Savannah nodded. "I was in the hall when he came out and saw Parker." She fanned herself, grinning. "And I second the idea that he's here for her."

I shook my head again, my face on fire. He couldn't be here for me? Could he? "The whole idea is insane," I muttered. "I'm still married."

"Is that your only objection?" Hope asked.

"Or was he a dud in bed?" Quinn looked at the pic on my phone again. "I don't believe it."

Sterling reached over and poked me. "Don't hold back,

Parks, tell us. Come on. I've sworn off men forever. I want to live vicariously through you. Give me the deets."

I sighed and drank more wine. "Okay. Fine. It was like this–We were on the way to the airport and I got a message saying my flight was canceled. Nash has a place in the city and he invited me to stay in his guest room so I wouldn't have to get a hotel. We cooked dinner together. And then–"

"And then what?" Sterling shouted. "Did he jump you?"

I shook my head and slugged back more wine. "No." Another gulp of wine. "I kissed him," I confessed in a rush. "I didn't mean to. I didn't. I was in the kitchen and I turned around and he was there and he was looking at me like... Like he wanted to devour me. And I kissed him."

"Then what happened?" Quinn demanded.

"How long has it been for you?" Sterling asked, staring at Quinn. "Can't you guess what comes next?"

Quinn shoved an elbow into Sterling's side. "I mean exactly what happened next. Did he do her on the kitchen island? Sweep her into his arms and carry her off to his lair? What?"

"Option two," I whispered, dizzy at the memory. "We didn't get a lot of sleep."

"How many times?" Hope asked, an amused glint in her eyes.

"You can't tell Griffen!" I shouted, sitting up in a rush, wine sloshing to the rim of my glass, every thought suffused with horror at the idea of Hope sharing this conversation with my brother.

Hope harrumphed at me, reminding me of Savannah and Miss Martha. "I can keep a secret. Griffen doesn't need to know everything. Now spill. How many times? He looks like he has stamina."

"Oh my god," I muttered to myself, shaking my head.

"Three times," I whispered. "And every one was spectacular."

"Woo Hoo!" Sterling cheered, pumping her fist in the air. "You go, Parker. I bet Tyler sucks in the sack."

"Sterling," Quinn hissed at her.

Sterling was unrepentant. "Tell me I'm wrong."

I couldn't. "Tyler only cares about Tyler, so..."

Sterling flopped back into the sofa. "Figures. Did you know?" At my questioning look, she clarified, "That he wanted you? Nash, I mean."

"I had an idea," I admitted.

Gently, Hope asked, "Did you have something with him while you and Tyler—"

I shook my head so hard I almost spilled my wine again, then took another gulp for courage. "No. Absolutely not. I never cheated on Tyler. Except–"

Everyone waited for me to finish my sentence. I went for more wine. I wasn't used to talking about this kind of thing. I'd gotten used to keeping secrets, had been away from my sisters for too long.

"Except?" Quinn finally prompted.

"Except for my wedding," I finished in a rush, bracing for the uproar that followed.

"What happened at your wedding?" Sterling screeched. "I can't believe Dad made me stay home, and I missed all of this."

"If something scandalous happened at the wedding," Quinn assured her, "no one had any clue. It was perfect."

"Ugh," I grunted, draining my glass again and flopping back into my chair. "I'm so sick of perfect. Perfect Parker. Perfect wedding. Perfect husband. Perfect life. It was all a fucking disaster. I'm a fucking disaster. And I'm so fucking tired of pretending I'm not."

Four sets of wide eyes stared back at me. "You don't have to be perfect, honey," Hope said. "We love you just the way you are. Disaster and all."

"I love you too," I blubbered, "I really do. I'm so glad to be home."

Sterling leaned forward and snatched my wine glass. "No more of this until you finish. I don't want you getting distracted. You love us, we love you, and we're all a fucking mess in one way or another. Now tell me what happened at your wedding before I lose patience and call Nash myself."

I laughed, wiping under my eyes. "He kissed me. We didn't meet until that night," I explained, drifting back in time to what had formerly been the best kiss of my life. Until Nash kissed me in his kitchen in New York. Unconsciously, my finger drifted up to press into my lower lip.

"He shook my hand in the receiving line and it was like—" I searched for the right word to describe something I still didn't understand. "Lightning. It was like being struck by lightning. He was so much. I'd never wanted anyone like that. Out of nowhere, needing him to touch me. Wanting to just be with him. Near him."

"Inconvenient since you'd married his brother only minutes before," Savannah commented, her eyes warm with compassion. "What miserable timing."

"It was awful," I agreed. "And there was no way I was going to do anything about it. Our father, the Kingsleys, all their friends. I wasn't going to run off with my brother-in-law at my wedding. The scandal would have been—" I shook my head. "That's just not me. That's never going to be me. But after we met, for the first time, it struck me that maybe I'd made a terrible mistake in marrying Tyler. So of course I ran as fast as I could in the opposite direction."

"How did that end with him kissing you?" Quinn asked,

refilling her own glass of wine. I wished I had mine back, but Sterling was right. Any more and I wouldn't be able to finish this. Plus, I hate being hungover.

"I was walking down a hallway, just trying to get some air, a minute to myself, and he pulled me into a dark closet. I'd never been kissed like that. He asked me to run away with him, but I couldn't bring myself to do it, even though a part of me knew that the real mistake was Tyler. I turned Nash down and he walked away. After that, I didn't see him until his father died. Nash stayed away from Tyler. Away from me. We barely spoke."

I shut my mouth, unable to share the rest. I couldn't tell them that every time I was near Nash, something deep inside me relaxed and sighed, *Finally, this is the one.* I'd been ignoring that voice for so many years. And now Nash was coming here. Was I going to keep ignoring that little voice?

Quinn read my mind. "What are you going to do?"

"We don't know that he's here for me," I protested, my mind still reeling at the thought.

"He doesn't strike me as a man who's going to wait around. If he is here for you, you'll know soon enough. You should have a plan, just in case." That was Hope, ever practical, always the woman with a plan. Savannah nodded along with her. I wasn't going to ignore two of the smartest women I knew. Except I didn't have a clue what to do about Nash.

I chewed on my lower lip, thinking, while voices raised around me. "She should just sleep with him until she figures it out." That was from Sterling.

Hope started to argue. I looked up to see Quinn studying me, her blue eyes heavy with melancholy. "What does your gut say?" she asked quietly.

"That I want Nash," I whispered, cheeks flaming at what I was saying. All the familiar arguments echoed in my head. I'm still married. He's my brother-in-law. It didn't matter. The truth was, I wanted Nash, and I always had.

Quinn gave a quietly decisive nod. "Then go for it. Life is too short. Believe me, I know. It's better to regret something that didn't work out than it is to regret missing an opportunity because you didn't have the courage to go for it."

Everyone turned to look at Quinn. Shifting uncomfortably, she tucked a wave of her shining dark hair behind her ear. Sterling nudged her in the ribs and said, simply, "Tell."

Quinn jerked a shoulder in a shrug. "There was a guy. After college. I took that whitewater training course, and he was one of the instructors. I had such a huge crush on him. I didn't think he had any idea. We always ended up hanging out after a long day on the water. We had the best conversations." She let out a long sigh. "I used to go to bed at night dreaming of kissing him, getting him naked, but I never had the nerve."

"What happened?" I asked, dreading the answer.

Quinn wiped a gleam of moisture from under her eye. "I finally worked up the nerve to ask him out, right before I left for home. He was interested."

She sighed again, the sadness pouring off of her. "He was really interested, said he'd been planning to ask me out once the class was over and he wasn't my instructor anymore. But he was leaving on a kayaking trip with some buddies and wouldn't be back for a few months. He was a pretty big name in that world and they were making a movie."

I knew what she was going to say before she said it.

"There was an accident. It's a dangerous sport on that

level, and they were filming on some major rivers. Big rapids. We were texting here and there. He sent me pics from the trip and we made plans for when he got back. The night before he died he was so excited about the section they had planned for the next day, even though the water was higher than usual. I waited for him to check in, and kept waiting, and finally one of his buddies who knew me called. As soon as his buddy's name showed on my phone, I knew.

"I understood the trip was risky. That was the point–no reason to film an easy paddle–but I never thought he wouldn't come home. After, I couldn't stop thinking about all the time I'd wasted, too afraid to go for it. I missed out on what we could have had."

"You couldn't have stopped him from dying," Sterling said, wrapping an arm around Quinn and tugging her close.

"I know. He still would have gone on the trip. That was his life. It was always going to be dangerous. But I missed out on the short time we could have had together. And for what? To spare my pride if he turned me down? To save myself from some future hurt?"

"It would have been worse if you'd had something with him, wouldn't it?" Savannah asked.

"I guess that depends on how you see it," Quinn said with a ghost of a smile. "Losing him hurt. It would have hurt more if we'd had a deeper relationship. But the regret was a pain of its own. I was heartbroken that he'd died, but it was worse that I hated myself for cheating us, for being a coward. If I'd had the guts to go after what I wanted, I still would have ended up with grief and a broken heart, but at least I wouldn't have blamed myself."

Sterling squeezed Quinn tight. Quinn leaned into her for a moment before lifting her eyes to mine. "If you have feelings for Nash, then you owe it to yourself to find out what you could have with him. Haven't you wasted enough time already?"

Quinn's words played in my head over and over in the days to come.

Haven't you wasted enough time already?

Every time I thought about it, the only answer I had was a resounding yes. Yes, I'd wasted far too much time when it came to Nash Kingsley.

The real question was, what did I plan to do about it?

Chapter Nineteen

PARKER

I wasn't stalking Nash. Not really.

It only felt like it.

Maybe because I was lingering in the library down the hall from Griffen's office, where Nash was in a meeting with Griffen, Hope, and Royal. The first of many, I assumed.

I'd missed his arrival that morning. I'd been tied up with Billy Bob and their Hawk-approved plumber, going over the issues at the cottage. Not that I should have been there to meet Nash. I wasn't his hostess. He hadn't even texted to let me know when he'd be at Heartstone Manor. And why should he?

I'd let all that wine cloud my head. Nash and I were family, kind of, who'd had a light flirtation that was seriously inappropriate, and one night we'd let it go too far. That was it. Any thoughts that Nash was here for me were just the product of too much wine and the hopeful wishes of my sisters and friends. That's all.

So why was I lingering in the library, listening for any hint of a sound from the office? Was I planning to ambush

Nash in the hallway? Follow him to the guest room? Of course not.

And I wasn't lingering. I was looking for a book of photographs of the estate that I recalled having some interior pictures of the cottage and gate house. Griffen wanted them restored to their original condition, or as close as we could get, and the photos would be helpful. That was all it was.

Once I found the book, I'd take it back to my room and go through it there. Or at the cottage. Yes, at the cottage. I needed to get out of the house so I could stop listening for Nash everywhere.

I almost threw my hands over my head and stormed out of the room. Was I crazy? I must have been crazy to think I could share this house with Nash as if nothing had happened between us. I'd seriously overestimated my emotional control.

Scanning the books in the library with unseeing eyes, my ears straining for a peep of sound from Griffen's office, I had to admit I was fresh out of any kind of control, especially emotional.

I checked my phone. 1:47PM. Sterling was still at work, running the shop and office at Quinn's guide service. This time of day, Quinn would be out with a group and the shop/office would be empty, except for the occasional tourist who wandered in off the street to book a future hike or rafting trip with Quinn. In my current mood, I completely understood why Sterling liked working for Quinn. Quiet isolation sounded great to me.

I could give up on finding the book, and go see Sterling. That would get me out of Heartstone, and maybe out of my head. My phone beeped with a text and I tapped it open, expecting to see Sterling's name. Instead, I puzzled at a number I didn't recognize. Tapping it, the message popped open on the screen.

Why are you doing this to me? I never agreed to any of this. Call off your bitch and come home so we can talk. We need to work this out. I know you love me.

Hands trembling, I took a screenshot, texted it to Angie, and blocked the number. Tyler was swinging from ugly abuse–fun stuff like *I'm going to fuck up that pretty face until you beg me to take you back*–to love bombing me with endless flattery–*you're my perfect dream, the only woman I'll ever love and I can't live without you*–to things like this most recent message. Passive aggressive pushing of blame on me while casting himself as the victim and insulting Angie. Jerk.

A shiver went down my spine and I shoved my phone in my pocket, suddenly less interested in the idea of leaving the estate to go see Sterling. Heartstone Manor was safe. There was no one here who wanted to *fuck up my pretty face*, for one thing. Wiping my damp palms on my bright linen capris, I moved to the next section of books and went back to looking for the photographs of the cottage.

I wasn't going to think about Tyler. I was not going to think about Nash. I was going to focus on my job, and my new life, and anything that was not the Kingsley men.

I lasted a whole four minutes, during which I did not find the book of photographs. I maybe read one title, my eyes on the spines of the books but my brain ping-ponging between worry about Tyler and annoyance at Nash. Who hadn't even done anything wrong. It wasn't his fault I was obsessed with him.

Ugh! I finally did it. I threw my hands in the air, spun on my heel and stormed down the hall, determined to get out of this house and find some way to quiet my racing mind. It might have worked if I hadn't slammed into a broad chest and bounced off. I was tumbling to the floor when strong fingers closed around my arm, drawing me back to my feet.

"Where are you headed in such a hurry?" Nash studied my face, his deep brown eyes heavy lidded, framed by thick sweeps of dark lashes that had always made me melt.

I stared at him, wondering for a second if I'd smacked my head on the floor and I was hallucinating. Maybe I'd passed out.

"I don't– When did you get here?" Even to me, my voice sounded weak, my breath caught in my lungs by my tight throat.

How had I forgotten how handsome he was? I hadn't. Of course I hadn't. It was just that he was so far beyond the normal level of good looking that sometimes I dulled him down in my memory. But here he was, in the flesh, and every inch of him was just...more. Larger than life. Those eyelashes, for one. I swear I've worn false lashes that aren't as thick as Nash's. And his shoulders. His forearms. When he rolled up his sleeves, oh my god.

My tongue was tied. I blinked up at Nash and words tumbled over themselves in my brain, not a single one leaving my lips. *I missed you. Where the hell have you been? Why aren't you kissing me yet?* Maybe it was a good thing I couldn't bring myself to talk.

Nash lifted his eyes from mine and glanced down the hall beyond my shoulder. In a quick move, he straightened, took my arm, and drew me down the hall into a small, dark room. The telephone room. No one used it anymore. Decades ago, when there hadn't been phones in every room, much less in every pocket, this room had housed the main telephone for the Manor. If someone wanted a private conversation, they could come here and make their call.

Nash left the lights off. I didn't care. I didn't need the light.

"I missed you," he breathed against my temple, echoing my own unspoken thoughts. His arms closed around me, pulling my body flush against the long, hard length of him. His strength never frightened me. My arms raised, fingers stroking the back of his neck, my face tilted up for the touch of his mouth.

Here in the dark I was catapulted back in time to that closet at my wedding, to the first best kiss of my life. Nash let out a low groan, his lips taking mine, arms crushing me to him. I kissed him back, all my uncertainty, my longing for him, poured from my body to his. I had a million doubts about what we were doing. When I was in Nash's arms, I just didn't care anymore.

Nash lifted me, spreading my legs and pinning me to the wall, the hard length of him pressing exactly where I wanted it. My legs wrapped around his waist, and I had the fleeting thought that I wished I'd worn a dress. His lips skated down the side of my neck, setting every nerve on fire. I was melting from the inside out, my body liquid and all his.

Was I really going to let Nash have sex with me in the telephone room?

No. I wasn't going to 'let' him do anything. I was going to–

Before I finished the thought, I reached for his shirt, pulling at the buttons. His hands caught me, tugging my arms to my sides as he carefully set me on my feet.

Mute, I stared up at him, my throat closed again, this time from lust and surprise and a flush of embarrassment.

Dipping his head, his lips grazed my ear, his breath coming hard and hot against my skin. Good to know I wasn't the only one who couldn't catch their breath.

"Do you have plans this afternoon?"

I shook my head. I hadn't expected him to ask that. Hadn't prepared an answer.

"Want to go for a ride?"

I nodded. I didn't know what kind of ride, or where. I didn't care about either. I just wanted to be with Nash. His hand took mine as he opened the door to the telephone room.

"I was wondering where you got to," Royal called out from down the hall, his blue eyes twinkling with amusement as they took in my flushed face, my hand captured in Nash's.

"I ran in to Parker in the library," he said, his eyes dropping to mine in a gaze so soft it had my knees going wobbly. Looking back at Royal, he added, "I'm stealing her for the afternoon."

Royal laughed, taking in the deepening flush on my cheeks. "Have fun," he said, turning down the hall, giving us a half wave over his shoulder.

I didn't say a word as Nash led me through the main hall to the butler's pantry and the mudroom, all the way through the garage to the courtyard beyond. As we stepped out of the garage into the bright afternoon sun, the gleam of chrome hit my eyes.

Nash turned to me, an unexpectedly boyish glint in his dark eyes. "Do you want to go for a ride?" he asked again.

I pulled my hand from his and moved closer, reaching out to stroke one handlebar. It was gorgeous. Vintage style, modern muscle. Looking back over my shoulder, I had to ask, "This is yours? How did you get it here?"

"I have my ways," he said, the side of his mouth curled in a smile. Plucking a helmet from the back of the bike, he held it out to me. "I bought you a helmet."

I took the heavy black helmet, realizing it was identical to the one he'd picked up, only a little smaller. He'd bought me a helmet. This wasn't his spare, shared with other women, or friends he might have ridden with. It was mine. For me alone. Cradling the helmet to my chest, I had to admit, "I've never been on a motorcycle before."

"I thought that might be the case," Nash said, easily. "Do you want to?"

I didn't have to think about it. "Yes. If it's with you."

"I'm hardly going to let someone else take you." He laughed, tucking a loose hair behind my ear before taking the helmet from my hands. "Not when I went to all the trouble of bringing the bike here to seduce you."

"You don't need the bike for that." My mouth was running without consulting my brain again.

Nash's lips curled as they landed on mine in a soft kiss. "I have a plan."

"Mmm, a plan? Don't let me get in the way then."

"I wasn't going to." Nash settled the helmet over my head. "Here, let me show you."

He put his own helmet on, and held up a leather jacket he'd pulled from somewhere. I stood still as he slid it up my arms and leaned close to zip the front, swooning a little at the care he was taking. Nash guided me in getting on the bike behind him, showing me where to put my feet, both of us letting out a sigh as I leaned into him, wrapping my arms around his chest.

"Comfortable?" he asked, his voice right in my ear. I started in surprise.

Nash tapped the side of his helmet. "Bluetooth. So we can talk to each other."

I relaxed against him, my heart speeding into ragged thumps at the growl of the engine, so close, far more immediate and visceral than a car engine. I'd always loved the roar of motorcycles, had longed to know what it felt like to ride one.

Tyler hated them. He'd said it was because the helmets ruined his hair. Maybe it was because Nash clearly knew what he was doing on a bike. It didn't matter. I didn't care what Tyler thought.

I was on a motorcycle with Nash, and it was better than my wildest dreams.

Chapter Twenty

PARKER

We were flying.

The bike hugged the curves of the road, Nash maneuvering the machine with complete control. I clung to him, my helmet pressed to his back, head turned to watch the scenery pass in a blur. Nash must have known where he was going. He'd said he had a plan, so I shouldn't have been surprised.

He'd taken a right out of Heartstone Manor. Not the way people normally went, as town—and almost everything else—was to the left. Nash followed the mountain road up and up, merging onto a narrow lane that ran along the ridgeline before dropping down to pick up a ramp onto the Blue Ridge Parkway. From there, we just rode.

I don't know how long we were on the bike. It could have been an hour, could have been a lot more. I didn't care. I couldn't remember the last time I'd felt this at peace. A funny thought to have against the backdrop of the bike's rumbling engine. But peace didn't have to mean quiet. I wanted this—to fly through the forest with Nash on roaring wings disguised by chrome and rubber, knowing he would never let me fall.

Gradually, I realized Nash had a specific destination in mind. Eventually, he slowed, taking an exit to a well-known inn and restaurant built right off the Parkway, hanging from the side of the mountain. Nash pulled into the parking lot and stopped. I climbed off the bike, immediately missing the heat of him pressed to my front.

Pulling off my helmet, I searched his face for a clue. "How did you know?"

Nash took the helmet. "You liked it, then?"

I thought I caught the faintest hint of uncertainty before his familiar, confident smile spread across his mouth.

"I loved it. How did you know I'd love it so much? That I always wanted to—"

Nash smiled down at me with the same soft expression he'd given me in the hall at Heartstone. Just like then, my knees turned to jelly. "I didn't know. I had a hunch. I have all sorts of hunches when it comes to you, Parker Sawyer."

"Really?" I looped my arm through his, letting him lead me up to the historic stone inn. "Pray tell? What's next?"

"Already want more?" Nash grinned, giving me another flash of him as a boy. Carefree and happy. My chest flooded with light at bringing that expression to his face.

"Maybe. Maybe I'm just curious to know what you have in mind." I paused as Nash gave the front desk his name. Had he gotten us a room? I hadn't brought anything... The thought dissolved as we were led, not to the stairs, but to a private balcony off the main dining room.

I let Nash help me into my chair, my gaze fixed on the endless view. Mountains, shaded in green, ridged in blue, row after row arrayed against the summer sky. I let out a sigh of pure joy. "I forget how much I miss this view when I'm away."

Nash settled in the seat opposite me, reaching out to take my hand in his, his eyes on my face. "It's the most spectacular view I've ever seen."

"You're not even looking at the view!" I shook my head, laughing and trying to pull back my hand. Nash didn't let go. I gave up. I didn't want my hand back, anyway.

Nash flicked his eyes at the mountains beyond our balcony. "That's nice too. But that's not the view I missed."

"You're very sweet," I demurred, not sure what to say.

Nash snorted a laugh, turning our hands over so mine was face up. His fingertips stroked the sensitive skin on my inner wrist. His voice heavy and low, he said, "I think we both know the last thing I am is sweet."

"You might think so," I said, the light touch on my wrist turning my insides to liquid heat. "But to me, you're always sweet."

Nash gave a low chuckle and started to argue. The arrival of the waiter had him sitting back, accepting the menu, reviewing the wine list, all without moving his fingertips from their slow stroke, stroke, stroke of my wrist. "Champagne or wine?" he asked, catching my eyes.

"Champagne," I answered.

I wanted to celebrate, to forget all my doubts and questions and celebrate being here with Nash. Everything was different. I was divorcing Tyler. I had a job. A life of my own. I'd had my first ride on a motorcycle and it was all I'd dreamed it would be. And most of all, Nash was here. With me. On a romantic date.

I should ask him what all this meant. Were we a couple now? What about Tyler? His mother? What about–

Internally, I closed the door on my questions. Later.

Maybe never. I wasn't going to ruin this by trying to figure out all the answers from the start. For now, I was just going to enjoy myself.

"Have you been here before?" Nash asked, glancing through the french doors back into the Inn's elegant dining room.

"Not in years. I forgot how beautiful it is up here."

"I'm looking forward to seeing more of the mountains."

"Is that why you brought your bike?"

"Partly. And partly because I thought you'd like it."

"Well, you guessed right on that one." Considering, I probed, "What else do you have planned?"

"It wouldn't be a surprise if I told you." Nash lifted my hand and kissed my fingertips, releasing me just as the waiter returned with our champagne.

The waiter did his dance, presenting the bottle and popping the cork with a flourish. Nash sipped and giving a regal nod. Once the waiter had disappeared again, Nash lifted his glass. "To new beginnings," he said, reading my mind once again.

"To new beginnings," I repeated, feeling the flush in my cheeks. To cover, I sipped the champagne, the sharp sparkle of bubbles breaking on my tongue.

"Griffen mentioned that you're working on renovating another of the outbuildings on the property, in addition to the cottage. Tell me about it. Are you still enjoying it?"

He seemed to be interested, so I told him, filling him in on my progress and what we had to get done. I was still talking when the waiter arrived to take our orders. Nash sent him a congenial smile and said, "We need a few more minutes," before turning his attention back to me.

I picked up my menu and chose something at semi-random, not really caring what I ate.

"What are you having?" Nash asked, taking my free hand in his again.

"The trout," I said, more interested in Nash, sipping champagne and holding my hand, grazing his thumb across my knuckles, back and forth. The waiter returned and took our orders.

I'd almost forgotten what we were talking about when Nash prompted, "When do you think the plumbing will be finished?"

"Billy Bob's guy thinks he can have it done this week, but I'm not sure. It's a small cottage, but it seems like there's a lot that needs to be replaced, and all of it is ancient."

As I explained about Billy Bob and the added complexity of security at the Manor shrinking my pool of available contractors, Nash seemed content to sit there, holding my hand and listening to me talk about my renovation project with what felt like genuine interest. For a few seconds, I had to wonder if I was dreaming. A smirk ghosted across my face.

"What?" he asked, his eyes fixed on my mouth.

I shrugged a shoulder. "Nothing. Just wondering if you're real."

Nash smirked. "I'm very real, and I'm far from perfect."

I laughed. No one was perfect, but Nash was giving me a pretty good approximation of it. Which made me nervous. I'd fallen for perfect once before, and I was still paying for it.

"Tell me what's wrong with you then," I challenged.

"That's easy." Nash took a sip of champagne before answering with a grin. "I'm bossy. Stubborn. Sometimes impatient. I can be a workaholic, especially with a new project. I hate bullshit and I'm rarely nice if I have to call people on it. I've also heard I'm a bed hog."

A slow smile curved my lips. I could attest to that after our one night together. He'd hogged the bed and the blankets. "I didn't mind."

My murmur sent the same slow smile to Nash's lips. "Good to know," he said in a low voice that sent shivers across my skin. "Now tell me what's wrong with you."

Oh, fun. But I'd asked for it. "I'm still married to your brother, for one."

Nash waved that away. "That's circumstance, not a character flaw."

"Okay, I married him in the first place."

"And you want me to blame you for that?" Nash asked, running his thumb over my knuckles.

"I blame me for that," I admitted. "I should have—"

Nash tugged at my fingers to get my attention. "Parker, stop." At the hard tone of his voice, I looked up.

"Bossy," I whispered.

"Exactly. And I'm telling you to listen to me. You were a very sheltered twenty-one year old and Tyler has always been great at the snow-job."

I raised my eyebrows in question. Nash gave an impatient shake of his head.

"You know what I mean. He puts on a great front. How many tantrums did he throw before he proposed?"

"None." He'd been the perfect boyfriend: attentive, thoughtful, romantic.

"And between your engagement and the wedding?"

I thought back. He'd proposed on Christmas in my senior year of college. We were married that June, only a week after my graduation. "Only one. He asked me to skip an exam, and I refused. The next day he was back to normal."

"And you decided you'd overreacted."

I nodded. "I was stressed about school, and he was so contrite after. I didn't think he–" I shrugged. "I didn't think."

"One tantrum before the wedding? That was it?" Nash raised a dark eyebrow. I nodded again in answer. "Then how were you supposed to know?"

"I should have known." I could be stubborn, too. "I grew up with my father. He would have shot anyone who said he threw tantrums, but that's what they were. At his worst, Tyler still isn't as scary as my father could be. I should have known what was coming. I should have seen the signs."

"We'll have to agree to disagree," Nash said. "Now tell me some real faults. Other than disagreeing with me."

"You're in for a disappointment if you think you're going to get your way all the time." My head spun with the giddy exhilaration of sparring with Nash.

Nash lifted my hand and pulled it to his mouth, pressing his warm lips to the back of my fingers. "I can't tell you how much I'm looking forward to disagreeing with you."

I was too breathless to argue. Trying to keep my head on straight, I laid it out. "Okay, fine. I'm naïve. I haven't done anything with my life. I'm trying to figure out my first job at twenty-seven. I'm stuck living with my family for the next five years. I'm–" I cut off abruptly at the amusement all over Nash's face.

"You sound terrible. Maybe I should leave." He shook his head in disappointment, the side of his mouth quirked in a smile. "And you forgot stubborn. We definitely have that in common."

"Don't make fun of me. You could do a lot better–"

"No, I couldn't." The laughter was gone from his face. I opened my mouth to argue. Nash squeezed my hand, shaking his head. "No, Parker. Don't. Neither of us is perfect. Agreed. But half the things you see as faults, aren't things I have a problem with. So what if you feel like you're just starting your life? So what if this is your first job? Do you like it?"

"Yes, actually. I love it." I didn't have to pretend on that one. But... "I'm not sure why I think I can do this."

Nash waved off my words again. "It looks like you *are* doing it. When you run into a problem, you'll figure it out. You have good taste, and that's an essential starting point with a renovation. Do you have pics of your progress?" I nodded. "Will you show me?"

Chapter Twenty-One

PARKER

I pulled my phone from the pocket of the leather jacket he'd given me. "Why the jacket?" I asked as I flipped to my 'Cottage' album.

"To protect your skin if we went down," Nash said easily. I hadn't thought about that.

"What about your skin?"

"I was more worried about you." Taking in my affronted expression, he smiled. "We'll get you your own jacket."

"Better." I pushed the phone at him. "You can see where I started. Griffen wants both buildings brought back to their original condition, except modernized where we need it. Take a look at the color scheme Savannah and I chose for the kitchen."

I was flipping to the pic where I'd laid out a painted cabinet beside the marble counter, the dull brass faucet and a sample of the dark hardwood. My phone chimed and a text notice popped on the screen. Before I could stop my finger, I'd tapped it open.

Don't block me you fucking cunt.

Chime.

I'm done playing nice.

Chime.

It's till death do us part you stupid bitch. get it?

Chime.

I'll make you get it. Until you beg me to take you back.

Chime.

No one else will want you when I'm done with you.

A low growl drifted across the table. I looked up to see Nash glaring down at my phone. He reached to grab it, but I snatched it up before he got there.

"Let me see your phone," he demanded, his voice deadly hard.

Closing my fingers around the phone, I shook my head. "There's nothing to see. Anything he sends, I screenshot and send to Angie. Then I block the number. You can scroll through my messages to Angie, but I don't think you should."

"Why?" Nash rumbled. The hand that had held mine so gently curled into a fist on the tablecloth. His knuckles were white, his jaw rock hard.

"For a few reasons," I said, reaching out to wrap my fingers around his fist, squeezing tight. "One, I like that phone and can't afford a new one. Which means you can't get angry and throw it off the balcony."

"And if I see his texts, I'll want to throw your phone?"

"You'll definitely want to throw my phone," I confirmed. "Two, I don't want Tyler to ruin this. We know he wants to make the divorce as difficult as possible. Let's not make that easier for him."

Nash stared at me for a long moment. I waited, frozen, expecting him to push, to insist I hand over the phone, or let him call Angie to get all the details. I expected him to do anything but what he did.

His fisted hand gradually relaxed, and he turned it to thread his fingers with mine, a hint of a smile pushing the grim expression from his eyes.

"Later," he said, "I'd like to look at the texts he's sent you. I promise not to throw your phone."

"Okay," I agreed, too surprised to protest.

"Have you shown the texts to Hawk or Griffen?"

My cheeks flooded with heat. No, I had not. I should have, but I didn't.

Nash didn't need my answer in words. "If you don't want to do it directly, you can ask Angie to send Griffen her file on Tyler's threats. She probably has the most useful accounting for Hawk's purposes."

Relief flooded through me. I could handle Griffen knowing about Tyler's texts. It was mostly the thought of actually telling them that had me procrastinating. "Good idea," I murmured, "One sec." I focused on screen-shotting the texts and sending them to Angie with a note asking her to forward her info on Tyler to my brother.

As I worked, Nash asked, "Just one question. How often is he texting you like this?"

I didn't miss the thread of tension in his gentle words. He was pretending to be calm, but it was an act. I appreciated it anyway. I wasn't quite as relaxed as I appeared, either. We both had reason to be on edge, but I wasn't going to let Tyler ruin this like he'd ruined so many other things.

"Here and there," I murmured, in a non answer to his question. He'd see everything later when I showed him my text thread with Angie.

I sent the text and set my phone on the table, face down, ringer silenced. Giving Nash my brightest smile, I said, "One of these days, when you have time, I'll walk you through the cottage and show you what I've been doing in person."

"I'd love that." Nash returned my smile and topped off my champagne. I noticed his own glass remained half full. I trusted him on the bike, but it was nice to know he wasn't planning to drink half a bottle of champagne and try to navigate our way through the mountains back to Sawyers Bend.

"Now," I said, changing the subject, "I want to hear how things are going in your venture with Sawyer Enterprises. At least, whatever you can tell me. I know it's top secret."

I didn't know much about programming or AI, but I knew enough to keep up as Nash filled me in on their progress. He and Royal were heading out the next day to look at the building Griffen had in mind for their new offices.

Our food arrived, and we ate, still talking, moving from Nash's business to his impressions of Sawyers Bend and my family, to our latest streaming obsessions. It was hard to believe that Nash and I hadn't talked much in the six years since we'd met. Once we started, we never ran out of things to say.

Just like that night in New York, we talked and talked, absorbed in each other. I could have stayed all night, not fully noticing as the air cooled and the sun dipped in the sky. Nash took care of the check–a good thing since I hadn't even grabbed my purse–and we got on the bike for the ride back to Heartstone Manor.

Again, it was like flying, the shadows deeper, the sun setting over the mountains drenching them in vibrant color. Orange, lavender, and streaks of red flashed by as we sped home, the heat of Nash's body against mine and the rumble of the engine lulling me into a state of relaxed bliss.

When we pulled into the courtyard, I got off the bike and took Nash's hand, leading him into the house, through the mudroom and up the back stairs. At the top, he came to a halt, glancing at the guest wing to our left. I shook my head and tugged at Nash's hand, pulling him across the center hall to the family wing.

Behind the thick door of my bedroom, I turned the lock and faced Nash. "I've been imagining having you here. In my room. With me." My fingers made quick work of the small buttons on my blouse, opening it enough to strip over my head.

Nash went for his own shirt buttons. "And what did we do in your imagination? Exactly?" Done with his shirt, his hands were at my waist, unzipping my capris and pushing them over my hips, taking my panties along with them. "I want you to be very specific."

"Mmm." I thought about that. How specific was I prepared to be? Tyler had never been chatty in bed. This kind of thing wasn't in my wheelhouse. But I was willing to try. I certainly had plenty of day dreams about Nash to work from.

"It depends," I said, unsnapping my bra and dropping it on the floor. I unfastened his belt. "Sometimes it starts here, with me stripping you, and admiring you naked for a while."

I pushed his pants to the floor, along with his boxers, leaving him bared to my greedy eyes. He was delicious, every inch of him. His muscles, the light dusting of hair on his chest. The wicked gleam in his dark eyes. And that long, thick cock between his legs. All of him was beautiful.

"Sometimes I do this." I reached out and wrapped my fingers around his cock, squeezing hard, moving closer to cup his balls with my other hand. He shivered under my touch and I leaned in, pressing my lips to his collarbone, tasting the salt and heat of him.

"And sometimes," I said, dropping to my knees, "I daydream about doing this." My lips closed over the end of his cock, his crown warm and velvet soft, filling my mouth as I sucked him in deeper. His fingers slipped into my hair, cradling my head, his thumb stroking the line of my jaw.

I had to touch, to get my hands all over him. Sinking my fingers into his tight ass, I drew him deeper, as deep as I could take, and sucked hard, dragging a groan from Nash, his fingers convulsively closing and releasing in my hair.

Stepping back in a jerk, he pulled me to my feet and swung me into his arms. I slung an arm around his shoulders and held on. "Was this on your to-do list?" he rumbled in my ear.

"Absolutely." I was laughing when he dropped me on my bed, the laugh turning to a giggle as I tilted and fell to the side, my eyes glued to Nash's long, hard body sliding onto the coverlet beside me.

My chest still shaking from giggles, I pounced. With Nash, just like the first time, I wasn't worried about doing the right thing, or being embarrassed. I was too hungry for him. I wanted him too much, leaving no room for restraint or second guesses.

I had about three seconds on top of Nash, working my way down until my mouth was even with his. He let me press one short kiss to his lips before he rolled us over, pinning me, his lips at the so sensitive juncture of my neck and shoulder.

I shivered in his arms, all coiled tension and desperate need. My giggles vanished. His mouth worked at my neck, his long fingers moved between my legs, finding the soft heat of me with unerring precision. My thighs fell apart in welcome, my hips surging up to meet him. Fingers sank into Nash's thick hair, holding him at my breast, his teeth nipping, lips soothing, sucking, sending bolts of fire to my heated core.

He was lazy, slow, lingering over my nipples, tasting my ribs, dipping his tongue into my belly button until I squirmed beneath him, every nerve overloaded until I couldn't tell pleasure from pain. "Nash, please," I begged, not even sure what exactly I was begging for. All of it. His mouth, his cock, my orgasm. I was begging for everything he could give me, and more. He slid back up to kiss me, my mouth drawing from his, desperate.

Hitching my leg over his hip, I opened my body to him, reaching between us. Nash nuzzled my ear. "Is this what you want?" He nudged the head of his cock against my wet heat. My hips rolled, drawing him closer in answer.

He pushed in just enough for me to feel the stretch, the sparking pleasure of him inside me. But not nearly far enough. "This? Because I was going to do other things first."

"Yeah?" I asked, breathless as he pushed another inch deeper. "Like what? Because this is pretty nice."

"Just nice? That's the best you have?"

He pushed in another inch. I gasped, trying for a nonchalant shrug that came out in a rough jerk of my shoulder. "So far, nice is it. Make me come and I'll give you something better."

Nash didn't answer in words. Hooking a hand behind my knee, he opened me and drove his cock in to the hilt, filling me so deep he slammed into my clit, the impact sending a knife edged shock of pleasure up my spine into my brain. I had no words left. Only instinct.

That night in New York, Nash and I had sex three times. He was slow and deliberate, teasing and aggressive. I thought I had an idea what he'd be like in bed. I'd had no clue. This wasn't like before. In a flash, Nash transformed from my gentle lover into a beast of instinct. He fucked me hard. There was no other word for it.

This wasn't making love or playing. This was no flirtation. This was a claiming. Nash's body took ownership of mine, opening me, filling me, over and over, driving me higher until I exploded in orgasm, my fingers gripping his shoulders as my body fell limp beneath him. Nash followed me with a deep groan, his lips covering mine, kissing and stroking me as the tension slipped from my body.

When I could breathe again, I rolled my head to the side, meeting his dark, satisfied eyes. "Would you accept 'very nice'?"

"I see I have work to do," He grinned back at me. "I accept the challenge."

Accept it he did. We cuddled, not really talking, mostly getting our breath back before Nash tempted me into a long, hot shower where we made use of the built-in bench. After, we snuck down the back stairs and raided the kitchen for a snack, long after everyone else had gone to bed. The last thing I remember was curling into Nash, my head tucked into his neck, his fingers playing in my damp hair.

I woke late to find myself alone.

Nash was gone.

Not just from my bed.

Nash had disappeared from Heartstone Manor completely.

Chapter Twenty-Two

NASH

T his was not part of my plan. I paced my mother's opulent drawing room, noting the increase in delicate china figures and ruffled silk throw pillows as I strode back and forth, irritation building with each step.

"Darling, would you sit, please?" My mother called from the settee, the teapot in her hand.

"No," I answered, shortly.

She sighed and poured a single cup of tea for herself. "I know you're annoyed by my summons, but this is important."

"Then tell me what's going on," I demanded. Narrowing my eyes, I examined her. She looked the same as always, dressed for a garden party, not a hair out of place. With steady hands, she poured the tea. "You're not sick, are you?"

"No, of course not. My doctor says I'm in perfect condition for a woman my age."

"Then what—"

"Patience, darling," she said, holding up her hand.

If a call for patience has ever resulted in anything other than making the recipient *less* patient, I'd love to know.

I shut my mouth, but sent my mother a glare I'm sure reminded her of myself fifteen years earlier. In general, I tried not to behave like a petulant adolescent, but if anyone could bring it out of me, it was Claudia Kingsley.

Her early morning summons via text had been vintage Claudia. High drama, little explanation.

You must come home immediately. It's of utmost importance. I'll explain when you arrive.

I'd tried calling, but her phone had gone straight to voicemail. Also vintage Claudia. Why explain over the phone when she could summon me to her presence? Usually I insisted she explain and work with my schedule. I love my mother, but if I gave her an inch she'd take over my life.

This time, between Tyler's recent unhinged behavior and our mother's fear of him, I couldn't bring myself to put her off. I'd taken a moment to watch Parker sleep beside me, every cell in my body fighting the idea that I was going to leave her side. I was finally exactly where I wanted to be, in every way.

The last thing I wanted to do was leave Heartstone Manor. Everything I wanted was here, Parker most of all. The day before had been a dream come true, and she'd loved every minute of it. I knew she had, from the bike, to dinner, to ending up together in her bed.

I'd debated waking her up or leaving a note, but decided to text her when I landed, giving her a chance to sleep in before I gave her the bad news that our plans for the day would have to wait. I'd emailed Griffen, Hope, and Royal to fill them in before my flight took off, but I'd wanted to talk to Parker personally.

The flight had been delayed, circling in the air above Manhattan, and I'd left it too late. Every time I tried to call, it rang exactly once and sent me to voicemail. My text messages went unread. I knew what that meant.

Parker had blocked me. Fuck.

I shoved my phone back in my pocket. A long-suffering sigh drifted over from my mother. "I am sorry, Nash. I know you're in the middle of important business. I truly wouldn't have asked you to come if it wasn't important."

I echoed her sigh and sank into the delicate armchair facing the settee, careful to land easily. These chairs looked barely substantial enough to hold my mother, much less a full grown man. This entire drawing room was packed full of delicate, ornate frippery, as my father had liked to call it.

The old-fashioned word fit. From the abundance of china figurines, to paintings and other objet d'art, the room was intensely feminine and jam-packed with stuff right down to the marble fireplace, which held an elaborate arrangement of flowers on this summer day, instead of cold logs. I shifted one of the fringed pillows behind me and accepted the china tea cup my mother handed me, resisting the urge to send her a sullen sneer.

She was sometimes silly and over-dramatic, but she was my mother and, clearly, whatever this was, it was important to her. I could behave like an adult for at least one more hour before I lost my patience and left. Maybe two hours. I loved my mother, even when she was driving me nuts.

I understood the reason for the meeting a few minutes later when the double doors of the drawing room slammed open and Tyler strode into the room. His face was fixed in a bland, genial expression aimed at our mother, until his eyes fell on me. In an instant his face twisted into a mask of rage, before unwinding back into something close to the Tyler he wanted our mother to see.

It wouldn't work. Claudia could be flighty and

dramatic, but she was not a fool. Tyler had made that mistake far too many times. He also mistook her love and subsequent indulgence for weakness. Another error on Tyler's part. He'd made far too many of them in the past few years. I was trying not to take too much satisfaction in his mistakes coming home to roost. It was a lot more entertaining now that Parker wasn't at his side, suffering from his stupidity along with him.

Knowing it would only annoy him, I nodded in his direction, but didn't acknowledge him otherwise. This was Claudia's show, after all. Given all I had to hide from both of them, I was going to say as little as possible. A good plan, since Claudia's words left me speechless.

"Tyler, please take a seat. I have some business to discuss with both of you."

Tyler dropped into a spindly arm chair, crossing one ankle over his knee, affecting nonchalance. The chair creaked ominously, and I waited to see if it would collapse beneath him. No such luck. Tyler's jaw flexed with poorly hidden irritation as we waited.

My mother set her empty teacup on the tray and folded her hands in her lap, taking a moment to look at both of us in turn. Clearing her throat, she began, "I've been doing a lot of thinking in the past few weeks. About your father, and what he would want if he were still with us. About what he left me, and what my responsibility is to his memory."

She sniffed delicately, dabbing a linen napkin beneath her eyes.

"I know you miss him, Mom," I said.

"I do, darling. I miss him every day. And it's very important to me to honor what he would have wanted."

"Which is?" Tyler prompted, a sneer ghosting across his face before he hid it with a smile. "I'm sure Nash has more important things to do than hang around here. Let's get on with it."

A chill ran up my spine when Claudia ignored Tyler's rudeness and turned to me. "I do know that you have important priorities, Nash, and I appreciate you coming at my request, as inconvenient as it must have been. I promise you'll understand shortly."

"It's okay, Mom," I said. It wasn't, but it was. She's my mom. She's allowed to be inconvenient.

"It's not," she disagreed, "but it is necessary."

"What about my important business?" Tyler pushed in, the sneer back in full force. "You're not sorry for inconveniencing me?"

Again, Claudia ignored him. This was not like her. Usually she bent over backwards to appease Tyler, believing that if she just gave him enough of everything—attention, love, money—it would fix what was wrong inside him.

"In thinking about your father and what he would have wanted," she said, "I've come to some conclusions. The first relates to Tyler." She shifted in her seat and met Tyler's eyes, her back straight, hands folded sternly on her knees.

"Tyler, I'm cutting you off. You'll still have access to the trust your grandmother left you. There should be enough there to keep a roof over your head while you get settled. I will not be funding your life any longer. Your credit cards have been cancelled, and the locks have been changed on the family homes. In addition, I've removed you from my will. If you can find suitable employment and maintain it, I'll consider reinstating your place in my will."

"What! You can't do that!" Tyler surged to his feet, toppling the chair behind him. It landed with a sharp crack.

I braced, considering the delicate breakables surrounding us.

"I can and I have," Claudia said, reminding me suddenly of my father, immovable and resolute.

I'd been cut off a few times. After the sting of the first, I'd stopped caring. I was my own man. My father hadn't been my provider. He'd always been my dad, whether I was in the will or out.

Tyler's jaw worked as he fought for a response. He tried begging first.

"Mom, why are you doing this?" A heated glance at me. "Did he talk you into this? I don't understand. You want me to find a job? It's absurd."

"No Tyler," Claudia said, a slight waver in her voice, "what's absurd is you expecting me to finance an extravagant lifestyle while you do nothing with yourself. It was one thing when you had a wife to look after, but you don't have that excuse anymore. Your credit card bill was thirty-two thousand dollars last month! You don't have rent, a mortgage, or a car payment. You don't even pay for your own phone! As your father would have said, the gravy train is over. Whatever you have left in your grandmother's trust, I suggest you make it last. You won't be getting another penny from me."

Tyler stood there, shoulders slumped, his eyes flashing from me to our mother, desperately trying to calculate his next move. I almost felt sorry for him. If it hadn't been for Parker, I would have. Remembering everything he'd put her through, I was all out of compassion.

"Can I at least go stay in the Hamptons until I figure out what to do next?" he asked, looking at her through lowered lashes, his most pitiful expression on full display. To my surprise, she didn't fall for it.

"No, you may not. There are too many valuables lying around, and I don't trust you anymore."

"Mom!" Tyler reared back, slapping his palm over his chest, his eyes wounded. "How could you say something like that! How could you think I'd steal from you?"

"Because you have before," she said crisply. "The, uh, exotic dancer you brought home a few weeks ago was caught trying to fence a few items that had gone missing while I was away. She confessed everything and played a recording for the police, in which you showed her what to take and offered to split the proceeds. I decided cutting you off was preferable to pressing charges."

I kept my mouth shut through sheer force of will. How could Tyler have been so stupid? Tyler caught the slight shake of my head and turned on me.

"Don't you shake your fucking head at me," he shouted, stabbing a pointed finger my way before swinging his eyes back to our mother. "Do you know he's trying to steal my wife? You're pissed I was screwing a stripper, but your own son is fucking my wife and you don't even care."

I waited for an interrogation from my mother, but her eyes never left Tyler. Her face drooping in a frown, she shook her head, her voice heavy with pity. "Tyler, I'm deeply disappointed that you chose to betray your marriage vows with Parker. I'm aware that it happened many times, most of them well before she finally left you."

"But Nash—"

"Nash is not your business," she said, her words unyielding. "Parker is no longer your business. I don't care what you think is going on with either of them. The only person you need to worry about is me."

"Mom," he wailed, "you can't do this to me! Is it because Parker left me? She's going to come back. I'll get her back, I promise. I'll never cheat on her again and everything will be like it was."

Our mother shook her head, the motion weary, her patience gone. "I don't want to find out that you've been bothering Parker. She's moving on. You need to let her go."

Tyler spun, snatching a shepherdess figurine off a side table and flinging it into the fireplace. It erupted in a fountain of porcelain shards that fell to the carpet, too far from my mother to do any damage. Lucky for Tyler. If he'd hurt her, I would have abandoned my restraint and beaten the shit out of him.

"I'll never let Parker go. She's not allowed to leave me!"

For the first time, alarm flashed across my mother's face. "Tyler! Stop this!"

Tyler turned to her, his chest heaving, eyes wild. "She's not allowed to leave me," he repeated, rage and desperation warring in his voice.

"She already has," my mother said, back to weary. "And if you agree to give her a divorce, I'm still willing to pay for your attorney. If you sign the papers today, I'll write you a check for five million dollars."

"Five million!" Tyler threw his hands in the air and stamped a foot. "Five million is nothing!"

What was he? A toddler? Then I remembered who I was dealing with. I knew toddlers more mature than Tyler.

"Five million is far from nothing," Claudia tossed back. "And that offer only stands until you walk out of this room." She gestured to an envelope sitting beside her. "Sign now and I'll hand you the check. If you walk out of here without signing, the offer disappears."

He tilted closer, as if already reaching for the check. Abruptly, he reared back, shoving both hands in his pockets and falling into a sullen slouch. "Just like Dad," he muttered.

"Trying to use money to get me to do what you want. Well, I won't fall for it. I still have Grandmother's trust. I don't have to let you control me!"

"This is your last chance, Tyler," Claudia warned, picking up the cell phone I hadn't noticed tucked beside her. "Until you're a parent, you'll never understand how much it hurts me to do this, but it's for your own good." She held out the envelope. "Just sign the papers. Let me give you the five million and you can get a good start on a new life. Please."

Tyler shot forward, snatching the envelope from her hand. I was on my feet in an instant, shielding my mother. My brother took a swing at me, one I easily blocked. Before I could hit him back, two hulking dark-suited men entered the room, headed straight for Tyler.

"I'm so sorry it came to this," Claudia said, her voice shaking with adrenaline and heartbreak. "Security will escort you from the building. Let me know where you settle and I'll make arrangements to have your things sent. You won't be allowed back into the house in the Hamptons, or any other family property. I've arranged for security, so I don't suggest you try anything. Do you understand?"

Tyler grunted in response, more concerned with getting free of the security guards than listening to my mother. We watched in silence as he was dragged from the room. At the thunk of the front door closing, quiet filled the penthouse.

"Well, that went well," Claudia said in a shaky voice, smoothing her skirt over her knees. "Don't you think?" She turned watery eyes my way. I risked the settee collapsing and moved to sit beside her, pulling her into a hug.

"I'm sorry, Mom."

"Why are you sorry?" she wept into my shoulder. "You've been a wonderful son. You tried to tell me and I

183

wouldn't listen. Your father tried to tell me. I thought Tyler just needed to grow up. And then I found out he hit Parker and I just couldn't–"

"Did she tell you that?" I asked.

"No, Parker would never tell me something like that. I hired a private detective. I had to know what he was up to. They talked to his women, who shared far too much. Apparently, Tyler likes to talk. I know about him raising his hand to Parker, how often he was cheating on her, that he likes cocaine and gambling. I know far more than I wanted, but I had to know everything before I made my decision."

I held her as she cried quietly. Finally, she whispered into my shoulder, "It was the right thing to do. I should have let your father do it years ago, but I hoped he'd grow up." She let out a long sigh before sitting up and dabbing the tears from her face. Standing, she walked to the door and pressed a button on the wall panel. "We'd like fresh tea in the drawing room."

Sitting back on the settee, she turned to face me, a resolute smile on her face. "I do appreciate you being here. I couldn't face him by myself. And we have business. I have papers for you to sign."

"You did the right thing," I said. "Though you could have let me know what was going on."

"I was concerned that you wouldn't come if you knew it was about Tyler."

A reasonable guess but–"Mom, I'm always going to look out for you, I just don't like being in the dark. And what papers?"

"You're already a trustee on several trusts your father left behind. I'm adding you to the rest. You're also my sole heir, aside from Parker. I created a provision to cover her in case her inheritance from her father turns out to be nothing." Shaking her head, she added, "Your father never trusted that man."

"Mom, I don't know what to say." I didn't. I'd expected none of this. "I don't want the money."

"I know you don't, darling," she said, patting my cheek affectionately. "That's why you're getting it all."

"And what about Tyler?"

Claudia sighed, then straightened as her housekeeper came in with a fresh tea tray. Setting the tray on the table beside the first one, she cleared the used tray and left as quietly as she'd entered. I snagged a tiny, crustless sandwich, wondering briefly if this was going to be lunch. I'd missed breakfast in my mad rush to catch a flight home.

"I think you should leave New York," I said. "Travel for a while. I know you just got home from Paris, but is there somewhere else you can go? Friends to visit?"

"You're worried about Tyler," she guessed.

"He's unstable, Mom. Until he figures out what he's going to do next, I don't want you anywhere he can get to you. If you're staying here, I'm going to get you a bodyguard."

Claudia shook her head in disdain. "Not a bodyguard, Nash. It's so crass. I'm not in entertainment."

"Mom," I protested, but she held up her hand.

"I agree. Your brother is unstable. Maybe it took Parker leaving, but–"

"I think he's been unstable for a long time."

She ignored my comment. "But I think you're correct. It will be better if I'm out of his reach as he comes to terms with these changes. Patricia–you remember my friend Patricia?"

"The senator's wife? That Patricia?" I vaguely knew who

she was talking about. I didn't keep track of my mother's friends any more than she kept track of mine.

"Yes, exactly. She's leaving on a month long safari in Botswana. Her daughter was supposed to join her, but had to cancel at the last minute and Patricia asked me to take her place. I accepted. As soon as you sign these papers and we have them couriered to my attorney, you can deliver me to the plane Patricia has waiting for me. My suitcases are in the hall by the door."

I sat back, amazed at her organization and planning. I was used to thinking of my mother as flighty and spontaneous. Clearly, she'd planned this maneuver down to the minute. I flipped through the stack of papers she'd set on the tea tray beside my cooling cup of tea. Ignoring the tea and the rest of the sandwiches, I scanned the papers more thoroughly.

Everything looked in order. The papers were exactly what she'd said they were—documents naming me her co-trustee. I signed where indicated, eager to finish this, get my mother to the airport, and head back to Parker and Sawyers Bend.

I should have known, given the way the day had unfolded so far, that nothing would go as planned. By the time I got back to Parker and Sawyers Bend, I was too late.

Chapter Twenty-Three

PARKER

I scrubbed at the tile in the first floor bathroom of the cottage, working furiously, my muscles aching, knees bruised despite the towel protecting them from the hard floor–though not as bruised as my heart. *Nash*. I couldn't even think his name without drowning under a wave of grief.

How could I have been so foolish?

Because I was a fool.

I'd married Tyler, hadn't I? And I'd stayed with him after he cheated, stayed after he hit me. I was a fool, and I deserved this. It's just that Nash had been so believable. His sincerity, his tenderness. It turned out his passion had been the only thing that was real.

After the most amazing night of my life, I'd woken alone. I was so naïve, at first I hadn't realized what had happened. I thought I'd overslept, that he was down at breakfast or in a meeting with Griffen. After a quick shower, I went down for my own breakfast and discovered Nash was nowhere to be found.

I couldn't bring myself to ask where he was. All it took

was imagining the pitying look I'd get from my brother, or Hope—from anyone who figured out that I'd slept with my brother-in-law and he'd left me without bothering to tell me where he was.

I'd given into my foolish heart and called Nash after I realized he hadn't been to breakfast and wasn't in the house. The call went straight to voicemail. I tried again an hour later and got the same. Enough. There was no note that had fallen off my pillow. No text, no message explaining his absence. Nash was simply gone.

Dodging the other inhabitants of the guest wing, I'd snuck in to Nash's room to find it empty. The closet held only bare hangers. The bathroom was devoid of anything personal. He was gone, and I was a fool. There was nothing more to say.

I was not chasing after him. Either he'd turned off his phone, or he'd blocked me. The ache in my heart was so deep it threatened to take my breath. I pulled up his contact on my phone and scrolled down to tap 'Block this Caller'.

I thought I'd feel better when it was done. A little revenge for the pain he'd caused. I didn't. He probably wouldn't even call to find out I'd blocked him. He got what he wanted from me. If he came back for more, I'd deal with him then.

I retreated to the cottage and set about scrubbing away my heartache.

First, I tried reminding myself that Nash didn't owe me anything. He hadn't declared his love for me, hadn't made me any promises. There had been that talk of 'plans', but maybe he'd meant taking me to bed. He certainly had plans once we got there.

Was I complaining about a night of mind blowing

orgasms? Maybe *that* was his plan; to bounce in and out of town, screwing me senseless when he was here.

I tried not to let the thought hurt. I could list a thousand reasons why I should not be pining for my brother-in-law. The whole thing was insane and inappropriate, and far better as a one-time fling. Well, two-time fling. But that was it. Never again.

My logical side said Nash was fun while he lasted, but he wasn't my future. He couldn't be, and his leaving was like ripping off a bandage. Painful, but necessary. I needed to get over him and get back to living my new life, in which I was soon to be divorced and did not need a complicated lover.

I knew my logical side was right. I could sulk here in the cottage, working out my hurt on these stained tiles, but eventually I'd have to get over it and get back to normal. A normal without Nash. The next time he sailed into town, I'd give him a cool smile and tell him I wasn't interested.

I ignored the tear that scalded my cheek as it slid down to splash the tile. I was not going to cry over Nash Kingsley. Just because I was inexperienced and got my heart tangled up in great sex did not mean I was going to keep acting like an idiot.

I worked through the afternoon and into the evening, sneaking into the dark kitchen to make a sandwich after everyone else was settled for the night. I didn't want to see anyone, didn't want to explain my swollen eyes and bruised heart.

When I woke in the morning, I still felt like hell after a night of broken sleep, plagued by dreams of Nash. His smile, the way he held my hand, the deep intimacy of feeling him skin to skin. All a lie.

I'd grabbed a granola bar and coffee in my room and fled

to the cottage. I couldn't force my heart back into one piece, but at least I could distract myself with work. One more day and the tile in the first floor bathroom would be back to its original condition. Just a few more hours of scrubbing.

Resolved, at least for the next minute, I went back to work, trying to think about my to-do list for the cottage, and the upcoming meeting with Billy Bob to talk about the gate-house. Hawk had insisted it was fine, but I'd talked my way into his living space and it was far from fine. He was sleeping on a fold out camp cot, his kitchen an ice-filled cooler and a camp stove. The bathroom was functional, but that was the best I could say about it.

We'd all agreed that the cottage was the priority, but the gatehouse was a close second. When it was finished, Hawk would have two floors of living space, a spacious bedroom that took up the whole second level and an open-plan kitchen and living space on the ground floor.

Unlike the cottage, it was going to need a lot more than elbow grease and a few new fixtures. I wasn't looking forward to telling Hawk he was going to have to move into the main house for at least a month. I had a feeling our taci-turn head of security/groundskeeper would not appreciate living with the rest of the family. Too bad. We couldn't always get what we wanted.

I bit my lip and shoved away that snarky thought. It wasn't Hawk's fault I was in a crappy mood. He wasn't the one who'd ripped my heart out of my chest and ground it into dust. It wasn't anyone's fault, but mine. And Nash's.

Tossing the scrub brush into the bucket beside me, I stood, my hands automatically going to my cramped lower back. Giving the tiles a critical look, I decided I'd gotten off most of the grime. Stains remained, but I had something for that. Retrieving a can from the kitchen, I carefully sprayed the tiles with a layer of white foam that stank of chemicals. It needed to sit until it dissolved.

Might as well head back to the house and pack up the things I'd sold in the last few days. Three pairs of very nice heels, four purses, and a cocktail dress. Day by day, my bank balance was growing and my closet was shrinking. It wasn't a ton of cash–anyone from my old life would have laughed at the sum I'd accumulated–but it was enough to give me some breathing room. I could pay for gas, my car insurance, and cat toys without asking for a loan. Right now, that little bit of independence felt very good.

I washed my hands in the sink, grabbed my notebook off the counter, and left the cottage. Striding across the lawn to the main house, I went in the back door to the mudroom, distractedly noticing that Savannah was mopping the back stairs to the second floor. "I'll go around," I called with a wave, diverting through the butler's pantry and dining room to the front hall and the main stairs.

I was so lost in my head, finally distracted from Nash by my plans for the rest of the day, that I didn't catch the voices until it was too late.

"What the hell do you think you're doing here?" Griffen. Why was Griffen shouting?

I quickened my pace and spilled into the entry hall to find Hawk just inside the front door, his big hand clamped over the back of Tyler's neck. Tyler? I glanced at Griffen to find him standing opposite me by the hallway that led to the library and his office, his face dark with rage. Hope hovered behind him, glancing over her shoulder.

"Tyler?" I asked, not understanding. "What are you doing here?"

As if he wasn't being held captive by Hawk, Tyler scanned me from head to toe, taking in my messy ponytail, worn jeans and stained t-shirt. "What the hell are you wearing? You look ridiculous. The maids are dressed better than you."

His narrowed eyes, the scorn dripping from his words, were all too much. I didn't want to deal with Tyler on a good day. Today, Tyler's crap was the last thing I needed.

"I was working," I said tartly. "I shouldn't be surprised you don't know what that looks like." I shifted my gaze to Hawk. "What is he doing here?"

"He says he's here to work things out," Hawk said, without expression. I knew him well enough by now to see the glint of annoyed amusement in his eyes.

"Not interested," I said to the room. Meeting Tyler's eyes, I went on, "I don't know why you're here, but I made it clear that I don't want you anywhere near me. Angie suggested I get a restraining order based on your texts. If you won't leave, I'll be forced to do that, and it won't look good for you when we finally get in front of a judge."

"There won't be a judge," Tyler insisted, jutting his chin out and glaring at me. "We aren't getting divorced. We're going to work this out, and you'll see we belong together."

A bitter, shocked laugh burst out of my mouth. Exactly how insane was he? I slapped my hand over my mouth, but the laugh kept coming, bubbling up until I doubled over, eyes prickling with tears of hilarity.

Maybe it was the emotional turmoil of Nash's desertion, or the idea of having to deal with Tyler after getting used to being free of him. I don't know, but once I started laughing, I couldn't stop.

It didn't help when Tyler whined, "Stop laughing at me! You're my wife, you have to be nice to me!"

"Oh my god, are you kidding me?" I gasped out, before another round of belly laughs had me shaking so hard I thought I might fall over. An arm went around my waist. My brother Royal. A glance showed Griffen was straining to get to Tyler, held back by Hope's hand on his arm in a death grip.

"Is she hysterical?" Griffen asked.

Royal answered, "Maybe? I vote she gets first swing."

That just made me laugh even harder.

Griffen shot an annoyed look at Hope. "Let go, I'm not going to hurt him."

Hope rolled her eyes. "I don't care about him, you moron. Hawk has him under control, and if you hit that jackass, I guarantee he'll press charges. West loves you like a brother, but he'll throw you in jail if he has to."

I tried to get myself under control so I could help Hope with Griffen. As much as I was delighted by the idea of anyone punching Tyler, Hope was right. Our police chief loved Griffen like family, but he'd loved Ford too and that hadn't stopped him from arresting our brother for our father's murder. Tyler would love to press charges. I wasn't risking Griffen's freedom on West looking the other way.

Gulping back my giggles, I straightened, leaning into Royal for a moment, smiling up at him. "Thanks, I'm okay. He's just–" I waved a hand at Tyler's outrage, succumbing to another wave of giggles.

"Stop laughing at me!" Tyler shrieked again, his gorgeous face twisted in a petulant scowl.

Grabbing Royal's arm for support, I collapsed into giggles again. "I'm sorry," I breathed, Royal's face blurry through my wet eyes. "I'm stopping, I am." I tried, sucking in a deep breath, then another, blocking Tyler from my sight by tucking my face into Royal's arm. He rubbed a comforting hand over my back.

"Are you sure he was old enough to get married?" Royal

whispered as he rubbed my back. "He's like Nicky when he goes to bed too late."

I hiccuped out another laugh and punched Royal lightly in the arm. "I can't stop if you keep making jokes."

Royal shrugged. "I think you should keep laughing at him. His head might explode and solve all your problems."

I peeked up from Royal's arm to see Tyler's face flushed tomato red, his jaw clenched in fury, his glare aimed directly at me. I didn't know what I saw in his eyes, but it was more than temper and impatience. I thought I caught a flash of true malevolence before metal creaked and all of us looked to the slowly turning handle of the front door.

"Did I forget to mention him?" Hawk muttered through a whisper of a grin.

The door swung open to reveal Nash, his features drawn tight with worry, his gaze homing in on me. "Parker," he breathed, relief washing over his face, softening his mouth into a smile.

I straightened, fighting the need to smile back at the lying bastard. I did not want to see Nash. My eyes flicked to my not-ex husband. I especially did not want to see Nash right now.

Nash's eyes followed mine, flying wide as they landed on Tyler.

"What the fuck is going on here?"

Exactly what I wanted to know.

Chapter Twenty-Four

NASH

At first, all I could see was Parker, her cheeks flushed with laughter, leaning on her brother Royal. She was vibrant, that spark inside her ignited into a flame everyone could see. I needed her in my arms instead of Royal's. It felt like I'd been away from her for weeks instead of a single day. I smiled at the sheer relief of being back here, and for half a second, she started to smile back.

Then her eyes slid away, and abruptly, the rest of the room came in to focus.

Griffen stood opposite Royal and Parker, his wife clutching his arm as if holding him back. To my left, I found the reason why.

Tyler.

How the fuck had he gotten here so quickly? Hawk had one hand around the back of Tyler's neck in a grip Tyler probably thought couldn't do much damage. From what I knew of Hawk, I would have bet Tyler was in a lot more danger than he realized. As usual, Tyler was too self-centered and stupid to notice.

"What the fuck is going on here?" I demanded, not sure who I was asking.

Hawk answered, his tone dry as dust. "Your brother came to win back Parker." Hawk's eyes snapped to Parker, whose face was granite, all laughter extinguished.

"Get out," Parker snapped at Tyler. "I don't want you here."

"You're still my wife," Tyler started, trying to shake off Hawk's grip on the back of his neck. Hawk's fingers tightened in an almost imperceptible squeeze. Tyler yelped and went still.

"Unfortunately," Griffen cut in, "until she can get you to sign the papers, she is your wife. But this is my house and you're not welcome here. Go back wherever you came from, and if you need to communicate with Parker, do it through her attorney."

"He doesn't have anywhere else to go," I interjected. I didn't see a reason to hide the situation from anyone. "My mother cut him off." Looking at Parker, taking in her wide eyes, I explained, "She texted me early yesterday, begging me to rush home. She said it was an emergency."

If I thought that was going to soften Parker, I was wrong. Understanding brightened her eyes, but her grim expression didn't yield.

"Shut up, you ass," Tyler hissed at me. "Mom didn't mean it, anyway. Once Parker forgives me, she'll let me come home."

I shook my head in disbelief. "How deluded are you, man? Mom doesn't want you to win Parker back. She wants you to leave us all alone, to get a job and show her you can support yourself and act like an adult. Then, maybe, she'll let you under her roof again. You harassing Parker is the last thing Mom wants."

"Claudia cut him off?" Parker asked. "What does that mean?"

"It means she kicked him out of all her properties. Changed the locks, alerted security, everything. She also cut off his credit card and access to her accounts."

"Oh my god," Parker breathed. "Is she—"

I knew what Parker was going to ask. "She's doing as well as she can be, given the situation."

Parker let out a breath, her gaze moving back to Tyler. I hated seeing them in the same room together, hated that she was still pissed at me. It had taken the long trip home for me to realize how badly I'd fucked up.

I hadn't meant to. For once, I'd had only good intentions. I'd known I should wake her and tell her I was leaving, but it had been so early and I'd kept her up most of the night.

I'd decided to let her sleep. In my guest room, I'd grabbed the duffel I'd never really unpacked, tossed in my toiletries bag, and left for the airport to catch my flight, thinking I'd be back before dinner.

Things had been so perfect between us, I'd taken her for granted. Since I realized she'd blocked me I'd been imagining her waking alone, probably convinced that I'd used her for sex and taken off. I knew she had far too much pride to ask Griffen where I was, and he wouldn't have thought to tell her.

We were both idiots.

I should have left her a note or woken her up, and she should know better than to think I'd ever use her and walk away.

"You need to leave Sawyers Bend, Tyler," Parker said. "I'm sorry Claudia cut you off, but you can't stay here."

Feet sounded on the main stairs opposite the front door.

Royal, Griffen, and Parker turned to see their cousin Bryce coming down the stairs, a wide, welcoming smile on his too handsome face. The guy looked like the crown prince of the country club, all golden blond hair, blue eyes and too many white teeth.

As if unaware of the tension in the room, he strode forward, hand outstretched. Hawk dropped his grip from Tyler's neck with a bemused expression, as if waiting to see what would happen next. Tyler took Bryce's hand, shaking it firmly, leaning in to pat Bryce on the back. "Good to see you again!" he said, with hearty cheer.

Bryce stepped back and scanned the room, his shit-eating grin stretching from ear to ear. "You decided to come home? Try to work things out with the wife?"

"He was just leaving," Griffen cut in, his glare divided between Tyler and Bryce.

Bryce turned the full force of his smile on Griffen. "Are you sure about that, cousin? I couldn't help but overhear your disagreement from upstairs, and I think you might want to consult Harvey before you toss your brother-in-law out on his ear."

Everyone froze.

Who was Harvey?

"What do you know?" Griffen demanded.

Bryce shrugged one shoulder and tossed his blond locks off his forehead. "Just a hunch."

Griffen slashed a sharp glance at Hawk. "Can you hold him until I talk to Harvey?"

Hawk gave a short nod. Closing his fingers around Tyler's neck for a second time, he wrenched his wrist, forcing Tyler to turn and face the door. "Outside," he ordered. Skewering Bryce with his eyes, he added, "You, too."

"What did I do?" Bryce asked the room, before following them out, that wide grin still on full display.

I wanted to know what the fuck was going on, but first, I needed to talk to Parker. Ignoring the thunk of the door closing behind us, I caught her gaze. "Can we talk?"

The pause was endless before she said, simply, "I don't think so."

Her words hit me like a fist to the gut. I'd expected her to make me work for it. I hadn't expected her to cut me off at the knees. I said nothing, staring at her, drinking in her face. Beneath the flush on her cheeks from the scene with Tyler, I caught the puffiness under her eyes, the dark circles. Had I made her cry?

The thought turned my stomach. I'd been overconfident and careless. I hadn't meant to be cruel. I'd forgotten that while I'd been waiting for Parker for years, she was not quite free of her marriage to my asshole, abusive brother. He was the only man she'd had a serious relationship with. Her only lover until me.

Parker had deep reservations about getting involved with me, reservations that wouldn't be erased by one night of romance and amazing sex. And I'd left her to wake up alone.

This wasn't about her making me work for her forgiveness. This was no game. I'd broken something fragile and precious. I had to fix it before she'd trust me again.

Fuck. I didn't know how to do this. "I owe you an apology," I began.

Parker was already shaking her head. "You don't. There's nothing to apologise for. I understand. Claudia needed you and you left. It gave me time to clear my head and—"

"Parker, please." I knew what she was doing. She was

trying to convince herself that we were over, that this was a mistake and I was nothing more than her soon-to-be-ex brother-in-law. I was back to square one, all the ground I'd gained in the past few months lost because I hadn't left a god damned note.

"I don't want to have this conversation with an audience—" I paused, giving her a second to agree to talk in private. I didn't want to have this conversation with an audience, but I would if the alternative was letting Parker push me away.

Parker lifted her chin and said nothing.

"I should have woken you up and told you I was leaving," I said in a low voice, as if that could stop Griffen, Hope, and Royal from hanging on every word. Parker stiffened, but remained silent.

"It was early, and we didn't get much sleep, so I thought I'd call you when I landed. It never occurred to me that you'd think I ran out on you." I glanced at Griffen, who watched me with blank eyes. "I should have asked Griffen to tell you where I was, but I didn't want to—" I gestured between us. "I didn't want to tell him about us if you weren't ready."

"Well, he knows now," Parker said, sourly. "And maybe I'm not mad at you for leaving. Maybe I'm just not interested." She lifted her chin, giving me her cool, polished shell.

Parker could try that act with me, but it wouldn't work. I'd hurt her, I got that, but I didn't believe for a second that she was finished with me. I knew this woman. She wasn't playing games. She never would have given herself to me the way she had—trusting me to take her on the bike, laughing and talking at dinner, sharing her body freely—if she didn't have serious feelings for me.

Plenty of women went wild after a breakup. More

power to them, but that was not Parker. I wasn't a rebound. I was hers. And she was mine.

"Parker," I said, softly, "I'm sorry. I fucked up. I was tired and worried about Claudia, and neither of those things excuses my not just waking you up and telling you I was leaving."

"Parker," Hope hissed from behind Parker. Parker turned and shot her sister-in-law a glare. Hope raised an eyebrow and returned the look. Parker shook her head. Hope stared back, not budging. "Remember what Quinn said."

"You're annoying," Parker responded.

"I know," Hope cheerily returned.

Parker turned to me. "Fine. I'll talk to you in the library." Turning on her heel, she marched from the room, regal and composed despite her ragged ponytail and stained t-shirt. I followed, thinking that I owed Hope Sawyer a debt. I didn't understand how she'd convinced Parker to talk to me, but I knew I owed her all the same.

Chapter Twenty-Five

NASH

"What did Quinn say?" I asked Parker as she closed the heavy door to the library.

"None of your business." Parker was hanging on to cool perfection. That was fine. I liked her shell as much as I liked what was inside. I loved every part of her. And I was in this for the long haul. She had a right to be mad at me, but I wasn't going to let her chase me off.

"Who's Harvey?" I asked. Parker jerked her chin up at the unexpected question before letting out a sigh. She sounded utterly exhausted. I fought the urge to take her in my arms. If I tried she'd probably take a swing at me.

"Harvey is our family's lawyer. He's also the only one who knows the ins and outs of my father's will."

Immediately, I understood. "Your cousin thinks something in the will gives Tyler the right to live here?"

"It's possible," Parker conceded. "We tried to kick Bryce and Ophelia out, or give them rooms at the Inn, but the will made that impossible. They're ours for the next five years, like it or not."

"And you don't like it?" I hadn't formally met Bryce or Ophelia, but I'd heard about Bryce from Griffen and Royal.

Parker waved a hand in the air in dismissal. "Aunt Ophelia is fine. She's sweet, usually, just way too indulgent with Bryce. Bryce is an asshole. He's hated all of us since we were kids, and we've always hated him back. It's just lovely having him in the house."

Her raised eyebrow and cool sarcasm told me Bryce as a houseguest was anything but lovely. Based on what I'd seen so far, I could imagine. "Parker," I began.

She cut me off. "Is Claudia alright? It must have devastated her to send Tyler away."

"She's fine. Off to Botswana to join a friend on a luxury safari for three weeks. It was hard for her, but she's resolved not to let him run amok like he has been."

Parker nodded, lost in thought. Her throat thick with emotion, she said, "I know how much she loves him. She's always believed he'd get himself together. I'm sorry she had to face the truth." Her warm hazel eyes met mine, her mouth turned down in sadness. "He isn't going to get himself together, is he?"

"I don't see that he has a choice," I said. Then, knowing my brother, I shrugged. "No, I don't think he will. I don't think he has it in him."

"What will he do?" she asked, with helpless worry.

"I don't know," I said, honestly. "He has what's left of our grandmother's trust. It should be enough to buy a place to live and a car, and maintain both if he gets a job and doesn't live extravagantly."

Parker sighed. "And the chances of that?"

"Not high," I admitted. "Are you feeling sorry for him? Because—"

"No," Parker interrupted, "I'm feeling sorry for your mother. He's going to break her heart."

"He already has," I said. "You know she loves you, don't you?"

Parker shook her head. "Not more than she loves her sons."

"She sees you as a daughter, not just a daughter-in-law. Finding out how Tyler has treated you, the way he's been behaving since you left, finally made her realize that he wasn't going to change."

"Does he really think he can get me back?" she asked, mostly to herself.

"Who knows what he's thinking? He's deluded enough to have convinced himself that he has a chance."

"He doesn't," Parker snapped, as if I were making a case for Tyler. Not in this lifetime.

"I know. Everyone knows that. Hopefully, we can get him out of Heartstone Manor, so you never have to deal with him again."

Parker turned, narrowing those usually warm eyes on me. Right then, they were anything but warm. Cool, assessing, calculating. That was okay. I could deal with calculation. And as frustrating as it was knowing Parker was angry with me, I liked that she was standing up for herself. But then, I can be a perverse bastard.

"And what about you?" Parker challenged. "Can I get you out of Heartstone Manor?"

"You could," I offered. "Griffen made it clear that family comes before business. If you want me out, I'm gone."

Parker turned and paced to the front window of the library, staring out into the courtyard at Hawk, who watched Tyler and Bryce engaged in a heated conversation. "I don't like the two of them having a private chat," she murmured under her breath. "They've been BFF's since the moment they met. Spoiled princelings squared. They're plotting something."

I followed her to the window. "Probably. Whatever it is, we'll deal with it."

Parker spun on her heel and glared up at me. "*We'll* deal with it? Since when are we a *WE*? How do I know I can trust you any more than Tyler?"

I tried not to let that sting. Shoving my hands in my pockets, I studied the woman in front of me, wearing her jeans and stained t-shirt as if they were a ball gown, defiance all over her. I'd loved her since the first moment I saw her.

Years of trying to talk myself out of it hadn't worked.

Seducing her hadn't worked. Playing it cool and giving her time hadn't worked.

It was time to try something else.

No more tactics. No more plans. I was going to give her what she deserved. The truth.

I drew in a breath, giving myself a moment to brace before I laid it out for her. It was time to stop protecting myself. If I wanted Parker to trust me, I had to trust her first.

"I love you, Parker. I was trying to take this slow, give you time to get used to the idea, but I see now that was a mistake. I shouldn't have left you without telling you where I was going, but I thought you understood."

"Understood what?" she pushed, her eyes wide, cheeks pale.

"That there's only you for me. Since the day we met, the day you married Tyler, there hasn't been another woman I wanted."

"But there've been other women," she pointed out, one blond eyebrow arched.

"You were with Tyler. If you recall, I asked you to come with me instead."

Parker shook that off. "I couldn't—"

"I know you couldn't. And yes, there were other women in my life. I'm not a monk and you were married. But I love you. I told myself it wasn't love, it was infatuation or lust or a crush. But it isn't any of those things. I love you. Just being near you makes me happy. You settle my soul. When I think of the future, all I see is you."

She crossed her arms over her chest, facing me. If I'd hoped she'd swoon in delight at my declaration of love, I was disappointed. "Did you come here for me? Was the business deal a ruse?"

"Yes and no," I answered with brutal honesty. Parker didn't need fancy words. She needed the truth. "The business deal is real. You know that. And I was hoping it would give me an excuse to be near you."

"What if it hadn't worked out?"

"Then I would have found another excuse. I don't want to wait anymore. You finally left Tyler. Maybe this is too soon. I know you're worried that it's inappropriate, that Claudia will be upset."

Parker nodded, but said nothing, her brow furrowed, eyes staring blindly out the window.

"Is that the only thing you're worried about?"

Parker turned to me slowly. "It's part of it. I don't want to lose your mother. I can't stand the thought of hurting her. But that's not the only thing."

It was torture to stand there and wait for her to put her thoughts together, to gather the courage to speak them aloud.

"I have feelings for you," she admitted, her golden hazel eyes wounded when they met mine. "I have since the day we met. You know that. But I can't–" She stopped, paused, and tried again. "I'm not even divorced yet, and–"

She stopped again. I didn't believe her marriage to Tyler was the problem. If we couldn't talk about this honestly, we weren't going to get very far. "You don't trust me," I said.

Parker's shoulders slumped in relief, and a shadow of a smile crossed her face. "I don't. I'm sorry."

Shaking my head, I let her off the hook. "Don't apologize for that, Parker. I don't know all the details of your marriage to Tyler. I've never understood how you could have stayed married to him for so long. But I do know that six years of being Tyler's wife would leave any woman reluctant to trust."

Parker nodded and looked away, her eyes brimming with tears. Fuck. Not how I wanted this to go. Then she shocked the hell out of me.

"This is why," she whispered, not looking at me. "I'm not the kind of woman you should be with. I'm not accomplished or ambitious. I let a man belittle me for years, and I stayed married to him, even after he hit me. What does that say about me?"

With that, I was done giving her space. Crossing the room, I pulled her into my arms. She went stiff, but didn't pull away. "That's ridiculous, Parker. All of it. I'm not the kind of man who falls in love with a resume. I don't want a woman who's perfect on paper. I want you. Do you think you're the only woman who stayed in a bad marriage and then felt like shit about it later? Life is complicated. You did the best you could. Isn't it time to let yourself off the hook?"

She shuddered against me, her face buried in my shoulder. Was she crying? I swear my chest was going to cave in if she kept crying. The last thing I wanted in the world was to make Parker cry.

Her words little more than a breath, she said, "You barely know me, Nash. How can you be in love with me?"

"Not know you? You're the woman who comforted me at my father's funeral. Who was most of the reason I could get through his death and everything that came after. You took care of everyone, even Tyler, who didn't deserve it. You're the best board game partner in the universe. Do you remember three years ago when Mom made us play that word guessing game and you and I blew everyone away?"

This time, her shudder was a laugh. "Tyler was so angry. You didn't even get the whole word out and I knew the answer."

"It was like you were reading my mind," I said, tightening my arm around her. "And I was reading yours."

Parker sighed and tried to pull away. I didn't let her get far. Reaching out, I took her hands in mine, looking down into her shimmering hazel eyes, taking in her tear-streaked face.

"Remember that Christmas two years ago, when mom strong-armed me into coming to the mountains with all of you? The Christmas movie marathon and all the popcorn?"

She nodded again, her eyes brimming with more tears. Claudia had gone to bed early, and Tyler drank himself into a stupor. Parker and I had stayed up all night watching every Christmas movie we could think of. We'd each been on our own sofa, tucked in with our own bowls of popcorn, but it had felt like we were right next to each other. Like we belonged together.

At the reminder, Parker sighed again, her eyes dodging mine.

"Parker." I tugged at her hands to get her to look at me. "I know you. I'm not asking for a declaration of love from you. I'm asking for a chance. I want to be with you. I want time. Can you give me that?"

Parker opened her mouth to answer just as the library door swung open. Savannah stuck her head in. "Sorry to interrupt, but Griffen asked me to come get you. Harvey will be here in a few minutes. He'd like to speak to you in Griffen's office." She narrowed her eyes on Parker, then shot me an assessing look. "Parker," she said, holding out her hand, "come with me, please."

Parker slipped from my arms and disappeared with Savannah. Not good. I wasn't sure if I was invited to the meeting in Griffen's office, but I didn't care.

Striding down the hall, I mentally prepared for battle. Parker might not fully trust me yet, but she needed me at her back, whether she wanted me there or not.

Chapter Twenty-Six

PARKER

Leaving Nash in the library was like tearing away a piece of myself. I'd been on the precipice of a decision, and like a coward, I took the reprieve Savannah offered. She dragged me up the back stairs to my room.

"We have ten minutes to get you presentable. Whatever is going on with Harvey and Tyler, you don't want to deal with it like this."

It showed how far I was twisted up in Nash that I hadn't considered what a mess I was. My clothes were bad enough, but my face was a puffy, red disaster. I pulled my hand from Savannah's and gave her a quick hug. "Thanks."

With a shove toward my closet, she said, "Anytime, Parks, you know that. Now you go pick out something to wear, and I'll run cold water on a washcloth."

As I rushed to my closet, her words followed me. "I'm only sorry I didn't get to eavesdrop on your conversation with Nash."

I sighed. Nash. What was I going to do about Nash? No time to think about it now, but Nash was all I could think about. Weird that I didn't care about Tyler. He'd showed up intending to get in my face and be a massive pain in my ass, and I didn't even care.

Tyler was the past. I had yet to determine my future.

That thought sank in, all the way to my bones, and the weight of the past lightened. Tyler could play his game. It didn't mean I had to play with him.

Letting out a deep breath, I scanned my closet, choosing a pale pink linen wrap dress that hit just above my knee, and deep pink sandals with a kitten heel and adorable roses on the straps. The dress was cool and elegant, the sandals fun and frivolous. Perfect.

Savannah met me in my sitting room with a cool washcloth. "Sit," she ordered, directing me to an armchair. Shadow jumped into my lap and curled up, purring softly. I stroked my hand over her soft fur and tipped my head onto the back of the chair as Savannah lay the washcloth over my eyes. "You have a few minutes until Harvey gets here. I get text alerts from the gatehouse when anyone comes on the property, so we'll know before he's in the house."

I felt Savannah move away, then return and tug at my ponytail. She pulled a brush through my hair, smoothing the tangled strands while we waited for the cold washcloth to work its magic. "So," Savannah began, "what are you going to do about the very sexy Nash?"

"I thought you didn't eavesdrop," I said without heat, lulled by the soothing strokes of the hairbrush and the purring kitten in my lap.

"I didn't eavesdrop in the library, but I heard everything that happened in the front hall."

Of course, she'd heard everything, she'd been mopping the stairs just around the corner. Anyway, I'd quickly learned there was very little that went on in Heartstone Manor that Savannah didn't know about.

"What would you do?" I asked, dodging the question.

"I don't know," she answered, honestly. "I'd like to think I'd go for it. He's hot, and he seems like a good guy. He definitely cares about you. But what I'd do isn't the question. Nash isn't interested in me. He wants you. What do you want?"

"To start over." The words slipped out. Before I could think about what they meant, Savannah let out a snort of laughter.

"Well, that's one thing you can't have. We can't erase the past, Parker. We can only decide what comes next. That's what my mom told me when I came back to Sawyers Bend with Nicky and no husband. I felt like I'd made a colossal mess of my life. Mom told me to stop dwelling on what I couldn't change and forge a new path for myself."

She fell silent after that, leaving me to think about the wise words of Miss Martha. I couldn't change what had already happened, but I could decide what I wanted next.

And yet, Savannah was wrong. The question wasn't, what did I want? The question was, did I have the courage to go after it?

I was about to find out.

Savannah secured my hair in a low, sleek tail, and went after my face with swipes of brushes and lip gloss. She set me free looking far better than I should after scrubbing tile all morning, followed by a crying fit. Lifting the kitten from my lap, she ran a rubbery wand over my dress, picking up any stray hairs. Her phone beeped from her pocket. "That's the gatehouse. You can meet Harvey in the front hall and walk in with him."

I loved that idea. This was my home, too. Tyler was

the interloper. And while Harvey was representing my father when it came to the will, he was still our family attorney. More importantly, he liked us better than he'd liked our father. Like West, he wouldn't subvert the law for us, but he'd look out for our interests as much as he was able to.

"You're the best," I told Savannah, giving her a quick hug as I headed for the stairs.

"I know," she called after me with a laugh.

I reached the front door just as Harvey rang the bell. Opening it, I took his offered hand, leaning in to press my cheek to his.

"Parker, you look lovely," he said, squeezing my hand with both of his before letting go. "I came as soon as Griffen called. I've been concerned this would be an issue. I'm sorry to say—"

"Don't be sorry, Harvey," I interrupted, taking his elbow and letting him lead me down the hall to Griffen's office. "I know dealing with the will has been distasteful to you. And I know you tried to talk my father out of most of this."

"Unfortunately, no one could talk Prentice out of anything." Harvey said, mournfully.

I gave his elbow a gentle squeeze. "True, and no one knows that better than his children."

Harvey smiled at me, his apple cheeks scrunching up to his gentle brown eyes. He was round all over, his belly straining the buttons of his vest. Add a white beard and he would have been a dead ringer for Santa in a three-piece suit. He'd always been kind to Prentice's children. That hadn't changed since my father's death.

Proving it, he went on, "Griffen said you're working miracles on the cottage he intends for Savannah and Nicky. Are you going to give me a tour when you're finished?"

"I'd love to. Would you believe I spent the morning scrubbing tile?"

Harvey aimed a shocked look at me. "I would not! Doesn't the budget allow for help?" He glanced at my hands with horrified eyes. "You don't need to do manual labor, Parker."

I laughed, pushing open the door to Griffen's office. As if we didn't have an audience, I leaned in and said, "I took the budget for help and put it toward the countertops I wanted. Absolutely worth it. You'll see."

"I can't wait." Harvey squeezed my shoulder with affection before reluctantly crossing the room to stand beside Griffen's desk.

Both Griffen and Hope sat behind the desk, side by side. Royal had taken the armchair opposite Harvey. Bryce and Tyler sat on the sofa facing the door. Nash stood in front of the cold fireplace.

I had a choice to make. I sure as hell wasn't joining Tyler and Bryce on the sofa. The other sofa, facing the french doors, was empty. I didn't take it.

Instead, I crossed the room to join Nash at the fireplace, standing just out of his reach, but beside him all the same. Harvey cleared his throat, and I braced.

"Your father," he began, looking at me, "made some provisions regarding marriage in his will. As Parker was the only one of Prentice's children who was married at the time of his death, this provision only applies to her."

It took everything I had to coolly raise one eyebrow and keep my mouth shut. My fucking father. He was dead, and he was still trying to control me. To control all of us. *Less than five years*, I reminded myself, *and we'll be done with him forever*. I could hang on that long.

Seeing I wasn't going to comment, Harvey continued.

"His will says nothing about divorce." Harvey aimed a quelling look at Tyler, who was grinning in triumph already. The grin dimmed a fraction but didn't disappear. "However, in terms of the occupancy requirements, it specifies that your spouse has the legal right to room and board here as long as you reside in Heartstone Manor."

"He was gone for more than fourteen days," Hope pointed out.

Harvey shook his head. "That restriction only applies to beneficiaries. As Tyler doesn't stand to directly gain anything from the will, he isn't bound by those terms. As long as Parker is in residence and they're legally married, Tyler has the right to live here."

Well, crap. That was inconvenient. Gracefully crossing my arms, I ignored Tyler and asked Harvey, "And if I choose to leave Heartstone Manor? Would that enable Griffen to evict him?"

"Parker!" Various male voices protested.

I shook my head at my brothers, ignoring both Tyler and Nash. "I'm only trying to clarify the situation."

"Yes," Harvey answered. "If you were to leave Heartstone, Griffen could kick Tyler out. However, you would also lose access to your home, as well as your eventual inheritance."

"I'm aware of that. And if Griffen legally evicted Tyler?" I aimed an arch look at Harvey. "Griffen is the owner of Heartstone Manor, after all."

"Yes, he is." Harvey cleared his throat and sent an apologetic look at Griffen. "You are the legal owner, and you can begin eviction proceedings, but that would have the same effect as evicting Parker."

"What you're saying," Griffen clarified, "is that if I kick this jackass out of my house, I'd be disinheriting my sister."

"Yes. That's what I'm saying." Harvey agreed with a dark look at Tyler.

The room erupted in argument, everyone insisting there had to be another way, that this was insane, and so on. I wasn't listening. Harvey wouldn't have put us through this if there was another way.

Out of the mayhem, Hope's voice rang out. "He can't stay. We don't have a room. Nash took the last guest room. Unless Tyler wants a cot in one of the empty rooms." Hope sent Tyler a furious glare. He smirked at me and opened his mouth. I knew what he was going to say.

Before he got a word out, I cut him off. "That's fine. Tyler can have Nash's room." I felt Nash stiffen beside me, but I didn't react. Everything would be clear soon enough.

"That's right, kick him out!" Tyler crowed. "But I don't need his room. I'll stay with you."

As if. Ignoring everyone except Harvey, I asked, "Is there anything in the will that specifies which room is included in Tyler's room and board?"

Understanding, Harvey smiled. "Only that he has a right to a room in the Manor. It doesn't specify which room."

"Lovely," I said, with as serene a smile as I could manage. "Then Tyler can take Nash's room."

"And what about me?" Nash asked, his tone as neutral as my own, his dark eyes locked on mine.

A thrill ran down my spine as I spoke the words my heart had been shouting ever since Nash came home.

"You? You'll stay with me."

Chapter Twenty-Seven

PARKER

Y ou'll stay with me.

A slow smile spread across Nash's face. "Excellent."

"I think so," I replied, my smile matching his.

There were shouts from around us, objections from Tyler, surprise from my brothers. From Hope, I got only a wide, satisfied grin. Through the insanity, she said to me, "Why don't you two get Nash's things moved while the rest of them fight this out?"

Flashing a smile at her in return, I grabbed Nash's hand and pulled him to the door. No one stopped us. Giddy joy flooded through me. If I'd known how good it would feel to finally make a decision, I might have done it a long time ago. Or maybe this had all happened exactly the way it was supposed to.

It didn't matter now. I'd made my choice, in a very public manner, and I couldn't have been happier about it. Whatever crap Tyler planned to shovel in our direction, we'd face it together.

Skidding to a halt in the hallway, I turned to look at

Nash. "Where are your things? When I checked the guest room, it looked empty."

Nash shook his head in remorse. "I hadn't really unpacked, so I just grabbed my bag. I don't think there's anything in the guest room, but my bag is in my car."

"Go get it and let's get you settled. Then do you want to get an early dinner? Or a late lunch? Or just get the hell out of here?"

"Yes. Definitely yes. Wait one second." Nash left me at the door, darted outside, and was back a minute later, his duffel bag in hand. With his free hand, he reached for mine.

We walked up the stairs like that, both grinning like idiots. Savannah came around the corner, a satisfied look in her eyes. "Moving into Parker's suite?" she asked.

"He is," I answered.

"Good for you," she said. "I checked the guest room and brought a few things I think you overlooked. They're in Parker's bathroom."

"Thanks, Savannah," I said. "We're going to get Nash moved in and then take off for a while. I'll let you know when we get back."

"One second." She handed me an old-fashioned brass key. "For your room. If Tyler is going to be in the house, you might want to keep your door locked."

I looked at the key in my hand. It must have been a century old, though the brass glowed against my skin. "You polish the keys?" I asked, turning it over in my palm. It was at least four inches long and heavier than it looked.

Savannah winked. "Not all of them. It's a little clunky, but it works. I asked Scarlett, and she said the door locks were hard to pick. Something about them being too stiff. This should keep him out."

"Scarlett would know," I mused. Tenn's girlfriend knew her way around a lock pick. If Tyler had a clue how to pick a lock, I'd still bet he wasn't as good as Scarlett. Something occurred to me. "One sec, Savannah. Can you do me a favor?"

I pushed open my door and clicked my tongue. Shadow's head popped up to peek over the arm of my velvet chair. I scooped her up and nuzzled the top of her head. "Aren't you a good girl? Aren't you the sweetest kitty?" Her purr was an outsized rumble against my neck.

Wishing I didn't have to, I handed her to Savannah. "Would you put her in Sterling's room? If I'm going to lock my door, I shouldn't keep her in here where no one can visit her."

Savannah dropped a kiss on the top of Shadow's head and tucked her into her arm. "Good thinking. I'll get her settled. You two get out of here and have a nice afternoon. You can't do anything about that mess downstairs anyway." She turned toward Sterling's rooms with a spring in her step, murmuring sweet words to Shadow as she went.

Once we were in my room with the door locked behind us, Nash dropped his bag and cupped my face in his hands, staring down at me, his eyes bright. "This is going to save me a lot of sneaking around."

"That's the plan." Sliding my arms around his waist, I said, "I'm sorry I blocked you. I overreacted."

"I get it," he said, lowering his mouth to brush his lips across mine. "I'm sorry I didn't leave a note."

"It's okay," I whispered. Despite the flutter of nerves in my stomach, I pressed on. "I feel like I should say I'm not sure about this. But I am. I don't know why or how, but I am. I want to give you what you asked for. Time. A chance.

I want to give us a chance. Tyler being here doesn't change that."

"You won't regret it," Nash promised.

I stared back at him, his heart shining in those dark eyes. "You know, I don't think I will."

I leaned into him, tightening my arms around his waist. "I really want to strip you naked and drag you to my bed." His eyes heated. "But I also don't want to be interrupted. So, for now, let's get the hell out of here and let the rest of them deal with Tyler and Bryce. Griffen's head is probably ready to explode by now."

"I'm with you all the way," Nash said. "But I want to do this first." He kissed me again, this time no gentle brush of his lips. Letting go of his waist, I slid my hands around the back of his neck, holding Nash close, kissing him with everything I had. His skin was hot, the spicy scent of him anchoring me. I was home. Here, in Nash's arms, I was home.

The sounds of raised voices filtered in through my heavy bedroom door. Nash's lips left mine. "We'd better get out of here while we can," he murmured into my hair.

I nodded against his chest, happy exactly where I was. His arms drew tight, and we stood there, just like that, for a long minute, breathing, holding on to each other.

"I wish he wasn't here," I said into Nash's shirt. "I wish we could just be us, together, without him in the way."

"We'll figure it out," Nash promised. "I say we ignore him. He's here to cause trouble. That doesn't mean we have to let him."

Doubtful, I studied Nash's resolved expression. "Do you think it could be that easy?"

Nash shook his head. "Probably not. Tyler isn't the type

to go quietly. But we can't leave, and we can't force him to leave."

"So we might as well ignore him as long as we can," I finished. "I'm in. I've spent enough of my life thinking about Tyler. For once, I want to think about me. About us."

"Good." Nash brushed another of those feather light kisses across my mouth, sending a shiver straight to my core. I was rethinking stripping him naked when he dropped his arms and stepped back. "Should we take the bike or my car? You'd have to change for the bike." The look in his eyes told me he liked my dress. So did I, but I also loved the bike.

"What kind of car?" I asked, considering.

"An Audi R8. Panther edition," he answered.

I grinned up at him. "Can I drive?"

"Hell, no." Nash smiled back at me, the happiness on his face filling my heart. "Not this time. I have to see you behind the wheel first. It's a lot to handle."

I hooked my arm through his and turned us to the door. "You can give me driving lessons then," I conceded. I wasn't entirely sure what an R8 Panther was, but I had a feeling it was one of those cars that belonged on the track, not cruising through town.

"That's a deal," Nash agreed, his grin stretching even wider.

I opened the door and the voices below rose in volume. Ugh. As quietly as I could, I closed the door and slid the key in the lock. The ancient workings resisted the key before turning with grudging slowness, the bolt sliding home with an audible clank. Tugging on Nash's arm, I led him in the direction of the back stairs. I wasn't going anywhere near the shouting crowd in the front hall if I could help it.

We ran down the back stairs like two teenagers sneaking

out, spilling out into the courtyard with a breathless laugh. Nash's car was before us in all its low slung, fierce glory. Deep black, with blood red accents, even at rest the car looked ready to devour the road. I was a little glad Nash wasn't going to let me drive. I was more than happy to be his passenger.

The engine roared to life, and I mean roared. I imagined the rough, aggressive sound stopping all conversation in the Manor as the arguing inhabitants realized we were making our escape. At the thought of their surprised faces, I laughed again. Nash put the car in gear and we took off.

We passed the gatehouse, and I remembered the shower I'd been cleaning in the cottage. I pulled out my phone to text the Billy half of Billy Bob and ask him to rinse off the tile. I wasn't sure if leaving the foam residue on too long would cause damage, but I didn't want to find out.

"Where to?" Nash asked, glancing over at me.

"How about the Inn? Have you been yet?"

"I've meant to, but I haven't made it over yet."

"Good. I haven't been since the fireworks on the fourth of July. You know how to get there?"

Nash nodded. I would have taken his hand, but he needed it to shift. I settled for resting my palm on his strong thigh, loving the way the muscle flexed as he shifted gears. The engine roared and my fingers squeezed in reflex. Nash slanted me a look, his eyes dropping to my hand.

"Am I distracting you?" I asked, with another squeeze.

"Definitely."

"Do you want me to move my hand?" I asked, the corner of my mouth lifting.

"Absolutely not."

Nash kept his eyes on the road, but mine were on him. I had something I needed to explain. "It's not you I don't trust, Nash."

His eyes skipped to me, narrowing in thought. "It's partly me."

"Not really," I said, knowing the words were true. "I don't trust myself." I took a breath, trying to put the words in order in my head. "I spent a long time second guessing myself. I wanted to leave Tyler so long ago, but I was afraid. I thought I was trapped, that what I wanted didn't matter, that I was just lonely and unhappy and that wasn't enough to end my marriage over. I don't know what I'm doing."

"With me?" Nash prompted, dropping his hand from the gearshift to curl his fingers around mine.

"With you. With myself. With my life. It bothers me that I didn't leave Tyler until after my father died and I had somewhere to go. I should have been strong enough to leave him a long time ago."

"Parker–"

I didn't let Nash cut in. "No, don't tell me it's fine. I'm not courageous like you are. Your father told you he'd cut you off if you didn't pick his college, his company. And you told him to go to hell. My father told me what to do, and I just said okay. Okay. Fine. I didn't want him to yell at me and I didn't know what else to do, so I did what I was told and it made me miserable. And I just lived with being miserable until–"

"Until you saw a way out," Nash cut in, "and you took it. Stop putting yourself down. My father also raised me to think for myself, to argue and fight back and make my own way. Even though he didn't like how that turned out a lot of the time. Your father's mission in life was to grind you down until you didn't have any fight left in you. Not the same thing at all."

"But–"

"And we aren't the same person, Parker. You don't have

to be like me to be worthwhile. You just have to be you."

"I don't know what that means," I admitted, as Nash slowed the car. Town was busy this time of year. The best we could do was a slow crawl down Main Street. Ahead, the stone facade of the Inn filled our view. "I don't know who I am."

Nash squeezed my hand before he let go to downshift. "You don't have to, Parker. You said you want to give us a chance?"

"Yes. I don't know what I'm doing, but I know that."

"Why don't you give yourself a chance while you're at it? Between the two of us, you deserve it more than I do. But you're willing to give me a shot. Give the same to yourself."

I shook my head. "I don't know what you mean."

Nash didn't answer, too focused on turning into the Inn and handing his keys to the valet. "Go easy with her," he advised the young man whose eager eyes roamed the car's curves. Considering he was going to park it right in front where everyone could ogle it, I don't think Nash had much to worry about.

Nash didn't say anything else until we were seated at a small table on the terrace overlooking the gardens. It was hot, but the fans moved the air and it was a beautiful day to be outside.

We ordered drinks and a charcuterie board to share. The waiter left and Nash turned the full force of his attention on me. "You're making everything too complicated. You're already doing what you need to do. You left a marriage that wasn't making you happy. You moved home, where you are happy."

He raised his eyebrows for confirmation, and I nodded.

"You wanted a job, and you got one," he went on.

"Working for my brother," I protested.

"So? Family is a good place to start. I didn't work for my father after college, but he still gave me my first job. And you're working your ass off. Griffen is proud of you. He said he's grateful you offered to handle the renovations, that you took off like a rocket and it's going to be beautiful when you're done."

"Griffen said that?" I sat back, rolling the compliment around in my head.

"I wouldn't be surprised if he puts you in charge of the rest of the renovations after you finish with the cottage and gatehouse."

"The rest of the renovations?" I echoed. I hadn't thought about that, but of course there would be more to do. Half of the house was empty. Griffen wouldn't leave it that way forever.

"Parker, sweetheart, the only person doubting you is you."

I didn't know what to say to that. I wanted to believe him. But that was going to take time. I had no words, but I knew what I wanted. Standing, I scooched my chair around the table until I was sitting beside Nash. Leaning into him, I picked up my drink and took a sip. Warmth shot through me when his lips pressed to the top of my head in a kiss.

"I'm glad you're here," I said with a sigh.

"Me too."

We didn't talk much after that. We ate and had another drink and watched evening take over the gardens. Later, we wandered down the street and stood in line with the tourists for an ice cream cone. Eventually, we headed back to the Inn and collected Nash's sexy car.

"Do you think we can sneak back into the Manor?" Nash asked.

"I don't know," I answered, "but we're going to try."

Chapter Twenty-Eight

PARKER

The house was quiet, dinner long over. We took the back stairs again, creeping down the hall in the family wing on silent feet. Once we were safe behind my bedroom door, the lock engaged, I texted Savannah and Griffen to let them know we were back.

That done, I tossed my phone on a side table and turned to face Nash. "I–"

That was all I got out. He moved in a blink, so close his shirt brushed the swell of my breasts, his dark eyes hot on mine. My throat went dry at the predatory gleam behind his thick lashes. His hands at his sides, he didn't touch me. With each breath, my breasts rose and fell, my dress touching his shirt and falling away. So little contact, yet he surrounded me.

"You're mine, Parker," he said, his voice rough. "I'm not fucking around anymore. Do we understand each other?"

Not the most romantic declaration. I didn't care. Nash was right. I was his. And I was tired of pretending otherwise.

I nodded, my throat too tight for words.

He didn't move. Didn't touch me. Just stared down at me. Waiting.

I reached up, tracing a fingertip along his full lower lip. "I'm yours," I agreed. "And you're mine." The words settled in my heart, exactly right. Nash was mine.

His head dipped, his lips brushing my ear. "I'm yours. It's all I've wanted to be. Since the first moment I saw you."

His mouth took mine in a rough kiss, his hands at the zipper of my dress. Stubble scraped my cheek. I scratched his neck in my haste to get his buttons undone. Fabric tore. I yanked my mouth from his so I could get to his belt.

Our clothes hit the carpet in a ragged pile as Nash swung my naked body into his arms and strode to my bed. He didn't bother pulling back the covers. I took him down with me, arching my neck to get my mouth close to his, kissing him with awkward fervor, chins bumping, his stubble scraping my lips.

I wanted to absorb him, to feel every inch of his skin on mine, to make him a part of me.

We rolled, Nash pinning me to the bed, his hips twisting until they were between my legs, spreading me wide, his hard cock against me. I was ready, desperate to have him inside me, to feel him filling me, stretching me–

I waited, but Nash was motionless, his hands pressing mine into the bed, our fingers twined, elbows braced beside mine, thick cock at my entrance. I was ready. So ready. What was he waiting for? His dark eyes fixed on my own, heated and intent.

"I'm going to show you what it means to be mine, Parker." His head dipped, and he took my mouth in a long, luscious kiss.

"I think I know," I said, inanely, after he broke away.

"You don't know." He ran his soft lips along my jaw. "You don't know yet, but you will."

Given the way we'd torn off our clothes, grabbing at each other in our desperation to get exactly where we were, I figured the sex would be fast and rough. I was wrong. Completely, blissfully, wrong. Nash didn't fuck me. This wasn't sex. It was worship.

Shifting to his side, Nash released my hands, leading them to the headboard of my bed. "Right here," he said, pressing them into pillows. "Don't move, or I'll stop."

I didn't have a chance to ask, "Stop what?"

He slid down my body, slowly. So slowly, I was dizzy with it. His mouth led the way, tasting me everywhere. The sensitive spot where my neck met my shoulder. The dip of my collarbone. The outer curve of my right breast. By the time he got to my nipple I was trembling with pent up need. I may have begged, just a little, when I could get my breath.

Nash only said, "Don't rush me."

I couldn't help it. He lavished attention on my breasts, each suck of his lips going straight to my pussy, bolts of pleasure that sent my head spinning. Still, he wasn't done, inching lower and lower until his mouth found my clit and the first orgasm exploded through me, leaving me gasping.

I definitely begged. It didn't do me any good. Nash tasted me, exploring every fold, finding each nerve ending and playing me like an instrument until I was limp and hoarse from crying out my pleasure. Only then did he push his way inside, the stretch of him against my swollen tissues almost painful. I welcomed it, welcomed him.

I hadn't planned to say it yet. Hadn't thought I was sure. But I was. He moved inside me in deep, slow thrusts, his fingers again twined with mine, his cheek pressed to my own. "I love you," I breathed, unable to keep the truth from him any longer. "I love you, Nash. I love you."

I couldn't stop saying it. Couldn't stop any of it. I didn't want to. I only wanted more. More of Nash. More of this glorious freedom to touch and love and be together. I came again, this time bringing him with me, welcoming the liquid heat of him inside me, his body covering mine, our legs tangled, his breath in my ear.

When we could move, he pulled me from the bed and into the shower, just long enough to rinse off before tucking both of us beneath the cool sheets. I fell asleep with the strong beat of his heart beneath my ear, knowing for the first time what love felt like in physical form. What it meant to be cherished.

I woke not long after dawn, the light pale and thin through the crack in the curtains. We both had busy days planned, and Tyler was in the house. I didn't care about any of it. Not quite yet. Instead of getting up and starting my day, I stretched against Nash, stroking up his body, delighting in the rise of his cock to my hand. Closing my fingers around his length, I whispered, "You awake?"

"That depends. If I am, are you going to stop?"

"Definitely not."

"Then yes, I'm awake."

Pushing the covers back, I rose to my knees and strad-dled Nash, leaning in to nip at his jaw. His cock rose to press against me, but I didn't take him inside. I had some cherishing of my own to do. "It's my turn," I said, raising up just enough to roll my hips, stroking his cock with heat and the gathering moisture between my legs.

Nash's hands closed over my hips, holding on, his eyes wide. I rolled my hips again, sliding my palms up my torso slowly, rounding my breasts, squeezing and lifting them, pinching my nipples and sending sparks through my entire body.

"Holy shit," he said, wonder suffusing his face. He started to move his hands from my hips. My fingers closed around his wrists.

"No." I wasn't sure who I was teasing more, me or Nash. I wasn't sure it mattered. Every nerve in my body hummed for him. I'd had a vague plan for more, to explore his body the way he'd explored mine. I didn't have Nash's discipline. Guiding his cock inside me, I took him to the hilt, and started to move.

I didn't last long. Nash tilted his hips, changing my position just enough for his mouth to find my breast and I was coming with a cry of surprised pleasure. Before it was done he flipped us, changing the rhythm with a hard thrust that set my clit to throbbing all over again. I closed my hands over his shoulders and hung on for the ride.

After, I rolled to the side, my hand finding his, and panted for breath, my heart pounding so loud it drowned out everything but the sound of our breathing. I'd planned to get up, but I turned into Nash and dozed, my head on his shoulder, his fingers tangling in my hair, the gentle tugging lulling me to sleep.

Later, I heard, "I have a meeting in ten minutes."

I let that sink in slowly. A meeting? A meeting that was with my brothers. And Hope. And if he was late... "What time is it?" I asked, my words slurred and drowsy.

"Almost nine," Nash answered, amusement in his voice.

"Almost nine," I repeated. Then again, as it hit me, "Almost nine!"

I jerked up, dragging the covers off us, and bolted for the bathroom. "I have a meeting in ten minutes, too. And it's at the cottage," I wailed. Not only would I miss my coffee, it would take more than ten minutes to get cleaned up, dressed, and over to the cottage.

Nash appeared in the door of the shower, leaning against the frame, watching me wash with lazy eyes. "A meeting with who?"

"Billy Bob and the electrician." I debated washing my hair. I didn't have time. I shoved my head under the spray, anyway. I hadn't bothered to wash it when I'd been in here the night before, and I had sex hair. Sex hair times two. I was not meeting with Billy Bob and the electrician with poorly disguised sex hair. I'd rather be late.

"I don't want you leaving the house or going anywhere alone. Not with Tyler here," Nash said in a suspiciously even tone.

I heard his words, but I couldn't have understood him. Not leave the house? I had a long list of things to get done so the cottage could stay on schedule. Rinsing the last of the conditioner from my hair, I looked at Nash, ignoring his ridiculous pronouncement. "Do you want the shower?"

With a grunt, he took my place under the hot spray, his eyes on me as I bent over to wrap my hair in a towel. Despite everything we'd done together, I blushed. I flew through brushing my teeth and took a second to text Billy Bob, letting them know I was running late.

By the time Nash was out of the shower, I was ready. I wasn't used to standing up for myself, but I had to start sometime. And this was Nash, who I loved. Nash, who loved me. "I'm not staying in the house. I have a job to do."

Nash sighed. "I know, and I know the schedule at the cottage is important, but you need to delegate for a few days. We don't know what Tyler is up to. You need to be careful."

"I'm tired of Tyler dictating my life. And I'll repeat, I have a job to do."

"Griffen would understand," he started. I wasn't having it.

"Of course he would. But I don't. I'll be with Billy Bob and probably the electrician all day. Working. Tyler won't want to come anywhere near the cottage. He'd take one look at all the dust and run screaming."

Nash pulled his shirt over his head. "I don't want to risk it."

"It's not up to you." I pulled on my own shirt, a clean but ragged t-shirt I'd stolen from one of my brothers with the logo of a local sandwich shop across the chest. I was working in Savannah's bedroom that morning, scraping old paint from the fireplace mantel, and it was going to get messy, as most things in the cottage did these days.

Nash clenched his jaw. "Sweetheart," he began.

"Nash. Stop." He did, but he wasn't happy about it. "I have no idea how long Tyler is going to string this out." I felt sick just thinking of him living in my house, especially when I couldn't leave. "According to Angie, this could go on for a while given how the courts are backed up and his refusal to cooperate. It could be a year. Or more. And I am not going to hide in my room until he decides to get the hell out of my house. I'm not going to let him take my life from me." I drew in a breath for courage. "And I won't let you do it either."

Nash reared back. "Parker, I'm not taking your life from you, you just—"

"I know you don't mean to," I interrupted, "But by asking me to stay in the house and never be alone, you are."

Nash pushed a hand through his hair, his eyes narrowed in frustration. "I want you to be careful."

"I will be," I promised. I hated making him unhappy, but I didn't have a choice. I took one more minute to shove a travel mug into my single serve coffee maker and press Go. I was not facing the day without coffee. That was a scarier thought than running into Tyler. By far.

Nash didn't argue while I made my coffee, instead spending his time getting dressed and brushing his teeth. He was ready when I was and followed me out the door. "There's only one key," I said, turning it in the lock.

"You keep it," he said. "If I need anything from the room, I'll come find you."

"Parker!" I looked up to see Griffen coming down the hall from the direction of the master suite.

Griffen strode closer, his eyes narrowing as he took in my clothes and the travel mug in my hand. "You're going to the cottage?"

"Don't you start," I said, pointing a finger at him. "I already argued with Nash about it. I have things to do at the cottage, a meeting I'm late for, and I'm not spending the rest of however long locked in my room. Deal with it."

Griffen shot a look at Nash. "What did you do to her?"

"Don't blame me, this is all Parker."

"Parks," Griffen started.

I walked past him. "Seriously, I'm late. Billy Bob and the electrician are waiting. I'll be careful. I promise."

Griffen said something under his breath. Probably better that I couldn't hear. Nash followed me, calling over his shoulder to Griffen, "I'm just going to walk her over to the cottage, hand her off to Billy Bob."

"Take your time," Griffen called back, sounding relieved.

We didn't say much on the short walk through the Manor and across the side lawn. I had my eyes out for

Tyler, but, aside from Hawk working in the barren gardens, we didn't see anyone. Tyler was probably still asleep at this hour. As long as he wasn't near me, I didn't care where he was.

"Be careful. Lock the door to the cottage when you're inside," Nash said before kissing me goodbye.

"I will, I promise." And I did, flipping the deadbolt as soon as I closed the door behind me.

Careful wasn't going to be good enough. Not when it came to Tyler. Careful wasn't even close.

Chapter Twenty-Nine

PARKER

"Sorry for the holdup, gentlemen," I said as I set my travel mug on the counter. "What did I miss?"

I almost wished I hadn't asked. They took me through the cottage, Billy Bob following in silence as the electrician explained what needed to be replaced and how extensive the damage was. When he was finished, I flipped to a new page in my notebook. "What's this going to do to my budget? And my schedule?"

The electrician, a whipcord thin man at least two decades older than me, tilted his head to the side and studied the ceiling before offering, "'Bout a week, all in. We can start today, unless you need to think on it."

He named a number that smashed my budget to smithereens. I sighed in resignation. I'd watched enough HGTV to know there was always at least one disaster in a renovation project. Hopefully, this would be the only one.

Doing a little mental math, I let out a breath that was almost relief. I'd move the furniture budget to the electrical work and still be under my top-line number. Savannah would much rather have reliable electricity than new furniture. Hope had said there was a lot we could use in the attics. I'd rely on that and put the money into working lights and air conditioning.

"Okay, sounds good. I was planning to work on the fireplace mantel upstairs today. Will I be in your way?"

The electrician swung his head from side to side. "Don't think so. Got enough light up there after we cut the power?"

"I should," I said. "If I don't, I'll figure it out." Shifting topics, I braced for the part of the conversation I'd rather avoid. "Did Hawk discuss security with you?"

A slow bob of his head. "We'll keep the doors locked. Won't bring anyone in who hasn't been cleared. Just me and my son, and Hawk already looked him over."

"Thank you. I know it's inconvenient. It's hard to secure this much space."

All of us looked out the front windows at the sprawling lawn between the cottage and the Manor, the vast lines of the Manor itself, and the woods surrounding all of it.

"Wouldn't want Hawk's job," Billy added. "At least in the cottage you can see someone comin'."

You could, as long as you were looking for them. The problem was, all of us had other things to do. I left the electrician, his son, and Billy Bob to their work and went back to the project I'd planned for the day; Scraping old paint off the fireplace mantel in Savannah's bedroom.

I was still debating what to do with the fireplace. It worked, which was cool, except Savannah would never use it. Not if it meant hauling logs into her bedroom all the time. There was a fireplace on the first floor, right below this one, and Billy Bob had suggested we run the gas line to both and give her a fireplace she could turn on with the click of a button. Much better, but I'd wait on that until I saw the final invoice for the electrical work. Either way, the peeling, faded paint on the mantel had to come off.

The work was boring and repetitive. It was also killing my fingers. I set music playing on my phone and zoned out, scraping and sanding, revealing inch after inch of rich, brown walnut. I'd been debating repainting the mantle, but now that I saw all this gorgeous walnut, I had other ideas.

I didn't stop until my stomach growled. I sometimes skipped lunch or snuck something from the kitchen later, but not today. For one thing, I'd gotten a lot more physical activity than I was used to the night before. I smiled to myself. Naked in bed with Nash was the best kind of exercise.

It wasn't entirely about my empty stomach. I wanted to see Nash, even if it was just at a family meal. Maybe I'd pull him into a dark hallway and steal a kiss. Or more.

I glanced at my phone, surprised to see that it was almost noon. Tapping to pause the music, I stood, working the kinks out of my back as I rose, gradually growing aware of the blanket of quiet surrounding the cottage.

Where was everyone? I stopped, holding my breath, and listened.

Nothing. I knew without checking that the electrician and Billy Bob were not in the cottage.

A whisper of unease snuck through me. The door was locked. Of course it was. The guys knew to lock it. It's just that it was usually so loud in the cottage between Billy Bob's power tools and whatever I was doing that the quiet felt wrong, that's all. Nothing to worry about.

I slipped my phone in my back pocket and leaned down to snag my empty travel mug. I'd get a refill when I was in the Manor for lunch, a little more caffeine to power me through the afternoon. Some food, more coffee, and I could shake this weird mood.

A faint creak floated up the stairs.

I froze, breath held.

The only sound was the frantic thumping of my heart.

Nothing else.

Letting out a breath, I ducked into the bathroom and pulled the clip from my hair, shaking it free before twisting the still damp strands into a knot and neatly re-clipping them. Patting my clothes, I tried to get rid of the dust and curls of aged white paint. Scraping paint and sanding were messy, messy work.

Savannah might kick me out of the dining room. Or she might not. My stomach growled again, the sound echoing off the tiles in the bathroom. I was hungry enough to roll the dice. At worst, she'd send me to eat on the terrace. As long as Nash joined me, I didn't care where we ate.

I was as clean as I was going to get without another shower and a change of clothes. Smiling, thinking of lunch with Nash, I jogged down the stairs. My eyes caught on the front door.

Closed and locked, as it should have been, the faint gleam of the deadbolt visible between the door and the frame. I would have thought the electrician and Billy Bob would tell me before they left for lunch, but it wasn't a big deal. They probably forgot.

Probably. It didn't matter. I was leaving anyway.

I shrugged my shoulders and strode across the room to the front door. I was just in a weird mood. A break from work and a little food would do the trick.

My hand closed around the deadbolt. Before I could turn it, he was there, sliding smoothly between me and the still closed door, staring down at me with his heart shining in his blue eyes.

Tyler.

Once upon a time, I would have melted at that look. He was a good actor. I'd give him that. If he hadn't used this look a million times already, if I hadn't found him in our bed with another woman, if he hadn't hit me, I might have fallen for it.

I didn't. I knew the aching love in those blue eyes was false. Tyler only loved himself.

I stared back at him, trying to keep any expression from my face, and waited to feel... something. Anything. This was my husband, the man I'd promised to spend my life with, the man I'd been married to for the last six years.

I got nothing.

No, that's not true.

I felt a faint wave of disgust. Of impatience. Of annoyance at the knowledge that I was going to have to put up with him until he had his say. I was so very tired of adjusting my life to suit Tyler's tantrums.

"Parker," he crooned, raising one hand to trail a finger down my cheek. "Tell me what I need to do to make this right and I'll do it. I love you, and I know you love me."

I resisted the urge to roll my eyes. I wanted to slap him. To scream how stupid he was and how I wasn't doing this anymore. Somehow, I held back. His face inches from mine, I couldn't help but be aware of how alone we were, the thick door still bolted shut behind me.

"Tyler, it's too late for that. I'm sorry."

The last part wasn't a lie. I was sorry. Sorry I'd stayed for so long. Sorry he was a shitty husband. I was sorry about a lot of things, but not about telling Tyler it was over.

I took a step to the side, relieved when he turned, but

didn't follow. Except now he had his back to the door, blocking my exit.

Glancing out the front windows, I looked for someone, anyone, who might be headed our way, but the grass stretched between the cottage and the house, a sea of emerald green, vibrant in the midday sun. The path winding through the grass was empty.

"Tyler," I said, hiding my frustration behind that serene, polished shell Nash liked to tease me about. "Why are you here? Really?"

Tyler shoved his hands in his pockets, trying for sheepish with a hint of apology. His dark hair fell over his forehead as he glanced up at me through thick lashes, white teeth sinking into his full lower lip. He was painfully beautiful, and I felt nothing more than faint revulsion.

"You know why I'm here," he murmured.

"I don't, Tyler. If there's any chance you think I still love you, you need to understand that I don't. I want a divorce. There's nothing between us anymore."

"Baby," he crooned again, melting away from the door, fluid as a hunting cat, closing the distance between us. "How can you say things like that to me? I never thought you could be so cruel. I love you. I've always loved you."

"And the other women?" I asked, stalling.

"Nothing. Distractions. You know I need sex and you weren't around." He stopped in front of me, his hands coming up to cup my face.

I couldn't let him touch me. My skin crawled at the thought. I dodged, trying to make it look like I tripped on a scrap pile of wood. Tyler's eyes narrowed as he caught the flash of disgust on my face.

I dug in my back pocket for my phone. I'd been trying to play nice, but I was done.

Tyler's hand shot down. In a neat twist of his fingers, he pried my phone away and dropped it into his pocket.

"Uh-uh." He wagged his finger at me like I was a disobedient child. "It was hard enough to get you alone. I'm not going to let you call your watchdogs."

The quiet. The electrician and Billy Bob's mysterious disappearance. "What did you do, Tyler?"

He gave an insouciant shrug, smirking with pleasure at his own cleverness. "There's a problem with the power in the Manor. It's completely out. You know how these old houses are. I don't understand why your father let it all go."

Neither did I, but that wasn't the point.

Not only had this asshole trapped me in the cottage for his big make-up scene, but he'd messed with the electrical at the Manor, which meant my electrician was going to have bigger priorities than the cottage until it was fixed.

Abruptly, my determined calm was a flash fire of rage. It was bad enough Tyler was here, in my face, in my house, causing drama when I just wanted to live my life. But now he was screwing with my work, the only work I'd ever had, work I loved and I was good at.

So far, the cottage was on budget and on schedule. I hadn't realized exactly how proud I was of that until Tyler took it away with one snotty shrug.

"I'm not doing this with you," I said, battling to restrain my fury. I was angry, but not stupid.

If I let loose, he'd explode. We were alone. The door was still locked.

A part of me still couldn't believe Tyler was truly dangerous, even after he'd hit me. But another part of me screamed that I was not safe with him. Especially if I pissed him off.

Right now he was all sweet words.

I couldn't afford for that to change.

I sidestepped, easing my way around to the middle of the front room. Tyler followed, just as I hoped, allowing me to lead him away from the door.

"Parker, baby doll," he cajoled. I cut him off.

"I'm done with this conversation, Tyler. I've made it clear, I only want to communicate through our lawyers."

Tyler leaned into me, crowding me, but not actually touching me.

"I just want to talk to my wife," he said, his tone all silky persuasion. "It's absurd to talk through lawyers when we're living in the same house. And you can't restrict my access to the Manor estate. I'm just trying to have a civilized discussion. You're the one flying off the handle."

I was not flying off the handle, and he knew it, but I understood what he was getting at just the same.

It was one thing to deny him entrance to private rooms, but the cottage didn't qualify. Harvey had explained that the will required that spouses be treated as any other resident of the Manor. If we tried to hold Tyler to standards we didn't impose equally, he could sue. And if he won...

At the least, I could lose my inheritance. I wasn't convinced there was much in there, anyway. More than the money, If I defied the terms of my father's will, I'd be banned from all family-owned property until the terms of the will were fulfilled. That was four and a half years during which I'd be cut off from not only Heartstone Manor, but most of Sawyers Bend.

The Inn, Avery's brewery, Quinn's guide business, everything owned by Sawyer Enterprises–even Nash's new offices–were all considered family-owned property according to the will. I'd only just found my family again. I would not let Tyler send me away.

I could almost hear his lawyer in the courtroom describing how I lost my temper, was emotionally abusive, how I was carrying on an affair with my brother-in-law right in front of my poor estranged husband.

I knew it didn't look good, but I wasn't giving up Nash.

For the first time in my life, I had love; I had work; I had family, and I wasn't going to let Tyler take any of it from me. Which meant I had to play it cool until we could figure out a legal way to get rid of him.

I wasn't sure I could pull it off.

Tyler eased closer, the side of his mouth curved in a hint of a grin. He had me exactly where he wanted me, and he was enjoying it.

I tried to be reasonable. "I don't understand what you think you'll get out of this. I have to allow you to live in the Manor. I'm not legally required to talk to you."

"True," he said, stopping only inches from me, again blocking me from the door.

What if I made a break for it? Would he try to stop me?

If he did, would it be assault? Could I press charges and make him leave that way?

If Nash or Griffen, hell if *anyone* heard what I was thinking, they'd kick my ass. Use myself as a target to get Tyler to commit assault? Oh yeah, no way that could go wrong.

Bottom line, we didn't have any witnesses. I couldn't record anything on my phone, because Tyler had it. Unless he really hurt me, any altercation would end up in a he said/she said, and only make everything worse.

I stuck out my hand, palm up. "Give me back my phone. The will gives you the right to room and board in the Manor, not permission to steal my belongings."

Tyler watched me for a moment, then turned and

placed my phone on the kitchen counter. No longer in his possession, but not in mine, either. I stepped forward to retrieve it and he slid in front of me. Not touching, but clearly blocking my way.

"Stop trying to run away from me, Parker. You're my wife. You owe me some consideration."

I didn't owe him anything, but I was wise enough to keep my mouth shut. Something occurred to me. He'd said consideration. Maybe he didn't mean emotional consideration. Maybe he meant the legal kind.

"How much?" I asked, trying to keep the edge out of my voice. I knew well enough, Tyler Kingsley did not like mouthy women.

"You don't have enough to buy me off." He sidled closer.

"Try me," I countered. He was right. I didn't have enough to pay my own car insurance, much less buy off a man used to flying in private jets, but it was worth asking.

Tyler's smug grin spread across his face. "It's too late for that. You think this is about money? If I wanted money, I could have charged Nash for access to that sweet pussy of yours and saved myself a lot of trouble."

"You're disgusting," I spat out, unable to hold back my revulsion. How had I been married to this man for six years?

"You want to know what I want?" Tyler waited for my sharp nod. "I want you to come home with me and convince Claudia that all is forgiven. Then, after everything is back to normal, I think we should have a baby."

"What?" I couldn't help it. My jaw hung open in shock. "Are you insane?"

Tyler didn't react, just cocked his head to the side and watched me with a predator's eyes. He was playing with me. He knew this had all gone too far for that. He knew I wasn't going to lie to Claudia or allow him to touch me, much less get me pregnant.

Was he waiting for me to make a mistake? Maybe he was recording this, trying to get evidence he could use against me. I wouldn't put it past him. I wouldn't put anything past him. That was the problem.

Fighting the urge to glance between my phone and the door, I tried to figure out what to do next. Nash and Griffen had been right. I should never have come to the cottage today. A flick of my eyes at the still deserted lawn and path to the Manor. There was no rescue in sight. If I was going to get away from Tyler without making everything worse, I'd have to handle it myself.

Making the decision and acting in the same breath, I lunged for the door, my fingers closing on the lock. It turned, the decisive click of the deadbolt music to my ears. A hand slapped on the solid wood above my head, holding the door closed.

"I'm not done with you," Tyler murmured in my ear. "You can go when I say you can go."

Chapter Thirty

NASH

"Let me know if you need any input on that cost analysis," Royal said as I packed up my laptop. We'd spent the morning working with Griffen and Hope on ideas for the new office space. It was almost lunchtime and the three Sawyers had their own business to focus on for the rest of the day. I had other plans. Parker related plans.

She'd be hungry, and wouldn't want to change for lunch in the formal dining room. I had an idea for that. On my way out the door, Griffen stopped me. "You going to check on Parker?"

"I thought I'd see if Savannah will pack us a lunch. Parker was scraping paint off a mantel and surround. She's probably a mess." I grinned at the idea. I loved seeing her wrapped up in her work, loved that she didn't mind getting dirty if it got the job done.

Griffen grinned back at me. "She's doing an amazing job with the cottage. I didn't know she had it in her."

"I don't think she did either." I stopped. I didn't want to gang up on Parker with her brother, but I had to say, "I know we can't get him out of the house, but I don't think she should be alone."

Hope, scrolling through emails on her laptop, looked between us, then spared a glance at Royal. "Normally, I'd protest that Parker is a grown woman and can make her own choices, but I don't like it either. There's something off about him coming here. I can't figure out what he thinks this will accomplish."

"He can't think she's going to take him back," Griffen said.

I shook my head. "It's possible," I admitted. "But it doesn't make sense to me either."

"Could it be as simple as needing a roof over his head?" Royal asked. "If your mother kicked him out, and he had nowhere to go, maybe he's just buying time until he has a better plan."

I tried to imagine it. Was free room and board worth the humiliation of moving into his estranged wife's home? Knowing no one wanted him there and, in fact, pretty much everyone at Heartstone actively hated him? "It could be. His ego is massive enough to convince him he has a right to be here."

"Thanks to my asshole of a father, he does have a right to be here," Griffen muttered. I knew it was killing him to let Tyler stay, never mind that he didn't have a choice.

"Maybe Bryce will keep him busy and they'll leave us alone," Hope said. The rest of us just stared at her. "But that seems unlikely," she finished.

"I'm going to go see Savannah about bringing Parker some lunch. Okay if I leave my laptop here? I'd rather it was somewhere secure, and Parker has the key to her suite."

Griffen scowled. "That's fine. Smart. I hate that we have

to lock the doors in the first place." Hope stroked a soothing hand down his arm.

"We'll figure something out," she said. "He can't plan to stay here long term. Can he?"

I didn't want to hear Griffen's answer. The truth was, we had no idea what Tyler's plans were. I'd learned he'd gone out drinking with Bryce after the meeting with Harvey. They'd come in late, drunk, and neither had been at breakfast. As far as I knew, Tyler was still passed out in bed.

I took the stairs to the lower level of Heartstone Manor at a jog, appreciating the way the formal woodwork of the main level shifted to rough stone and arched barrel ceilings as I descended. It felt like I was traveling further back in time with each step.

The wide hall of the lower level ran from one end of the Manor to the other, the ceiling high, pipes and electrical conduit exposed, but out of reach. The air here was a good five degrees cooler than above, the light bright in spots, and dim where the bulbs couldn't reach.

The main kitchen bustled with activity, the staff preparing for lunch. Savannah spotted me as soon as I stepped through the doorway, setting her clipboard on a windowsill and crossing the room. "Nash, how can I help you?"

"I can see you're all busy, but I was thinking about bringing Parker lunch. Maybe a picnic? She's been scraping paint off that mantel–" I didn't get any further. Savannah knew exactly what I was getting at.

"Let's keep her out of the dining room then, and spare April and Kitty the vacuuming. I'm sure she'd prefer a romantic picnic with you than a family lunch, anyway. Why don't you–" Savannah's eyes sharpened as something behind me caught her eye. "What do you think you're doing here?"

I'd never heard that edge in her tone. Turning, I saw Finn, Parker's older brother, lurking in the hall. He lifted his chin at Savannah, his usual chill demeanor nowhere in sight.

"You didn't answer my text," he said.

Savannah's eyes narrowed so far they were almost slits. "I was getting to it. We're preparing for lunch down here, in case you can't tell."

"You can do seventeen things at once, Savannah. If anyone else had texted, you would have answered by now."

"True," she agreed with saccharine sweetness. "But I like everyone else. And I'm helping Nash. I'll get to you later."

"I texted before he showed up," Finn protested.

"Technically," Savannah drawled, "I already answered your question. You can have kitchen time on Saturday, when the cook is off. Otherwise, you're banned from the kitchens. No exceptions."

"That's ridiculous," Finn protested. "I'm not going to start a fight with this one. She's completely adequate—"

Savannah raised a hand, palm out. "Don't say another word. Just turn around, walk away, and you can come back on Saturday. Otherwise, I'll get Griffen to ban you from the lower level entirely."

They stood facing each other, Savannah's sharp grey eyes locked to Finn's green. They reminded me of two cats, facing off before one of them pounced. Finn backed down first. Interesting. He turned and stalked off without another word. Savannah saw me watch Finn leave and explained.

"He's a classically trained chef and a real snob about it. So far, he's run off two perfectly good cooks. Griffen told him if he does it again, he either takes over the job or he has to leave Heartstone. And you know what that means."

Her head tilted to the side as she considered. "I think it's driving him nuts not having access to a kitchen. But he made his bed." Straightening, she refocused. "Give me twenty minutes to put something together for your picnic. Maybe thirty. I have to—"

From down the hall, a loud pop filled the air, and everything went dark. For just a moment, all movement stilled in the busy kitchen, the light from the windows set high in the walls the only source of illumination.

"God damn it!" I heard from deeper in the kitchen, joined by, "Not again!"

A scuffle of feet sounded in the hall. A second later, Scarlett, Tenn's girlfriend, appeared in the doorway, her red hair curling wildly around her face, a metal clamp in her hand. Parker had told me she was a glass artist and had her studio down here somewhere. Glancing around the kitchen, she asked, "Is it the entire house? Or just down here?"

Savannah's phone beeped with a text, giving us the answer. Her shoulders slumping, she confirmed, "It's the entire house. Damn it. Last time it took all day to get it back on." She typed a quick reply to the text.

"Where's the panel?" I asked. "I can take a look. I'm no electrician, but I can change a fuse." At Savannah's raised eyebrow I said, "The house I grew up in wasn't this size, but it was about this old and the fuses used to blow now and then."

Savannah nodded at Scarlett. "Could you show Nash where it is? I have some calls to make."

Scarlett flicked on the flashlight on her phone and I followed her down the long hallway to a narrow door at the far end. It hung slightly ajar. Scarlett hummed in the back of her throat, considering. "This is always closed. Whatever blew was loud. Maybe it forced the door open?"

Turning on the light from my own phone, I shone it in the small room. Several electrical panels lined one wall, all of them neatly closed. The wiring leading to all three was a mess, tangled and scorched. The faint scent of smoke hung in the air, though nothing was on fire.

"What the fuck?" I said into the dark, studying the wild knot of wiring. I knew better than to touch any of it.

"This is way over my pay grade," Scarlett murmured.

"Mine too," I admitted.

Scarlett ran her light over the closest section of wiring, examining it without getting close enough to touch. "I can't tell if this is deliberate or an accident. Something about the way it burned doesn't look right."

My brain kicked into gear. When the lights had gone out, it hadn't occurred to me that it could be deliberate. I'd heard all about the electrical problems at Heartstone. But this wasn't what Scarlett had been expecting. Which meant it wasn't the usual power outage. Shit.

"I have to get to Parker," I said, turning for the door. Scarlett moved out of my way, following me out.

"Do you think her husb– Uh, your brother could have–"

"I don't know, but–" I cut off as feet pounded down the stairs at the far end of the hallway, voices raised. Billy Bob came into view, a tall, thin stranger behind them. By the way the stranger was huffing and puffing, they'd come on the run.

Parker was alone.

Without another word, I raced for the cottage.

Chapter Thirty-One

NASH

The cottage wasn't far from the Manor. Only a few hundred feet down a winding gravel path. It felt like miles. From a distance, the cottage looked peaceful, a two-story stone building tucked into the trees. The door was closed. The windows dark. My feet hit the gravel in skidding slides, my shoes meant for polished floors and not a sprint on an uneven surface.

I didn't care about my shoes; I cared about getting to Parker. Nothing about the scene in front of me indicated she was in trouble. Just my gut, urging me to run faster, faster, until I hit the porch in a final lunge. The doorknob turned under my hand, the door giving the barest inch before slamming shut.

Fuck. I swung back, giving myself some space, and flew into the door, turning the handle as I hit, using every pound of my body weight, every inch of leverage to force the door open. I heard them before I saw them, the thump and roll of bodies hitting the floor, the door suddenly swinging wide to crash into the wall once the resistance was out of the way.

I dove for Parker, laying on her back on the hardwood,

her chest lurching as she gasped for breath. I hit my knees beside her, spotting Tyler face first on the floor a few feet away. "I'm sorry, sweetheart. I didn't mean to knock you down." I ran my hands over her body, looking for injuries.

Parker caught one hand in hers, her voice a whisper as she fought to fill her lungs with air. "Breath knocked out of me. I'm okay."

"I'm sorry," I said again, sick at the knowledge that I'd put her on the ground. I'd burst in thinking I was saving her from Tyler and instead I'd tossed her halfway across the room.

She squeezed my hand hard, her eyes sliding to where Tyler was slowly getting to his feet, fury turning his face a deep shade of red. "He wouldn't let me leave." She sat up, leaning in to press a soft kiss to the side of my mouth. "You were just in time. Now we have to get out of here without killing him. Can you do that?"

To be honest, I wasn't sure I could. He wouldn't let her leave? I wanted to kill him for coming this close to Parker, much less for trapping her here. For making her feel unsafe. I saw the fear in her eyes, felt the way she gripped my hand.

But I knew my brother. If we gave him the slightest excuse, he'd use his meager funds to find a lawyer willing to fuck with us until he drove us all mad. Or worse.

I helped Parker to her feet before I turned to face Tyler. "Stay away from Parker," I said, trying to sound like a reasonable adult. Even I heard the growl in my voice. I was pretending to be civilized, but inside I was anything but.

"You can't tell me to stay away from my own wife," he whined.

A rumble filled the room. Shit, that was me, growling again.

Parker squeezed my hand hard. "It's no use trying to

reason with him," she said. "He just wants to cause trouble. He can't unless we let him."

Tyler ignored her words, and me, focused again on Parker. "You know Nash is only using you, right? He's jealous because mom always loved me more. And because I slept with his girlfriends when we were younger." Turning his attention back to me, he said, "Why don't you just find someone else to fuck and let Parker and I work this out between us? Our marriage has nothing to do with you. And, honestly, sleeping with my wife is just tacky."

Tyler swung back to Parker. "I thought you were better than this, Parker. I can't believe mother disowned me when you're the one fucking your brother-in-law while you're still married. Such a fucking whore."

I lunged at him when he called her a whore. Parker yanked me back, but said nothing. Only she could have stopped me. My chest heaved with each breath. I knew throwing a punch was a disastrous idea. I knew it. My fingers curled into a fist, anyway.

I was not going to escalate this shit show. I was not.

Parker leaned into my side, her arm going around my waist. I reached for calm. It eluded me, but I managed not to annihilate Tyler.

Tyler set his hands on his hips, sneering at both of us. "I can't believe you're falling for his bullshit, Parker. He's going to dump you as soon as he's bored with you. You know that, don't you? And then what'll you have? You'll be alone, used up, and no one will want you. If you don't get rid of him and come back to me, you won't have another chance."

"And if I stay with Nash? You'll walk away and leave me alone?" she asked serenely.

Tyler saw his mistake. If he'd thought to undermine her by poking at her confidence, he'd chosen the wrong woman.

Parker had her own insecurities, but she was long past letting Tyler's insults break the skin. He turned his rage on me.

"I'm going to sue you for alienation of affection!"

"Go ahead," I replied, easily. "I'll give you the name of a good lawyer. In the meantime, stop harassing Parker."

Tyler rolled his shoulders back and lifted his chin, trying his best to give us a withering glare. "I'm not harassing her. She's still my wife."

"Not for long," Parker said. "And I'll say one more time, I only want to communicate with you through our lawyers. I can't make you leave Heartstone, thanks to my father's insane ideas about marriage, but I don't have to talk to you."

Tyler lifted his chin even more, making me wonder, for just a second, if he was going to tip over backward. My lips curved in a faint grin, the need to hit Tyler draining away. He was a miserable human being, but he was only a speed bump. We just had to tolerate him long enough for him to get bored and leave Heartstone. Knowing Tyler, that wouldn't take long.

Which reminded me, as long as I had him here... "Why did you come to Heartstone, Tyler? I can't figure it out."

"I came to give Parker one last chance to come back to me."

"If that's it," Parker said, "you might as well leave. I'm not going anywhere with you. Ever."

The petulant look faded from Tyler's face, leaving his eyes sharp and assessing as he studied Parker. Something about that look left me feeling uneasy. Maybe it was the sudden feeling that the accusations, the tantrum, were all an act. He knew Parker was done with him.

"Are you leaving, then?" I pressed. "Now that you know all she wants is a divorce?"

Tyler crossed his arms over his chest, a smirk twisting his mouth. "I don't think so. Thanks to our dear mother, I no longer have a home. Might as well use this one, for now. Even if the Manor is a dump. You two can keep playing house. I'll get what I want in the end." He lifted his chin again and strode past us, taking the porch steps in one leap and striding down the path to the Manor.

We followed him out, making sure he really was gone. Beside me, Parker said, "I wish I knew what the hell he wants. I know it's not me. I thought it was money, but I offered to buy him off and he wasn't interested."

"He wants to win," I answered, my gut speaking instead of my brain.

Parker leaned back and looked up at me. "I don't know what that means."

"Neither do I," I said, more to myself than to her. "He trapped you in here? Did he touch you? Hurt you?"

Parker shook her head. "He all but admitted he did something to the electrical at the Manor. He was a jerk, and a bully, but he didn't touch me. Or threaten me." She fell silent, thinking. "He didn't do a single thing we could bring to West or Harvey. Sadly, being a raging asshole isn't illegal."

"Sadly, it's not," I agreed. "If it were, he and your dad would have been out of our hair a long time ago."

Staring at the summer sky, the green grass waving in the breeze, Parker mused, "It's so typical of Prentice that he set up his will to try to keep us from leaving our spouses when he died, while he discarded wives like they were used tissues." She shook her head. "God forbid any of us use the inheritance to get out of a bad marriage. 'Till death do us part, except for him. The worst thing is realizing that, in a way, I married my father. All those years of wanting to escape, and I did the opposite."

I squeezed her into my side, pressing a kiss to the top of her head. "Don't do that, sweetheart. The past is the past. We're moving on."

Parker turned into me, wrapping her arms around my waist. "Yes, we are."

"Could you do me a favor?" I asked, deciding to press my advantage while I had her feeling affectionate.

"Mmm?"

"I don't want you alone. I don't care what Tyler says, he clearly targeted you today. I–"

"Okay. We'll have to figure something out, because I have work and so do you, but you're right. Until we understand what he's up to, I think we should be careful. He might come after you next."

I hadn't considered that. Until we figured out what Tyler really wanted, we wouldn't be able to predict what he'd do. "I don't believe this is as simple as Tyler needing a roof over his head, or wanting you back," I said, thinking out loud.

"Neither do I," Parker agreed. "I think this just turned into a game of wait and see. All we can do is stick together and hope he finds something else to entertain him."

I thought about the calculating look in Tyler's eyes as he'd watched Parker and me. I was all about sticking together. At the moment, I could work anywhere as long as I had my laptop and a cell signal. I'd bring a folding table to the cottage and set up here, or work in our suite.

I wanted to think we could wait Tyler out. He'd never stuck with anything for long, even the marriage he was so determined to preserve. But something about the way he'd looked at us, the way he'd shifted gears so abruptly, had my radar pinging hard.

He wants to win.

I'd said it without thinking.

Deep down, I knew that's what this was about.

This time. Tyler was determined to win. To finally beat me at something. The real question was, win at what? He wasn't going to get Parker back. He didn't jump at the chance for cash when she offered it. So what did Tyler consider a win? What did he really want?

Until we found the answer to that question, I wasn't leaving Parker's side. I finally had everything I'd dreamed about from the day I met her. I wasn't going to lose her now.

Whatever Tyler had planned, he was going to have to go through me first.

Somehow, I didn't think the idea of that would bother Tyler in the slightest.

Chapter Thirty-Two

NASH

"One second, baby, I just need to check the tracking on this order." Parker reached up to kiss my jaw before turning her attention back to the data on her tablet screen.

I didn't love that she was selling her things, but I was so fucking proud of the way she took on every challenge. The stock in her online shop was cleverly photographed and displayed, and she was moving inventory at a brisk pace.

It was the same with the cottage. She might not have had experience with renovation, but she was relentless, researching or asking Billy Bob about everything, learning in leaps and bounds.

Her slender body curved into mine, her velvet couch more than big enough for the two of us to stretch out together. I'd already set my laptop on the coffee table, finally finished with work for the day and ready to distract Parker. Preferably a naked distraction.

Nuzzling the top of her head, I reached down to cup one full breast. Her swift intake of breath had her pausing, the tablet in her hand wavering. I pressed my advantage, reaching across to–

Parker swatted my questing hands away. "Don't you have more email to deal with?" she asked, her starchy tone ruined by a breathless laugh.

"Nope, all done." That was a lie, but I'd long given up on the idea of inbox zero. I'd handled everything I needed to get to, and that would have to be good enough. I was more interested in Parker than my email. By far.

"Find something else to occupy yourself for five minutes and then I'll be done too."

I pulled her down the couch, turning on my side so I was reclined and she leaned against me as a backrest. "Good?"

"Umhm," she murmured, settling in, her eyes on the screen.

I let my eyes close. A nap would do until Parker finished her work. I'd learned she was hard to distract when she was focused on a project. That was fine with me, since I was her project more often than not. I'd quickly learned that being the subject of Parker's focus was better than I'd dreamed.

For most of the time I'd known her, Parker had been more concept than reality. We'd had moments together, sure. Those moments had fed my feelings for her, kept them going during the long stretches of time when I only heard about her from my mother. There were things I knew were true–that Parker was kind, intelligent, loyal, loving, and far more than Tyler deserved.

But I didn't know the little things. That she always hung up her clothes. That her fixation on her morning coffee was a little intense. She was affectionate with the people she loved, hugging her siblings and friends often, touching me whenever we were close enough. Even now, her free hand lazily stroked my hip as she worked.

I'd wondered so many times over the years if the real Parker could possibly live up to the dream. Sex was one thing. After that night in New York I had no doubt we were compatible in bed. Really, I'd known after that kiss on her wedding day, but New York had proved it.

The last week together had been proof of a different nature.

I'd already known we were perfectly matched in bed. The few dates we'd managed away from Heartstone had been better than I'd imagined. But it was one thing to plan a romantic date and another to share a bathroom. We'd gone from years of dancing around each other to living together in a few short days. The risk of implosion was perilously high, especially when you added in Tyler living under the same roof.

So far, there hadn't been an implosion. When it came to the domestic aspects of life, Parker and I fit just as well as we did everywhere else. She could live with me hogging the bed. I didn't mind that her stuff took up most of the bathroom counter.

Those minor issues aside, we were pretty much in sync. We both rose early. We both made the bed in the morning. Neither of us liked to leave stuff lying around, but neither of us was obsessively neat, either.

In the last week, we'd fallen into a comfortable rhythm. Parker's renovation was off schedule, thanks to the ongoing electrical problems in the manor. She still went to the cottage every day to work on her smaller projects, like refinishing the mantel in the upstairs bedroom and sanding down the kitchen cabinets in preparation for repainting.

Savannah found me a folding table and chair, and I

brought my laptop to the cottage, tethering to my phone for internet. While Parker worked in the cottage, I worked at my makeshift desk. If I had a meeting or had to leave the Manor, Parker worked in the main house, or came with me.

I'd worried being joined at the hip would wear thin. Not so far. More than the sex, which was fucking spectacular, I just liked being with her. Hanging out, watching a movie, helping her scrape paint. It didn't matter. If Parker was in arms reach, I was good. Better than good. I'd never been this happy.

The only real problem was Tyler. He was still in the Manor, at the dining room table for every meal, acting like a welcome houseguest instead of a despised intruder. Inexplicably, he'd been staying out of our way. After he'd cornered Parker in the cottage, I'd been on high alert.

His words echoed in my brain.

I'll get what I want in the end.

And since then... nothing. He hung out with Bryce, playing golf, fly-fishing, raiding the family liquor cabinet and playing endless rounds of pool. He ignored the rest of us. As often as we could, I took Parker out for dinner to spare her having to share a table with Tyler.

It wasn't enough that he was ignoring us. Sitting beside Parker at the expansive Heartstone dining table, watching Tyler drink endless glasses of wine, droning on and on with Bryce, I could feel Parker's nerves fraying thin. Around Tyler, she kept her shell polished to a shine, never letting him see how much he was getting to her. On the surface she was serene, as cool as moonlight, impervious to his drunken comments and constant presence.

I saw beneath her shell, always had, and I could feel the strain. It was too much, being constantly on edge, waiting for the other shoe to drop. Tyler was ignoring us, but he was always there. Around. Sucking all the air from the room. If his plan was to slowly torture Parker, it was working, and there was nothing I could do to stop it.

At least the clock was ticking on their divorce. As far as Angie knew, Tyler still didn't have an attorney. Even without one, he was expected to file the next motion. If he didn't, Angie could ask the judge to rule. Tyler was a raging asshole, but he wasn't stupid. He had a plan. I just couldn't figure it out. Ignore us to death?

Tyler left my mind the second Parker closed the cover of her tablet case and put it on the coffee table. "I'm done—"

I lifted her, laying flat out on the couch and pulling her on top of me, her sundress riding wonderfully up the backs of her thighs. I followed it, stroking my palms over her soft skin, spreading her legs so her knees ended up on either side of my hips. Exactly where I wanted her.

She sat up, reaching behind her to pull at her zipper, tugging it just low enough for her dress to slide down in the front. I didn't waste any time, baring her breasts, filling my hands. Her cheeks pink, eyes glittering down at me, Parker leaned in, her mouth on my neck, sucking, nibbling, working on that sensitive spot that made me crazy.

I skimmed my hands down her back, searching for the hem of her dress, pulling it up to reveal her panties. I had my hands underneath in a second, my fingers splayed over her soft, round ass, squeezing, kneading her flesh, dragging her against the erection trying to bust through my jeans. I wanted to be naked, but her mouth was doing amazing things to my neck, my jaw, working up to my lips. When Parker's on a mission, I'm the last person to get in her way.

Instead, I went on my own mission, my fingertips searching between her legs, grazing her clit with a featherlight touch, loving the way she moaned, the heat of her shuddering breath on my skin. With one hand, I dipped into her from behind, pushing two fingers into her damp heat, rolling my thumb on her clit from the front.

Her hips rocked, close to dislodging my fingers, her body moving on its own, out of her control. Abruptly, she shifted, making space for her own hands to dive to my belt, fumbling to get it open.

"Wait," I managed, "you're coming first."

"I want you inside me," she said, her teeth closing over my stubbled jaw, the heat of her tongue a brand on my skin.

I pushed a third finger into her pussy and turned my head to kiss her. She'd get my cock, but I wanted this first, to feel her pussy clamp down on my fingers as she came, pulsing and drawing me deeper, until I was a part of her.

Her mouth moved on mine in frantic pleasure, her breath hitching, hips rolling as I drove her higher, my thumb working her clit until she tore her mouth from mine and cried out, the delicious heat of her closing on my fingers in a painful possession.

When she'd caught her breath, I raised my head to promise, "Once you can get up, I'm going to take you to bed and eat that sweet pussy until you come again. And then I'm going to—"

I never got the rest of it out. I barely remembered what I was going to say when Parker slid off me, hitting the floor in an awkward thump, catching herself by grabbing my belt. She yanked, finally getting it open, and pulled at my jeans, wrapping her fingers around my cock the second she shoved my clothes out of the way.

"Move," she ordered, and I wasn't going to argue. Not with Parker on her knees in front of me, her lips swollen and parted, aimed at my cock.

I shifted, sitting up, splaying my knees, making room for

her to get in close, close enough for her mouth to slide over the head of my cock, sucking hard. I saw stars. Fucking hell, she was good at that.

At first I thought the flicker of light was my brain shorting out from too much sensation. When the room went black and the house fell silent, I realized it was another power outage, but I didn't move. Neither did Parker. I'm not sure she noticed. I sure as hell wasn't going to say anything. Lately, the power going out wasn't anything new.

I wasn't going to last. Parker was fucking with all of my plans, and I couldn't have been happier about it. I cupped her face in my hands, the feel of her jaw moving, her tongue stroking, the hollow of her cheeks as she sucked all swirling into a whirl of exquisite sensation driving me closer and closer to to the edge.

"Parker, I'm going to–"

Parker planted her hand on my hip, pinning me in place, and took me deeper, sucking hard, her hand closing around the base of my cock in a tight grip, squeezing and twisting, sending me headlong into a fierce orgasm that had me reeling.

For a second I thought the high-pitched wail was inside my head, an after effect of coming so hard. A breath later, I realized it wasn't me.

"Is that the alarm?"

Chapter Thirty-Three

NASH

Parker raised her head from my thigh, blinking up at me. When she registered the sound, she jumped to her feet. "I haven't heard it since we tested it. I forgot how loud it is."

Pushing her hair off her face, she crossed the room to her phone. Standing, I got my clothes in order and went in search of my own phone. Both of them chimed with a text.

Hold tight. Checking on the alarm. Don't leave your rooms.

Hawk. In the last week we'd gotten used to the power going in and out. "This is the first time you've heard the alarm since it was installed?" I asked Parker. She nodded. "What are the odds this has to do with the power going out again?"

"Given that the alarm system has its own power, separate from the house? I doubt the power outage tripped the alarm, if that's what you're asking. But it doesn't mean someone is trying to break in."

Staring at the screen of her phone, she made her way

back to the couch. Just as she was turning to sit, we heard it. A voice in the hall, familiar but indistinct.

Parker froze, waiting. We heard it again. Closer, definitely a woman, a voice I'd heard before, but still too muffled to make out the identity or what they were saying. Parker thought she knew. Whirling to face the door, she called out, "Sterling? Are you okay?"

"Parker, wait!" I don't know what tipped me off. It very well could have been Sterling out there. No reason to think it wasn't.

Except that Hawk had told us to stay in our rooms. Sterling had her reckless moments, according to the things I'd heard, but she wasn't stupid. She wouldn't be roaming the halls when Hawk told her to stay put. Unless she thought she had a good reason. Or...

I lunged ahead of Parker, shouldering her away from the door, knocking her outstretched hand out of the way. Then I heard it too. Sterling, calling for Parker. Fuck.

My fingers closed on the brass handle of the door, and I was out.

I fell over like a log, my muscles locked stiff. I couldn't blink, couldn't talk, couldn't think. Seconds of nothing, followed by a fiery pain surging up my arm, spreading through my body, my brain in a centrifuge, spinning, thoughts cascading, nothing making sense.

My frozen body sank into waves of pain, bees on bladed wings slicing through every nerve, my muscles cramping in agonizing surges. I blinked, a shadow falling over my eyes, something wet on my face, and all was still. Black. The blare of the alarm forced its way through the cacophony of sound in my brain.

And her. "Nash! Nash!" Parker, screaming, her hands fluttering over me. I tried to bat them away, terrified whatever had me in its grips would transfer to her. "Nash, stop! Stop! Just stay still. Breathe. Take a breath for me."

Her cool fingers brushed my hair off my forehead. My lungs unlocked. My vision cleared. Muscles that had seized and cramped so furiously went limp. I'm not sure I could have moved if I'd tried. I didn't. I lay there, letting her soft strokes ease me back into the world.

When I thought I could talk without squeaking out sounds of pain, I whispered, "What happened?"

"Are you okay?" Parker's hair trailed over my skin, silken soft, her warm hazel eyes wet with tears.

"Think so. Going to lay here for a minute." Or a year. I wasn't sure I could sit up yet.

"What happened?" I repeated, this time at a normal volume.

"I don't know. I–" She shot a glance at the door. "I think you got shocked. Like you grabbed a live wire. You touched the door and went down. And you–" She shook her head, stroking her fingers over the line of my jaw. "It sounded like it hurt." Her voice caught. I grabbed at her hand, squeezing hard.

"It did, but I'm okay." I thought I was telling the truth. I was definitely telling the truth about the pain. And I was fairly sure I was okay. "What happened to my phone?"

"I don't know. It was in your hand. I think you dropped it." Parker shoved hers at me. "Use mine."

Taking her phone, I tapped the call icon and pulled up Hawk.

"Status?" he barked.

"It's Nash," I said slowly, hoping my brain and my vocal cords would stay online long enough to fill Hawk in. "Not sure exactly what happened, but I think the door handle in Parker's suite just shocked the hell out of me. I went down like I'd been tased." I said it before the thought was fully formed. I'd been tased once years before, and while this hadn't been exactly the same, it was pretty damn close. Just a lot worse.

"Shit. Are you okay? Still in her suite?"

"I'm fine. And we're not going anywhere near that door. But Hawk? There was a voice outside the door. It sounded like Sterling. Check on her?"

"On it. Stay put. I'll head up there and deal with the door."

I handed Parker back her phone. Desperately hoping I wasn't about to fall flat on my face and scare the hell out of her, I braced my hand on the floor and levered myself into a sitting position. It felt like lifting an elephant, every muscle in my body wrung out as if I'd just finished a punishing workout.

"Water?" Parker asked. I don't know if she was just trying to be helpful, or if I looked as thirsty as I suddenly was.

"Please," I said, my voice hoarse. A moment later she was pushing an open water bottle into my hand.

"Do you want anything else? Tea? Or–"

I shook my head, patting the carpet beside me. "Just sit here with me for a minute."

She did, coming to the floor and tucking herself against me, giving me something to lean on. I drained the water bottle and pushed myself up further, leaned forward over my knees, soaking in her comfort. Minutes later, I lifted my head, ready for the next step.

"Give me a hand?"

Parker stood, reaching down. I closed my fingers around her wrist. She did the same on mine, leaning back as I levered to my feet, swaying as my legs protested carrying any weight.

"I think we should take you to the hospital, have them check you out," she said, leading me to the sofa. I collapsed into it, welcoming the pillows helping me stay upright.

Parker went back to her mini fridge, rummaging around until she emerged with a bright blue bottle of sports drink. "Try this. You still look thirsty."

I was, and I was halfway through the blue drink when the alarm finally cut off. In the silence we caught a rustle in the hall outside the suite. Parker's phone beeped with a text.

Door disarmed. Coming in.

A few seconds after the text alert, the handle of the door turned, the door swinging open to reveal Hawk followed by Griffen. I'd almost forgotten that Griffen used to be an Army Ranger, and later in private security. His eyes hard, face without expression, he looked more like Hawk than the billionaire head of Sawyer Enterprises.

Those calculating eyes scanned his sister, then me, and finally the room. "We recovered a homemade device from the door handle. You said you heard Sterling in the hall?"

"Is she okay?" Parker cut in. "I was going to open the door and Nash stopped me." Remembering, she swung her head in my direction. "How did you know?"

I shrugged, the motion sluggish. "I don't know. It sounded like Sterling, but not like Sterling. Is she okay?"

"She's fine," Hawk said. "Whatever you heard, it wasn't her." He was still scanning the room. I had no clue what he was looking for.

"You recovered a device?" I prompted.

Hawk gave a short nod. "You were tased by the door."

The words didn't compute. "Say again?"

Griffen shot Hawk a look. "There was a rigged up device on the door, basically wires jacked into an overpowered taser. Whoever set it did it shortly before you grabbed it, based on the after effects. Not a lot of time for the battery to run down."

"They lured you with the voice, probably a recording of one of your sisters," Hawk said to Parker. "Then they activated the device and took off. I'll get it to West for prints. Maybe whoever set it up was stupid enough to leave some."

"Do you think–" Parker began.

Griffen shook his head. "We aren't making assumptions. The last time we did that, Daisy and JT almost got killed. It could be another attack by whoever sent Vanessa and the others after us. Or it could be coming from inside the house."

"You mean Tyler," Parker said. Her eyes flashed to mine, heavy with remorse. "Nash."

"No." I raised a finger and pressed it to her lips. "Not going there."

"He wouldn't be here if it weren't for me. And neither would you."

"Don't be a dumbass, Parks," Griffen said. "I'm not sure Tyler could pull something like this off. But even if he was behind it, he is not your responsibility."

Seeing that Parker wasn't going to argue further, I asked, "Did the device take a lot of skill?"

Hawk shrugged, sharing a glance with Griffen. "Not necessarily. You can probably find the instructions on the internet. It's just hard to imagine your brother planning something like this."

"He's not as stupid as he looks," I said, remembering what Tyler had said.

I'll get what I want in the end.

The last week played out in my head in fast forward, and something clicked into place. "He might not be working alone. He and Bryce have been inseparable."

"Fuck," Griffen said, just as Hawk swore under his breath.

"I need a bigger team," Hawk said to Griffen. "I know you don't like security in the house, but—"

"Do it," Griffen cut out in a low voice. "Whatever you need, just do it. This can't happen again."

Hawk's phone buzzed. After a quick check of the screen, he looked to Parker and me. "Nash has to go to the ER. I'm assuming you won't stay here?" he directed to Parker.

"I'll take him," Parker said in answer. I started to protest, and she pressed her finger to my lips, just as I'd done to her. "I'm not staying here while you're in the hospital." She dropped her hand and turned worried eyes to Hawk. "Why does he have to go to the ER? Is he in danger?" I caught her hand in mine at the worry in her voice.

"Probably not," Griffen answered. "But after a shock like that, he needs his heart monitored." He shared a look with Hawk, who nodded.

"You take them," Hawk said. "Call West on the way. He needs to know what's going on. Stay at the ER and call Cooper, see if he can free anyone up in the short term. I'll run the team here. We have to find out what set off the alarm."

With a nod at Hawk, Griffen stepped forward and pulled me to my feet, shoving his shoulder under my armpit, taking my weight. "Too bad we can't use the elevator," he said. "You're a heavy bastard."

Parker grabbed her purse and retrieved my phone from

the floor, her brows knitted together. Moving to my other side, she slipped her arm around my waist for support.

"I can walk," I grumbled. I was almost sure that was true.

"In the dark? Down the stairs? Let's not take any chances," Parker said lightly.

"I'm fine, sweetheart, don't worry," I reassured her.

My muscles were jelly and my brain was sluggish, but my heartbeat was steady and strong. I didn't want to go anywhere, but I saw the wisdom in heading to the ER. That had been a hell of a shock. Better safe than sorry.

And, more importantly, whoever set the trap on the door was probably still in the Manor. Which meant the best place for us was anywhere else.

Chapter Thirty-Four

PARKER

Griffen sat with me in the waiting room while they took Nash back for an EKG, and after that, to another monitor to ensure nothing was going to pop up the EKG hadn't caught. I didn't mind waiting for Nash–there was nowhere I'd rather be–but I knew Griffen had a big pile of headaches back at Heartstone.

"You don't have to wait with me," I said. Griffen didn't bother to respond. "I know you have a lot to do with Hawk back at the Manor."

"Nothing more important than being here with you," he said, putting his arm around me. "Nash is going to be fine, you know. This is just a precaution."

"I know," I said, though I wouldn't feel good about the whole thing until a doctor told me Nash was all right.

We were silent for a few minutes. Then, Griffen said, "I like him. Nash. He's easy to work with. Confident, but not arrogant. Willing to compromise if its better for the project. He cares about his team. And he's a geek behind the high profile and the motorcycle. When he talks about the code behind his AI tech, my brain shuts down."

I smiled through my worry. "You're not exactly a slouch in the brains department, Griffen."

"Different kind of brains. I love running Sawyer Enterprises, and I'm your man if you need help with a hostage rescue or kidnap prevention. I'm good with a security system, but the kind of code he's working with might as well be Greek for all I can make sense of it. You picked a smart one this time."

"He pushed me out of the way," I confessed, even though Griffen already knew. "I was reaching for the door. I thought Sterling needed me, and I didn't think. I just went for the door, and then he shoved me out of the way and touched the handle and he was out."

My voice trailed off. I hadn't processed. It happened so fast. The alarm and hearing Sterling and then Nash on the floor convulsing and those terrible, agonized groans.

"I'm glad he shoved you out of the way. Makes me like him more."

"Griffen!" I tried to pull away so I could glare at him, but he tightened his arm in a hug.

"I know you feel guilty," he said. "That's a normal reaction to seeing a loved one go through trauma. But as your brother, I like that he protected you. He's head over heels for you."

"I'm head over heels for him, too."

"I know. And I know it's a little weird and awkward that he's your brother-in-law and you aren't divorced yet, but it doesn't matter."

"It kind of does. Doesn't it?" I wanted to stop worrying about all of that, but I couldn't. I kept thinking of Claudia and how she would feel about all of this. We hadn't talked since she'd left for her safari, conveniently letting me dodge the issue a little longer.

"If you let it matter, I guess it does," Griffen said. "But I don't think you should. I figure you married the wrong brother. Now you're rectifying that mistake. No big deal."

"No big deal?" I laughed in the somber waiting room. Another squeeze from Griffen.

"You got a good one this time. Don't overthink it."

I rolled that thought around in my head for the next few days. While I spent the night in the hospital with Nash, dozing in a pleather recliner to the constant beep of monitors and machines. Through the weekend, while Tyler and Bryce golfed and drank and pretended we didn't exist.

I was so tired of overthinking my life. Couldn't I just let things be simple? I was finally with the man I loved, doing work I loved, living at home with the family I loved. I suddenly had so much of the good in life. Why was I tarnishing it with worry?

There was the whole issue of the door that could have killed Nash. That was something worth worrying about. The doctors had pronounced his heart perfectly healthy, but it could have been worse. I'd assumed Tyler did it, but there wasn't any proof. Certainly not wires or tools in his room or a handy notebook with instructions on how to wire a taser to a door handle. No fingerprints. Nothing definitive.

Hawk and his team were on high alert. He and Griffen suspected it was someone in the house, but without proof, they weren't making any assumptions. My gut said it was Tyler, but, like everyone else, I remembered Daisy's friend JT almost dying after Vanessa mistook him for Royal and stabbed him. In retrospect, Vanessa had raised plenty of red flags, but no one had thought she'd be crazy enough to kill someone. We were all wrong.

The weekend dragged by in a stalemate. I tried not to

flinch every time I opened the door of my suite. Nash and I went out for dinner Saturday and Sunday, avoiding the rest of the family, including Tyler. By early the next week, the tension was getting to me. When Tyler had headed out first thing this morning in Bryce's car, laden with fly-fishing gear, I'd breathed a sigh of relief. It was wearing on me, having him in the house all the time.

I'd forgotten how Heartstone Manor could feel like a prison, the walls closing in, filled with malevolence. When I'd lived here before, it had been my father who brought the darkness. When she was alive, my mother could chase off the cloud he carried with him some of the time. After she was gone, Miss Martha had done her best, but Prentice Sawyer had been a force of nature, casting a pall over the entire estate. No, the entire town.

Tyler was no Prentice, but he still made his presence felt. With him safely on the other side of the closed gates, I felt less hunted. Free, if only for a few hours.

"I want you to stay in the house," Nash had said after we got word Tyler had gone fishing.

"But he's not here," I protested. "I can head over to the cottage and finish the cabinets in the kitchen."

"Can you wait a few hours? I have that meeting with Griffen, Hope, and Royal, and you have packages to mail out. Why don't you take care of that this morning and then I'll help you with the cabinets in the afternoon."

I stared Nash down, wanting to argue and not sure I should. "You don't think the door was Tyler?"

"I don't want to take any chances. I can't stop thinking, what if I hadn't stopped you? What if you'd grabbed the handle? The doctor said I was lucky I didn't have any permanent damage and you're a lot smaller than me. If—"

"I'll stay in the house," I said, immediately. I wanted

freedom, but not at Nash's expense. Stepping into his arms, I wrapped mine around his waist, pressing my cheek to his chest, soaking in the healthy thump-thump of his heart. "Don't think about what ifs. It'll drive you crazy. We're being careful. Nothing is going to happen to either of us."

"Hopefully, the meeting won't run too long. We can get some lunch after and then finish those cabinets so Billy Bob can re-paint them once the electrician is done."

"Sounds like a plan," I agreed, pushing him out the door of our suite with a long, lingering kiss.

We were right, and at the same time, horribly wrong. We were being careful. True. But careful hadn't been good enough with the door, and it wouldn't be good enough today.

The morning started out quiet. Tyler stayed away. Nash was in his meeting. I packed up several orders, post-marked them, and arranged them in a repurposed cardboard box I'd been using to carry orders to the post office. Maybe Nash and I could catch lunch in town after I dropped them off.

Occupied with thoughts of a trip to town, I strolled down the hall. Stopping at the top of the main stairs, I spotted April damp-mopping the front hall. Diverting, I headed for the back stairs. The house was quiet, save for the quickly fading sound of April's mop swishing across the hardwood floor.

I stopped just before the stairs, eyeing the elevator. I rarely used it, the stairs faster than waiting for the elevator to come from the main level, where it returned after use. Lately Nash had been helping me carry my packages to the car. Shifting the box of orders, I reached out to hit the call button. Why not take advantage of the elevator since we had it?

I never heard him coming. From the strength and size of

the hand that slapped over my eyes, I assumed it was a 'him'. It happened so fast I couldn't brace, didn't know how to resist. The hand came over my eyes, the inside of an elbow over my mouth, and I was dragged against a body, pulled off my feet, backwards, into the dark.

I twisted, fought, scrabbled at the man holding me captive. Stomping my foot into an instep, I hoped I'd hurt him enough to make him shout so I could figure out who I was dealing with. Nothing. It wasn't Tyler. That's all I knew. Bryce? Or someone else? How did he get in the house? Unless he was already here...

It didn't matter. Nothing mattered but getting away. My mind was racing, my feet kicking and hands wildly slapping, all to no avail. I was dragged back into the second floor utility closet. The door shut, leaving me without sight. I broke free when he moved the arm that had been covering my mouth. He slapped the wall, and a motor whirred to life.

He grabbed me again, one arm around my chest, the other under my knees, pulling my legs up until I was compressed in a tight ball. He didn't feel that much bigger than me. How was he so strong? A sliding sound and I was flying, tossed into a metal box, arms and legs shoved in, the slam of a door ringing in my ears.

It took me a minute to remember. The dumbwaiter. I was in the dumbwaiter. Seconds after I realized what had happened, the dumbwaiter began to move. If it stopped on the first floor, I'd be in the butler's pantry off the dining room. Further down and I'd be at the far end of the lower level.

Neither location was close to where anyone would be working. Savannah and the staff only used the dumbwaiters for food service or, once a week, for moving laundry.

I caught a slice of dim light on one end of the dumb-waiter. The butler's pantry. The dumbwaiter continued its slow descent. One more minute and I'd be at the lower level. I could get out. This was a stupid prank, but I'd be fine once I reached the bottom.

Except the dumbwaiter stopped. No slice of dim light from the lower level pantry. Just inky black silence.

I was trapped between floors. Even if I could get the door to slide open, there was nowhere to go. And this wasn't an elevator. There was no hatch in the ceiling. No emergency call box or alarm. Laundry and food didn't care if it got stuck. The darkness was complete, oppressive, extending forever past the tight walls.

I won't lie. I lost it for a few minutes, maybe longer. The dumbwaiter was made for trays of food and laundry baskets. Not a fully grown adult. My knees were jammed into my chest, my arms held to my sides. I tried kicking, but my feet only made low thuds against the solid wood and metal interior of the dumbwaiter. Slamming my elbows into the walls had the same effect.

Sucking in a deep breath, I screamed as loud as I could. "Help! Help! Get me out of here!"

I screamed for a while.

No one answered.

There was no comforting lurch of the dumbwaiter starting back up. No shouts coming up the shaft. Nothing but silence and infinite darkness.

Chapter Thirty-Five

PARKER

Lightheaded from my screams, I drew in another deep breath, trying to calm down. Someone was going to find me. Someone would hear. Feeling around the tight box, I found an inch wide gap along one end, and felt warm air moving against my fingertips, air from the shaft of the dumbwaiter. I wasn't going to suffocate.

Wiggling my hand down to my hip, I felt for my phone. Too late, I remembered I'd left it on my desk. I was only running the box of packages down to my car. I didn't need my phone for that. Squeezing my eyes shut, I tried to breathe, tried to think. It was mid-morning. Nash's meeting wouldn't be done until noon, at least.

I had hours until anyone would miss me. Hours. In this tight, dark box. In this tight, dark, *hot* box. The air from the shaft would keep me from suffocating, but it was warm, maybe from the motor that powered the dumbwaiter. Drops of sweat gathered under my arms and along my spine, dripping, soaking into my sundress.

Hours of waiting for Nash to notice I was missing, and

then how long until they found me? Heartstone Manor was tens of thousands of square feet. Hawk would be able to tell them I hadn't left the house, but that didn't narrow it down much. I was going to be stuck in here for hours and hours and hours if I didn't do something.

I went back to screaming, calling out until I was hoarse and pouring sweat, my dress sticking to my skin, my throat on fire. Nothing. No movement. No response. Just more endless dark and silence. I let my forehead drop to my knees, trying not to think about the heat, my cramping hips, and the insatiable need to stretch out my legs.

I drifted for a while, dreaming of water, of moving, of cool air and freedom. How long had I been stuck? I couldn't tell. An hour? Two? Surely not longer. I might have fallen asleep. It was so hot, the air heavy, humid from my own sweat. So dark. So quiet.

A few times I opened my eyes, not sure how long had passed, and gave a half-hearted attempt to kick and scream, to catch someone's attention. There was never a response, and I drifted off again. And again. I think. I wasn't sure if I fell asleep, or I was just lost in the dark.

Time stretched. It was hard to think. I cried at some point, hot tears only making everything worse, but it hurt not to move and it was so hot. I was drifting again when I heard them. Voices. So faint in the dumbwaiter, but they must have been shouting, wherever they were, for me to hear them. Voices. If I could hear them, maybe...

I went wild, kicking and screeching with everything I had left, my wails those of a desperate animal gone feral. My elbows spiked with pain every time I slammed them into the metal walls of the dumbwaiter, but I didn't stop. Time had become liquid, stretching forever, just like the darkness. This might be my only chance.

I only got louder as the faint hum of vibration shook the walls around me. Movement. I was moving. As if whoever had hit the call button might stop, I begged, "Please, please, please let me out." It didn't occur to me that the man who'd put me in here might have pressed the button. I just wanted out. At any cost.

The dumbwaiter came to a stop, and the door slid open, fresh cool air swirling around my sweat soaked body. I started to shake, blinking into the bright light blinding me. Arms reached in and I heard a voice further away.

Savannah. "Get down to the lower level pantry. We just pulled Parker out of the dumbwaiter. I don't know how long she was in there, but she doesn't look good."

Strong arms hooked around my back and under my knees, dragging me from the hot metal box. "Shh, I've got you, Parks. I've got you."

Finn. My brother Finn. Only a year older than me, Finn had always been distant. Reserved. Rebellious and angry when I worked so hard to be perfect. I never would have guessed Finn would be the one to cradle me to his chest and whisper, "I've got you, Parks. I promise. Everything is okay. I've got you."

I sobbed into Finn's shirt, still blinking against the light, my head spinning, my body shaking with tremors. A cool hand touched my forehead, and I flinched.

"Do you have her?" Savannah asked. A grunt from above in the affirmative. "She's so hot." Another cool touch. "Not enough for heatstroke, but from the way she's shaking, I think she has heat exhaustion. Poor baby."

Savannah disappeared, then returned and pressed something into my ear. Not back to myself, eyes stinging and my throat too sore to talk, I jerked my head away.

"Shh, honey," Finn murmured, "let her take your

temperature, okay? We just need to see how bad off you are."

The thermometer beeped. "102 degrees. Not heat stroke, I don't think, but we need to get her cooled down."

Pounding feet approached, voices raised.

Nash's voice hit my ears, and I tried to raise my head, so dizzy, but I wanted Nash. I loved Finn for saving me, for holding me, but I wanted Nash.

"Parker!" He took me from Finn. "What the fuck happened to her?" he demanded.

Savannah took charge. "We don't know. We were in here, arguing about the cook's spices, and we heard sounds coming from the dumbwaiter. I called it down, and we found Parker inside. I took her temp and I don't think she has heat stroke, but you need to get her cooled down before it gets any worse."

Griffen ordered Nash, "Use the elevator. Take her up to your suite and get her in a cold shower. We'll be up soon to check her temp again, see if we need to bring her to the hospital."

Savannah's voice was fading. "I'll get her water. Some sports drink. Did you call Hawk?"

I didn't hear the answer. I was limp in Nash's arms, breathing slowly, watching the rough stone hallway transition to the tight confines of the elevator. I braced as the door slid shut, not ready to be boxed in again.

"It's okay, sweetheart. I've got you. I need to get you cooled down and the stairs are too slow."

I wanted to say something, to tell Nash I was okay, that I loved him, but all that came out was a whimper. Tears leaked from my eyes. Relief, love, fear, I didn't know. I was still shaking, still so hot, and I hurt from head to toe.

Nash reached the door to our suite and braced me

against the wall, rummaging in my pocket for the key. I tried to help, but he gently nudged my hand out of the way. "I've got it, Parker." The door opened, and he carried me straight to the shower, not bothering to take off our clothes.

Setting the water all the way on cold, he stepped inside, holding me against him as the freezing water soaked us both. I drifted again, the cold shocking and wonderful. Eventually, after someone poked their head in the bathroom and Nash said we were okay, after we stood there a little longer, I lifted my head and rasped out, "I can stand. Want to get this dress off."

"How about you try sitting instead?" Nash asked. He didn't wait for an answer, setting me on my feet and bracing my back against the wall. He unzipped my sundress and peeled it off, guiding me to the wooden bench I usually used to brace my foot when I shaved my legs.

I sank on to it, leaning back into the cold tile wall, blearily watching as Nash stripped off his sodden clothes, watching to make sure I stayed put.

"Can you talk?" he asked, taking a soft bath poof and wetting it under the spray, adding a generous dollop of body wash. The scent of fresh watermelon surrounded me as he stroked it over my skin, washing away the sweat and stink of the dumbwaiter.

"I was screaming," I whispered, surprised at how hoarse my voice was. "Throat hurts."

Nash grunted in reply. "Then don't say anything. Hawk and Griffen will have the same questions I do. We'll deal with them all at once."

I closed my eyes, letting him wash me, my body, my hair, gradually adjusting to the cool water as my body temperature eased down. "I'm ready to get out now," I whispered as Nash drew a wide-tooth comb through my clean hair.

Giving me a long look, Nash agreed. Turning the water off, he said, "Stay there. I'll get your robe and some clothes, and we'll go deal with the crowd in our sitting room."

I nodded, my throat still raw from screaming. Absently, I thought that I liked how he called it *our* sitting room. It wasn't just my suite anymore. It was ours. Nash returned with a gauzy thin-strapped night gown and my robe. He'd changed into cutoff sweatpants and a faded t-shirt, his dark hair combed back off his face.

I was still wobbly on my feet, but much better than when Finn had hauled me out of the dumbwaiter. With Nash's arm around my waist, I walked into the sitting room, ignoring the flood of questions until I was seated on the couch, tucked into Nash's side.

Griffen went first. "Did you see who trapped you in the dumbwaiter?" I shook my head. Before I could explain, he kept going. "Do you know what time it was?"

That question I could answer. "A little before ten." He started again, and I held up a hand to stop him, appalled at the way my arm wavered. Fortunately, Griffen shut up.

Savannah shoved a bottle of orange sports drink in my hand. "Drink that," she ordered. I took a long sip, swallowed, wincing at the stabs of pain in my throat. I wouldn't be screaming again anytime soon. Before anyone else could start with more questions, Savannah snapped, "Give her a second." They did, waiting until I finished half of the sports drink and handed the bottle to Nash.

"I was taking the packages to the elevator. Someone grabbed me from behind. Covered my eyes. Pulled me back into the closet. I couldn't see and he grabbed me, shoved me in the dumbwaiter and shut the door. I tried screaming, but no one could hear."

Such paltry words to describe the last few hours of terror and delusion. I'd never forget the heat and the darkness. Not being able to move or see.

"How did he grab you, Parker?" Hawk asked, leaning closer. "Are you sure it was a he?"

"I'm sure it was a man. His hands were big."

"Callused?" Hawk asked.

I tried to remember. "No, not really. Smooth, but big. He covered my eyes first, then his arm was around my throat and he dragged me backwards to the closet. I tried to kick and pull his arm away, but he was so much stronger."

I pushed my brain to think back. I didn't want to, my mind veering away from what had happened in the hallway. But I had to. This was important. Slowly, the memory unfurling as I spoke, I said, "He was so strong, and I remember thinking how could he be so strong when he wasn't that much bigger than me." I looked at the men ranged around the room. "Shorter than all of you. My head was at his shoulder, but he was pulling me down."

Hawk looked at Savannah. "Do you mind?" She shook her head and crossed the room to where he stood. Moving behind her, Hawk covered her eyes with one hand and wrapped his other arm around her throat, pulling her back against him. Savannah was a good five inches taller than me. Her head hit Hawk right on the shoulder, her temple aligned with Hawk's jaw.

I nodded. "Like that. Exactly." Hawk let Savannah go while I considered the way he'd grabbed me. "He didn't want me to see his face. He should have grabbed my hands, but he was more worried about covering my eyes."

"So it's someone in the house." Griffen looked from me

to Savannah to Hawk. "And based on your heights and Parker's, he's about 5' 10."

Hawk pulled out his phone, flipping through screens. "Not a lot of men on the property that fit that description. The electrician's son. Bobby, maybe. And Bryce." He shoved his phone back in his pocket. "Bobby and the electrician's son were at the cottage this morning. Bryce left in his mother's car at 9:52."

"I wish I'd seen him," I murmured. "So I could say for sure. It could have been Bryce. I just don't know."

"West is on his way," Griffen said. "At the least, you need to make a report. Cooper has his plane headed this way with a team of five. We'll have more coverage in the house. I want someone on Parker and Nash around the clock until we get a handle on what's going on."

I wanted to argue. By the tension in his body, I guessed Nash felt the same way.

Neither of us voiced a protest. I wanted freedom. I didn't want to be trapped, or never alone. But more than that, I wanted to stay alive.

It was looking like someone in the house very much wanted the opposite.

Chapter Thirty-Six

NASH

I didn't want to leave Parker, but I had to see Bryce's face when Hawk questioned him. Hawk didn't love the idea, making me promise I'd stay in the background and resist the urge to beat the shit out of Parker's cousin. I'd agreed, mostly because I wanted to see the asshole's face, and Hawk wouldn't let me in any other way.

My phone beeped with a signal a few hours after Finn had pulled Parker out of the dumbwaiter. Parker was asleep, wrung out by her ordeal. Hope sat beside her, keeping watch.

"Hawk just messaged that Bryce is here. Do you mind staying with Parker?" I asked.

"Yes, because I want to be the one to punch him after Hawk gets him to confess," Hope said, "but I'll take pity on you and sit with Parker while you go do it."

"Hawk made me promise not to hit him," I confessed.

"Then what use are you?" Hope asked, her words light but her eyes somber.

"I guess we'll find out," I said. "Be back soon."

I jogged down the stairs to meet Hawk in Griffen's

office. As I opened the door, I heard Bryce, whining already.

"I don't know what this is about. I was just out fishing. I'd like to change, if you don't mind."

He could have been telling the truth. He was dressed in a t-shirt and cargo shorts, definitely more appropriate for fishing than most of Bryce's clothes, as far as I'd seen. A faded cap obscured his blond hair, his blue eyes sullen and annoyed.

"Just a few questions, Bryce," Griffen drawled, "And then you can go."

"What's going on?" Bryce demanded. "I didn't do anything!"

"What time did you leave to go fishing?" Hawk asked.

"I don't know. Around nine thirty? I wasn't paying attention," Bryce said.

"Why didn't you leave with Tyler?" Griffen asked.

"Because I was hungover and didn't want to get up yet." Bryce crossed his arms over his chest and sneered at Griffen.

Blandly, Hawk asked, "So it wasn't you who trapped Parker in a dumbwaiter around that time this morning?"

"What are you talking about? That's crazy, of course not!" Bryce's face was the picture of astonished innocence. "Why would anyone trap Parker in a dumbwaiter?"

"You mean, why would anyone other than Tyler trap Parker in a dumbwaiter?" Hawk pressed.

Bryce shook his head. "Look, Tyler is pissed at Parker. He doesn't understand why she left him, and her fucking this asshole isn't helping," he said, tossing his head in my direction. "Yeah, he's angry, and pretty broken up that his marriage is over, but he wouldn't do anything to Parker. He wants her back, he doesn't want to hurt her! You should hear him moan about how she broke his heart. The guy is miserable."

"Then he had nothing to do with the device on Parker's bedroom door handle? The one that almost killed Nash?" Griffen cut in.

I hadn't been near death, but I wasn't going to get in the way of the interrogation. Bryce's gaze cut to me, his eyes flaring wider for a second before he got control and pulled off his ball cap, tossing his hair with an insolent flick of his chin.

"I really don't know what you're talking about. I think you two miss your old jobs or something. You can't find the guy who killed Uncle Prentice and Vanessa, who keeps trying to kill the rest of you, and instead of getting out there and looking for him, you're blaming Tyler?"

Bryce raised his chin and crossed his tanned arms over his chest. "The poor guy just lost his home, his wife is fucking his brother practically in front of him, and now you two are trying to make him out to be the villain in all this? Get a life!"

I couldn't figure out if he was lying, or if he really believed the bullshit he was spouting.

Hawk's voice was calm when he spoke again, as if Bryce's outburst hadn't happened. "Parker was in bad shape when Finn and Savannah found her. She'd been in the dumbwaiter for a few hours. Trapped in that tiny box, unable to move, in complete darkness, while it got hotter and hotter. She was close to heat stroke when Finn pulled her out. Too much longer and she'd be in the hospital. She could have gone into shock."

The blood drained from Bryce's face as Hawk spoke, until he was gray under his tan. Shaking his head wildly, he insisted, "It wasn't me. I like to fuck around, but I'd never hurt anyone. I'd never hurt Parker. She's always been–" He swallowed hard, his Adam's apple bobbing. "She was always–" He shook his head, backing toward the door. "I'd never hurt Parker."

When no one moved to stop him, Bryce whirled and bolted from the room. The three of us watched him go. "I know we can't prove it," Hawk said, "but he's the one who shoved Parker in that dumbwaiter."

"Agreed," Griffen added. I only nodded and excused myself to go sit with Parker.

After her close call that morning, I needed to be with her, needed to see for myself that she was fine. Hawk had exaggerated the danger I'd been in, but not Parker's. She'd been close to heat stroke. If Finn and Savannah hadn't been in the storeroom, if my meeting had run later, if she'd been in there much longer, she could have died.

I'd taken her from Finn and the second I touched her, I'd known genuine terror. The heat had baked off her skin, her body shaking so hard it had been difficult to keep her in my arms. And most of all, she'd seemed barely conscious, withdrawn, tears leaking from her eyes. I'd never forget any of it. I couldn't stand how close I'd come to losing her.

The seed of an idea took root as I let myself back into our rooms, sending Hope away to rest herself. I thought about it all that day, and the next, and the day after that. Finally, by the middle of the week, I called my lawyer with a set of very specific instructions. Within another few days, papers were signed and my plans carried out.

My original plan had involved romantic dates with Parker, new adventures, and lots and lots of sex. Then Tyler had shown up and blown that plan to hell.

Now I had a new plan. One that would eliminate the Tyler problem for good. I just had to talk Parker into it.

I stalled through the weekend, waiting for her to get back to full strength. By Sunday, we were both going a little stir crazy. So stir crazy that we were joining the rest of the family for Sunday dinner. Parker had insisted that she was finished with hiding. She felt fine, and we weren't running from anything. I'd agreed. But before we went downstairs–

"Parker, I have a proposal for you."

She turned, a laugh in her eyes as she screwed on the back of a diamond earring. "I hope not! I'm not divorced yet. "

I was glad she could laugh about it. I tried for a smile. "Not that kind of proposal. When it's time for that kind of proposal, I won't announce it ahead of time."

"Good to know," Parker said with a smile, coming closer to reach up and pull me down for a kiss. Something about the incident in the dumbwaiter had changed her. She'd lost her reservations about our relationship, wasn't worrying about whether it was inappropriate or awkward.

Parker was mine. She loved me, and she didn't care who knew it. I had to hope that was going to work in my favor.

Unaccustomed to the nerves skittering up and down my spine, I broke our kiss and reached behind me for a white rectangular envelope. Handing it to Parker, I waited.

Raising one pale eyebrow, Parker pulled out the stack of papers inside and reviewed them. Her brows drew together as she scanned page after page, mouth pursing in a scowl. Flipping the last page to the back of the pile, she shoved the papers back at me.

"What is this supposed to be? I don't want this, Nash."

The honest distress in her eyes gutted me. I was doing this all wrong. "I want you to leave Heartstone Manor with me. I know that means you'll lose your inheritance. That's what the money's for."

Parker stared at me, her face blank for a moment as she tried to absorb what I was saying. Then she laughed, tossing the papers onto a nearby table.

"Fifteen million dollars, Nash? You have a very optimistic idea of what I was worth to my father." She shook her head, her certainty and sad eyes turning the knife in my gut. "Fifteen thousand, maybe. Nothing is more like it. But there's no way there's fifteen million in my inheritance. Maybe for Griffen or Ford, but not for me or my sisters."

"I want you to leave with me, Parker," I said, trying again. I had to make her understand. "It isn't safe here. Even with the extra security, we're living like prisoners. I want you in an environment I can control. As long as Tyler is here, I can't keep you safe, so let me take you away from Tyler."

"And in return for leaving my home, my family, I get fifteen million dollars?"

"Will you forget about the money?" I said, painfully aware I was too loud, my frustrated anger leaking out. "This isn't about money, it's about keeping you safe."

Once, Parker might have flinched from my raised voice. Instead, she planted her hands on her hips and glared at me. "Listen to yourself. Do you know who you sound like?"

What? Why wasn't this going the way it was supposed to? I didn't answer her question, just glared back at her.

"Your father, Nash. You sound like your father. He did things like this to you all the time. *Do what I say and all this will be yours.*' You hated that crap. I can't believe you'd do it to me."

The disappointment in her voice was too much. "It's not the same! I'm trying to keep you alive, not manipulate you."

"It's exactly the same! I used to listen to him worry about you and your startups. He just wanted you to spend your time on something secure, like the business he'd built. But that wasn't what you wanted."

Her words sank in, weighing on my heart. Shit. She was right. "I'm not trying to control you. I just want to keep you safe." I didn't know how to put it more plainly than that.

Parker's eyes softened, but she crossed her arms over her chest. "I don't like the situation either, but I'm not leaving Heartstone Manor. I'm not forfeiting my inheritance." I opened my mouth to protest, and she held up a hand. "It's not the money, Nash. I don't care about the trust or what's in it. I don't think there's much, and it doesn't matter. I have a roof over my head, and food in my stomach. I'll figure out the rest."

"Then what is it, Parker? It's not safe here. If you'd been hit with that device on the door, or been stuck in that dumbwaiter any longer, you could have died. That's twice already. And I know you hate feeling like a prisoner." I threw my arm out at the door to the suite. On the other side was an armed guard, courtesy of Sinclair Security. "Make me understand why you're risking your life to stay here if it isn't about the inheritance."

"It's about my family," Parker shouted back, her hands clenching into fists. "It's my family! This is the first time in my entire life that I feel like I have a real family. Before it was always little moments, what we could steal together without Prentice seeing. I couldn't just love any of them. He was always trying to come between us. He sent Griffen away. He ran Finn off. If he sensed my sisters and I were growing close, he'd orchestrate some betrayal and set us against each other. But now he's gone, and we're all here together. We're a family for the first time. I can love them, and laugh with them, and no one is going to take that away from me. Not Tyler, and not you!" Her words cut off in a sob.

I moved for her, but she threw her hand up and stepped back, blocking me.

"You can still see them, Parker," I promised. "I'm not asking you to cut off your family, just to leave Heartstone Manor. For a while. Until it's safe." I shifted toward her and she took another step back.

"It's the same thing, Nash. Don't you understand? If I violate the terms of the will, I don't just lose my inheritance. I'm barred from all family properties. That's the entire Heartstone Manor estate, The Inn at Sawyers Bend, your new offices, Quinn's guide shop, Avery's brewery, and most of the shops on main street. Hell, if I violate the terms of the will, West can practically throw me out of town. I'll be exiled. For five years."

A tear rolled down her cheek. I felt like a real asshole. I understood, I did, but all of that didn't change the fact that she was not safe at Heartstone Manor. "Parker," I began. She shook her head.

"I'll wait for you," she said, her voice small and tight with pain. "I understand if you want to leave. You could have died last week. If you want to go, I'll wait for you. I love you, Nash. You're it for me. But I won't be driven from my home. I can't do it."

My heart cracked right through the center. I was across the room in a second, pulling her into my arms. Parker sank into me, holding on, her shoulders jerking in a sob.

"I'm not going anywhere without you, Parker."

Her arms squeezed my waist, holding on tight, her face buried in my shirt. "I don't understand why he's doing this," she said, her voice muffled. "What's the point? To scare us? To be a jerk? It doesn't make sense. I can't figure out how to stop him if I don't understand what he's doing."

"I don't know, sweetheart. It doesn't make sense to me either. Hawk thinks it could be whoever killed your father."

Parker pulled away, shaking her head. "It's Tyler. I know it's Tyler. He put Bryce up to pushing me in the dumbwaiter. And all week Bryce has been weird with him."

I didn't argue. What was the point when I agreed with her? Bryce was still hanging out with Tyler, but there was a distance between them that hadn't been there before Hawk and Griffen confronted Bryce about the dumbwaiter.

At the end of the day, none of it mattered. We knew Tyler was responsible, knew Bryce was helping him, but until we could prove it, until West could make an arrest, we couldn't get Tyler out of Heartstone Manor.

"Parker, I'm not going anywhere without you," I said again. "But I can't keep you safe. I'm not sure Hawk's team can keep you safe. I don't want you to lose your family or your home, but I can't live with the thought of losing you."

Looking down at her, my throat tight, I tried to force the words out. "We've had two close calls already. I can't stop thinking about what would have happened if we'd found you too late in the dumbwaiter. I've waited for you for six years. No, I've waited for you my entire life. It's only the last six years that I knew who I was waiting for. Nothing I have is worth anything if you're gone, Parker."

She stared up at me, silent, thoughts turning over behind her wary eyes. "I need to think about it. Please? Can I think about it?"

All I could do was nod, my heart in my throat, threatening to shatter in a million pieces. I loved this woman more than my own life, and she was willing to think about giving up what she loved the most, for me. Now, knowing what this place meant to her, I wasn't sure I wanted her to agree to my plan.

How could I live with being the reason she lost five years with her family? How could I go on if we stayed, and I lost her?

She slipped away, saying something about fixing her face, and I stood there, staring after her, rolling the puzzle around in my mind, trying to come up with a way to keep her safe and let her stay at Heartstone Manor. I didn't have an answer by the time she returned. Probably because there wasn't one.

"Are you angry with me?" she asked, her head tilted back to look up at me, worry clouding her hazel eyes.

Cupping her cheek in one hand, I pressed a long kiss to her lips. "No, Parker. Never. I'm just frustrated."

She let out a sigh. "Me too."

"Are you sure you want to do this?" I asked, holding out my arm.

Parker took it, following me to the door. "It's Sunday dinner. All he can do at dinner is get drunk and be annoying. I was married to him for six years. I have plenty of practice handling Tyler when he's drunk and annoying. We're not hiding anymore. If he wants to live here, he'll have to get used to us. I can be annoying, too."

Famous last words. Tyler could do a lot more at dinner than be drunk and annoying, but it turned out, dinner wasn't the problem. The problem was what came later.

Chapter Thirty-Seven

NASH

Sunday dinner was a command performance at Heartstone Manor. Almost everyone was there, except for Braxton and Ford. Brax, Parker's youngest brother, was ever absent, preferring to spend most of his time in Asheville, focused on his real estate business. Brax slept in the Manor, but that was it. His seat, and the one assigned to Ford, who remained in prison for Prentice's murder, were the only seats empty. Otherwise, the entire family was in attendance. Including Tyler. Unfortunately.

The dining room at Heartstone Manor is one of the most impressive I've seen. The room itself was massive, paneled in walnut, the dark-beamed and white plaster ceiling a full two stories above us. Great iron chandeliers cast a golden glow on the beautifully set table. Crystal sparkled, snowy white napkins folded intricately sat in the center of antique Meissen place settings. My mother would have been in heaven.

Griffen sat at the head of the table, as usual, Hope on his right. From there, the Sawyer siblings were arranged in order by age, though Royal had Daisy in between him and his younger sister Avery. In violation of the age ordered seating, Hope had moved Parker and I in front of Tenn and Scarlett, putting more distance between Parker and Tyler, who was at the opposite end of the table, closest to Parker's aunt Ophelia, who sat at the foot.

Bryce had the seat beside Tyler, which had suited them well so far. They both lounged carelessly, sipping from the only full wine glasses at the table. They must have hit the bar in the billiards room before dinner. Not a surprise.

Sterling was the unfortunate soul forced to sit closest to the pair. She ignored them both with steely grace. Everything was the same as the last Sunday dinner we'd attended, with three exceptions. The guards, Thatcher, and Bryce.

Hawk wasn't bothering with subtlety. He had the extra team of guards working in shifts, one within arm's reach of Parker at all times. Two of them stood at attention on either side of the door, ten feet from Parker, reminding me of the footmen that might have once served in the dining room, years ago.

Thatcher, Scarlett's thirteen-year-old son, was the other recent addition to Sunday dinner. I'd heard Scarlett say with a throaty laugh that he had to practice his table manners before he lost them completely. Thatcher had given her an excellent teenage glare, but hadn't argued.

On the surface, Bryce appeared exactly as he had at the few meals Parker and I had attended since Tyler had shown up. Half drunk, his fingers curved around the wine glass in front of him, tapping a beat on the crystal, a familiar sneer on his face as he observed his cousins. But something was off. The distance I'd sensed all week between him and Tyler was more obvious than ever.

Tyler's grin was exuberant, Bryce's a shade forced. When Tyler tipped his glass of wine over Sterling's empty glass and filled it, Bryce shook his head, murmuring something I'd swear was, "Cut it out." Tyler only laughed. Sterling slid the wine glass away, ignoring Tyler completely.

Tyler leaned closer and whispered something that brought an angry flush to Sterling's cheeks. Bryce kicked him under the table. This time, his words were audible. "Leave her alone."

Tyler kicked him back with a lazy swing of his foot, his attention focused on Sterling. Parker hadn't missed the byplay. Before she could shove back her chair and come to Sterling's rescue, Sterling rescued herself. She stood with icy composure, still ignoring both Tyler and Bryce. Striding around the end of the table, she slid into Brax's empty seat beside Thatcher.

"Mind some company?" she asked the teenager with a bright smile.

Thatcher shot her an engaging grin. "Will you eat my asparagus?"

Sterling laughed, the sound clear and bright. "Asparagus, yes. Peas or green beans, no way."

"Fair enough," Thatcher agreed. He held out his hand, and Sterling shook it, sending him a wink. Beside Thatcher, Scarlett shook her head, grinning down at her plate. Across the table, Tyler sulked, all his targets out of reach. He grabbed Sterling's rejected glass and drained it of wine.

Bryce leaned in and said something–I thought a word of caution–and Tyler's eyes narrowed. There was a flash of something calculating in his expression. Just as I was turning it over in my mind, Parker whispered, "He's not as drunk as he seems."

I watched more closely. No, Tyler wasn't as drunk as he seemed. And Bryce might be more drunk than I'd guessed. Bryce toyed with his empty wine glass, his eyes shifting from the empty glass to Tyler, an air of apprehension hanging over him.

Now that Sterling had moved out of range, Tyler was done toying with lesser targets. His eyes were on Parker, absorbing her every move, as if he were waiting for something.

The dining-room door opened. Savannah and one of the day staff entered with wine and a pitcher of ice water. As they made their way around the table, filling glasses, Griffen looked to Tenn. "I heard you had a freeloader in the cottage again. Was this one as interesting as Scarlett?"

Scarlett elbowed Tenn in the side. "Another freeloader in my cottage?"

Tenn shook his head. "Teenagers. They were with one of the family groups and wanted a quiet place to drink the beer they liberated from the minibar."

"They didn't do any damage," Royal added. "I was almost sorry I had to rat them out to their parents."

Tyler shifted in his seat as Savannah reached Parker and leaned in to pour her wine. "Nice to see you two at dinner," Savannah murmured.

"Not sure yet if it's nice to be here," Parker murmured back.

Bryce clocked Tyler's shift and his eyes shot to Parker's wine glass. As she reached for it, Tyler leaned forward.

Bryce's eyes widened, shooting between the glass and Tyler, finally landing on Parker. Something changed in Bryce's face, hesitation morphing into resolve.

As Parker lifted her glass, Bryce grabbed a dinner roll from one of the silver baskets set around the table. Bryce leaned back and winged the roll straight at Parker, knocking the glass from her hand with an explosive crash, drenching her with wine.

I wouldn't have expected that kind of aim from Bryce, especially considering how much he'd been drinking. Parker sprung to her feet, as her aunt Ophelia cried, "Bryce! What on earth?"

Bryce didn't acknowledge his mother. Grumbling, "Asshole," at Tyler, he stormed from the room without another word to anyone. Tyler grinned at his departing back, calling out, "You're wasting your time, man."

"Are you all right, Parker?" Griffen asked, rising from his seat. Parker waved him back down.

"I'm fine. It's just a little wine." Glancing down at her dress, she shrugged. "I'm glad it's white. Red would have given the dry cleaner a challenge." Looking around at the concern on her siblings' faces, at the embarrassment coming off her aunt Ophelia in waves, she said firmly, "I'm fine. Really. No harm done."

"Parker," Ophelia said, her cheeks flushed, "I'm so sorry, I don't know what's gotten into Bryce lately—" She trailed off. Ophelia knew Bryce wasn't well loved by his cousins, but I wasn't sure she knew exactly why. She reminded me of my mother, so blinded by love for her son, she couldn't see clearly who he was. "I'll have your dress cleaned, of course," she finished weakly.

Parker waved her off. "You'll do no such thing, Aunt Ophelia. Really, it's just a little wine. Please, don't worry about it."

I grabbed a napkin and helped Parker dry her dress. When I was close enough not to be overheard, I murmured, "Tyler did something to your wine glass."

"Seems likely," Parker agreed. She eyed the broken glass on the floor. As soon as we'd mopped up most of the wine from her dress, she took one of the damp napkins, crouched down and piled the broken pieces of glass in the center.

Savannah arrived with a fresh wine glass. "You didn't have to clean that up. What happened?"

Parker shook her head, bundling the pieces of the glass in the napkin and tying off the ends to make a little pouch. Under her breath, she said, "Can you keep this aside? I'd like Hawk to take a look."

Savannah stared at the pouch of glass shards for a few seconds before Parker's request made sense. With a brisk nod, she took the pouch, saying only, "I'll just take care of this. I'm about to bring in the salad. Do you want me to hold it while you change?"

"No, I think I'll stay. It's only a little wine."

Her voice so low only Parker and I could hear, Savannah said, "None of the food was left unattended. Only the table settings. I'll get you a fresh setting and put the rest of this aside in case we need to give it to Hawk."

Her eyes carefully avoiding Tyler's end of the table, Savannah set the pouch of glass pieces on top of Parker's place setting, gathered her silverware and water glass, and carried it all from the room. Moments later, she returned with the day maid in tow and began to serve the dinner salad. Parker's place setting was quietly replaced. Only Griffen and Tyler seemed to note the change.

Conversation resumed. I shot a quick look at Tyler, to find him sullenly staring at his mostly empty glass of wine. Had he tried to poison Parker? It seemed obvious to me that he'd been waiting for Parker to drink that wine, and since it had been served to the rest of the table, it couldn't have been the wine itself.

I'd noticed that Savannah often set the table for dinner early in the afternoon, when she had more free time. Parker's glass could have been sitting on the table for hours.

Plenty of time to drop something inside. Time for it to dry unobserved, waiting for the wine to disguise its presence.

"Am I being paranoid?" Parker asked in a low voice.

"If you are, so am I," I said. "Even with the extra guards, I don't like this. You're too vulnerable."

Parker sighed. "I know. I want Hawk to find out if there was something in that glass."

"He will." I picked up my own glass, then set it back on the table. Suddenly, I wasn't in the mood for wine. "After dinner, I want to talk to Griffen about my proposal."

Parker straightened, her brows pulling together. "I haven't agreed to leave," she whispered.

"I know." I took her hand, squeezing her fingers with mine. "But I want Griffen's take on all of this. He has the same training as Hawk, but he's also your brother. He won't want you exiled any more than you want to be sent away. But I need to know if he sees a strategy we've missed. Because if Tyler did what I think he did to that glass, I don't think you can stay here."

Eventually, one of Tyler's schemes was going to work. I had to get Parker out of Heartstone Manor before Tyler got lucky and took her out himself.

Chapter Thirty-Eight

PARKER

Tyler left Heartstone Manor after dinner, saying something about finding better company in town. Standing in the front hall with Nash and Griffen, my personal guard lurking in the background, I kept an eye on Tyler. I didn't relax until he disappeared down the hall to the garage. The slam of the door echoed all the way to where I stood, the sound easing my nerves. Tyler was out of the way, at least for a while.

A good thing, because I had some thinking to do, and it would be easier on my own.

"Parker?" Griffen's raised eyebrows told me this wasn't the first time he'd said my name.

"Sorry, I'm just distracted." I dragged my eyes from the hall to the garage and focused on my brother and Nash.

"Do you want to come with us?" Nash asked. "You should be part of this conversation."

I looked between them, taking in their concerned faces, knowing they needed to feel like there was something they could do to solve the problem of Tyler. Nash was right. I should be a part of any conversation about my future.

Nash was right about a lot of things. I wasn't safe in this house. As long as Tyler was here, I would never be safe. Every time I thought about leaving, being exiled from my family, my home, I wanted to bawl like a child. It wasn't fair. I didn't want to go.

I shook my head. "I need to change out of this dress. You two go ahead. You don't need me for this, and I need some time by myself."

Nash didn't like that. "It isn't safe for you to be alone."

"I won't really be alone. Len's on duty for a few more hours, and Tyler just left." I tried to explain, "I know you two need to talk and problem solve. I need to think. Especially after that dinner. I need to think."

Griffen raised a hand, gesturing to Len, my guard for the evening. "Don't let her out of your sight unless she's in her room with the door locked."

"Got it, boss." Len gave a brisk nod. He reminded me of a cross between Griffen and Hawk. He was more chatty than Hawk, less charming than my oldest brother. He wasn't here to be charming, he was here to keep me safe.

I rose up on my toes to press a kiss to Nash's jaw, fitting myself against him, his arms holding me tight. "We'll figure this out. I promise."

"I know," he whispered back, letting me go.

I followed Len to the stairs, staying by his side, as instructed. Len watched me unlock my door. As soon as it was open, he ordered me to wait just inside the re-locked door as he cleared the rooms. When he was sure no threat lurked in my suite, he took his position just outside the door, saying, "Lock it behind me."

I did, trying not to feel trapped. I was alone, but only if I stayed in my rooms. I'd never thought of myself as someone who needed solitude, but after four days with a full-time bodyguard, I already knew I needed more privacy than this. I could handle it for the short term, but for however long Tyler was going to drag out this divorce? I might go crazy by then.

Ready to get out of my wine-damp dress, I wandered into my closet, lost in thought. What did I want? A life with Nash. Absolutely. No question there. If I left with Nash, Tyler would find it hard to follow, considering his lack of funds. Nash could do most of his work remotely, and I'd be able to visit my family when we came back to the area for Nash's on-site work in his new headquarters.

If I left, Griffen could evict Tyler. And without a roof over his head, Tyler wouldn't have the luxury of hanging around to harass me. He'd be too busy dealing with his own problems. We could come back to Sawyers Bend. That would be complicated, given that I wasn't allowed to be on family-owned property. But maybe we could get a place in Asheville for the rest of the terms of my father's will.

I'd be close to home, and family property would be easier to avoid in Asheville than Sawyers Bend, though under Brax's stewardship the family concerns had expanded in the bigger city. The more I thought about it, the more certain I was—I couldn't go further from home than Asheville. Not happening.

I tried to imagine what that would be like. I could see my siblings occasionally, if they made the drive into the city. Hours with my family snatched here and there, like when we'd been growing up. Only hours at a time, never longer, the will demanding they return to Heartstone Manor each night. No more making hot cocoa in the kitchens with Sterling late at night. No more walks with Quinn in the morning before her first group.

I wouldn't be here to see Hope and Griffen's child born.

To watch Royal and Tenn fall more deeply in love with Daisy and Scarlett. Royal and Daisy seemed to be taking their time, but I'd seen the way Tenn watched Scarlett and her boys. He wanted to put a ring on her finger sooner than later. I was going to miss that, too.

My heart weighed heavy in my chest, tears pricking my eyes as I absorbed everything I'd give up if I left Heartstone Manor. If it weren't for Nash, I'd take the risk and stay. If it weren't for Nash, Tyler might still be a self-centered, egotistical ass rather than the homicidal prankster he'd become.

And that was the other issue. I couldn't quite convince myself that Tyler was trying to kill me.

Why? If this was about money, he wouldn't get a penny if he got rid of me now.

Everything came back to Nash.

I could almost understand how Tyler felt. Not his trying to hurt me, but being angry and humiliated because his wife left him for his brother? As much as I loved Nash, that part still made me cringe, though I knew I'd made the only choice for us.

Griffen had been right. I'd married the wrong brother. It was awkward and weird and painful, but my marriage to Tyler hadn't ended because of Nash. It had ended because Tyler was an immature, spoiled, controlling alcoholic who'd been cheating on me for years. If Nash hadn't been in the picture, I still would have left Tyler.

Pulling on loose knit lounging pants with a matching tank and light cardigan, I wandered back into my sitting room, contemplating a cup of tea. I wasn't having any more luck sorting out this mess than Nash and Griffen were likely having downstairs.

There were only two choices. Exile and safety, or family and possible death. Both choices stunk.

I was halfway to the electric kettle when voices filtered through the closed door, followed by a firm knock I recognized as Len's.

"Come in," I called out.

Len followed Sterling in, shutting and locking the door behind him. "This is a bad idea," he said, his eyes on Sterling.

My youngest sister was pale, her vibrant blue eyes stricken. "I can't find Shadow. Len said she didn't come this way–" She paused, waiting for a response.

"She isn't here. Len checked the room when we came in, and the door was only open for a few seconds." Worry seized me at the thought of our tiny kitten wandering the house alone. So many closets and small spaces to get trapped in.

"I asked Savannah," Sterling continued, "and she's looking. One of the day staff thinks she might have left my door open."

"Let's go look for her," I said, the weight in my chest heavier at the tears in Sterling's eyes. We both loved our little Shadow, but Sterling and the kitten had bonded on a level that went beyond human and beloved pet.

Sterling had taken a lot of hits in her short life, some of the worst this year, and she'd given all she had to recovering. She'd lost her father, the only parent she'd ever really known. She'd quit drinking, fallen in love, and been terribly betrayed.

I hadn't protested when our shared pet loved her more. How could I? Every time I saw Sterling with Shadow, I understood that lavishing affection on the tiny kitten anchored her in her new life, gave her a way to love and be vulnerable without risk.

If Shadow got hurt, I'd be devastated. Sterling would be destroyed.

Turning to Len, I said, "Tyler is out, and you'll come with us. We're just going to check the rooms on this floor. She probably got stuck in a closet or bathroom when someone shut the door and didn't realize she was inside."

"Absolutely not," was Len's reply.

"Are you supposed to keep me prisoner in my room?"

"No," Len conceded, his dark eyes narrowed in irritation, "But I was told you were going to be reasonable, so I wouldn't have to keep you prisoner."

"I am being reasonable. We're not going to run around in the dark, we're just going to look for our kitten. She's too small to wander the house by herself." I grabbed a bottle of her favorite treats. "I'll shake this a few times and she'll come running."

"I already tried that," Sterling said.

Len huffed and strode ahead, checking the hall before he ushered us out and locked my door behind him.

"Where have you looked already?" Len asked Sterling, his eyes scanning the hallway.

"All the rooms in this hall except Parker's."

"Do you want to check the guest wing?" I asked, heading in that direction. "We should ask Griffen and Hope to check their room. And—"

We came around the corner where the family wing intersected with the main house. Planning on crossing the main house to the guest wing on the other side, I stopped. "Did you hear that?"

We all paused, ears straining. I caught it again; A faint meow. We stood at the base of the staircase that began in the lower level and continued up through the house, ending in the attic over the family wing.

"Aren't those stairs too big for Shadow?" I asked Sterling, looking at the wide staircase.

Sterling shook her head, eyes wide with worry. "She was jumping on and off my chair yesterday."

"What's up there?" Len asked.

"Just the attic," Sterling said, not waiting for permission to find her missing pet. I flipped on the light switch, and the dark length of stairs was suddenly less ominous. Despite the age of the house, the attics were in good shape, well lit and clean. Nothing to worry about.

With a glance behind us, Len jumped ahead, reaching out an arm to block Sterling. "Stay close, but let me go first."

We obeyed, letting Len lead the way, Shadow's meows growing louder with every step.

"She's up here," Sterling said, breaking into a jog as we rounded the landing. Len reached out to grab her arm, but she slipped away, desperate to find Shadow.

Len and I raced to catch up, hitting the attic at a run, Shadow's meows distinct now that we were on the same level. Sterling slapped the light switch as she ran, the first room of the attic filling with a golden glow. I skidded to a halt, listening. Over the sound of Sterling's footsteps, I caught Shadow's meows coming from deeper in the attic.

Even as I followed my sister, Len at my side, doubt crept in. It sounded like Shadow, but the night Nash had been electrocuted by the door, I'd been sure I heard Sterling in the hall. I'd been wrong.

I'd seen Tyler leave earlier, but what if Bryce was still helping him? After the incident with the wine glass, I'd been sure Bryce was angry at Tyler, but what if I was wrong?

It was too late for questions. Sterling disappeared deeper into the attic, and I followed, beginning to think we'd made a mistake. I caught the click of another switch and the next room filled with light. Here, Heartstone's attic spanned the width of the family wing and was divided into rooms, one leading to the next. The first had an open doorway, the second two rooms had doors that closed and locked, the third little more than a closet.

I spilled through the second door to see Sterling reaching for the third. It was open a few inches, Shadow's meow coming from inside.

"Sterling, wait!" I shouted. Len sprinted ahead, following Sterling into the dark room. I didn't hesitate, shoving the door wide, reaching for the light switch.

In the dark, a hand closed over mine, yanking me away from the switch. I lost my balance, tumbling to the floor, the sliver of light revealing a familiar face before the door slammed shut, trapping all of us inside.

Chapter Thirty-Nine

PARKER

Tyler.

He reached over and turned on the light. Shadow's meow filled the room, the sound emanating from the phone in Tyler's hand. Sterling lay on the floor beside me, her eyes closed, a smear of red on her temple. Len was face down closest to the door, blood streaming from the base of his skull to pool around him.

"You left," I said, inanely, staring up at Tyler, a gleam of metal at his fist. Had he hit Sterling and Len with something? They needed medical attention. I couldn't help them until I got away from Tyler.

He laughed as I struggled to my feet. "I let you think I left. I figured you'd be too stupid to verify it with the gatehouse."

I swallowed my angry retort, trying to think. It burned that Tyler had been right. I'd heard him say he was leaving, saw him go to the garage, and I'd assumed he'd left.

It had been less than a week since the dumbwaiter, and I was already making mistakes. If I survived this one, I was leaving Heartstone Manor. Assuming that assaulting Sterling and Len didn't get Tyler kicked out. I eyed the growing pool of blood under Len's head. I wanted to be rid of Tyler, but not at this cost.

"Why are you doing this?" I demanded, fed up with all of it. "Hurting my family isn't going to get me to come back."

"I don't want you back, you stupid cow." Tyler flipped his hair off his face, glaring at me in disgust. "You were a drag as a wife. Nag, nag, nag, bitch, bitch, bitch. Until you came around, Mom loved me the best. Nash was always off working, and so was Dad, but I was there and mom fucking worshipped me. I took her to tea at the club and played tennis with her, and she gave me everything I wanted. Then she said it was time I married, that you'd settle me down, and instead she loved you best, more than she loved me."

"What are you talking about? Claudia loves you, Tyler. You're her son. Of course she loves you."

"Not enough!" He screeched, spittle flying from his lips. "As soon as you showed up, you were the daughter she never had, and no one loved me the best anymore. You were both supposed to love me. And you never did. Don't lie and say you did."

No, I wasn't going to lie and tell Tyler I'd loved him. That I thought I had when we married didn't matter. "Tyler," I started, trying to soothe when all I wanted was to scream. "Your mother loves you so much. You know she does."

"Not enough! It's never been enough since you showed up. She cut me off! I have no money. No home. Don't you get it? She did it for you, said I was treating you horribly, blah blah. Like I should care about you. Your own father couldn't get rid of you fast enough, and there you were sucking up to my mother, stealing her from me, fucking my brother behind my back–"

"I never slept with Nash when I was with you!" I knew I shouldn't argue with the crazy man, but I couldn't help it. "Not until after I filed for divorce. Never! And you were cheating on me the whole time! For years, you were cheating on me."

"So what? It's not the same. You were mine. I was the only man to fuck you, and then you ruined it. You took everything."

"Then sign the divorce papers and get rid of me if I'm that awful. Why all this drama?"

Tyler stretched his right hand out in front of him, the metal wrapping his fingers coming into focus. Curling his fingers into a fist, he smiled at me, his mouth stretching slowly wider, the gleeful menace in his eyes freezing my soul.

"If I divorce you, I get nothing. I'll be homeless and poor. But when you're gone–you and Nash both–then mother will have to take me back. She'll be all alone. I'll be there to comfort her, and she won't be able to stand the idea of sending me away again. Everything will be back to the way it was, only better. I wish I'd thought of this years ago." He grinned maniacally. "When you're gone, everything will finally be perfect."

"You're insane," I whispered. How had I been married to this man? "How do you think you're going to get away with this? Maybe you can kill me, but you'd still have to deal with Nash, and he's not going to fall for your tricks."

Tyler cocked his head to the side, studying me and nodding, that manic grin still stretching his mouth out of shape. "You'd think so, wouldn't you? Nash is smart when it comes to business and computers, but he's a fucking idiot when it comes to you. Trust me, once he thinks you're in danger, he'll be easy to take out. And one thing I've learned in the past few weeks—it doesn't matter if they think I did it, it only matters what they can prove. They're not going to pin your death on me. Yours or Nash's."

He leaned in, his face only inches from mine. "I win," he whispered with glee, right before he swung his fist at my head.

The moment I felt it coming, I ducked. Too slow. Pain exploded in the back of my head and I fell, smacking my forehead into the wood floor. I let myself go limp, so Tyler would think he'd knocked me out like he had Sterling and Len.

I was hoping to buy myself time to make a plan.

I wasn't expecting Tyler to leave, flipping off the light and closing the door behind him.

Even after he was gone, I waited, laying still, listening. I caught shuffling sounds on the other side of the door. Something being dragged. And finally, after endless minutes in the dark, his footsteps striding away.

Carefully, I got to my feet, easing around the bodies on the floor to reach the light switch. Getting rid of the dark was a relief, even if it didn't get me out of this room. My voice had recovered from the dumbwaiter, but screaming wasn't going to do me any good here. I was well over a hundred feet from the stairs, and the rooms at this end of the family wing belonged to Brax and Tenn. Brax, who only came home to sleep, and Tenn, who'd moved into a room in the guest wing to be closer to Scarlett and the boys.

I yanked at the door handle, throwing my weight back, trying to force the door to give. The handle turned, but the door didn't open. Was there a lock on the outside? I had no idea. I could count on one hand the number of times I'd been in the attic. With the delays on the cottage, Savannah, Hope, and I hadn't gotten around to looking for furniture up here. If there was a way to open the door from the inside, I didn't know what it was.

Spinning around, I searched the room for something to break down the door. It was too much to hope there was a spare hatchet lying around. I found boxes of papers, a trunk filled with ancient bolts of fabric and dressmaking patterns from the twenties. An equally old sewing machine. A long, sturdy pair of fabric scissors.

Snatching up the scissors, I jammed them in the seam where the door met the frame, wedging them in as close to the lock as I could and pushing back to pry the door open. It shifted, just a little. Widening my stance, I jammed the scissors further into the gap, throwing my weight against the handle, shifting the door a little more. Not enough. It wasn't enough.

Glancing back over my shoulder, I checked Sterling and Len, still unmoving, the smear of blood on Sterling's temple welling up, dripping down her face. Len was looking grey, the pool of blood beneath his head spreading wider with each second that passed.

We were running out of time. I shoved at the scissors again, wrenching them back, begging the door to give. If this didn't work, I was going to have to try something else. I was not going to let Tyler kill me, and I sure as hell wasn't going to let him kill my baby sister.

Drawing in a breath, I choked. Something in the air was wrong. Acrid, heavy, rising from the floor. Smoke. Dropping to my knees, I pressed my hands to the bottom of the door, my heart sinking as heat spread through my palms.

Of course. Locking me in here wouldn't kill me. Smoke inhalation absolutely would. And it wouldn't take long. Tyler had bought himself enough time to get away, but the fire on the other side of the door would devour the attic as soon as it hit critical mass. Backing up in horror, I watched as the smoke trickling beneath the door thickened, rising into the air, gradually filling the room.

Diving for the trunk of fabric, I yanked yards of velvet off the first bolt I came to, packing it into the crack beneath the door, temporarily blocking the smoke. That done, I threw myself at the door, shoving the scissors at the lock, knowing I only had this one chance, and then it would be over.

If I couldn't get the door open, I was going to die, and I'd take Sterling and Len with me.

Chapter Forty

NASH

"I don't see a way around this," Griffen said, his eyes grim as he stared past me to the barren gardens outside. "I don't want Parker to leave, for all the reasons she doesn't want to go, but she can't live as a prisoner. And as long as Tyler's in the house, as long as he has access to her, we can't keep her safe. This isn't any kind of life for her."

"Hawk is going to have the wine glass tested?" I asked.

"The glass, the place setting, the silverware—all of it."

"Even if he finds something, we can't prove it was Tyler," I said.

Griffen shook his head. "No, we can't. I wouldn't have guessed he'd be smart enough to cause this much trouble and not get caught."

"Me either," I agreed. "He's my brother. I should have known what he was capable of, but he spent so many years doing nothing but drinking and playing and fucking around on Parker, I just assumed that was all he had in him."

Griffen let out a long breath. "It's kind of fucked up that I wish she'd run off with you at her wedding. It would have caused a shit storm, but she would have been happier in the end."

"Happier," I agreed, "and a hell of a lot safer."

"Want a drink?" Griffen asked, pushing back his chair and striding over to the crystal decanter and matching glasses on the sideboard.

"Why not?" I said. "I could use a drink. I'm not looking forward to the conversation I have to have with Parker when I go upstairs."

Griffen returned with a crystal glass filled with two fingers of whiskey. I took a sip, letting the smoky burn of the liquor distract me for a minute.

"Look," I said, "I know this is inconvenient and asking a lot, but I need you to figure out a way to bring her family to her after we go. I can't talk her into leaving Heartstone Manor unless I know she'll still have all of you. I figure we can set up a base in Asheville, so I'm close enough to be at the new offices and she isn't isolated."

"That's a good idea. Easy to visit and Brax is there most of the time, so she won't feel completely exiled."

"I feel like a real asshole, pushing her to leave," I confessed. "Do you know what it means to her to have a family again?"

Griffen took a long sip of his whiskey. "I can guess. I know what it means to me. For most of our lives, we were family, but we weren't. Prentice was always getting in the middle. Ford and I were best friends until Prentice drove us apart. He did the same with the rest, finding reasons to pit us against each other. Bribing and tempting and lying until none of us trusted anyone, least of all our own family. Now he's gone, and finally, we're building something here. Something real. I gotta tell you, man—Taking Parker away? It's going to gut me. I want her here—when Hope has the baby–" Griffen trailed off. "I just want her here. With her family."

Griffen took another slug of the whiskey. "I know this asshole is your brother, but I've had a few fantasies about teaming up with Hawk and luring him into the woods." Griffen gestured at the mountains beyond Heartstone's formal gardens. "There's a lot of acres of forest out there. Pretty sure we could lose a body."

I laughed, the sound bitter but tinged with genuine amusement. "I don't give a shit that he's my brother. If you need any help, I'm your man."

Griffen's mouth curved in a smile that faded as quickly as it arrived. "Don't joke. I may knock on your door in the middle of the night–"

"I'm not joking," I interrupted, completely serious. "If your police chief wasn't such a goddamn boy scout, I might have done it already."

Griffen gave a slow nod. "I'm with you on that one. West was my best friend growing up, aside from Ford. He was Ford's best friend, too, and he still put my brother in jail for killing our father, even though he doesn't believe Ford did it. But his job is to follow the evidence, and everything he has points straight at Ford."

Griffen drained his glass. "If anyone could get rid of Tyler and not get caught, it's me and Hawk, but–"

I took another slug of whiskey, welcoming the burn, and finished for him. "–but you've got a wife and a baby on the way and a family that needs you. And as good as you two are, you can't guarantee you won't leave something behind."

"Exactly," Griffen agreed. "I don't know how Parker lasted six years married to your brother. He's only been here a few weeks, and he has me casually talking about murder."

"Believe me," I said, "no one understands like I do. I've

been holding back for years. I think–" I leaned forward, planning to suggest we go up and talk to Parker.

The office door slammed open. Bryce rushed into the room, his golden hair a snarled mess, his eyes wild. "Have you seen Parker? Where is she?"

"I'm not telling you," Griffen said, one eyebrow raised at Bryce.

"No," Bryce rushed on, "you don't understand. Tyler didn't leave. He didn't leave! I went to the garage to see if my car was there and it is. All the cars are here. He's still here. Why did he make us think he was leaving if he's still here? I went upstairs to talk to Parker. She's not answering the door, and the guard is gone."

Griffen and I were on our feet in an instant, the two of us racing for the door. Bryce followed behind, babbling, "I thought it was just a game, a little fun. I didn't mean anything with the dumbwaiter. But now I think he really wants to hurt her, maybe kill her."

Filing away Bryce's words for later, I focused on Griffen. "She was in our rooms," I said as we bolted for the stairs. "I don't have the key. Maybe Hawk–"

As if I'd conjured him out of thin air, Hawk came tearing around the corner, headed for the stairs to the second level. "I lost contact with Len," he said in explanation. "Where's Parker?"

"We don't know," Griffen answered, "And Tyler is still on the property."

Hawk cast us an incredulous look. "You thought he left?"

"We should have confirmed," Griffen admitted. "That fucking bastard. With Len on Parker–"

We never made it to the family wing. Once we hit the

end of the main hall, we all stopped for a split second. I'd never seen the lights on in the stairwell to the attic.

"This way," I called out, racing up the stairs.

The attic was flooded with light, flickering red at the furthest end. The acrid stench of smoke hit me a second later. No! I sprinted for the fire, but when I got there, I couldn't get close enough to the door to open it.

I lunged for it anyway, losing my balance as a hand closed over the collar of my shirt and hauled me back. Hawk.

"Wait," he said, "Griffen's got this."

Then Griffen was there in front of me, a red fire extinguisher in his hands. He pulled the trigger and, with a violent hiss and a cloud of white, attacked the fire.

The second the fire was out, I pulled my shirt over my mouth to filter out the smoke and reached in to unlock the door, ignoring the burn of the deadbolt on my skin. Nothing mattered but getting to Parker.

Chapter Forty-One

PARKER

The clock was ticking, running down faster than I could keep up.

I yanked at the length of velvet still wrapped around the bolt and pulled it over Sterling's face, doing the same for Len with another bolt of fabric, this one lighter than the velvet, but thick enough to keep out the smoke. For a while. Despite the fabric I'd shoved in the crack at the bottom of the door, smoke was infiltrating the closet, displacing the breathable air.

I'd done my best with the scissors, working at the lock, desperately trying to pry the door open. I wasn't surprised Heartstone Manor was still standing after a hundred years, even with my father's recent neglect. Every inch of the fucking place was solid as a rock, even the door to a forgotten closet in the attic.

Smoke burned in my lungs, sending me into a spasm of coughs that doubled me over, body heaving. I needed air. I should be on the ground. I was supposed to get low in a fire, to stay away from the smoke. Not going to happen. We only had minutes until there was more smoke than air in here.

I'm no fire expert, but I knew it wouldn't be the fire that killed us. No, by the time the greedy flames ate through the door, Sterling, Len, and I would be long dead from smoke inhalation. Funny how that wasn't the least bit comforting.

I wasn't ready to die. Of fire, smoke, it didn't matter. I wasn't going anywhere. I had a life to live, a beautiful future I wanted to grab with both hands, a family I needed to get to know, and a man I'd been waiting for since the day we met.

I was not going to let Tyler take any of it from me. He'd taken enough already. I spun around, looking one more time for something, anything, I could use to get through that door. The same trunk of fabric, boxes of papers, and ancient sewing machine stared back at me. Nothing.

I took shallow breaths through my cardigan, my body shaking as I struggled to fight back the next coughing fit. Almost out of time, and I had nothing. Sterling and Len needed me to save them and all I had was a pair of scissors.

I heard something outside the door. The fire? The rest of the attic was likely already engulfed in flames, I realised with a wave of nausea and another wracking cough. Even if I got the door open, we'd never make it all the way to the stairs through the fire. Was it better to die of the smoke? Did it matter?

I leaned against the wall beside the door, dizzy, sweat and tears stinging my eyes, and wished I'd had more time. With Nash. With my sisters, my brothers. My knees folded, my back sliding against the unfinished planks of the wall, sinking to the floor, head spinning.

I wanted more. Instead, it was all over. Too soon.

At first, I thought the wash of air across my face was a dream, the white cloud my entry to heaven. My eyelids were too heavy, glued shut, burning. Sounds crowded around me, shouts, all delusion. Was there shouting in heaven?

"She's breathing. That's three. Call went out to an ambulance. We need to get Len moving now."

"I've got him. You get Sterling. Parker can wait for the ambulance. These two need to go. Rest of the team will find him. He's not going to make it off the property."

"Come on baby, you're okay. Open those eyes for me. Parker. Come on."

I knew that voice. Knew all those voices. But this one, bossy, domineering, and underneath, utterly terrified. Nash. My Nash.

This time, my eyelids cooperated. My voice a croak, I managed, "I'm okay. Tyler hit them. Locked us in. Fire." I blinked rapidly, a sudden swell of tears stinging and clearing my vision. Nash came into focus, his face streaked with soot, eyes shattered.

"Parker." He dropped his forehead to mine. "Thank god," he breathed into my hair. "Thank god."

Pulling me into his arms, he stood, ducking his head through the doorway. "I'm taking you out of here. An ambulance is on the way."

"The fire?" I asked, shocked to see that, except for the haze of smoke in the air, the attic looked much the same as it had when we'd come in searching for Shadow. Someone had opened the windows and fresh air was rapidly clearing the haze of smoke.

"Only at the door. Thanks to Savannah sticking fire extinguishers all over the place, it didn't get very far."

"Put me down," I said, pushing at Nash's shoulder. "I'm fine. I just need a sec." Nash set me gently on my feet, his arm around my waist to steady me. I wasn't going to argue. My knees were wobbling more than I wanted to admit.

"It was Tyler," I said. "He lured us up with Shadow and locked us in. He hit Sterling and Len in the head, knocked them out." I glanced around wildly.

"Griffen and Hawk have them. An ambulance is coming for you, but—"

"Len was bleeding a lot," I said, glad he and my sister were on the way to the hospital. "I don't need an ambulance." As if my body took exception to my rash statement, an inhale caught on my ragged throat and sent me into another coughing fit. Nash's arm wrapped around my waist, holding me steady as my lungs heaved.

"The hell you don't. Let's get you downstairs."

"Where's Tyler?" Another voice cut in. Bryce?

When the coughing fit eased enough for me to stand, I turned to see my cousin Bryce, streaked with soot, his golden hair a tangled mess, his blue eyes stark with shock and pain. "Bryce?" I croaked. "Why are you here?"

"Parker, I'm so sorry about the dumbwaiter. I never meant—I didn't know he wanted to hurt you. I thought he was just messing around." Bryce swung his head from side to side. "Did he leave after he set the fire?"

"Funny you'd be the only one to wonder about me," Tyler said, stepping through the haze of smoke, the gun in his hand pointed at Bryce. "I thought you were an idiot, and most of the time you are, but you have your moments."

"Tyler, what the fuck are you doing?" Nash asked, angling his body to shield me.

Curling my fingers around his belt for support, I took my place at his side. If we were going down, it would be together.

"He wants to kill us," I said, my eyes on the barrel of the gun pointed at Nash. "He thinks if he can get us out of the way, your mother will love him best."

"Are you insane?" Nash asked his brother, tightening his arm around my shoulders and trying to push me behind him again. I stayed where I was. "You can't think you'll get away with this. What are you going to do with our bodies?"

Tyler rolled his eyes, shaking his head as if wishing for patience. "I can set more than one fire, and this time, the calvary won't be here. Hawk and Griffen are racing for the hospital. The ambulance will take a while to get here. Much longer than it'll take for me to shoot you, shove you in the closet, and get that fire going again. All that fabric lying around in there will go up in seconds. By the time they find you, there won't be anything left but your bones."

"What the hell is wrong with you?" Bryce shrieked. "You said we were going to play some pranks, get back at Parker and your brother. You can't shoot them! You can't—"

Tyler's eyes narrowed. He shifted the gun a few inches to the right and pulled the trigger. It was loud, so much louder than I thought it would be, the air in the attic pulsing from the shot, my ears ringing. Bryce went down, red blooming across his abdomen, his eyes and mouth wide with surprise.

I dove for him, pulling off the cardigan I wore over my tank top and wadding it into a ball to press to Bryce's midsection. He groaned, his head rolling against the floor, but his eyes didn't open.

"I wouldn't bother," Tyler drawled, sounding completely unconcerned that he'd just shot his friend. When I risked a glance, it was to see him grinning down at us, his eyes lit with surprised glee, maybe even joy.

"No need to save him," Tyler went on, his voice oddly light-hearted. "You'll all be dead soon enough. It's what you deserve. And I'll get what I deserve. The life I used to have."

"What life?" Nash asked, his voice devoid of emotion.

"What is it you want, Tyler? What do you think you'll get out of this?"

"The life I had before."

"Before what? Before Parker left you?" Nash pressed.

"Before I married her!" Tyler spit out. "Before Mom decided I needed a wife, before Parker ruined everything. I want the life I had when you were off with your startups and Dad was at the company all the time, and it was Mom and me, and she gave me everything I wanted. Back when she loved me the best."

Nash stared at his younger brother with no expression. "You're going to kill us so Mom will put you back in the will?"

"The will, the penthouse, the Hamptons, her accounts, everything! She didn't have the right to kick me out! I'm the one who paid attention to her, who spent time with her. I deserve all of it."

Nash's shoulders shook. Was he laughing? Now did not seem like the right time to laugh at the homicidal maniac holding the gun.

"Taking Mom to tea once a week after a game of tennis doesn't entitle you to drain the family coffers, you fuckhead. She loves you. God knows why. If you put in the tiniest effort to get yourself together, she would have given it all back. Only in your fucked up brain is it easier to kill three people than to get a job."

Tyler raised the gun, making a production of pointing it at Nash's head. My insides froze. The tiniest squeeze of his finger, and it was all over. Tyler liked skeet shooting. No way he'd miss at this range. The bullet he'd put in Bryce hadn't been luck.

Nash didn't seem to care. He rolled his shoulders back, as if we had all the time in the world. "A fire won't erase the shell casings. They'll still know someone shot us."

Tyler shrugged, his eyes flashing to Bryce and the rapidly spreading pool of blood beneath him. "Then I'll put the gun in his hand and everyone will think he did it. It's common knowledge he hated his cousins, and he admitted he was behind the dumbwaiter prank."

"Everyone knows the dumbwaiter was your idea," Nash countered. "Bryce told us everything. Why don't you put the gun down? You can still get out of Heartstone. We'll stay right here, and you can run. The rest of Hawk's team is still in the house. You know they heard that gunshot."

A tremor went through Tyler, his white teeth biting into his lower lip as he digested Nash's words. "Maybe. Maybe not." He shrugged again, shaking off his unease. "But you're right, I might as well get this done. Eventually, that ambulance will get here and someone will come looking for you. Good thing I brought this."

Tyler pulled a small metal can from his pocket, the label faded, rust eating away at the bottom. "Sewing machine oil," he said, his eyes bright with laughter. "I found it right next to the sewing machine in the closet. A little of this and the fire will take your bodies in no time. Won't even look suspicious."

His grin reminded me of a boy looking for a pat on the head at having aced a tough math problem. If he hadn't been about to shoot me, I might have felt sorry for him.

"You're pathetic," I said, resisting the urge to flinch as the gun swung to me. "You don't have the first clue about love or family. Poor Claudia. You think you love her when all you want is to bleed her dry." A cough seized me and I pulled my hands from Bryce, afraid I'd press too hard as I gasped for breath.

"It's going to be nice," Tyler mused, "to never hear your nagging voice again. You ready for that divorce you've been begging for? Here it comes."

His arm raised another inch, his finger tightening on the trigger. I looked at Nash, his face the one I wanted etched in my mind as I died. Weirdly, he took a step back, edging to the side of the room. Tyler, eagerly soaking in my fear, didn't notice.

"I love you," I said to Nash, not caring that Tyler would hear. I had one breath left, and I needed to say it. Needed him to know.

"Shut the fuck up, you stupid little whore," Tyler spat out.

He pulled the trigger.

I flinched, eyes squeezing shut, keeping them closed even after the room shook with a thud, even after Nash was there, hooking his hands under my arms and pulling me to my feet.

"You're okay. Hawk got him. Parker, look at me."

I forced my eyes open and looked up at Nash. "Tyler?"

Nash's eyes shifted to the floor, then back with a wince. "Hawk got him," he repeated.

"He didn't shoot me?" I asked, pretty sure he hadn't, but I couldn't erase the barrel of the gun aimed at me, the squeeze of his finger on the trigger.

In answer, Nash stepped back. Hawk was there, running his hands lightly over my body, his sharp eyes taking in every detail. "Too close," he grunted, "but we got lucky. Now we need to get you to the hospital." Before I could argue, Hawk slanted a dark look my way. "Smoke inhalation. Hospital. Now."

"Okay," I whispered, looking at Nash. "Can you give me a ride?"

"Anywhere you want to go, sweetheart. Always."

Chapter Forty-Two

PARKER

I didn't look at Tyler's body as Nash rushed me from the room. It was enough to know he was wasn't getting back up. Hawk stayed with Bryce, waiting for the ambulance I could hear in the distance.

Nash ignored my protests that I was fine, that I wanted to change clothes, hauling me into his arms and carrying me to his car. I finally shut up as he buckled me in, my lungs seizing in a new series of coughs. Maybe they were right about the hospital.

My brain couldn't keep up. Reaching across the center console of the car, I took Nash's hand. "Is Tyler dead?"

"I don't know. If not, he's close to it. It looked like Hawk got him in the chest."

"You didn't see?"

"I had my eyes on you," Nash said, squeezing my hand in his.

"I'm sorry." I wasn't sure I *was* sorry, but Tyler was Nash's brother. Claudia's son. I wasn't sorry for Tyler, but I was sorry for his family.

Echoing my thoughts, Nash said, "I'm sorry for my mother. That's the best I can do."

We fell silent for the rest of the ride to the county hospital. They were ready for us, bypassing the regular procedure and taking me straight to a semi-private room, where they stuck an oxygen mask on my face and treated a burn on Nash's hand.

"Sterling," I asked the closest nurse. "My sister? She had a head wound, And Len–" I paused, shook my head. "I can't remember his last name. Also a head wound, worse than Sterling's–"

The nurse cut me off. "They're both in imaging. Your sister was conscious, the male patient was not. I can't tell you more than that. For now, we're going to check your pulse ox, get an x-ray of your chest, and take a look at your head. Then we can go from there."

I opened my mouth to ask another question. The nurse held up a hand. "No talking. Lay there, breathe in that oxygen, and rest. When we have more information, we'll share it with you."

I kept my mouth shut. When Nash's hand was bandaged, he took a chair beside my bed, sending me a look when I tried to say anything. I might have closed my eyes for a few minutes. I heard the ambulance arrive with Bryce. Another one came a few minutes later. I thought it might carry Tyler.

Mostly, we waited. I got my x-rays, was thoroughly checked over, and pronounced mostly okay. Griffen and Hawk finally showed up with West, who took our statements.

They stayed long enough to tell me that Sterling was awake, with a hell of a headache, but otherwise okay. Len was still unconscious. He was stable, but had some swelling in his brain. Bryce was in surgery. So was Tyler. I was staying overnight, whether I liked it or not.

I didn't argue. I wanted to know what was going on, and if I was here, I could badger the nurses in person. After West left, I closed my eyes for a few minutes, Nash's hand in mine. When I opened them, Griffen was there, his expression grim.

"Sterling? Len?" I asked, my heart in my throat.

Griffen didn't make us wait. "Sterling is going to be okay. Serious concussion. They want her to stay another day. She'll need to take it easy for a while, but she'll be fine. Forrest is here. She won't see him, and he won't leave."

Sterling had dumped Forrest when we discovered he was using her for access to the Sawyer family in a bid for revenge. To our surprise, Sterling convinced Royal and Tenn to keep Forrest on as CFO at the Inn, though she refused to have anything to do with him.

"And Len?" I prompted.

"Still unconscious. They may have to transfer him to a bigger hospital if the swelling in his brain doesn't go down. We'll see."

"We shouldn't have–" I began.

Griffen cut me off with a shake of his head. "This is part of the job. No one made Len do anything he didn't want to do."

"What about my brother?" Nash asked. I squeezed his hand, knowing he couldn't possibly feel as neutral as he sounded. Before anything else, Tyler was his brother.

Griffen let out a breath. "He's dead, Nash. I'm sorry–" He cut off, then shook his head slowly. "I'm sorry it worked out this way. I'm sorry for your mother."

"Me too," Nash agreed, letting out his own sigh. "I hate that I have to give her this kind of news over the phone."

"And Bryce?" I asked.

"Still in surgery," Griffen said. "That's all I know. I'm going to go sit with Sterling. I'm just down the hall if you need anything." To Nash, he added, "I assume you're staying?"

"Until they release Parker, yes."

"Nash–"

"Can it, sweetheart. I'm staying."

I didn't argue. I felt bad for him, stuck in that recliner all night, but I was too grateful for his company to argue. The next morning, I snuck down the hall to Sterling's room. Forrest still sat outside, his dark curls rumpled, his face pale, eyes sad. I wanted to offer him a word of comfort, but out of loyalty to my sister, I walked by in silence. I might forgive him one day. After Sterling did. Not before.

Sterling was sitting upright in bed, her golden hair pulled back in a ponytail, a scowl on her face. "They won't let me go home," she complained.

"They want another look at your brain," I reminded her.

She rolled her eyes. "You going home? You're okay?"

"I'm fine, just a headache and a sore throat. I'm supposed to rest."

"I'm sorry I talked you into looking for Shadow," Sterling said after a minute. "I was so worried, I didn't think–"

"Savannah found her. Tyler shut her in a laundry hamper. She's fine."

"I know. I wouldn't go to sleep until Griffen found out where she was. I'm sorry. If we hadn't–" Sterling's eyes filled with tears. "Griffen said Len isn't awake."

"It's not your fault, Sterling. It's Tyler's. And he's dead. Did you hear Bryce pulled through surgery? And even though Len isn't awake, the swelling on his brain has gone down, which is a good sign." I moved to sit on the side of Sterling's bed. "They're both going to be okay."

"I feel like I should say I'm sorry about Tyler." Sterling avoided my eyes. "But I'm not."

I nudged her shoulder with mine. "I get it. I feel awful for Claudia. It was terrible listening to Nash tell her." I'd been able to hear my mother-in-law's wails of grief over the phone, the answering pain in Nash's face breaking my heart for both of them. "But Tyler tried to kill us. If he got what he wanted, four people would be dead. Every time I feel bad, I remember that, and I'm not sorry Hawk shot him."

"You sure you're okay?" Sterling asked.

"I'm fine," I assured her. And I was. Extremely fine. I walked out of Sterling's room and into Nash's arms.

"Ready to go home?" he asked.

"I am. I really am." Belying my words, I stayed where I was for a moment longer, wrapped in Nash's arms, exactly where I belonged.

We arrived at Heartstone to a household prepared to fuss, especially over me. Savannah waved them all away, ushering me to our rooms, where she'd already run a bath. Ordering us to call when we wanted food, she left, shutting the door firmly behind her.

"Join me?" I asked, tipping my head toward the steaming tub, fragrant with lavender and vanilla.

In answer, Nash stripped off his clothes, baring his gorgeous body. I drooled, just a little, before letting him help me in to the tub. Sinking down in the deep, hot water, I let it wash away the antiseptic stink of the hospital layered over the yuck of old smoke from the fire. It felt like the fire and the attic were a million years ago instead of the night before.

Dunking my head, I scrubbed my fingers against my

scalp, surfacing to slick the water from my face and hair. Nash lounged against the end of the tub, a smile teasing his lips. "You look like a water nymph," he said, his eyes raking over my naked form.

"Is that so?" I asked, turning in the water, straddling his waist. An hour ago, I would have said sex was the last thing on my mind. But that was before the tub and naked Nash. His hands closed over my hips, pulling me snug against him, his mouth teasing my neck. I rocked into him, moaning as his length fit perfectly against me, stroking over my clit hard enough to pull a gasp from my throat.

"Not yet," Nash murmured against my wet skin. Nudging me back, he soaked a washcloth, wringing it out and adding a liberal sploosh of bath gel. With long, slippery strokes, he washed every inch of my skin, turning me to work lather through my hair, even combing through conditioner. By the time I was clean, every nerve in my body was on fire.

I grabbed a fresh washcloth and went to work on Nash, taking my time exploring his body until he smelled like grapefruit instead of lavender and was every bit as turned on as I was. He didn't argue when I slid into his lap again, wrapping my fingers around his hard cock and fitting it against my pussy, sinking down so slowly, raking my teeth across his jaw. The catch in his breath as he hilted inside me was perfection.

He leaned me back, closed his mouth around one nipple and sucked hard, sending spikes of bliss through my body, my hips rolling faster, splashing soapy water over the edge of the tub. Neither of us cared.

Later, Nash helped me out, tossing towels on the floor so we didn't slip, urging us both into the shower to rinse off before bundling me into my robe and leading me to our bed.

"It's barely lunch time. I don't need a nap," I protested.

Nash nuzzled my neck before saying, "I do. After we beg Savannah to send up some food. Neither of us got much sleep last night."

That was true. As exhausted as we'd been, it had still been impossible to sleep in the hospital between our worry and the constant interruptions. Despite my protests, my mouth opened in a jaw cracking yawn.

Nash sent a quick text to Savannah and patted the mattress beside him. I was there in an instant, no place I'd rather be than next to Nash. His phone beeped.

"Lunch will be here in a half hour," he said, pulling me to his side.

I rested my head on his chest and let out a long sigh. Finally, after so many years of dreaming, of denial, of heartbreak and misery and hope, I was exactly where I wanted to be. With Nash, our future stretching before us, nothing but possibility.

Another jaw cracking yawn got me, punctuated by a laugh from Nash. "Take a nap, love. I'll be here when you wake up."

"You too," I mumbled into his warm chest, his heartbeat strong under my ear, lulling me to sleep.

"I'm already asleep," he promised, his arm tightening around me, keeping me close. I drifted off, knowing that when I woke, we'd have all the time we needed to figure out what came next.

Epilogue
PARKER

When I fell asleep that day, I'd imagined our future stretching before us, free of conflict now that Tyler was gone. I'd been both right and wrong. Right in that Nash and I got along as well as we always had, in and out of bed. And wrong in thinking we'd cruise through life without butting heads. Most of our disagreements were garden variety couple stuff, and we muddled our way through as well as any other couple, compromising and talking things out until we were both happy.

Except when it came to one thing. Marriage.

I was free, finally, and found myself reluctant to change my single state too quickly. I couldn't quite figure it out. I didn't have a single doubt about Nash. He was it for me, my one and only love, better than I'd dreamed. Even so, I wasn't ready. I had a lot to figure out.

I'd told Sterling the truth that day in the hospital. I couldn't bring myself to feel sorry about Tyler, except in the abstract way I'd feel sorry for anyone whose life went badly wrong. He'd brought it on himself, and I could only be glad he hadn't taken anyone else with him.

Claudia was the one I felt for, her bewildered voice slicing through my heart when I called her after they released me from the hospital. I convinced her to come to Heartstone Manor instead of going to New York, where she'd be alone in her grief. Nash left my side long enough to meet her flight, help her pack, and escort her to Sawyers Bend.

Griffen and Hope welcomed her with open arms, and she settled in more easily than I expected. I hadn't thought of my aunt Ophelia, hadn't considered that she might enjoy having another woman her age in the house. It turned out they'd crossed paths a few times over the years, knew some of the same people, and they spent long afternoons playing cards in the sunroom or going out on day trips to explore the small towns scattered through the mountains.

Aunt Ophelia was especially grateful for Claudia after Bryce left Sawyers Bend. A week after the doctor pronounced him mostly recovered, he showed up in Griffen's office to let us know he was going.

"I'm sorry I helped Tyler," he'd said, shoving his hands in his pockets with a shrug, looking almost sorry about being such an ass. "I got caught up in old grudges, and being a shit-head, and I didn't see the signs that he was a total psycho."

"He paid you back for it," Griffen said with a wry smile.

"He did," Bryce agreed with a laugh. "And I guess I should say I deserved it, but getting shot hurts like a bitch and I don't think I deserved it that bad. Anyway, I'm flying down to Miami. A friend fronted me the ticket. He needs help sailing his boat to the Caribbean. I told him I'm not up to full speed yet, but he doesn't care. I'll probably stick around for a while. See if I can pick up some work. I don't know." He shrugged again, avoiding our eyes. "Figure my shit out. You know."

"Good luck," Griffen said, standing and holding out his hand.

Bryce took it with a flash of surprise, shaking it a few seconds longer than normal. "Thanks, man. I'll see you around."

Aunt Ophelia was the only person in Heartstone Manor who missed Bryce. With him and Tyler both gone, life settled into a peaceful rhythm. I worked on the cottage, then the gate house. We watched Tenn marry Scarlett, eagerly looked on as Finn took his fall, as Quinn went after her heart's desire. With each one, Nash asked, "Are you ready yet?" And each time, I shook my head.

I wanted to be, but I wasn't. Part of it was about Tyler. He'd been a miserable husband and a terrible excuse for a human being, but I still couldn't bring myself to jump into marriage so soon after burying him. Not out of respect for Tyler, but for Claudia. She was glad I was with Nash, and made sure I knew it, but she grieved for her youngest son, the child she hadn't been able to save, and I couldn't help but feel that watching me marry Nash would rub salt in the wound.

When she took me aside, six months after Tyler's death, and said, "When are you going to put Nash out of his misery and marry him?" I knew it was about more than protecting Claudia.

It was about me, about my marrying Tyler right after college graduation, then moving in with Nash before I was free of Tyler. I'd never stood on my own. Not really. I still wasn't–living in my brother's house and with Nash at my side–but I wasn't moving out or leaving Nash. I just needed some time to be me, Parker, without being anyone's wife.

Nash, for his part, was both understanding and persistent. We had our shorthand well established. Every once in a while he'd ask if I was ready, and I'd shake my head, answering, "Not yet."

And then one day, I woke before Nash, rolling over to see the rising sun gilding his sleeping face, and I knew. I would never be more myself than I was at that moment, and I'd never love another man the way I loved this one. I waited until the sun prompted his eyes to open, waited for him to turn to me, blinking until he was fully awake.

When I was sure he was conscious, I said, "I'm ready."

Nash knew exactly what I meant. A blinding smile spread across his face, his kiss full of love and lust in equal parts. When he pulled away, he rolled over, opened his bedside drawer, and rolled back to slide a ring on my finger.

"You were prepared," I managed to say, tears of love blurring the sparkle of the ring.

"I've had it for months," he said. "And now, unless you want to elope, you're going to have to be ready to deal with my mother, and Savannah, and every other wedding crazy woman in Heartstone Manor."

My heart full of love, I kissed him. "Do you want to elope?" I asked when we broke apart.

"Hell no. I want the entire world to watch me marry you."

"Maybe something slightly smaller than that?" I offered, my mind racing with thoughts of marrying at Heartstone, and security. Maybe the Inn? I'd have to check with Hawk, and see what Claudia had in mind, and...

"I don't care," Nash said, pressing another kiss to my lips. "As long as you're at the end of the aisle, and you say *I do*, I'll be a happy man."

"Ditto," I said back, punctuating my agreement with another kiss.

We'd figure out the wedding details later. Much later. For now, I was going to celebrate being with Nash, our future spread before us, filled with the love I'd dreamed of, and the man I'd always wanted to be mine.

Wicked Heart

SNEAK PEEK

PROLOGUE
SAVANNAH

He was out there again, skulking around the kitchens of Heartstone Manor in the middle of the night. None of the kids at school would believe it.

Finn Sawyer, the undisputed king of our high school, cooking? For fun? No way.

Watching him bent over a copper saucepan, his dark hair falling in his eyes, I wished with desperate rage that I'd told his secret before he'd told mine. Now it was too late.

If I said anything now, everyone would think I was lying in revenge. The more I thought about what he'd done that day at school, the more I wanted to bash him over the head with that copper saucepan. I hated no one on this planet as much as I hated Finn Sawyer.

The day he'd transferred to the local high school, he'd become the bane of my existence. Before that, no one much cared that I lived in the big house. I was the daughter of the housekeeper, a townie, just like everyone else. I'd made it clear early on that I barely interacted with the Sawyers, and everyone pretty much forgot I had anything to do with them.

Then Finn got himself expelled from Laurel Country Day, and even his father's generous donations hadn't been enough to convince the school to take him back. Setting fire to the principal's office tended to make school administrators cranky. Coming into our rural public high school from an elite prep school like Laurel Country Day should have been hard for Finn. After all, he didn't know a soul, except for me, and by unspoken agreement, Finn and I pretended to be strangers.

It wasn't an act. Not really. We might have slept under the same roof, but I could count on one hand the number of conversations we'd had. Prentice Sawyer did not encourage chit chat between the family and staff. I might have been young, but I knew enough about life to understand how it was.

My mother had a good job. She worked her ass off, but Prentice Sawyer paid her well, especially considering she didn't have to worry about room and board. I love Sawyers Bend, but it's not exactly bursting with jobs. If I got my mother fired, we'd go from comfortable to desperate in a heartbeat. Which was the only reason I hadn't bashed Finn with that copper saucepan. Yet.

He flicked the whisk in lazy swoops, his t-shirt stretching across his back as he leaned over the pan and drew in a long breath, savoring the rich scents of vanilla and cream. He was so absorbed he hadn't noticed me lurking in the dark hall that led to our small apartment off the kitchens.

This wasn't the first time Finn had snuck into the kitchens late at night to cook. His relationship with the family chef was an anomaly in Heartstone Manor. He'd pestered Chef Guérard to teach him to cook for years, until the chef had agreed to a single lesson if Finn would promise never to bother him again. I don't know what Chef Guérard saw in Finn, only fourteen at the time. It must have been something extraordinary, because he never argued about teaching Finn again, even though he knew he'd be fired if Prentice ever found out.

I'd seen Finn during his lessons a few times, barely recognizing him as the boy who ruled our high school with disdain and sullen apathy. With Chef Guérard he was all intense focus, seeming to absorb the chef's instructions into his very cells.

That wasn't the Finn I knew from school. Another kid might have been bullied after making the transfer from his cush private school to our rural public one. Not Finn. In the perverse way of teenagers, he rose to the top of the social hierarchy, powered by the sheer force of his indifference. He slouched around school, sullen and sneering, impervious to anything the other kids might throw at him.

His third day, two boys in his class jumped him behind the gym, thinking to teach him a lesson about the pecking order. He'd pummeled them both, walked away, and never said a word to anyone. That was all it took. Within two weeks of his transfer, he'd become the bad boy every girl swooned over, and every boy wanted to be. Ugh. I tried to pretend he didn't exist.

Until recently, it had worked out fine. He ignored me. I ignored him. Problem solved. Until today. Today, Finn Sawyer ruined my goddamn life and, for once, I had something to say about it. Stepping forward, I left the dark of the hall for the dim light of the main kitchen.

"Why did you do it?" I demanded, keeping my voice low, so it didn't carry down the hall and wake my mother.

Finn's shoulder jerked a fraction of an inch, the only sign that I'd surprised him. Then, with a careless flick, he tossed his hair off his forehead and shrugged.

"What do you mean, why did I do it? I was bored."

He was bored? That was all he had to say? *He was bored?* "Why do you hate me so much? We barely know each other. I've never done anything to you!"

Another flick of that dark, shiny hair and he turned his attention back to whatever he was whisking in that stupid copper saucepan. "It wasn't about you. You don't have to take everything so personally. I was bored, and it was fucking funny. You should have seen the look on your face."

I ground my teeth together, hurtled back to that afternoon in the cafeteria when I'd passed Finn's table carrying my lunch tray.

I heard one of Finn's asshole buddies ask, "Is she a hot fuck? I know she plays the good girl, but that rack is fuckin' sweet."

Finn had leaned back in his chair and shrugged, noting that I'd slowed to hear his answer, already reminding myself that I couldn't beat him over the head with my lunch tray.

Then he said it. "Savannah? Hell no. She's gonna be a virgin till the day she dies. Trust me, she's a complete prude. It's the fucking Sahara in that cunt. Don't bother wasting your fucking time."

Then he'd slashed me a look with those green eyes, a vivid mossy emerald I'd never seen on anyone else. I'd recoiled at what I saw there; Equal parts amusement and vindictive pleasure.

"You did it because it was funny?" I struggled not to scream. The last thing I needed was my mother waking up to see what was going on outside her door.

Another shrug. "Yeah. Obviously. It was fucking hysterical. I thought Murphy was going to cry. He was practically salivating at the idea of getting in your pants."

"Murphy's a pig," I shot back, "but my prom date dumped me because of you. Now the whole school thinks I'm a dried up prude who'll never put out."

Finn slanted me a look under his thick lashes. "You *are* a dried up prude who'll never put out, so really, I wasn't lying. I was just saving Murphy the time."

"Do you know how long I saved up for that prom dress? And it's not like I can go with someone else. No guy in school will go anywhere with me now," I wailed in furious despair.

Looking suddenly far older than his years, Finn flicked off the burner under his saucepan and turned, crossing his arms over his chest. He leveled that deep green gaze on me. "That's the kind of guy you want to take you to prom? The kind that's only looking to get laid? If anything, I did you a favor."

"You made me a freaking social pariah, you dickhead. And you get to head off to college and start over. Meanwhile, I'm stuck here for another year and I'm never going to get another date. They all think you're the fucking king of the universe, and if you say I'm a dried up prude, it might as well be gospel."

"Not really my problem."

That was it. That was one more smartass comment than I could take.

I lunged forward, smacking him hard across the face, my hand burning at the impact. Finn didn't even flinch, just placed his palm flat on my chest and pushed me back out of reach. He didn't shove, just gently but firmly moved me out of his way. That pissed me off even more.

"I am not a dried up prude! And I do not have the Sahara in my–" My voice trailed off. I didn't have a problem with swearing, but I couldn't bring myself to say that word to Finn. Never mind that he'd said it in front of the whole freaking cafeteria.

He dropped his arm and studied me, his green eyes appraising, glowing with amusement. I was getting very tired of being the butt of Finn Sawyer's latest joke.

"You sure you're not a dried up prude?" he asked with a lift of his chin. "Prove it."

I tossed my hair back over my shoulders, setting my hands on my hips so I wouldn't slap him again. "What kind of moron do you take me for? *Prove it?* Fuck you. You're the last person I'd ever–"

Finn's hand shot out, closing over my arm, yanking me toward him. His mouth hit mine with a fury, his palms coming down on my cheeks, holding my face still.

I was too surprised to stop him. Then I didn't want to.

He kissed me like he wanted to consume me, his mouth raw and rough and hungry. My lips opened under his, my mouth, my body. All of me wanted to kiss Finn Sawyer.

He smelled of vanilla and sugar, of decadence and the dark. His lips were sweet, his tongue stroking, demanding and cajoling until I was pressed to him, my head tilted back, one hand clutching his T-shirt at his waist, my head spinning. I didn't remember him backing me up to the big table in the middle of the kitchen.

I should have stopped when his hands closed over my hips and he lifted me to sit on the edge, making a place for himself between my knees.

I should have stopped when his hand slid under my shirt, his rough palm sliding up my ribs, fingers curling around my back, his thumb grazing the side of my breast through my tank top.

I'd never been kissed like this. My knees clamped his sides, holding him close, until his hand dropped to my hip, dragging me almost off the edge of the table, close enough for the thick bar of his erection to grind into the growing heat between my legs.

Fuck the Sahara, I could feel how ready my body was, my breasts tight and swollen, pressing against his chest, that callused thumb stroking, stroking until I wanted to beg. He never stopped kissing me. He didn't press me back to the table, didn't try to strip off my clothes. Just kissed me until I was liquid in his arms, ready to do anything for more of Finn Sawyer.

I don't know what would have happened if we hadn't heard it.

A door shut somewhere. Maybe my mother getting up to use the bathroom in the middle of the night or one of the family coming downstairs. Neither of us stuck around to find out.

All that delicious liquid heat evaporated in an instant. I shoved Finn back and leapt off the counter, bolting for the door.

His mocking voice chased me down the hall. "Like I said, a complete prude."

My body hummed with a kind of desire I'd never known before. His cruel words sliced right through me. I thought I hated him after that scene in the cafeteria, but now I knew what hate really was. Knees trembling, body aching with unfulfilled need, I escaped into the only space that was mine.

Our small apartment was dark and quiet, my mother still asleep. Splashing cold water on my face, I tried not to look at myself in the mirror. The glimpse I caught was enough. Swollen, red lips, my grey eyes too bright.

What had he done to me? How could I have let Finn Sawyer kiss me like that? How could I have–

I was not going to think about it. I tried to go to sleep, but couldn't stop the merry-go-round in my brain. I lay awake until the sun came up. When I finally gave up on sleep and crept into the kitchen for some juice, I found a small white ramekin of crème brûlée in the staff refrigerator, topped with a card that read, *Sahara*.

I took out the ramekin, turning it in my hand. The crust of sugar was perfectly browned. Even through the chill of the fridge, I could smell the night before. Vanilla, sugar, and Finn. The memory hit me like a freight train; The heat of his body, his rough mouth. His hand on my hip, pulling me closer, so close our bodies were almost one. Almost.

A sticky mess of emotions assaulted me. Desire. Regret. Fury. Humiliation. I pitched the delicate porcelain cup in the trash, wincing only a little as it shattered.

If I never saw Finn Sawyer again, it would be too soon.

I almost got my wish.

Less than a year after that night, Finn Sawyer disappeared off the face of the earth.

It would be ten long years before I saw him again. And I'd been right.

It was still too soon.

ARE YOU READY FOR FINN & SAVANNAH'S STORY?

Visit IvyLayne.com/WickedHeart

to see what happens next!

Never Miss a New Release:

Join Ivy's Reader's Group

@ ivylayne.com/readers
&
Get two books for free!

Also by Ivy Layne

Don't Miss Out on New Releases, Exclusive Giveaways, and More!!

Join Ivy's Readers Group @ ivylayne.com/readers

THE HEARTS OF SAWYERS BEND

Stolen Heart

Sweet Heart

Scheming Heart

Rebel Heart

Wicked Heart

THE UNTANGLED SERIES

Unraveled

Undone

Uncovered

THE WINTERS SAGA

The Billionaire's Secret Heart (Novella)

The Billionaire's Secret Love (Novella)

The Billionaire's Pet

The Billionaire's Promise

About Ivy Layne

Ivy Layne has had her nose stuck in a book since she first learned to decipher the English language. Sometime in her early teens, she stumbled across her first Romance, and the die was cast. Though she pretended to pay attention to her creative writing professors, she dreamed of writing steamy romance instead of literary fiction. These days, she's neck deep in alpha heroes and the smart, sexy women who love them.

Married to her very own alpha hero (who rubs her back after a long day of typing, but also leaves his socks on the floor). Ivy lives in the mountains of North Carolina where she and her other half are having a blast raising two energetic little boys. Aside from her family, Ivy's greatest loves are coffee and chocolate, preferably together.

For More Information:
www.ivylayne.com
books@ivylayne.com
Facebook.com/AuthorIvyLayne
Instagram.com/authorivylayne/

Made in the USA
Coppell, TX
13 October 2024

38602881R00213